Seven

Days

in

May

By FLETCHER KNEBEL

and CHARLES W. BAILEY II

HARPER & ROW, PUBLISHERS
NEW YORK AND EVANSTON

For Marian and Ann

. . . In the councils of government, we must guard against the acquisition of unwarranted influence, whether sought or unsought, by the military-industrial complex. The potential for the disastrous rise of misplaced power exists and will persist. We must never let the weight of this combination endanger our liberties or democratic processes.

—President Dwight D. Eisenhower, January 17, 1961

Sunday

The parking lot stretched away to the north, cheerless and vacant. Its monotonous acres of concrete were unbroken except where the occasional shadow of a maple tree speared thinly across the pavement. In the nearby lagoon that opened out into the Potomac, small craft lay in rows at their moorings as though glued to a mirror. No ripple disturbed the surface of the water where it reflected the early-morning sun that was now rising over the silent domes and roofs of Washington across the river.

Colonel Casey parked at the River entrance of the Pentagon. He stood beside his car for a moment, jingling his keys absently as he eyed the old Ford with disgust. Age had settled upon it. Its enamel, once a deep blue, was faded down to a kind of neutral smudge. A rear windowpane was cracked and the fenders were nicked and dented.

Turning away from his car, Casey looked at the great building. The Pentagon loomed up, opaque and formidable, rows of identical windows marching away around its corners without a single touch of grace or humor, as bleak and grim as the business that kept men busy inside it year after year.

Ordinarily Casey approached Sunday duty with a kind of sunny resignation. But this morning a vague uneasiness had ridden with him, an unwanted passenger as he drove to work.

He couldn't diagnose it. Certainly there were plenty of possible causes. The country at large was in a sullen mood—apprehensive over the treaty, wary of Moscow, angered by the prolonged missile strike, worried about unemployment and inflation, not quite sure of the man in the White House. An immediate irritant, in his own case, was the strike. Only Friday General Seager, the commander of the Vandenberg Missile Center, had warned in a biting, almost sarcastic message that if the strike did not end in a few days the entire Olympus program would be derailed for months.

Casey stepped briskly across the special parking area, trying to shake off his mood. As each foot swung forward, a glint of high polish intruded on the lower fringe of his vision. If a man learns nothing else in twenty years in the Marines, he thought, he learns how to shine shoes.

Colonel Martin J. Casey was director of the Joint Staff, the select group of two hundred officers that served as the research and planning agency for the Joint Chiefs of Staff. Once a month Casey took on the chore of Sunday duty officer, a post potentially as vital to the defense chain of command as it was boring to the temporary occupant.

He trotted up the broad steps to the River entrance and pulled open one of the tall wooden doors. The guard at the reception desk put down his newspaper to inspect Casey's pass.

"Tough luck, Colonel," he said. "Nice day for not working, isn't it?"

As Casey entered the Joint Staff area, with its big "restricted" sign, he passed through an electric-eye beam which triggered a two-tone chime to alert another guard. This one, a Navy chief petty officer, sat behind a logbook. Casey signed his name and wrote "0755" in the time-in column of the log.

"Morning, chief," he said. "Everything running smoothly?"

"Dead calm, sir." The guard grinned at him. "But I imagine the colonel would rather be out on the golf course today."

Casey could never quite get over the accuracy of the data which a good enlisted man acquired on the personal preferences of his officers. He winked at the sailor.

"So would you, chief. But someone's got to stand the watch."

"Right, sir." Then, taking a little Sunday-morning license, the guard added: "And probably more gets done, sir, without so many topside."

Casey followed a corridor through the jungle of cubicles and offices which was the cloister of the Joint Staff. Once manned by more than four hundred officers and headed by a lieutenant general, the Joint Staff had in recent years been halved in size and reduced to little more than a personal planning agency for the chairman of the Joint Chiefs. This morning the area was as bare as the parking lot. Casey could hear one typewriter; the halting rhythm of the keys told him it must be an officer trying to finish an overdue paper. Casey turned into the large office that went with his job as staff director. The washed-out pale green of the walls told him he was once again at work in the impersonal labyrinth of the Pentagon. With a sigh he hung up his jacket and sat down to look over the Sunday papers he had brought with him.

He skimmed the Washington *Post*, read two columnists, looked at the baseball scores, and then settled into the *New York Times,* starting with a line-by-line reading of the weekly news summary.

There was trouble everywhere, from Malaya to Milwaukee. The Chinese Communists accused the West of nurturing "spies and saboteurs" in Singapore. A conference of midwestern industrialists denounced the newly ratified treaty. A citizens' committee demanded, in wires to every member of Congress, that striking missile workers be drafted.

But however sour the world's mood, Jiggs Casey had to admit that his own should be bright enough today. For one thing, he felt fit and rested. Beyond his physical well-being, Casey at the age of forty-four had developed a protective skepticism about the woes of the world. It had been going to hell in a handbasket since the year zero zero, as he frequently put it, and if it weren't, who'd need to hire a Marine? His country, which he tended to view with a sort of vexed affection, had managed to survive for almost two centuries and with luck it might sidestep any irreparable injury for the three additional decades which he figured were about the span of his personal concern. But this morning his customary tolerance for the shortcomings of his nation had somehow been strained, if not quite broken. Casey felt uneasy, and he didn't like it.

Colonel Martin J. Casey, USMC, himself seemed built for survivability, as Pentagon jargon would have it. He wasn't handsome, but women had once found him irresistible and still admitted to each other that he was appealing. Men had always liked him. He stood just a hair over six feet and weighed one-ninety now, after almost a year behind his desk. He was about ten pounds overweight by his reckoning, but there was no obvious fat anywhere. A crew cut still masked the beginning of a thinning-out on top. Quiet, green eyes and a short neck gave him a solid look that was mirrored in the photograph of his two sons on the back corner of his desk.

Casey wasn't a crusader and he wasn't brilliant. He had learned at Annapolis, long before the end of his plebe year, that neither was necessarily an attribute of successful military men. But he was a good Marine who had never once pushed the panic button. He hoped he'd make brigadier general before he retired. If you asked him for more, he'd say: That's Casey, period.

It took him nearly an hour to read through the *Times,* and he made it without interruption. Not that he had expected any. On his once-a-month trick as Sunday duty officer and theoretical alarm bell for the chiefs in case of war, natural disaster, or telephone calls from the President or congressmen, nothing ever happened. The White House had called once, but on a matter so minor that Casey had forgotten its nature. As for the more frequent Congressional calls, it was a matter of working up the proper tone of sympathy, interest and alertness while jotting down the gist of the complaint for someone else's attention on Monday morning.

He was eyeing a stack of old personal mail when Lieutenant (jg) Dorsey Hough, the regular Sunday watch officer in the all-service code room, made his usual casual, and distinctly unmilitary, entrance. The code room handled the Pentagon's radio traffic, and Hough was responsible for encoding and decoding all classified dispatches. He carried a sheaf of flimsies, the carbon copies of messages sent from commands around the globe to the Joint Chiefs.

"No sweat, Colonel," he advised. "All routine. But I'll stay for coffee and thanks for inviting me." He dropped the messages on Casey's desk and slid down into a nearby chair, all but hibernating until one of the enlisted men on the guard detail brought in two big white china mugs of coffee in response to Casey's request.

Dorsey Hough, permanently slouched, wore a perpetual hint of a yawn around his mouth. He was the kind of young officer about whom Casey felt, as his wife Marge put it, "excessively neutral." Hough's level of interest in the Navy stood only a notch higher than his concern for the rest of the world. Life would always bore him, Casey had decided long ago, and he would never wear the scrambled eggs of a commander on his cap visor. But Casey seldom had any pressing duties on Sunday and small talk with Hough had somehow become the custom every fourth weekend.

"So what's new, Dorsey," he asked, "besides girls?"

"I wasted twenty bucks on one at the Hilton last night," Hough replied, ignoring Casey's minor premise. "And no sport. But speaking of sport, Gentleman Jim must have the horse in the Preakness. At least, if he doesn't, he's going to a lot of trouble to collect bets from his pals."

Casey thought absently that in his days as a company-grade officer, he would never have referred to the chairman of the Joint Chiefs of Staff by a nickname in the presence of a senior officer, especially one who was the chairman's direct subordinate. "Gentleman Jim" was General James Mattoon Scott, U. S. Air Force, holder of the Distinguished Service Cross, the Distinguished Service Medal, and the Distinguished Flying Cross with two oak leaf clusters. He was by all odds the most popular public figure in uniform and probably in the United States, a fact that was of considerable concern to friends of the President. A brilliant officer, Scott demonstrated perfectly that mixture of good will, force and magnetism that men call leadership. The nickname had been hung on him in high school because of an early eye for meticulous personal appearance and a rare ability to grasp the niceties of adult manners. It had stuck to him at West Point and ever since.

Hough rattled on, with Casey giving him no more than half his attention.

"The General's aide, that Colonel Murdock, brings me in a message at oh seven two five this morning before I hardly got my eyes open," Hough said. "He's got five addressees on the thing and it's all about some kind of pool bet on the Preakness. Ah, if the House appropriations committee ever found out about some of the traffic through my little madhouse—especially on Sundays."

Casey eyed young Hough, slumping in his chair, and idly picked up the conversation.

"Well, General Scott knows his horses. What does he like?"

"He didn't say. It was all about getting the entries in to him on time."

Hough reached into the pocket of his newly starched shirt. At least he wears clean shirts, thought Casey. Hough fished out a half-sized message form and read it aloud:

" 'Last call annual Preakness pool. My $10 already deposited with Murdock. Give lengths your pick will win by in case of ties. Deadline 1700Z Friday. Post time 1900Z Saturday 18 May. Scott.' "

Casey reached out for the slip. He noticed it was written in Hough's hand and decided it was time for a small lecture on discipline.

"Dammit, Dorsey, you know the rules. It's a breach of security regulations to take a personal copy of all-service radio traffic out of the code room."

It didn't take. "That'll be the day, Colonel," Hough drawled, "when they convene a board of inquiry to break me for cracking security on Gentleman Jim's bookie operations."

Casey had to grin despite himself. "This must be some annual custom of Scott's. Who's on his sucker list?"

Hough threw him a mock salute. "Sir, I have filed dispatches in Secret Code Blue, the chairman's personal cipher, sir, to the following-named officers:

"General George Seager, Vandenberg Missile Center, California.

"General Theodore F. Daniel, Strategic Air Command, Omaha.

"Vice Admiral Farley C. Barnswell, commanding Sixth Fleet, Gibraltar.

"Admiral Topping Wilson, CINCPAC, Pearl Harbor, *and*

"Lieutenant General Thomas R. Hastings, commander First Airborne Corps, United States Army, Fort Bragg, sir."

Casey grunted. He had tired of the chatter—and of Hough. He reached for the pile of messages the youth had brought him. Each had to be read, logged and marked for routing to the proper desk in the morning.

"Beat it, Dorsey," he said. "I'll see you later."

The incoming dispatches ranged across the spectrum of military minutiae: Colonel Swain, detached Embassy Buenos Aires, proceeding Washington for permanent change of station, requests permission make personal report General Scott. . . . R/Adm LeMasters, chief of staff CINCPAC, requesting clarification JCS Directive 0974/AR4 23 April 74. Does this mean doubling submarine patrols Sundays and holidays as well as regular duty days? . . . Brig Gen Kelly, commanding Lagens AFB, Azores, urges JCS appeal SecDef ruling limiting Officers Club liquor issue. Ruling damaging morale this station . . . Commander 101st Airborne Division, Fort Campbell, requesting explanation subparagraph (c), paragraph 15, JCS critique of airborne performance in last All Red alert . . .

Casey made it a practice to do the secretarial chores himself whenever he pulled a Sunday shift. It gave him a chance to see firsthand some of the raw material that came into his shop. So he rolled a typewriter over and typed answers to some of the queries, in triplicate. These were routine matters on which the chiefs had given him discretion to act. The rest of the messages went into a separate box for action by the five top officers themselves. On each of the latter Casey clipped a memo, noting time of receipt in his office. On some he added the number of the applicable JCS order or directive. In the process he had to turn occasionally to one of several loose-leaf notebooks, each stamped TOP SECRET, which he pulled from his personal safe.

It was almost noon when Casey finished and headed toward the code room with a manila envelope full of replies to be sent. But first he had to put in his daily appearance at the Joint Chiefs' war room. In this big room, with its global maps and smaller "crisis spot" blowups, duty officers maintained a 24-hour vigil for the nation's military leaders. Direct command lines linked the war room to more than a hundred major combat posts, including the Strategic Air Command near Omaha, the North American Air Defense Command at Colorado Springs, and NATO Headquarters in Paris. A "gold" phone and a red phone, for instantaneous transmission of battle commands in case of war, stood on a separate table.

Casey chatted with the duty officer. The charts were almost bare of special military activity, save for a rectangle marked in red crayon in the South Pacific. Six atomic submarines would begin firing Polaris missiles there tomorrow in a routine exercise. Casey left the war room after a few minutes.

As he walked into the Pentagon's central corridor, he paused to look out the window at the sun-filled courtyard. With its small wooden pergola and high concrete walls, the court seemed a strange hybrid, half prison exercise yard and half village common.

The world may be in a mess, he thought, but it's a swell day outside. Down below, a shirt-sleeved civilian sat on a bench with a girl. She has nice legs, Casey thought. I wonder why we get all the old maids? Maybe they're better security risks.

He lingered at the window a moment or two longer. The mild May sun filled the courtyard. Except for tatters of cloud in the southwest, the sky was clear blue. This was the kind of day when a man wished he had a country place, a chair under a big shade tree, and maybe a couple of horses.

Horses. So Gentleman Jim had a pool on the Preakness, huh? Casey grinned. That was the fox in Scott, lulling his top field commanders with a line of chatter about a horse race which would be run off the same day as the All Red alert.

The last All Red, six weeks ago, had pleased no one. Two carrier attack forces were caught in port, half their ships tied up for minor repairs that should have been completed weeks earlier. Only a little more than a third of the SAC planes got into the air on time. Bits of snafu had leaked into the press from half a dozen bases around the world. President Lyman had telephoned twice to find out what was the matter and Scott, who rarely lost his temper, got mad.

The result was a decision to schedule another no-warning exercise this week. For this one the time was closely held. The Joint Chiefs set the date only last Thursday and so far only the five of them, plus the President, Casey and Colonel George Murdock, Scott's personal aide, knew of it. Scott himself picked out the time: this coming Saturday, May 18, at 1900 hours Greenwich Mean Time, 3 P.M. daylight time in Washington.

Not even the Secretary of Defense knew of the plan. Casey had asked Scott about this, only to be told that the President specifically ordered it that way. There was a growing coolness between the Secretary and the President. Perhaps Lyman thought he would catch the Secretary off guard.

Casey believed Saturday's All Red would be a pretty good test of the remedial measures that had been rushed since the fiasco in late March. Certainly the timing would show whether the field commanders had performed as ordered. By 3 P.M. Saturday in Washington, most United States commands would be well into their usual peacetime weekend cycle. If Moscow ever did push the button, you could be sure it wouldn't be between 9 A.M. Monday and 4:30 P.M. Friday.

Now Scott was handing five of his top men in the field a little extra tranquilizer with his message on the Preakness, even setting the "post time" to coincide with the hour he had picked to blow the whistle for the alert. Pretty cute, Casey thought. Some of those people might relax an extra notch, surmising that Scott was sure to be up at Pimlico for the race.

The girl in the courtyard had slipped her head onto the shoulder of the shirt-sleeved clerk as they lazed away their lunch hour in the sun. Casey pulled himself away from the window and continued along the corridor to the guarded door of the all-service code room. Inside, it was largely a Navy operation. Four sailors with headsets manned typewriters. Another door, this one black with "No Admittance" painted on it in large white letters, led into the cryptographic center where young Hough spent most of his time. But today Hough was slouched at an empty desk in the outer room, reading the Sunday comics.

"Hiya, Colonel," he offered. "You got some work for my tigers?"

Casey handed him the envelope. Hough riffled through the messages, pulled out those which he would have to encode himself, and distributed the rest to the operators. Casey nodded to him and started to leave, but Hough tapped his elbow.

"Take a look at this, Colonel."

Casey took the flimsy. It was a copy of an incoming dispatch:

> SCOTT, JCS, WASHINGTON
> NO BET. BUT BEST RGDS AS EVER.
> BARNSWELL, COMSIXTHFLT

"Which proves," Hough said, "that even an admiral sometimes can't get up ten bucks for a bet. Or maybe he thinks it would set a bad example for the fleet."

"If you don't quit sticking your nose into Scott's business," Casey said, "you're likely to wind up setting a good example by being shipped off to the Aleutians."

"Come on, Colonel. Hawaii would be far enough. In fact, Pearl would be just swell. I told Murdock this morning that instead of worrying about horses, he ought to do this stinking town a favor and get me a transfer to the islands. I'd reduce the confusion, don't you think?"

"You sure would, Dorsey, but what have we got against Hawaii? The Aleutians need men like you," Casey said, "to make the Eskimos safe for democracy."

Casey sauntered along the hall and entered the senior officers' dining room for lunch. It was, like the rest of the building, almost empty. A cluster of Navy and Air Force officers crowded around one table. An Army officer, alone at a table in the rear, stood up and waved at Casey.

"Hi, Jiggs!" Casey walked over, pleasantly surprised to see a friend, Mutt Henderson, a Signal Corps light colonel he'd met in the Iranian War three years ago. Only now, judging from the insignia, it was Colonel William Henderson.

"Hey, Mutt, when did you get the chickens?" Casey snapped a finger against the eagle on Henderson's left shoulder, then thumped him on the back. "Good to see you. What brings you here?"

"Somebody's got to straighten you chairborne soldiers out once in a while," Henderson replied. His black eyes were wide and a familiar impish grin creased his round, red face.

Casey ordered a sandwich and iced tea and the two men settled back to look each other over. This, Casey thought, is what I like about the service. A civilian has three or four close friends at the most. A military man can claim them by the dozen. At almost every post a man could find an officer or a noncom with whom he had shared a few seconds of danger, a few months of boredom, a bottle or perhaps a girl. Your past was always around you. You could never pretend you were something you were not; there were always too many who knew too much.

For Casey and Henderson the sharing had included both danger and boredom, as well as a few bottles. They first met on a rainy night in Iran when Henderson, pulling the lead end of a field telephone wire, slid into the foxhole from which Casey was trying to run his battalion. They remained neighbors, and became fast friends, in the months that followed.

Casey bit into his sandwich and leaned forward.

"All right, Mutt, give me the current statistics. Where're you stationed?"

Henderson dropped his voice. "I haven't given a straight answer to that in four months. But with your clearance you know it all anyway. Hell, Jiggs, you probably got me my orders. I'm exec of ECOMCON."

Casey managed a knowing smile. He had never heard of ECOMCON, but if he had learned anything since Annapolis in addition to the techniques of bootblacking, it was never to let on when you didn't know. Not that there was much of that now, with such unhappy little items as the location of every nuclear warhead in the nation stuffed into his head. A director of the Joint Staff couldn't very well function without knowing these things. Casey surmised Henderson must be using some trick local name for a unit he would know by another designation. He probed lightly.

"So you hate the assignment. Well, don't blame me for your orders, pal. You live on the base?"

Henderson snorted. "Christ, no. Nobody could live in that hellhole. It's bad enough when the Old Man makes me stay there four or five days at a time, the ornery son-of-a-bitch. No, Mabel and I got a little house in El Paso."

He pulled a memo pad out of his pocket and scribbled on it.

"There's my home phone in case you get down there. You know Site Y hasn't got an outside phone on the place except the C.O.'s personal line."

Casey prompted again. "I hear you're doing a pretty fair job for a country boy. How many men you got now? Seems to me I remember you're not up to strength yet."

"Sure we are," Henderson said. "We got the full T.O.—100

officers, 3,500 enlisted. The last ones came in a couple weeks ago. But you know, Jiggs, it's funny. We spend more time training for seizure than for prevention. If I didn't know better I'd think someone around Scott had a defeatist complex, like the Commies already had the stuff and we had to get it back."

What's Scott holding out on me? Casey thought. Maybe he's got orders from the President to keep the lid on. But what is the thing? Some kind of sabotage-control outfit?

Aloud, he responded in a tone that he hoped covered his curiosity.

"Foresight, Mutt, foresight. You tell 'em Washington looks ahead—even if it's in the wrong direction. How long you going to be in town, anyway?"

Mutt grimaced. "Just till tomorrow, while the Old Man briefs Scott and I back him up. We've got a cubbyhole and a phone up on the fifth floor." He consulted another scrap of paper from his shirt pocket. "72291, in case you want me. But we're flying back tomorrow night."

Casey wondered who Mutt's commander was, but didn't ask. Henderson would expect him to know. Instead, he turned the conversation into other channels, first their families, then the war and the politics that flowed from it. They agreed again, as they had the day the word reached them on the line in Iran, that the partition of that country was the blackest mark in American diplomatic history. The Communists had attacked in force and won half a country. Casey and Henderson had joined the top-heavy majority of Americans who unseated Republican President Edgar Frazier in the 1972 election, with the partition of Iran almost the sole issue.

"Jordan Lyman got me with his acceptance speech," Henderson said. "First Democrat I ever voted for. I'll never forget that line of his—'We will talk till eternity, but we'll never yield another inch of free soil, any place, any time.'"

"Me too, cousin," Casey said. He chuckled. "But he wasn't my first Democrat."

"I'm getting a little worried, though," Henderson went on.

"Is he going to stand by it? I don't like that new treaty worth a damn, and from what I read and hear I don't think the country does either."

"The treaty's signed, sealed and ratified," Casey said, "so don't fight it. But if you want to know how some people think the President's doing, ask Scott tomorrow. You'll get an earful."

Henderson laughed as he got up from the table. "I don't talk to four-star generals—yet," he said. "I listen."

Casey won the toss for the check and they parted, Henderson heading upstairs while Casey returned to his office.

Casey wondered again about Mutt's ECOMCON. He spent the better part of an hour leafing through JCS orders and directives for the past year, searching for a clue. Nothing turned up. Oh, well, he thought, Scott will tell me when he thinks I need to know about it.

The phone rang. First call of the day, he noted happily. The bland voice of Colonel Murdock came over the line. It was the routine Sunday afternoon check by the chairman's aide.

"Nothing stirring, Colonel," Casey informed him. "The only flap of the day was all yours. You got young Hough all lathered up about race horses."

As Casey anticipated, Murdock was not amused.

"Somebody ought to gag that kid," he snapped.

"Give us all a break and get General Scott to assign him to Pearl Harbor," Casey suggested lightly.

"You've got something there," Murdock said, not at all lightly. "Dammit, that was the General's personal business."

"That's exactly what I told him, Colonel. But as a good aide you might want to check Admiral Barnswell's credit rating. He sounds like he's fresh out of ten-dollar bills."

There was a silence on the line. When Murdock spoke again there was a film of frost on his customary suave purr.

"I'll be at home the rest of the day if any important business comes up." There was just enough emphasis on the adjective to convey Murdock's disapproval of Casey's attempts at humor.

"I've got you on the call list, Colonel," Casey answered, and hung up without saying good-by. As usual, George Murdock had succeeded in irritating him. Casey had never found it easy to like the kind of men who made their careers out of opening doors and carrying briefcases for the brass, and Murdock's cold efficiency made it twice as hard in this instance.

Casey spun the dial on his office safe, placed the red "open" tag on the handle and took out a hand-typed planning book. On its cover, between two TOP SECRET stamps, were the words "All Red 74-2." Since Scott, in his present mood, would have little else on his mind all week, Casey felt it behooved him to go through the plan once more. He read slowly, trying to commit it to memory.

The President would go to Camp David, his occasional weekend retreat in the Maryland hills, at ten o'clock on Saturday. He would then get back in his helicopter and fly south to the underground command post at Mount Thunder in the Blue Ridge of Virginia. The five members of the Joint Chiefs would drive to Mount Thunder in separate automobiles, arriving not later than 11:15, shortly before President Lyman was due. Murdock was to go with Scott. Casey was to drive up alone. When the President and chiefs were all in, a mock briefing would begin, setting out bits and scraps of "intelligence" indicating the possibility of hostile action by the Soviet Union. Scott would conduct this briefing. At the proper time, about 2:45, it would be assumed that early-warning radar had picked up the track of missiles rising from Soviet launching pads. At this point the alert process would begin, with Scott and the service chiefs ordering the regular Mount Thunder duty crew to open emergency communications lines. At 3 P.M., President Lyman was to give the order for the All Red. If it went off properly, all missile bases would be armed within five minutes, all SAC bombers would be in the air within ten minutes, all Nike-Zeus antimissile missiles would be armed and tracking, and every warship in the fleet would be either on its way to sea or raising steam. The Army airborne divisions at Fort Bragg and Fort Campbell were each supposed to have a regiment combat-loaded and ready to take off in a half hour. The Air Defense Command's interceptors, loaded with air-to-air missiles, were allowed ten minutes to get their flights to 50,000 feet. And so the specifications ran on, down through all the services. On paper, the nation was ready to meet an attack in minutes. The test would show how much of a gap there was between paper and people.

Also to be tested Saturday was the master communications control system. A flick of a switch at Mount Thunder would cut into every radio and television network, placing control over broadcasting in the hands of the command post. For the alert, it would mean only a 30-second blackout of regular scheduled programs. Viewers would get a "network trouble" sign on their screens while the command post held the circuits open just long enough to be sure they were working properly. In the event of a real attack, the lines would be kept open to allow the President to go on the air. The communications cutout was being tested this time simply for practice. It had worked perfectly the last time—about the only part of the alert that had, in fact.

The plan included a list of officials to be alerted. The list was shorter than usual. Casey's footnotes explained why: Vice-President Gianelli would be out of the country, halfway through his good-will visit to Italy. Congress, which had missed its usual Easter recess this year because of the debate on the treaty, would be in adjournment from Wednesday, May 15, to Monday, May 27.

Casey was still mulling over the plan when his relief arrived at four o'clock. He quickly covered the folder and replaced it in the safe. Casey felt silly, for Frank Schneider was at least as good a security risk as he, but one violation of the need-to-know rule could ruin this alert. Nothing spread faster through the Pentagon than a hot tip on an upcoming operation. Schneider played the game, fussing at the desk and pretending there was no such thing as a private safe in the room.

Even fewer cars stood on the parking lot now than there had been in the morning, and Casey realized unhappily that his old Ford sedan stood out like a soldier out of step. The engine wheezed when he pressed the starter, then coughed like a protesting flu victim as he let in the clutch.

Damn the civilians who run this government, Casey thought as he headed out Arlington Boulevard. Ever since he went to Korea as a second lieutenant fresh out of Annapolis, they had whittled away at the pay and prestige of the military. Half the fringe benefits were gone. There had been only two general pay raises in twenty years. If he'd been passed over for colonel he'd be making more money on the outside. Some of his old pals were pulling down $30,000 a year. Instead, he struggled to make ends meet, paying the mortgage late every month, driving this old crate two years after it should have been scrapped. If it weren't for the little income Marge had from her mother's estate she wouldn't even be able to dress decently in Washington.

The Pentagon had prepared a new, comprehensive bill to give the services a pay raise and reinstate some of the old benefits. General Scott had pressed the matter with the President, Casey knew, but so far Lyman had refused to buy it.

And people wonder, Casey mused wryly, why service morale is bad, why re-enlistment rates are too low, why we aren't as efficient as we ought to be. Oh, well, if civilians had any sense, they wouldn't need guns—or Marines.

The boys were shooting baskets in front of the garage doorway when Casey turned in behind the subdivision house he and Marge had bought in Arlington when this Pentagon assignment came up. Sixteen-year-old Don, already as tall as his father, was a first-stringer on the high school team. Bill, two years younger and six inches shorter—he had Marge's chunky build—never would be as good as his big brother but never would quit trying, either.

"Hi, mob," Casey called, getting out of the car. "Where's the boss?"

"Over at the Alfreds'," Don said, nodding his head toward the next house. He flipped the ball to his father. "Shoot one."

Casey gripped the ball in 1950-vintage style, aimed carefully, and bounced it off the rim of the basket.

"Gee, Pop," Bill complained. "What's the other team do while you aim? Salute, maybe?"

"Lay off," Don said. "You want to talk like a taxpayer, grow up and pay taxes."

Casey grinned at his first-born. Don flipped the ball to his brother and addressed himself to more serious matters. "Say, Dad, can I have the car to take the gang to the movies tonight?"

His father played the tough Marine. "You want to drive your own car, grow up and buy one." It was Bill's turn to laugh. "Seriously, Don, your mother and I are going out tonight. One of the other guys will have to provide transport."

Don shook his head. "That means Harry's old crate. I hope it's running."

Casey took two more turns with the ball and then went inside to change into more comfortable clothes. Midway in the process he decided to lie down for a minute and relax.

When Marge Casey came home a half hour later she found her husband sprawled on the bed in his shorts, sound asleep. With a sigh for the bedspread—for almost twenty years she had been asking him to turn it down—she sat down at her dressing table to repair her nails for the party that night.

She was still sitting there when Casey opened his eyes. He looked at her back, bare now except for the thin strap of her bra, and thought half of lust and half of love and of his luck that with Marge he couldn't tell them apart. At forty-two she still had the small, neat beauty of the girl he met in Newark during his tour there as a recruiting officer right after Korea.

Marge looked up into the mirror and now he saw the wide-set dark eyes and the sprinkling of freckles across her nose. When she smiled, as she did on seeing him awake, a little space showed between her two front teeth. The gap gave her a little-girl look that Casey liked.

"If you were more woman and we had more time," Casey drawled, "this might be a pretty good afternoon for rape."

Marge wrinkled her nose at him, glanced at the clock on

her dressing table, sniffed, stood up and closed the bedroom door.

"I sometimes wonder," she said, sitting down on the edge of the bed, "if Marines don't talk more than they fight." They both laughed as Casey growled and reached for her bare shoulder to pull her to him.

The sun had set and the coolness of a spring evening was rising as they drove across Western Avenue toward Chevy Chase. Marge was talking, but Casey heard little of what she said. He wasn't intentionally tuned out, just pleasantly oblivious. Once his mind brushed against business, reminding him of something he should have done before leaving home.

"Oh, dammit. I forgot to call Scott. Marge, will you please remind me to call the General when we get home? I've got to get his okay for changing one of his appointments tomorrow."

"Aye, aye, sir," she replied briskly. "The fate of the nation is in good hands. The only thing we have to fear is the day I forget to remind you of the things you can't remember. Hey!" Marge squirmed as Casey's hand squeezed her leg. "Two hands on the wheel, Colonel."

The Stewart Dillards lived in a five-bedroom house on Rolling Road in Chevy Chase. Two towering oaks set off the brick colonial architecture fashionable when the house was built in the late forties. There might as well have been a tag reading "prestige" on the street-number sign beside the flagstone walk.

For a lobbyist like Dillard, who looked out for the interests of Union Instruments Corporation in its continual contract dealings with the Defense Department, it was perfect. It gave him a good northwest address, it was close to the Chevy Chase Club where he did much of his entertaining and played his golf, and there was enough backyard for the big outdoor parties like tonight's at which Dillard from time to time entertained the crowd of casual acquaintances he had to maintain.

The street was already well filled with parked cars. Casey eyed the California license plate on a cream-colored Thunderbird: USS 1. Must belong to Senator Prentice, he thought. He'll probably be Stewart's ranking guest tonight.

Casey parked the elderly Ford a bit down the street and waited while Marge twisted the rear-view mirror, fussed with a curl, and wiped lipstick from the corner of her mouth. Casey held the door open for her.

"Damn girdles." She wiggled and took his arm. "What rating do you give it, Colonel?"

It was their private pre-party game. Casey looked at the other cars. "Oh, upper lower middle," he said. "One senator, from the license plate there. Probably one White House assistant. One military man of some importance. That's me, of course." He went on despite her snort. "Two-three newspapermen, a couple of congressmen, one regulatory commission member, and six couples you never met and will never find out anything about."

"How about a society writer from the *Star?*"

"Nope. But I'll bet Francine has already called the papers with the guest list. There'll be items tomorrow on the women's pages."

A Filipino in a white coat opened the front door and waved them through to the back lawn. A clatter of conversation burst on them as they stepped off the side porch. The aroma of perfume and new-mown grass hung in the air, and such symbols of the cookout as cigarette stubs and the tiny punctures made by spike heels were already marking the Dillards' sloping lawn. Francine's teeth flashed and she was beside them, bubbling, delighted, shoulders thrown back, hips thrown forward.

"Marge!" Both hands came out as though she were presenting a loving cup. "You look lovely."

Stew Dillard moved over to do the introductions and Francine peeled off to greet another couple at the back door. As they moved around the yard, Casey found he had been slightly off in his estimate, for he saw no congressmen. But his rating stood. The senator was indeed Frederick Prentice, California Democrat, chairman of the Senate Armed Services Committee, a power in his party and a virtual overseer of the Pentagon. The commissioner was Adolf Koronsky of the Federal Trade Commission, a Republican holdover from the Frazier administration. The ranking newspaperman was Malcolm ("Milky") Waters, who covered the White House for the Associated Press.

The identity of the White House staffer brought a smile to Casey's face. He was Paul Girard, President Lyman's appointments secretary. Casey and Girard had been friends since the days when Girard played basketball for Duke and Casey was a Navy substitute. They had seen each other in Washington, on both business and pleasure, and Casey had sized Girard up several years ago as a man you could trust. He was shrewd, knew where all the bodies were buried on the Hill, and had Lyman's absolute confidence. He was almost ugly, with a head too large for his body, flaring nostrils and sleepy eyelids. Girard was often put down as a clod by strangers who frequently woke up the next morning wondering who had stacked the cards.

"Hi, Jiggs," he said, shifting his whisky to his left hand and offering his right.

"Glad to see you here, Paul. When I get investigated for taking favors from a defense contractor, at least I'll be in good company."

"You know the rule, Jiggs," Girard returned. "Anything you can consume on the spot is okay." He held up his almost empty glass. "And I'm a pretty good consumer."

Casey took a gin-and-tonic from the tray brought over by a waiter who responded to Girard's signal. He looked around for Marge, but she had been swirled away into an eddy of women near the azaleas at the foot of the garden. The pitch of conversation rose steadily, buoyed by alcohol and reinforcements. Casey and Girard found themselves in a group that included Waters and Prentice. The newsman was bracing the senator.

"Did you hear about the Gallup Poll coming out tomorrow?" Waters asked, his voice as noncommittal as it always had been through two administrations at the White House.

"No," said Prentice, "but let me guess. It's about time for another reading on Lyman's popularity, and I'd say he's lucky if he gets 40 per cent."

Prentice oozed the self-assurance that comes with years of power, unencumbered by responsibility, as a Congressional committee chairman. He could attack, second-guess, investigate and chide with never a fear of being proved wrong, for the making and executing of policy was always someone else's job.

The senior senator from California was not a particularly striking figure, but he successfully conveyed the impression of being a man who expected to dominate a gathering and usually did. If he was a bit heavy across the midriff, that gave him a certain advantage over men of less ample bulk. If his gestures were a trifle broad, his voice a shade too strong for ordinary conversation, these characteristics seemed appropriate enough in a man more used to being listened to than listening.

Now, as he looked at Waters for confirmation of his guess, there was a hint in his bearing and glance that he did not expect disagreement—and would not welcome it. He got no contradiction from the reporter.

"You're on the right track, Senator, but too high. The poll out tomorrow will show only 29 per cent saying they 'approve' of the way the President is doing his job. The Gallup people say it's the lowest popularity rating for any President since they started taking the thing."

Prentice nodded and stabbed the air with his forefinger.

"It's this simple," he lectured. "The President trusts Russia. The American people don't. The people don't like this treaty. They don't believe the Russians will take those bombs apart on July first and neither do I."

The treaty, the treaty, the treaty. Casey, and indeed all

Washington, had heard nothing else since Congress met in January and President Lyman forced the pact through the Senate with only two votes to spare over the required two-thirds majority. It seemed as though everybody in town had chosen sides in the argument, and letters-to-the-editor pages in newspapers all over the country indicated that the same thing was happening everywhere. Casey sneaked a look over his shoulder to see if he could slip away, but he was hemmed in.

He had heard all he wanted to, and then some, about the nuclear disarmament treaty that would go into effect on July 1. On that date, under the agreement reached by Lyman and Soviet Premier Georgi Feemerov in Vienna last fall, identical moves would be made at Los Alamos and Semipalatinsk. Each country, under the eyes of Indian and Finnish inspectors, was to disarm ten neutron bombs. Each month more bombs would be dismantled, not only by Russia and the United States, but also by the other Western and Communist nuclear powers. All of them, including Red China, had subsequently ratified the treaty. The process would continue until the nuclear lockers of both East and West were bare. The target date for completion was two years hence.

"Don't you think there are other factors affecting the poll, Senator?" It was Waters again. "I mean the high unemployment, inflation, and the mess over the missile-base strikes?"

"Don't you believe it, young man," retorted Prentice. "Every President has had troubles like those. But, my God, Lyman negotiated this treaty in defiance of the facts of life. The Russians haven't kept an agreement since the end of the Second World War. You know I fought the treaty with every fiber of my being and I'm proud of it."

"Yeah," said Girard sourly. "We Democrats really stick together."

Prentice swung toward him, his face twisted with irritation and his forefinger in motion again.

"It was the President who left the Democratic party, Girard," he said. "And I say that as a man who went down the line for him at the convention."

"Well, after all, is the President's position so unreasonable?" The new participant in the debate was a man in a cream-colored sports jacket whose name eluded Casey. "I mean, if Russia reneges or cheats, we know it immediately and the deal is off."

"I've listened to that argument for thirty years," Prentice said, "and every time I hear it used to justify a policy we lose something more. The last time was the summit conference in '70 that was supposed to settle the Iran business. Six months later the country was flooded with Soviet guerrillas and now we're left with two Irans, one of them Communist."

"I don't know, Senator. I don't think I can agree with you so far as President Lyman is concerned." The man in the sports jacket wasn't to be put off so easily. "He may be taking a calculated risk, but it seems to me we're protected. And if the President is willing to risk some of his popularity right now to do the one thing that might save the world, I say more power to him."

You know, I think he may be right, Casey thought. Several others in the group nodded silently. But Prentice wouldn't let it go. He leaned toward the President's defender.

"Don't talk to me about Lyman's 'popularity,' young man. He hasn't got any to lose and he doesn't deserve to have any, either."

The temperature of the discussion was rising along with the intake of cocktails. Dillard bustled over to exercise his pacifying functions as host and adroitly turned the talk to pure politics.

"Leaving the merits of the treaty out of it," he said, "I'll make a bet at reasonable odds that the Republicans nominate General Scott in '76. It's a natural. He's got the personality. If anything goes wrong with the treaty, he's solidly on record against it. And if it works, people will be worrying about Russia's conventional forces and will want a strong man like Scott."

"Oh, Christ," said Girard. "I can see the slogan now: 'Scott, the Spirit of 'Seventy-Six.' "

"You White House boys better not make too much of a joke

out of it," Prentice said. "I agree with Stew. Scott's far and away the obvious Republican choice. If the election were today, he'd beat Lyman hands down."

"May I convey the compliments of the senator to the leader of *his* party?" asked Girard with some heat.

"I'm talking facts, sonny," Prentice shot back. "We simply wouldn't stand a chance against Scott."

The porch floodlights blinked on, signaling dinner. Francine Dillard shepherded her guests to the rear of the garden, where a caterer's man in a tall white hat had been grilling steaks. With each steak went a baked potato. When the guests found their seats at the little tables set up on the porch, there was a green salad and a bottle of beer at each place.

Casey's dinner partner was Sarah Prentice, a cheerful, plump woman who spent much of her time in Washington applying salve to the wounds opened by her husband.

"Fred is awfully worked up over this treaty," said Mrs. Prentice, "but I think he'd admire your General Scott anyway."

"He isn't exactly *my* general," Casey said, with appropriate military neutrality. "I just work for him."

"But don't you think he's a darling?"

"I think he is an extremely competent general."

"Oh, you Marines!" She laughed as if on cue. "I couldn't expect you to say a good word for an Air Force man."

After dinner the guests moved out across the lawn again. Casey passed up a proffered highball in favor of a second bottle of Stew's excellent pale India ale. He had taken a single swallow when Prentice came up, took his elbow and steered him out of a group.

"Colonel, I meant what I said earlier. You're lucky to be working for the one man who commands the confidence of the country and who could lead us out of this mess."

Casey answered in his best light party tone. "I'm a military officer, Senator, and it sounds to me as if you might be pushing me pretty near the brink of politics."

"Let's not kid ourselves, Colonel," Prentice said snappishly.

"This country's in trouble, bad trouble. Military man or not, you're a citizen, and every citizen has his duty to politics."

Casey laughed, but he felt increasingly uneasy in this conversation. "You'd never make a professor at Annapolis, Senator," he said. "I'm in mufti tonight, but the uniform's in my closet and I put it on tomorrow at 0700."

Prentice peered at Casey in the half-light. The hortatory forefinger came up again.

"Well, if you get a chance, you have a talk with General Scott. I'm serious, Colonel. I'm sure you'll find his ideas on the situation are close to your own—and close to what most good Americans are thinking today."

Casey hadn't the faintest idea where this insistent politician was trying to lead him, but wherever it was, Casey wasn't going. He switched the subject.

"I hope you and Mrs. Prentice enjoy the recess, Senator. I forgot to ask her at dinner where you plan to go."

"I'm staying right here. There's plenty of work to be done." Prentice glanced around. "Besides, somebody on the Hill has to stay alert. Especially on Saturday, right, Colonel?"

The word "alert" took the Marine by surprise.

"Why, yes, sir. We should be, always," he said lamely. Prentice slapped him on the arm and walked away.

The party was about ready to break up. Casey found Marge and threw her an inquiring look. He got an answering nod and they said their good-bys, walked back through the house and along the street to their car. Casey drove home with only half his mind on the traffic. Now, just where had Prentice learned of the alert? Only eight men were supposed to know and he wasn't one of them. Of course, Prentice headed the Armed Services Committee and was told just about everything. But Scott had been adamant on security this time. If Prentice knew, did someone else? One thing was sure: he better take it up with Scott first thing tomorrow.

Marge was chattering about the party.

"Who did you have as a dinner partner, Jiggs?"

"Mrs. Prentice. The senator's wife. Nice woman, I guess,

but you sure can't say as much for her husband."

"I noticed he was bending your ear at the end there. What was it all about?"

Casey decided not to go into details. "Oh, just the usual Hill gripes."

"He's on the Armed Services Committee, isn't he? . . . By the way, Jiggs, don't forget to make that telephone call."

Casey looked at his watch as they passed under a street light. "Oh, hell. It's too late now. I'll have to get up early and call him in the morning."

Bill was asleep when they reached home. Don was still out at the movies. Casey relaxed in the living room while Marge used the bathroom. It was their routine arrangement; he got priority in the morning. He could still hear water running upstairs when the phone rang.

"Dad?" It was Don. "Listen, we just came out of the movie and there's a flat on Harry's car. It's Sunday night and I don't know what we can do, and we live closest, so . . ."

"I'll tell you one thing you can do," Casey said. "Change the tire."

"Dad." Don's voice was heavy with pity for the limits of adult comprehension. "Harry doesn't *have* a spare."

I've been had again, Casey thought. "Where are you?"

Rolling down Arlington Boulevard after getting the theater location from Don, Casey decided to swing by Fort Myer. Scott might possibly be up and, if so, he could tell him about the British Chief of Staff's request to move his appointment up from 9:00 to 8:30 tomorrow morning.

The wide, elm-shaded streets of the old post at Fort Myer were dark and vacant. Scott lived in the sixteen-room house traditionally reserved for the Chairman of the Joint Chiefs. The brick structure, built almost seventy years ago in the bulky, ugly style of officers' quarters of that period, had once been bleak as a county poorhouse, but renovation had left it serviceable and comfortable, if hardly elegant. Set up on the ridge, old Quarters Six commanded a panoramic view of Washington across the Potomac. From his second-floor windows, Scott could look out and down on the Capitol, the Lincoln Memorial and the White House, the residence of his commander in chief.

Casey slowed almost to a stop as he turned the corner and came around in front of the house. His headlights glinted on a rifle barrel where the sentry paced along the walk. The lights also picked up the rear of a cream-colored Thunderbird parked in front of the house. Its license plate, designed to reflect light, jumped into Casey's vision. It was California USS 1.

Hey, that's Prentice's car, Casey thought. He glanced up at Quarters Six. A light was on in a window which he knew was in Scott's study. Otherwise the house was dark.

He accelerated and swung wide into the street past Prentice's car. If Scott was conferring with the chairman of the Senate Armed Services Committee, he would not welcome an interruption. Better to call him early in the morning.

On his way home, after rescuing Don and his two pals from the darkened theater parking lot, Casey's thoughts were still on the car in front of Quarters Six. He hadn't known Scott and Prentice were such close friends, although God knows the General had spent enough time testifying before the senator's committee to cement a dozen lifelong friendships. Maybe Prentice rushed over to tell Scott about the Gallup Poll. Scott took no pains to hide his dissatisfaction with Lyman, and Prentice had been pretty outspoken tonight for a man who was supposed to be a leader of the President's party. But why all this in the middle of the night? Casey looked at his watch again. Five minutes after midnight. Pretty late for political chitchat.

And Prentice obviously knew all about the All Red too. So what did it add up to?

Back home, he set his alarm for 6:30, just to be on the safe side. He had to call Scott before seven on the British appointment. Casey thought wearily that his decision not to leave a message had cost him at least a half hour of sleep.

When he crawled into bed, Marge stirred but did not quite

waken. Casey tried to settle down, shifting from side to side, then onto his face, finally onto his back. Sleep would not come. The vague uneasiness of the morning had returned and in the small hours of night had become a puzzling anxiety.

"Something wrong, Jiggs?" Marge's voice was thick.

"I don't know, honey," Casey said. "I don't know."

Monday

Even as he groped for the button that would shut off the alarm clock, Casey knew it was going to be one of those days. A small ache at the back of his head told him that he had missed too much sleep, and the bitterness in his mouth made him wonder why he always smoked three times as much at a party as he did in an evening at home.

The shower helped. Wrapped in his towel, he went downstairs and dialed General Scott's quarters. There was an answer on the second ring.

"Colonel Casey, General," he said. "I hope I'm not too early."

"Not at all, Jiggs." Scott was already in full voice. "What's up?"

"Sir Harry Lancaster requested that his appointment be moved up to eight-thirty, sir. I didn't think you'd mind. I'll have the briefing papers for you by 0800."

"That's perfectly okay, Jiggs."

"I meant to call you yesterday, sir," Casey said, "but it slipped my mind, I'm afraid, and by the time I came to last night I was afraid you might have been asleep, so instead I—"

Scott interrupted. "Well, you were right. I turned in early and dropped off right away. Must have been asleep by ten-thirty. I haven't had such a good rest in months."

"Yes, sir," Casey said. "I'll see you at the office, sir."

Unless I was dreaming last night, Casey thought as he climbed the stairs again, that's a big fat fib, General.

Why would Scott lie to him? He couldn't remember a single time in a year when the chairman had told him a false-hood or had even tried to mislead him. Scott was sometimes devious—perhaps a better word was cautious—with Congress or the White House, but with his own staff he seemed to go out of his way to lay out all the facts.

And why conceal a meeting with Prentice? The senator obviously seemed to know about the alert. Perhaps there was something going on at higher echelons.

But that would be odd too. As director of the Joint Staff, Casey was supposed to know everything involving the military. Supposed to? He had to.

Marge peeked out from the bathroom, her face dripping.

"Throw me a towel, Jiggs. A dry one, please. Someday, dear, maybe you'll be famous and wealthy and we won't have to get up with the birds any more."

Casey said little at breakfast. The puzzle over Scott's re-mark had brought the ache back to the base of his skull and hot coffee only dulled it. He scanned the front page of the morning newspaper, but couldn't concentrate, not even on a speculative story about a "new direction" in military policy to fit the treaty. Marge fussed a little over him.

"You didn't get your sleep, Jiggs," she said.

"Not enough of it, anyway," he said. "Thanks to Don. For want of a spare, an hour was lost, or something like that."

Five days a week a Pentagon sedan called for Casey. The olive-drab car from the motor pool was one of the perquisites of the director of the Joint Staff. It let Marge keep the family car and let Casey get his paper read before he reached the office. But today he left it folded on his lap while the early-morning breeze, funneled in through the driver's open window, blew on his face. When he finally picked up the paper, his eye fell on a small headline: "V.P. to Visit Ancestral Village." Casey read the story:

Vice-President Vincent Gianelli, who flies to Italy Wednesday for a good-will visit, is planning to spend the weekend in the remote mountain hamlet where his grandfather was born, it was learned.

The story went on with a description of Corniglio, a village high in the Apennines south of Parma. Perched on the mountains at the end of a dirt road, it contained only a few hundred residents. Gianelli would sleep in his grandfather's hut Friday and Saturday nights, and return to Rome on Sunday.

Casey thought again what an ideal weekend it was for an alert: no Congress in town, no vice-president. Not one in a dozen field commanders would suspect such a time might be chosen for a readiness exercise. No wonder the Joint Chiefs picked it.

Casey arrived at his office at 7:45. He made the customary check of his appearance in the washroom, then collected the briefing papers on Sir Harry Lancaster's appointment and walked down the E-ring corridor to the office of the chairman of the Joint Chiefs of Staff. He had been seated in the waiting room only a moment when Scott strode in.

"Good morning, Jiggs," he said as he swept by. "Come on in."

Casey couldn't help admiring his boss as the four-star General took his morning ration of cigars from a box on his desk and laid them neatly alongside a large green blotter. At fifty-eight he was all military. His lightly tanned face was unlined except for the tiny network of creases at the corner of each eye. He was six feet two and carried close to two hundred pounds without the slightest trace of softness. His hair was salt-and-pepper gray, a full thatch, combed neatly from a side part. A strong jaw and high cheekbones gave him a handsome, rugged face.

Casey had no doubt that those who called Scott the most popular military man since Dwight D. Eisenhower were right. Feature writers had praised him for almost thirty years: as the World War II fighter pilot who once downed seven ME-109's in a single day, as one of the first jet aces in Korea, as the brilliant air commander in Iran whose pinpoint bombing and resourceful use of tactical air cover almost made up for the inadequacies of our ground forces there.

Magazine articles often claimed to see in Scott a blend of the best of Eisenhower and MacArthur. He had, they said, Eisenhower's warm personality and appealing grin, plus MacArthur's brilliant mind, tough patriotism and slightly histrionic flair for leadership. Casey knew something else that the writers generally did not realize. Scott had an intuitive sense about politics and was widely read in the literature of that art. Casey had yet to see him make a major blunder in tactics, either military or political. When Scott protested the Korean War policies that prevented the Air Force from bombing across the Yalu, he managed to make his case without getting into the kind of trouble that ended MacArthur's career. Scott's recommendations had gone through channels, to his superiors, and had never been made public until someone (Casey guessed Murdock) slipped them to the Scripps-Howard newspapers a few months ago. Again, Scott bitterly dissented from President Frazier's decision to sue for peace in Iran rather than risk a nuclear war, but he kept his disagreement in proper bounds. Even on the subject of the disarmament treaty, when his position as chairman of the Joint Chiefs allowed him to speak publicly, he never quite crossed the line into forbidden territory.

Now he was concentrating on his work, reading rapidly through the briefing packet, wetting his thumb as he turned the pages.

"For once the British offer more than they ask," Scott said. "What do you think of this proposal that they shift an airborne regiment to our command in Okinawa?"

"I like it, sir. Those Highlanders are first-rate troops and the regimental commander is a good friend of General Faraday. They ought to work well together."

"I'd forgotten that. I think it's a pretty fair idea. Thanks, Jiggs. I think I'm up on everything now." Casey turned to go. "By the way, please tell the officers who drafted these papers that I thought they were excellent."

Now, who would think a straight guy like that would lie to a fellow before breakfast? Casey closed the door quietly behind him. Scott was already into the pile of papers awaiting his attention. The routine workday of the Joint Chiefs had begun.

Across the river at the White House the day's work was also well under way. President Jordan Lyman, like his chief military adviser, started early, and by 8:30 he had been hard at it for an hour. The difference was that Lyman was still in bed. Around him lay the jumbled sections of a dozen newspapers, evidence that he had finished his self-imposed weekly chore of sampling the press. He chose Sunday editions for their fatter letters-to-the-editor pages and the "big" editorials that publishers for some reason liked to print on the weekend.

This week's batch gave him a pretty clear picture of the mood of the country, and it definitely was not an optimistic one. The Atlanta *Constitution*'s lead editorial, for example, began:

As the date for the first stage of disarmament draws near, our skepticism as to Russia's good faith mounts. We hope, of course, that President Lyman's trust in Moscow proves justified, but . . .

There was a similar rumble in the *New York Times* judgment, delivered in customary doomsday style:

We supported the nuclear disarmament venture with grave reservations. These reservations have by no means been diminished in recent days by the pronouncements in *Pravda,* the official Soviet party organ . . .

My God, Lyman mused, you'd think editorial writers were the only people in America who ever had grave reservations. He climbed out of bed, walked into the big oval study, and poured himself a cup of coffee from the carafe that had been left there a few minutes earlier.

Through the tall windows overlooking the south lawn Jordan Lyman could see the steady morning rush of cars along Constitution Avenue. It's a funny thing, he thought. The people in those cars work for the government, just as I do. I can tell them what to do. I can make their jobs or wipe them out. But they have the power to undo what I do, by simple error, or by omission, or even by design.

He was President and famous. They were little bureaucrats and obscure. But they were, by and large, secure and befriended in their obscurity, while he stood vulnerable and alone in his fame.

Lyman had read more than enough American history to have known, on the day he returned from his oath-taking to enter the White House, that he faced loneliness. But his pre-inaugural comprehension had been academic, born of memoirs and legends. (Harry Truman said: "The buck stops here.") No reading, no advice from those who preceded him, had prepared him for the crushing emotional load of the Presidency. Jordan Lyman would never forget the hour he had spent, shaken and depressed, after receiving his first full briefing on the mechanics by which he alone could, in some fatal moment of crisis, open the floodgates of nuclear war.

He took a gulp of hot coffee. "Cut it out, Lyman," he growled out loud. "You're feeling sorry for yourself again."

The President picked up the morning paper from the tray beside the coffee jug where the mess attendant left it for him each day. He glanced at the front page and found the headline he knew would be there: "Lyman's Popularity Drops to Lowest Point in Poll's History."

He had expected some temporary slump in his rating. The acrimony of the Senate debate on the treaty had made a lot of headlines, which in turn couldn't have failed to hurt him. But he had been unprepared for the actual figures given him last night by his press secretary. Twenty-nine per cent, he thought, we're really getting clobbered on this one. We? Don't kid yourself. It's you, y-o-u.

He returned to the bedroom, dropped his pajamas on the floor, and went into the bathroom to wash and shave. He allowed himself to dwell a moment longer on that godawful Gallup Poll, then chided himself out loud again.

"Cheer up, world leader. Don't forget the *Literary Digest* picked Alf Landon in '36. You must be doing all right."

Ten minutes later he was on his way to breakfast. As he crossed the big upstairs hall, he nodded to an Army warrant officer sitting in a chair outside his room.

"Good morning."

"Good morning, Mr. President."

Nothing in the entire Presidential routine depressed Lyman quite so much as his exchange of morning greetings with these soldiers. There were five of them, and every night one sat outside Lyman's bedroom while he slept. The man on duty held a slim portfolio on his lap throughout the night. Inside it was a thin black box containing the complicated codes by which the President—and only the President—could give the orders sending America into nuclear war.

The first morning glimpse of his "atomic shadow," as Lyman called the unobtrusive warrant officers, always seemed to hurl him back into the duties of the Presidency, as though he had plunged nude into icy water. But he had learned to live with the facts of nuclear terror, and except for this first shock every day he paid no more attention to it than he did to the three-inch-thick plates of bulletproof glass set inside his office windows. The glass shields were insurance against a madman with a hunting rifle 500 yards away; the warrant officers were insurance against a madman with a ballistic missile 5,000 miles away.

Now Lyman was breakfasting in the small white-paneled family dining room downstairs, and the most pressing problem on his mind was how to teach those idiots in the kitchen to loosen the segments of a grapefruit before serving it. There was a knock on the doorjamb.

"Ah'm workin' foh the Gallup Poll," said the newcomer in the richest Georgia drawl he could manage, "and ah wantuh know how yuh feel about Jordan Lyman. *Someone* must like the guy. Hiyuh, Mistuh President!"

Raymond Clark's grin was as wide as his face. Even the flesh along the jawbones seemed to crinkle. Lyman laughed out loud. As always, he felt better at the sight of the junior senator from Georgia, this morning, as often, his breakfast partner.

"Put me down as undecided," Lyman said. "How about you?"

"Oh, Ah think he's a smaht ol' boy," Clark replied. "He's jes' ahead of his time, that's all." Then, dropping his heavy accent, he added: "But you'll come out okay, Jordie."

The waiter appeared with eggs, bacon, toast and fresh coffee, and the two men turned their attention to eating. As they ate, Lyman wondered if Clark ever realized how much this friendship meant to him. The Georgian was almost unique among Lyman's friends in Washington, for their relationship, though politically intimate, was only incidentally so. The bond between the two men was really almost entirely a personal one.

The public knew Ray Clark as Jordan Lyman's political manager, the man who got Lyman the presidential nomination on the third ballot at Chicago by making a deal with Governor Vincent Gianelli of New York to throw his strength to Lyman when his own momentum was checked.

But neither the public at large nor anyone at all, for that matter, knew that Clark, twenty years earlier, had given Jordan Lyman an infinitely more precious gift.

It happened in Korea where the two men—both reserve officers recalled in 1951 and assigned as infantry platoon leaders—commanded adjacent outfits on Heartbreak Ridge. They had returned together to the line after a final preattack briefing one foggy morning when Lyman simply froze, teeth chattering, eyes filling with helpless tears, in the grip of that utter exhaustion of body and spirit known as combat fatigue.

Clark joshed him gently at first. "Come on, Yankee boy," he said, using the old stand-by with which he kidded his Ohio-born buddy. "Let's go."

Lyman did not move.

"For Christ's sake, Jordie, snap out of it," Clark said, deadly serious. He spoke quietly so Lyman's men couldn't hear.

Again there was no reaction.

Clark put himself between Lyman and the troops, shoved him into a dugout and slapped him, left, right, left, right, four times, swinging his open hand as hard as he could. The two men stood there, nose to nose, staring at each other, for half a minute.

Then Clark asked: "You okay, Jordie?" and Lyman replied: "Yeah, Ray. Let's go."

Clark took a mortar fragment in his elbow that day, just after Lyman guaranteed the success of their attack by personally silencing two Chinese machine guns with hand grenades. As soon as he could, Lyman located Clark in a field hospital and visited him.

"Ray," he said, "I want to thank you for yesterday morning. You saved my life, and a lot more, when you socked me."

Clark lowered his voice, for the hospital tent was crowded, but his words were intense.

"Jordie," he said, "as far as I'm concerned I saw nothing and did nothing. What happened to you has happened to millions of men, and if you're as smart as I think you are you'll forget it ever did happen. I'm never going to mention it again —to you or anyone else."

In the years that followed, Clark kept his word. In fact, on a couple of occasions when Lyman seemed disposed to rehash the incident Clark wrenched the conversation into another channel. No phrase that might reawaken the memory of that morning, not even the nickname "Yankee boy," was ever again used by him in talk with Lyman.

But Lyman had not been able to follow Clark's advice, although he tried to. For months the incident regularly plagued his dreams. Even now he would relive it in his sleep once or twice a year. The very fact of his close political ties with Clark, their constant association, kept it in the back of his mind. The Georgian had been on hand for all the political crises—the key television speech in Lyman's race for governor of Ohio, his nomination for President, election night, and even the evening last winter when Lyman decided to fight his treaty through a balky Senate without accepting any reservations. Lyman never admitted to himself, much less to Clark, that he needed him. Each time he called on his friend he found other reasons— Clark's judgment, his easy humor, his common sense and common touch. But he was always there at the right time.

Now the President rubbed the last crumbs of toast from his fingers and reopened the conversation.

"I'd be less than honest, Ray, if I said the poll didn't hurt. It sure does. But I know this treaty is the right thing to do. Wait till you see the polls this fall."

Clark again assumed his drawl. "Ah'm not arguin' with you, Mistuh President, Jordie, suh. If Cousin Feemerov ovuh in the Kremlin pulls a fast one, we holluh 'foul' an' staht stackin' the bombs again." He reverted to normal accents. "Either way, by fall, you'll be in better shape."

Lyman laughed. "Ray, if I didn't know you better I'd think George Bernard Shaw picked you as the model for Eliza Doolittle. How do you decide when to turn that cracker dialect on and off?"

Clark's smile was slow and lazy. "Mr. President, a man has to keep in practice. In Georgia I'm a country boy trying to keep Sherman from coming back. In Washington I am a graduate of the Harvard Law School engaged in the practice of political science and high statesmanship."

"Okay, professor," Lyman replied. "Now suppose you give me a little lecture on the state of the Senate these days, with special reference to my program."

"I'm not sure yet, Mr. President, but I think it will be sticky. I think it might be smart to put off the big domestic stuff till next year. I know there's an election coming up, but we senators of the United States are feeling a little pushed around after that row on the treaty."

"Spoken like a true Senate man, Ray," Lyman said. "I don't suppose you did any of the pushing?"

"Why, Mr. President, I wouldn't say that, now. I may have helped some of my colleagues reason together a bit, but no more. Anyway, there won't be anything much doing on the Hill for three weeks now, with the recess starting. I'm in the clear myself except for an armed services meeting tomorrow to find out what will be left of our defenses after you take the bombs away."

"Scott going to be there?"

"Yessir, Gentleman Jim himself is going to deliver the overall report and then we'll hear in detail from the Navy on its plans."

"Well, if Prentice gets Scott to open up on the treaty again, keep an eye on him. Give me a ring if he says anything interesting, will you?"

Clark got up from the table. "Sure will. By the way, what do you hear from Doris and Liz?"

"Doris called last night from Louisville," said Lyman. "Liz's baby is due in a day or two. Certainly this week. Potential grandpas get kind of excited, Ray."

The Lymans' only child, Elizabeth, had been married a week before his own inauguration.

"We could use a little one right now," said Clark. "Why waste your first grandchild on a week when you're riding high in the polls?"

"Liz is a great little politician," said Lyman affectionately. "I think she's timing it perfectly for Pop."

"Give 'em both my love," said Clark.

The two friends headed for the west wing. Lyman dropped off at his office and Clark sauntered out through the visitors' lobby. There were only two reporters on the job at this early hour, but they both wanted to know how the President felt about the new Gallup Poll.

"I never quote the President," said Clark. The lazy smile spread over his face. "But you can quote me, if you're hard up. Twenty-nine per cent of the people still think Truman lost to Dewey in 1948."

Lyman settled himself behind the big desk in his office. A moment later Paul Girard popped his head through the door from his adjoining cubbyhole. Lyman looked at him and shook his head.

"I can tell by those eyes, you didn't get to bed early," he said. "Where were you last night?"

"In the camp of the enemy," Girard said, shaking his big, ugly head morosely. "I dined, or rather drank, at the home of Stewart Dillard, lobbyist for Union Instruments."

"Watch it." Lyman's grin belied his tone. "Remember Sherman Adams and Matt Connolly."

"If I promised anybody anything last night, I can't remember it this morning," Girard said. "Anyhow, I spent most of the time listening to that bastard Prentice proclaim his undying loyalty to you."

"I'll bet he did. Well, we can console ourselves in the knowledge that no one else likes him either."

"General James Mattoon Scott ought to love him, the way Prentice was talking about *him* last night," Girard grumbled. "Christ, the way he makes it sound, you'd think Scott could walk on water."

He pulled a white, five-by-seven card out of his pocket and slipped it into a holder on Lyman's desk.

"There's today's line-up, Mr. President. The first batter is Cliff Lindsay. He's due at 8:40, or a minute and a half ago."

"Hold him up for a couple of minutes, please, Paul," Lyman said. "I want to make a call."

He flicked the switch on his intercom box as Girard left.

"Esther? Please get me the Vice-President. Yes, he's probably still at home."

A red light winked beside his phone and he pushed the proper button.

"Vince? Yeah, I know. I saw it too. How about coming down for lunch? You can cheer me up. I want to talk about your trip, too. 12:30 okay? Fine. Thanks, Vince."

Cliff Lindsay, president of the AFL-CIO, bowed slightly to the President as Girard ushered him in. He said nothing as they shook hands and Lyman motioned him to a chair.

"You sent for me, Mr. President?" Lindsay's tone was totally noncommittal.

"Yes, I did, Cliff. Those strikes at the missile plants on the Coast don't make any sense at all to me. The men are getting good wages. There are no valid grievances that I can see. Maybe there's something I don't know. I thought maybe you could fill me in."

"You've been getting your story from the Secretary of Labor," Lindsay said stiffly. "We don't consider him exactly an unbiased source."

Lyman smiled. "You mean he's too pro-labor?"

"If that's intended as a joke, Mr. President, I can assure you the executive council won't take it that way."

"I can assure *you* this is no time for jokes," Lyman answered, his own tone now sharp too. "I want you to tell me why those men are on strike."

"It's no secret, Mr. President. Sure, it's a jurisdictional dispute. The sheet-metal workers get into a row with the aluminum workers, the Teamsters side with the sheet-metal guys and next thing you know the jobs are picketed. Maybe it's not the best beef in the world, but that's no cause for your Secretary of Labor to start hollering that labor is irresponsible. He knows damn well that's no way to get people back to work."

"The Secretary made the statement with my approval," the President said. "Cliff, I'm sick and tired of the Federation's all-or-nothing attitude."

Lindsay's face was passive, but his blue eyes darted around the room angrily.

"If we were all last time," he said slowly, "we could be nothing next time."

"If that's a threat," Lyman said, "I must say your timing is poor. If we don't show some unity now, with the Russians watching us over this treaty, there might be no next time."

"You got to give me time to work this thing out," Lindsay said, less aggressive but still stubborn.

"I'll give you a week," Lyman said. "If you can't clean it up by next Monday morning, I'll have to send the Attorney General into court."

He escorted Lindsay to the door. Again the union chief took the offered hand but said nothing. Lyman let it pass. Cliff was all right, and he had a few political problems of his own.

Lyman buzzed for Girard. "Paul, tell those West Virginia people that the Secretary of the Interior will handle the Rhododendron Queen. Tell them I've got a special Security Council meeting or something."

"Any real reason, Mr. President?"

"Yes, dammit. I need to plan some strategy and if I'm going to do it, I need to think—for a change."

Girard bowed slightly, grinning. Lyman knew no other man who could smile with quite that mixture of cynicism and warmth.

"I know, boss," he said. "It comes over all of us now and then."

Jordan Lyman knew he had handled Lindsay right and was sure he had come out ahead, but he was angry and frustrated. I came into office after that mess in Iran had this country's stock down to almost nothing, he thought. I had to do something about that and I did. I sat down to negotiate a disarmament treaty, something every President since Teddy Roosevelt tried to do, and I got one. What do I get? Labor is down on me. Business has always been hostile, and now that they'll have to make something besides nuclear warheads they're madder than ever. And if you believe Gallup, the public—whatever *that* is—is mad too.

It was hard for Lyman to understand the country's apparent hostility toward the treaty. Neither he nor anyone in his administration would ever forget the wave of relief that swept the nation and, in fact, the world the day the treaty was signed. A photographer had snapped a picture as Feemerov left the United States embassy in Vienna after the all-night session that buttoned it up. Lyman and the Russian, shaking hands on the steps, were haggard and unshaven after the final bargaining, but morning sun flooded the scene with the promise of a new day. The picture was printed in every city in the world. Men looked at it, felt the weight of nuclear holocaust lift from their shoulders, and wept.

But later the reaction set in. He began to understand how Wilson felt after Versailles. No matter how many times you explained, publicly or privately, the safeguards so painstakingly built into the treaty, someone always made a splash by charging "appeasement" or "sellout." The Senate debate on ratification gave every member of the lunatic fringe plenty of chance to rant. People started to worry about their jobs, as if the United States couldn't prosper without making bombs. As if Marx and Lenin and Khrushchev had been right.

God knows, Lyman thought, I don't trust the Kremlin either. That's why it took seven weeks to negotiate that treaty instead of seven days. But how can we possibly lose? If they cheat, we know it and we're back in business on twenty-four hours' notice. We don't dismantle a single bomb until they do.

And it had to be done. That was the one thing that finally compelled the Russians to sign a self-policing treaty and force their Chinese allies to do likewise. With atomic weapons already stacked like cordwood and Peiping boasting of a third hydrogen test, there wasn't much time left. This country will understand that eventually, he thought. I hope to God it doesn't take too long, but they'll understand.

President Jordan Lyman could lament the fickleness of public opinion, as this morning, and still retain his faith in the eventual soundness of collective public judgment. He had thought it out often during a public career that ran from district attorney through state senator, state attorney general and governor to the White House. Question: How do you know that the electorate will wisely exercise the power it is given in this republic? Answer: You don't—but it always has, in the long run. Lyman's wrestle with the problem was no matter of past decades, either. Even now the windows of his study were lighted late on many nights while he sat inside, feet propped up, shoulders pushed back in an easy chair, reading anything that bore on the American government, from Jefferson's letters to Eisenhower's press conferences. He rarely went back from his office to the mansion at night without picking a volume off the shelves in the Cabinet room that held the writings of the Presidents. Most people took the American system for granted even while they proclaimed its perfection. Lyman pondered it, questioned it, wondered about it, and so knew why it worked so well.

The intellectual curiosity that led Lyman into this long study, and the knowledge gained from it, also gave him a poise and balance that served him well now. He could lose his temper, but he never made an important decision when he was angry. He would weigh the pros and cons of an issue until his aides were in despair, then make up his mind and never waver again. Yet even as he stayed on a course so carefully charted, Lyman could always make himself see the other side. This was not modesty but breadth of understanding, although it did not always seem so. He would candidly concede, for instance, that under certain circumstances General Scott or Secretary of the Treasury Christopher Todd, the "brain" of his Cabinet, might have made a better President than he. Lyman did not find it necessary to add, on such occasions, that under existing circumstances he was better fitted for the job than they. He knew it. Those who heard his remarks, however, sometimes wondered whether he was afflicted with self-doubt. Lyman, having thought it out, would have been willing to disabuse them of this notion if they had asked about it. But they did not, for the associates of the President of the United States do not voice such notions to him, and so the question lingered in their minds—and perhaps in the mind of the public too.

Certainly Lyman was a good deal more complex than one

would guess from a glance at his record, a record of unbroken political triumphs in every election he ever entered
and of consummate skill as well in the art of back-room
politics. He obtained the presidential nomination by making a
deal with the man who came to Chicago with the greatest
number of first-ballot votes. Lyman, accompanied by Clark,
simply took a back elevator to Vince Gianelli's room and
told him he could not possibly win the nomination. Gianelli
exploded indignantly, but Lyman, who of course had thought
it all out before, explained the situation to Gianelli so precisely that the only remaining question was whether the New
Yorker would accept second place on the ticket. He did,
within the hour.

Lyman's race against President Edgar Frazier that year was
never a contest. He won it at the very start with a single sentence in his speech accepting the nomination: "We will talk
till eternity, but we'll never yield another inch of free soil,
any place, any time." The Republicans could never overcome
the public distaste for the Iranian War and the national revulsion against the partition that ended it. They privately
derided the Lyman-Gianelli ticket as "The Cop and the Wop,"
trying to turn Lyman's pride in his Ohio law-enforcement
record and Gianelli's ancestry against the two Democrats. The
analysts guessed later that this whispered slur cost the G.O.P.
more votes than it gained. The Democratic ticket carried all
but seven states in the first real landslide since Eisenhower.

Yeah, Lyman thought, I carried forty-three states a year
and a half ago. Now I'm trying to do something for all those
people, and I don't think I could carry ten states today.

He walked into his lavatory, splashed cold water on his
face, and wiped it dry.

"Listen, Lyman," he said aloud, "there's life in the old
bird yet. You'll bring this thing off. You've got to. You can't
let the world down."

There you go again, he thought, talking to yourself, trying
to sound like the big shot. Knock it off, Jordie, you're making
an ass of yourself.

Lyman went back to his desk and began reading the intelligence reports left for him by his military aide. A stranger seeing him now might have taken him for a college professor. At fifty-two, his rather long face was less wrinkled than seamed. His curly hair was thinning back from the temples and was streaked with occasional strands of gray. Although he had it trimmed weekly and kept at it with a comb, the hair had a wiry quality that made it appear perpetually tousled. Colorless plastic frames held his glasses on a prominent nose. He was not a tall man, standing an inch under six feet, but oversized hands and extremely big feet, appended to a rather thin body, gave him a gangling appearance. No one would call him handsome, but he looked like a man who could be trusted—and no politican could ask more of his own physique.

The President read and signed the stack of mail his secretary had left for him, holding out a couple of letters that weren't quite right so that he could dictate new versions. He was well into another pile of mail when Esther Townsend came in. She had come to work for him as his personal secretary when he was attorney general of Ohio, moved into the governor's office with him and inevitably accompanied him to the White House. No one else on his staff knew Jordan Lyman as well as this tall, blonde girl with the light-brown eyes and the wisp of hair falling over her forehead. She knew him so well that she rarely had to ask what to do with a problem. He knew her so well that he never had to worry about her judgment.

"The Vice-President is here," she said. "Do you want some more time to yourself?"

"No, thanks, Esther," he said, "I've done all the thinking that a man can stand in one day. Tell the kitchen they can bring lunch over here."

Over that lunch the two leaders commiserated on the evident ebb in the administration's popularity.

"I haven't sold the treaty to the country, Vince," Lyman said. "I've been too busy selling it to the Senate. But by the time you come back from Italy I'll have a plan. We'll work out of this, don't worry. We can. We have to, because we're right."

"I'm not faulting you, Mr. President. So Gallup puts us down. So what? It's one of those things. A couple of months from now, you'll be a hero."

"You'll be the hero this week, Vince. Home-town boy makes good." Lyman blew him a kiss, *bravissimo.* "Say, where'd you dream up that weekend in your grandfather's village? That's a great idea."

Gianelli beamed, winked and waved his arms, never missing a beat as his fork propelled meat loaf into his mouth. Lyman could never quite get over Gianelli's appetite and the haste with which he appeased it. But as Vince had once said: You want Ivy League manners, you should have picked someone from Princeton to run with you—and lost, maybe.

"I should take credit, but you know who cooked that one up? Prentice, that's who. I had it worked out to stop Saturday in Corniglio, you know, just run up on the way from here to there, make a little speech. So last Friday Prentice comes up to me in the cloakroom and says what am I going to do in the old country? And I give him a rundown. All of a sudden he sticks that finger in my face, the way he does, and gives me a big song and dance about tradition and sentiment and the Italo vote. He should tell me about *that.* But he says why not give the home-town thing a little more moxie and spend a couple of nights there? It's a natural if I ever heard one, no matter who thinks it up, so I buy it quick and yesterday the boys leak it to the papers."

"Prentice is sharp, all right," Lyman conceded dryly. "He made enough trouble for us over the treaty."

"Ah, he'll be okay when this simmers down some. I know, I'll never trust the bastard either, but an idea's an idea. Right?"

"Right, Vince. You going up to what's-its-name has real charm."

"Moxie," Gianelli corrected.

"Okay, moxie," Lyman agreed with a grin. "And moxie we can use right now."

Their talk drifted into small political gossip. Gianelli frequented the Senate cloakroom and the Speaker's rooms over in the House and he regularly brought Lyman an assortment of useful, if not always particularly elevated, nuggets of information. The Vice-President stowed away a pineapple sundae, patted his stomach, and rose to go.

"Cheer up, chief. From now on, things will start looking up." He waved from the door. "*Arrivederci,* Mr. President."

After he left General Scott's office, Casey concerned himself with strictly military matters in the strictly routine way with which he began each day. While the chairman conferred with Sir Harry Lancaster, Casey read methodically through the pile of messages, inquiries and receipts for orders that had accumulated since his relief from duty the day before. Selecting those that required Scott's attention, he added them to the Sunday stack and presented himself at the E-ring office shortly after the British Chief of Staff had left.

Scott, puffing on his first cigar of the day, was in good humor. Casey could almost feel himself basking in the General's radiance, as though he were standing on a beach in the first full heat of the morning sun. It was a rare man who, once within range of Scott's personality, failed to feel better for it.

"You look pretty chipper, Jiggs, for a man who had the Sunday duty."

"Marge and I stepped out last night, General. Pretty good party at the Dillards'. I think you've met him. He's Union Instruments' man here."

"Anybody I know there?" Scott asked.

"Yes, sir. Paul Girard from the White House and Senator Prentice, I guess, were the ranking guests."

Scott examined the thin column of cigar smoke wavering in the uncertain eddies of the air-conditioning currents. He chuckled.

"With those two," he said, "I'll bet there was a small go-round over the treaty. Prentice uphold our side all right?"

"He was pretty candid, sir. Also quite complimentary about

you." Now, why this line of questions? Casey wondered. Scott must have covered all this last night with Prentice at his quarters.

Unsure of his ground, Casey turned to business.

"Here's the message file, General. And I wondered if you wouldn't want to invite a couple of Congressional people to observe the All Red, sir? It might not hurt us on the Hill if the leaders saw just how smoothly we can work when we have to."

Scott pressed his palms hard against his desk, fingers spread, the nails white where he pushed them against the wood. Casey had long ago noted the General's unconscious habit of flexing his hand muscles, sometimes clenching the fist, sometimes pressing on an object, often simply pushing the heels of the hands against each other.

He looked at Casey for a moment, then studied the ceiling briefly before he answered his question.

"No, Jiggs. I want to test our security as well as our readiness," he said. "Right now, nobody in Congress has a hint of it, and I want to see if we can keep it that way."

Casey was on the verge of blurting an objection—that Senator Prentice already knew about the alert. But, again remembering the odd meeting at Fort Myer last night, he decided not to.

Scott looked at his watch. "Time for the tank. Walk over with me, and then wait awhile. We may have some questions you can help us on."

"The tank" was the big conference room used by the Joint Chiefs. The name memorialized the depressing effect it had had on several generations of occupants. Pentagon wags described the furniture as "dismal brown," the rug as "disappointed mustard," and the walls as "tired turquoise." Although it was on the outer side of the building, the Venetian blinds were usually closed, further emphasizing the room's cheerless atmosphere. Between the windows a cluster of flags provided the sole touch of bright color. There were nine of them: the personal flag of each service chief and the standard of each of the four services, plus the chairman's own flag—a blue-and-white rectangle divided diagonally with two stars in each half and an American eagle, wearing a shield and clutching three gold arrows, in the center.

A changing array of wall maps lent the proper military tone to the room. Today, Casey noted, a map of the United States had been hung.

As Casey retired to a chair outside, the service chiefs arrived, one at a time, from their own offices.

First in was General Edward Dieffenbach, the stocky paratrooper who was Army chief of staff, wearing the black eyepatch that made him famous in Iran. He walked as if he also had on the jump boots with which he liked to emphasize his continuing rating as a qualified parachutist.

General Parker Hardesty, Air Force chief of staff, needed no such sartorial trademarks. His wavy brown hair and long cigar served the purpose equally effectively.

Next was General William ("Billy") Riley, commandant of the Marines, owner of the most innocent blue eyes and the most belligerent jaw in the military establishment. Unlike the others, who had only a nod for Casey, Riley paused and winked.

"Into the tank again for the Corps, Jiggs," he said. "Outnumbered as usual."

Scott appeared again, but only long enough to close the door. Wait a minute, General, Casey thought, you haven't got the Navy with you yet. But the meeting began and wore on, and there was no sign of Admiral Lawrence Palmer, the chief of Naval Operations. Scott must have known he wasn't coming.

The four chiefs met in private for twenty minutes. As they filed out, Scott beckoned Casey into the room and motioned him to a chair. Casey sat down in the "Air Force seat" just vacated by General Hardesty. Scott pressed his hands together and strode over to a window to raise the blind. Casey, tapping the big brown ashtray in front of Hardesty's place, squeezed his thumb against a crumpled ball of paper. He fingered it idly as Scott sat down and lit a fresh cigar.

"Jiggs," the General said, "Colonel Murdock told me you heard about our Preakness pool. As a personal favor, I'd appreciate it if you'd keep that to yourself."

Casey could not quite hide his surprise.

"Don't worry, sir," he said, grinning. "All I want is the right horse. Seriously, General, I always respect your personal messages."

"I trust you'll keep Admiral Barnswell's reply in confidence too."

"Of course, sir."

Scott cocked an eyebrow. "Rank has its privileges, Colonel, as you'll realize when you get your star." He smiled at Casey. "Which I hope won't be too long coming."

The reference to his career genuinely flustered Casey.

"Actually, General, I make it a point on the Sunday duty to limit myself to official traffic. I don't inquire about the chairman's personal messages, but this time—well, sir, the young jaygee in all-service radio is something of a gossip."

"So I've heard. Name's Hough, isn't it?"

"Yes, sir."

Back at his desk, Casey found he still had the little wad of paper from the conference table. He unfolded it absently as he mused on Scott's mention of a possible promotion for him. By the book, he wasn't due for consideration for another three years. By then there might not be so many stars to hand out, thanks to the disarmament treaty. At least that was the way a lot of hungry colonels around here had it figured. Better not waste a lot of time thinking about it.

Why such a flap about those Preakness messages? Scott seemed a little uneasy even talking about them. Casey couldn't remember the chairman's ever being on the defensive that way before. He flattened out the little piece of paper, which turned out to be a page from one of the memo pads on the chiefs' table.

Something was written on it, in pencil, in General Hardesty's scrawl. Casey squinted to make it out. It seemed to say: "Air lift ECOMCON 40 K-212s at Site Y by 0700 Sat. Chi, NY, LA. Utah?"

The K-212 was the newest of the military jet transports,

big enough to handle a hundred troops in full battle dress with light support weapons. There was that queer ECOMCON thing again. Now, just what the hell is going on? Casey asked himself. That's Hardesty's writing, all right. Why would anyone need a big jet airlift for the Saturday alert? Casey felt strangely unsettled and a little irritated as he stuffed the paper into his pants pocket. Why is a whole operation being kept secret from the director of the Joint Staff, who is supposed to know everything?

On his way to lunch a couple of hours later, Casey met Dorsey Hough in the corridor. The bored look was gone from his sallow face. Instead, he wore a triumphant grin.

"Hey, Colonel, you know that transfer I was telling you about? Someone must have heard me talking. It came through a few minutes ago and it's good old Pearl for me."

He did a poor imitation of a hula twist and winked at Casey.

"And say, by the way, Big Barnsmell turned out to be the only party poop on the chairman's racing form. All the others came through with their IOU's."

He swaggered off down the hall, whistling "Sweet Leilani," without waiting for a reply. Good God, Casey thought, a man needs more than four hours' sleep to cope with the characters around this place. What a flatheaded flannelmouth that kid is. How does a man like that get cleared for code duty? Thank God the Japanese aren't threatening Pearl Harbor this semester.

In mid-afternoon, after delivering a folder of papers to Scott's secretary, Casey met another colonel—this one Army —as he was leaving the chairman's office. The two men all but collided head on in the doorway.

"Well, well, if it isn't my favorite jar-head himself," said the soldier, pulling Casey into the corridor and looking him up and down appraisingly.

"Hello, Broderick," Casey replied, trying to hide his distaste for the other man's use of an epithet that was generally intended to provoke a Marine to blows. "I thought you were in Okinawa, or maybe worse."

A heavy hand came down just a bit too hard on Casey's shoulder. "Not me, Jerome, not me."

Instantly the old dislike for this man came flooding back over Casey. Colonel John R. Broderick was as ugly a man as he knew. His eyebrows merged in a dark line over the bridge of his nose, a scar marked his right cheek, the backs of his hands were covered with thick black hair. Casey had seen Broderick's face contorted with contempt and had long ago decided this was the most arrogant officer he'd ever met.

They had fallen out the first time they had seen each other, in the officers' club at the Norfolk Naval Base during joint amphibious exercises years ago when Casey was in the basic officers' course at Quantico and Broderick was a new second john in the Army. They were standing at the long mahogany bar when Broderick made some sneering remark about the Marines. Casey suggested he hadn't meant it and when Broderick repeated his gibe, Casey invited him outside. Instead, Broderick swung at him right there and Casey swung back. Luckily two friends broke it up and there were no senior officers in the room.

Their paths crossed occasionally during the years, the last time in Iran, where Casey remembered Broderick, by then a Signal Corps battalion commander, growling that the country would never be worth a damn until we got a President "with enough iron in his spine to shut down the goddam Congress for a couple of years." Ironically, their wives met and become friendly while they were overseas, and Casey later suffered through a couple of strained social evenings while Broderick inveighed against the President, both parties, and politicians in general. A few months ago the Brodericks disappeared from Washington and Casey hadn't bothered to find out their whereabouts.

Somewhere along the line Broderick had learned that he could always rile Casey by using his middle name.

"Jerome, my boy," he said now, "I hear you're doing a fine job as director of the Joint Staff, a fine job."

Casey felt like swinging again. Not the least of Broderick's poisonous traits was his habit of saying everything twice, as though his listener were either deaf or a moron, or both.

"Where you stationed now, Broderick?"

"Uh . . . oh, no you don't, no you don't. I'm top secret, pal, all the way. Just in town for the day to report to the chairman." He nodded toward Scott's office and smiled condescendingly at Casey.

"Have it your own way, Broderick," Casey said. "You usually manage to, anyway."

"How right, Jerome, how right. See you around sometime."

Casey was back at his desk a few minutes later, still irritated, when Marge called. She had just finished a round of golf at the Army-Navy Country Club and was about to pick up the boys at school.

"Jiggs," she asked, "who do you think I just saw in the clubhouse?"

"Abercrombie and Fitch."

"Monday's your bad day for jokes, honey. I saw Helen Broderick. Very mysterious, like Mata Hari. Wouldn't say what John's doing. Something very hush-hush down near Fort Bliss. Don't you know all the hush-hush things, dear?"

"Oh, sure," Casey said. At least I used to, he thought.

"Well, I'm dying to know. Sounds all hot and sandy and deliciously secret. What time will you be home tonight?"

"The usual, more or less, I guess. Say about six."

Casey toyed with a pencil on his desk. So Broderick is head of some secret command near Fort Bliss, eh? That checked with what Mutt Henderson was talking about yesterday. On a hunch, he fished out of his jacket pocket the paper Mutt had given him and dialed the number. Henderson answered.

"Hi, Mutt. Jiggs. Just checking on you. When you leaving?"

"In a couple of hours, after the C.O. gets through with Scott."

Casey kept his tone casual.

"Hope you get along better with Johnny Broderick than I do," he said. "The guy rubs me the wrong way."

"Yeah," Henderson said, "he takes a lot of getting used to.

But he's one hell of a C.O., Jiggs. Our outfit really moves. The men don't like him, but they work their butts off for him anyway. Big morale man."

"Well, good luck, Mutt. Let us know next time you come up here."

My God, Casey thought as he hung up, Scott sure picked a fine Fascist son-of-a-bitch to run his ECOMCON—whatever that is.

Casey pulled the stack of papers out of his "in" box and doggedly set to work on them. He couldn't keep his mind on the job. The events of the past two days kept intruding on his concentration. Finally he gave up trying and just sat, wondering why he was so addled. Suddenly he got up, cleared his desk, locked his safe, and picked up his cap.

"Miss Hart," he said to his secretary, "call the car for me, please. I'm going home. If there's any flak, I'll be there."

His car was in the driveway when the Army chauffeur delivered Casey at his home. The boys were nowhere in evidence. He found Marge in the kitchen.

"It's only four o'clock, Jiggs," she said, startled. "Are you sick?"

He answered with an embrace whose vigor and duration were sufficient to convince her of his good health. He grinned at her when she wiggled loose.

"Nope, I'm doing fine," he said, "but I need to take the car for an errand. I won't be long."

He changed into slacks and sport shirt, then drove down to the Potomac and out the George Washington Parkway, past the fashionable homes on the bluffs, all the way to Great Falls. He parked and walked down along the dirt path to a rock ledge overlooking the cascades.

Casey sat on the rocks and watched the brown water of the Potomac careen over the falls, disappearing into dark eddies at the bottom, then bursting into new rapids. He watched this, but he did not really see it, for he was thinking.

Prentice talking about being "alert." Admiral Barnswell refusing to put up ten bucks for the chairman's betting pool. That bastard Broderick. ECOMCON. General Hardesty's crumpled memo: a big airlift to New York, Chicago, Los Angeles and . . . and maybe Utah. Why Utah? In fact, why an airlift? What was Site Y anyway? And why was Scott suddenly cutting him out of things? Bits and pieces from the past two days swirled in Casey's mind like the water at the foot of the falls. He struggled to sort them out. The Vice-President's trip, for some reason, kept intruding on his thoughts, but he was at a loss to know why. Casey again felt the uneasiness of Sunday morning and the anxiety that had kept him awake last night. He sat by the falls and stared down at them, and he tried to make some sense of it.

Casey sat for almost an hour, oblivious of the strolling couples and the racketing children who passed him. Then he stood up, stretched, and walked slowly back along the path, his eyes on the ground.

He was still preoccupied as he drove along the river toward town. In Langley the sight of a telephone booth at the corner of a service station lot broke the spell.

Casey pulled off the road, dropped a dime into the coin box, and dialed.

"White House." The operator was simply stating a fact.

Casey took a deep breath, started to speak, then hesitated.

"White House?" The phrase had become a question.

"Paul Girard, please," said Casey, finding his voice.

"May I tell him who is calling?"

"Colonel Martin Casey."

"Just a minute, Colonel."

There was a delay of more than a minute before Girard came on.

"Jiggs, if you offer to buy me a drink, I'll cut your throat."

Casey had no answering wisecrack. "Paul," he said, "I want to see the President."

"Oh, fine," Girard scoffed. "What did you do when you got home last night? Pick up where I left off? You really must be flying by now."

"Paul," Casey repeated, "I want to see the President. No kidding."

"Sure. All you have to do is invent a forty-hour day and we

can take care of you and everybody else too."

"Paul, I'm serious. I've got to see him."

Girard chuckled patronizingly. "Okay, pal. How about my saving you a few minutes the next time your boss comes over here? I'll slip you in afterwards if you can hang around."

"Uh-uh. I have to see him right away. Today."

For the first time there was the slightest hint of professional wariness in Girard's voice when he answered. "Today? Come on, Jiggs, what's this all about? Some hot-shot Pentagon business?"

"Paul, I can't talk to you about it now."

"You can tell your uncle Paul, Jiggs. These phone lines are okay."

"No, no, I don't mean that." Casey was sweating inside the stuffy phone booth, but the heat was not the cause. "I can't tell you about it, Paul. It's . . . it's a national security matter."

Casey knew there was much defense information to which he had access but which was denied to Girard on the theory that he didn't need to know it. He hoped the phrase would be enough. It wasn't.

"Jesus, Jiggs, aren't you pretty far out of channels? How about doing it through Scott or the Secretary of Defense?"

"I can't, Paul."

Girard again chose to see the funny side. "Ah, I'm beginning to get it now," he bantered. "Looking for a backdoor promotion? Or are you after the chairman's job?"

Casey squeezed the phone hard.

"Paul, listen to me. Please. You know I'd tell you about this if I could. I'd like to. I think the President would, and will, but he's got to decide that. There are things involved that I'm sure you don't know about and it isn't up to me to tell them to you." He stopped.

"Go ahead, Jiggs." There was no jesting in Girard's voice now and Casey knew he had broken through.

"I said it was a national security matter. What I really mean is, it involves the . . . the security of the government. The President has to know about it as soon as possible."

Girard was silent for what seemed to Casey like half an hour. Then he spoke again, all business.

"Well, how about tomorrow morning? I can fit you in at eight-thirty."

"That'll be twelve hours wasted," Casey said. "Besides, I can only come at night."

"Oh." There was another pause. Then: "Hang on, Jiggs. Let me talk to The Man and see what I can do."

Casey loosened his shirt, pushed the door of the booth open a foot or so, and lit a cigarette. It was half gone when Girard's voice came through the phone again.

"Okay, Jiggs. Be here at eight-thirty sharp tonight. Come in the east entrance. I'll be waiting for you. And I sure hope it's as important as you said, because the President hates any nighttime stuff."

"Thanks, Paul," said Casey. "It's important. And Paul, tell the President all you know about me. He's got to hear me out."

Monday Night

Casey left his car in a garage on F Street and walked around the block past the Treasury building. The softness of evening had dropped over the city like a veil, blurring the sharp edges of daytime. The statue of Albert Gallatin in front of the Treasury seemed friendly, almost lifelike, in the dusk. There were few people on Pennsylvania Avenue, for Washington, unlike Paris or London, withdraws into itself after sunset. It is a habit that Europeans patronize but which Americans feel lends a kind of lonely dignity to their capital. Casey was simply thankful for the lack of pedestrians on the streets; he did not care to be seen just then.

He had viewed the scene scores of times: the great elms arching over the sidewalk from the White House lawn, the last white-capped guide still prowling the corner in quest of a late tourist, the handful of bench sitters dozing in Lafayette Park, the glow from the great hanging lantern on the White House portico. Tonight the calm setting seemed somehow unreal, strangely detached from his own mission.

Casey turned the corner down East Executive Avenue and walked quickly to the east gate, where a White House policeman stood outside his cubicle. In the semicircular driveway beyond, Girard was waiting, his eyelids half lowered like tiny curtains in the big head, his hands jammed in his pants pockets.

"Here's my man, officer," he said. "He's okay."

Girard made no effort to suppress his curiosity as they walked along the wide ground-floor hallway through the east wing to the mansion itself.

"What the devil is this all about, Jiggs?"

"Paul, I told you I can't tell you about it. That's got to be up to the President. Did you brief him on me?"

"Sure." Girard paused before he pressed the elevator button. "Listen, Jiggs, I hope this isn't more trouble. The Man's got all the headaches he can stand right now."

The elevator doors slid open and they stepped into the little car. With walnut paneling, rich brown carpeting, and two oval windows in the doors, it seemed almost like a small room. Girard motioned Casey off at the second floor and led him across the cavernous hall—actually a great room in itself —that swept almost the whole width of the mansion.

The President's study was oval in shape. Casey guessed that it must be directly above the ornate Blue Room on the first floor. Here, in the living quarters, the colors were warmer, thanks to soft yellow carpeting and slip covers, but the study was still far too large for Casey's taste or comfort. Its high ceiling, pilastered walls, tall bookcases, and shoulder-high marble mantel combined to make him feel a little less than life-size.

President Lyman was reading, his big feet all but hiding the footstool on which they rested, when Casey and Girard entered. An Irish setter with silky red-brown hair and sad eyes lay curled on a little hooked rug beside the President's chair. Lyman laid his glasses on a table, stood up quickly and came forward smiling, his large hand extended. The dog accompanied him and sniffed gravely at the cuffs of Casey's trousers.

"Hello, Colonel. It's a pleasure to see you outside of business hours."

"If this isn't business," Girard said, "I'll strangle him." He returned to the door. "I'll leave you two alone."

"Colonel," said Lyman as the door closed, "meet Trimmer. He's a political dog. He has absolutely no convictions, but he's loyal to his friends."

"I've read about him, sir," said Casey. "Good evening, Trimmer."

"Ever been up here before, Colonel?"

"No, sir. Just social occasions downstairs. Awful big rooms, sir."

Lyman laughed. "Too big for living and too small for conventions. I don't blame Harry Truman and the others for getting out of here every time they had the chance. Sometimes it gives me the creeps." Lyman swept his arm around the room, his bony wrist thrusting out of the shirt cuff.

"Still, for a place big enough to hold a ball in, this room is about as cozy as you could expect. They tell me it used to be pretty stiff until Mrs. Kennedy did it over in this yellow. And she found that old footstool somewhere. The Fraziers left it that way and Doris and I decided we couldn't improve on it either."

Casey was vastly ill at ease. He was no stranger to high officials, including this President, but somehow even Lyman's small talk, though obviously intended to relax him, made the nature of his errand suddenly seem to dwindle in dimension. What had been real and immediate in the roar of Great Falls now looked fuzzy and a bit improbable. He stood somewhat stiffly.

"Drink, Colonel?"

"Why . . . yes, sir. Scotch, please, sir. A little on the pale side, if you don't mind."

"Fine. I'll keep you company."

The drinks mixed, the two men sat down in the yellow-covered armchairs with a little end table between them. Trimmer settled down again on his rug, his eyes on Casey. Over the white marble mantel, the prim features of Healy's *Euphemia Van Rensselaer* looked down on them, not altogether approvingly. Casey was facing the tall triple windows which provided, through sheer mesh curtains, a vista of the darkening Ellipse. The fountain on the south lawn raised its stream of water below the balcony. Far away, down by the tidal basin, stood the domed colonnade of the Jefferson Memorial, its central statue softly spotlighted. A little to the left, and much closer, rose the gray-white shaft of the Washington Monument, red lights at its top as a warning to low-flying aircraft.

"And now, Colonel. That matter of national security." Lyman's eyes were on Casey.

Casey licked his lips, hesitated a moment and then began just as he had rehearsed it on the drive from home.

"Mr. President," he asked, "have you ever heard of a military unit known as ECOMCON?"

"No, I don't believe I have. What does it mean?"

"I'm not sure, sir, but in normal military abbreviations, I'd think it would stand for something like 'Emergency Communications Control.'"

"Never heard of anything like that," the President said.

Casey took his second step.

"I know a colonel isn't supposed to question his commander in chief, sir, but have you ever authorized the formation of any type of secret unit, regardless of its name, that has something to do with preserving the security of things like telephones, or television and radio?"

Lyman leaned forward, puzzled. "No, I haven't."

"Excuse me again, sir, but one more question. Do you know of the existence of a secret army installation that has been set up somewhere near El Paso recently?"

"The answer is 'no' again, Colonel. Why?"

"Well, sir, I hadn't heard of it either, until yesterday. And as the director of the Joint Staff I'm fully cleared and I'm supposed to know everything that goes on in the military establishment. That's even more true of you, sir, as commander in chief."

Lyman sipped his drink for the first time. Casey reached gratefully for his own highball and took a swallow before he went on.

"In a way I'm relieved that you said 'no' to those questions,

Mr. President, but in a way I'm not. I mean, if you had said you knew all about ECOMCON, I'd have said thanks and apologized for bothering you and asked permission to go home. I'd have been pretty embarrassed. But the way it is, Mr. President, it's worse. I'm frightened, sir."

"We don't scare easy in this house, Colonel. Suppose you let me have the whole story."

"Well, sir, yesterday I learned from an old Army friend, a Colonel Henderson, that he's executive officer of ECOMCON. Today I learned that the commanding officer is another man I know, an Army colonel named John Broderick. Both of them are Signal Corps, which means their outfit has something to do with communications. They've had a hundred officers and thirty-five hundred men training secretly at a desert base near El Paso for six weeks or so.

"I ran into Henderson by accident and naturally he thought I knew all about it, because of my job. He said one odd thing that got me thinking, something about how they spent more time in training 'on the seizing than on the preventing.' He complained that somebody up here must have a defeatist attitude because their book seemed to assume that the Communists already had the facilities."

"What facilities?" Lyman broke in.

"He didn't say."

"Who set up this outfit?"

"I assume General Scott did, sir. At least Henderson and Broderick were up here to report directly to the chairman today.

"Of course," Casey went on, "when I heard, I assumed that I had been cut out of it for some perfectly logical security reason. It didn't occur to me then that you might not know about it. It just seemed odd. Then this morning I got another jolt. Look at this, sir."

Casey took the memo-sized paper from his wallet, unfolded it carefully, and handed it to the President. Lyman reached for his glasses. He studied the note for a minute.

"I must say I can't make much out of this scrawl, Colonel."

"That's General Hardesty's writing, sir. I know it pretty well. The paper comes from one of the memo pads they use in the Joint Chiefs' meeting room. It was rolled up in a ball in an ashtray and I happened to pick it up this morning."

"What does it say? I can't make sense out of the part of it I can read, let alone the rest." Lyman held out the note.

Casey took it again and read the note out loud: " 'Air lift ECOMCON. 40 K-212s at Site Y by 0700 Sat. Chi, NY, LA. Utah?'

"It looks to me, sir, like Air Force jet transports—that's the K-212—are scheduled to lift this whole command out of Site Y—that's what Henderson called the base near El Paso—before the alert Saturday, and take the troops to Chicago, New York, Los Angeles, and maybe Utah. The telephone company has big relay facilities for its long lines, you know, sir, in Utah."

Lyman eyed Casey closely. Casey, in his turn, noted a frown on the President's face. He wondered whether it was a sign of concentration—or of suspicion.

"Just what are you leading up to, Colonel?"

"I'm not sure, as I said, Mr. President. But let me try to tell you the other things that have happened in the past two days. It's all very hard for me to sort out, even in my own mind."

Lyman nodded. Slowly, carefully, and in detail, Casey recounted every oddity that had occurred since Sunday morning. He began with Scott's invitation to the five field commanders for wagers on the Preakness, Admiral Barnswell's curt "no bet" reply, and the unusual emphasis that Scott had put on the need for silence on Casey's part. He told of meeting Senator Prentice at the Dillard party, of Prentice's outspoken condemnation of Lyman and praise of Scott, and of his use of a phrase that indicated knowledge of the alert. He explained how he had seen Prentice's car parked outside Scott's quarters at midnight, and how Scott had lied to him about that visit by saying he had been asleep by 10:30. He told of Scott's apparently lying again when he said no one on Capitol

Hill knew of plans for the alert. He mentioned Dorsey Hough's sudden transfer. He quoted Broderick's previously stated views on the desirability of a government without a Congress, and cited his bitter disdain for civilian leaders. He reminded Lyman that the Joint Chiefs had set the alert for a time when Congress would be in recess, when the Vice-President would be abroad—and when the President would be in the underground command post at Mount Thunder. He told of his surprise when he noted in the paper that Gianelli would be in a remote mountain hamlet in Italy Saturday night.

By the time he had finished, the White House was in the full embrace of night. Only the street lights and the glint of water in the fountain could be seen through the windows. Casey glanced at his watch. He had talked for almost an hour without interruption.

President Lyman stretched and ran a big hand through his wiry hair. He walked over to a small table, selected a pipe, and went through the fussy little preparations for smoking it. Casey, uneasy again in the silence that followed his long recital, drank off the last ice water in the bottom of his glass.

"Colonel," said the President at last. "Let me ask you a question or two. How long have you worked with General Scott?"

"Just about a year, sir."

Lyman struck a match and pulled at the pipe until he had it going.

"Have you mentioned what you've just told me to anyone else?"

"No, sir. Paul asked about it, but I thought you were the only one I should talk to, under the circumstances. I haven't said a thing to anyone else."

Lyman, back in his chair, crossed his feet on the stool and tried several smoke rings. There was a little too much draft from the open windows.

"What is Scott's real attitude on the treaty?" the President asked. "I know he's been against it in his testimony on the Hill, and I gather he's leaked some stories to the newspapers. But how deeply does he feel?"

"He thinks it's a terrible mistake, sir, a tragic one. He believes the Russians will cheat and make us look silly, at best, or use it as a cover for a surprise attack some night, at worst."

"And you, Colonel, how do you feel?"

Casey shook his head. "I can't make up my mind, Mr. President. Some days I think it's the only way out for both sides. Other days I think we're being played for suckers. I guess I really think it's your business, yours and the Senate's. You did it, and they agreed, so I don't see how we in the military can question it. I mean, we can question it, but we can't fight it. Well, we shouldn't, anyway."

Lyman smiled.

"Jiggs, isn't it?" he asked. "Isn't that what they call you?"

"Yes, sir, it is." Casey began to feel almost normal.

"So you stand by the Constitution, Jiggs?"

"Well, I never thought about it just that way, Mr. President. That's what we've got, and I guess it's worked pretty well so far. I sure wouldn't want to be the one to say we ought to change it."

"Neither would I," Lyman said, "and I've thought about it a lot. Especially lately, after this row over the treaty. How do the other chiefs feel about the treaty, Jiggs?"

"Just like General Scott, sir. They're all against it. The C.N.O., Admiral Palmer, sometimes even gets a little violent on the subject."

No sooner had he finished the sentence than Casey felt a rush of guilt. Criticizing a ranking officer inside the service was one thing, but outside quite another.

"I didn't mean to single out the Admiral, sir. They all feel that way. It's just that he—"

Lyman cut him off. "Forget it, Colonel. By the way, at that meeting this morning—the one where you think that note was written—were all of them there? All five chiefs?"

"No, sir. As a matter of fact, Admiral Palmer wasn't in it." Now Casey was thoroughly confused.

"Anything unusual about that?"

"No . . . Yes, sort of. Now that I think of it, he didn't have a representative there either. I mean, it's not unusual for a chief to miss a meeting, but they always send someone to sit in for them. In fact, I can't remember another time when a service just wasn't there at all."

Lyman thought for a minute, then apparently dismissed this line.

"By the way, Colonel, who are Scott's special friends in the press and television? Do you know?"

The question startled Casey. He glanced at the President's face for a clue, but Lyman was studying the bowl of his pipe.

"Well, sir," Casey said hesitantly, "I'm not really sure. He knows some of the big columnists, and he has lunch or dinner occasionally with a group of Washington bureau chiefs, but I don't know of any of them being a special friend. The editor of *Life* has been in a couple of times, and of course the military writers for the Baltimore *Sun* and the *Star* here.

"I can't think of any others . . . Wait a minute. He's very close to that television commentator, Harold MacPherson. I think he's with RBC. MacPherson has called several times when I've been in the General's office, and I know they've seen each other socially. Frequently, I'd say."

"And that horse pool business?" The President seemed to be going over the things Casey had told him. "I don't quite get your point on that."

"I wouldn't have thought anything," Casey said, "except along with everything else. Frankly, sir, I think that message could be a code for some kind of . . . well, action, on Saturday, and not about the race at all. And then, if that's right, Admiral Barnswell has included himself out."

Again there was silence.

"Well, to sum it up, Jiggs, what are you suggesting?"

"I don't know for sure, sir." Casey fumbled for the right words. "Just some possibilities, I guess. What we call capabilities in military intelligence, if you know what I mean. I guess it all sounds fantastic, just saying it, but I thought it was my duty to lay it all out for you."

The President's voice was suddenly hard.

"You afraid to speak plain English, Colonel?"

"No, sir. It's just that—"

Lyman interrupted harshly.

"Do you mean you think there may be a military plot to take over the government?"

The words hit Casey like a blow. He had avoided the idea, even in his own thoughts. Now it was there, an ugly presence in the room.

"I guess so, sir," he said wanly, "as long as you use the word 'may,' making it a possibility only, I mean."

"Are you aware that you could be broken right out of the service," Lyman snapped, "for what you have said and done tonight?"

It was Casey's turn to stiffen. The cords stood out in his short, thick neck.

"Yes, sir, I am. But I thought it all out pretty carefully this afternoon and I came here and said it." He added quietly: "I thought about the consequences, Mr. President. I've been a Marine for twenty-two years."

Lyman's sudden harshness seemed to slip away. He went over to the little bar, mixed himself another Scotch and asked Casey if he wouldn't like a second. Casey nodded. God knows I need one, he thought.

"You know," Lyman said, "I can never get over the caliber of the service academy graduates. The officer corps, the professionals, have been good to the nation. And they've been good *for* it. The country has believed that—look at the rewards military men have been given, even this office I happen to hold right now. There's been a real feeling of trust between our military and civilians, and damned few countries can say that. I think it's one of our great strengths."

Lyman went on, looking at the liquid in his glass, not so much talking to the other man in the room as musing aloud about the generals and admirals he had known and admired. He spoke with something like awe of the combat records of Scott, Riley and Dieffenbach. He said he agreed with the people who thought Scott might be the next President.

Casey listened respectfully, sipping his drink. He hadn't realized the President felt this way. He seemed to know everything about the military. He was generous in his evaluation of men. When Lyman told an anecdote about General Riley, a story of which the President was the butt, Casey laughed with him. But he also was becoming aware that this man was far more perceptive and sensitive than he had realized.

"Maybe that's why our system works so well," Lyman concluded, "fitting men with the brains and courage of Scott and Riley in near the top, making use of their talents, but still under civilian control. I'd hate to see that balance upset in some hasty action by men who'd come to regret it until the day they died."

"So would I, sir," Casey said.

"Have you any bright ideas on what I ought to do, Jiggs?"

"No, sir." Casey felt inadequate, almost as if he'd let this man down. "I'm just a buck passer on this one, Mr. President. The solution is way out of my league."

The President unhitched his big feet from in front of him and stood up in an angular series of motions that seemed to proceed one joint at a time. He grasped Casey's hand. There was no perceptible pull, but Casey found himself moving toward the door as he returned the handshake.

"Colonel," Lyman said, "I very much appreciate your coming in to see me. I think perhaps I ought to know where I can reach you at any time. Could you call Miss Townsend, my secretary, in the morning and keep her up to date on where you'll be? I'll tell her to expect the call. Thanks for coming in. Thanks very much."

"Yes, sir. Good night, sir." Casey was out in the big hall. Lyman came after him as he started for the elevator.

"One other thing, Colonel. Now that you've talked to me there are two of us who know about your thoughts. I think maybe I'd better be the one to decide from now on whether anyone else should know. That includes your wife, too."

"I never tell her anything that's classified, sir."

"This conversation has just been classified by the Commander in Chief," Lyman said with a quick smile. "Good night, Jiggs."

When Girard came back to the President's study after meeting Casey on the ground floor and escorting him out, he found Lyman walking restlessly around the room.

"Get a drink in your fist, Paul," the President said. "You'll want one. Your friend Casey thinks he's discovered a military plot to throw us out and take over the government."

"He what?" Girard gaped in disbelief.

"That's what the man says. A regular damn South American junta."

"Oh, Christ." Girard groaned in mock horror. "Not this month. We're booked solid with troubles already."

Lyman ignored the opening for light repartee. He spoke slowly.

"Paul, I'm going to tell you everything he told me. First, there's one thing you need to know. Another All Red alert, a full readiness test, has been scheduled with my approval for Saturday at three P.M. I'm supposed to go up to Mount Thunder for it. Under the security plan, you weren't to know, and neither was anyone else except the chiefs, Casey and Colonel Murdock, Scott's aide. Now remember that and listen to me."

Lyman recounted Casey's full story. He showed Girard the creased scratch-pad sheet with General Hardesty's scribbles, and copies of Scott's message and Barnswell's reply, all of which Casey had left with him. As Lyman talked, Girard sank lower in his chair, his sleepy eyes almost closed, his head cradled between his hands.

"Now let me add a few things *I* know that I didn't tell Casey about," Lyman said when he had finished. "Several months ago I got a call from General Barney Rutkowski, the chief of the Air Defense Command. I've known Barney awhile and I guess he thought he could speak freely to me. Anyway, he said General Daniel, the SAC commander, had sounded him out on making a trip up here to talk with Scott about 'the political mess the country's in and the military's responsibility,' or something like that. Barney asked me what to do. I told him that I could use a little advice from Scott, but the upshot was that Barney stalled off the invitation and nothing came of it. At least, I never heard any more about it."

Girard pulled his ear. "I gather your point is that Daniel is one of the men on Scott's betting list."

"That, and the wording of the invitation Barney got," Lyman said. "Now, second. Vince Gianelli told me at lunch today that Prentice was the one who suggested he spend Friday and Saturday nights at his grandfather's place in the mountains. Fred suggested it to him last Friday, Vince says, and he changed his plans to do it. Of course, it's a good publicity gimmick, but it's funny that Prentice would be thinking up ways to help the administration, especially just one day after the Joint Chiefs fixed the date for the alert, which Prentice obviously knows about, if we can believe what Casey says."

"Don't worry about that part of it, boss," Girard said. "Jiggs is solid. He never makes anything up, and he's got a good memory to boot."

"A third point," Lyman went on. "A week ago Sunday, I watched the Harold MacPherson show on RBC. He spent twenty-five minutes blasting me and the treaty and five minutes praising the bejesus out of Scott. I hadn't seen him in quite a while. Actually I watched because Doris had been raving about his sex appeal and it made me curious. The fellow's a spellbinder all right. His style reminds me of Bishop Sheen or Billy Graham years ago. Afterwards I realized I didn't know much about him and I asked Art Corwin to run me a quiet check."

"You could have told me," complained Girard. He, not the head of the White House Secret Service detail, normally did the confidential political chores.

"I meant to, Paul, but I just forgot, frankly. Well, to my surprise, Corwin came back with word that the FBI has quite a file on MacPherson. It seems he belongs to several of those far-right-wing groups. A couple of them have a lot of retired military men in their memberships. You know the kind of thing they advocate."

Girard grunted. "Yeah, stamp out everything. Some of these military guys seem to hate what they call 'socialism' more every time they get another free ride out of it, from the academies on. If you took them seriously, we'd have to indict ourselves for treason—and them with us."

"That's about it. Anyway, Casey says Scott and MacPherson are close friends. That kind of surprised me, but if it's right, then Scott may be playing around with the lunatic fringe.

"Now, fourth. This afternoon Scott called me up about the alert. He wants me to shake off the press at Camp David and take a chopper down to Mount Thunder. I said I'd like to take a newspaper pool man to play square with the boys, but Scott insisted that this alert had to be worked just like the real thing. So I gave in. But you can see what that means. I'll be going to the cave Saturday with only Corwin and one or two other agents, at the most."

"The way you make it sound," Girard commented dryly, "you better take along a couple of divisions of Secret Service men, to say nothing of the Alcohol Tax Unit, the FBI, and anybody else who can fire a gun."

"I take it from that crack that you don't believe Casey's story?" Lyman asked.

"I don't say he isn't telling the truth, boss. I'm sure he is. I just don't agree with the conclusion. I don't think there's any military plot cooking. It's absurd."

"Yes, it is," Lyman said, "but the string of coincidences is getting pretty long."

"The thing that seems unlikeliest to me," Girard said slowly, "is the e-co-hop business, or whatever Casey calls it. How in the devil could Scott set up a big outfit like that, with all the people and supplies involved, without your hearing about it? It may only have been operating six weeks, but they must have started construction right after you signed the treaty last fall."

"On the other hand," Lyman said, "it ought to be easy enough to check."

Girard got up and went over to the phone beside the curved sofa by the windows.

"Sure it is. How about giving Bill Fullerton a call? He's a career man with no ax to grind. And he knows where every dime in the Pentagon is spent."

"Go ahead," Lyman said. "By the way, Paul, you pronounce the name of the unit 'e-com-con.' "

Girard reached Fullerton, head of the military division of the Bureau of the Budget, at his home.

"Bill," he said, "keep this one confidential, because it's from The Man. Have you people ever cleared any money for something called ECOMCON? It's supposed to be an Army outfit with about thirty-five hundred men. That's right. . . . You haven't, huh?"

Lyman scribbled a note and held it up for Girard: "Any unallocated JCS funds?" Girard was still talking to Fullerton.

"You ever hear of this ECOMCON yourself, Bill?" Girard put his hand over the mouthpiece and spoke to the President. "Never heard of it, he says." He spoke to Fullerton again.

"One other thing, Bill. Do the Joint Chiefs have any unallocated money? . . . Oh, yeah. No other way, though? . . . Well, listen, Bill, thanks. Hope I didn't get you out of bed. And keep it under your hat, okay? Right. See you."

Girard hung up and turned to Lyman.

"He never heard of it. He says he'd have to, because every new project has to be justified before him first, no matter how highly classified it is. The Joint Chiefs have a hundred million for emergencies, but they're supposed to get your approval in writing and so far as he knows the money hasn't been tapped. Hell, if there are thirty-five hundred men down at that base, that's somewhere around twenty million bucks a year just to feed, pay, and put clothes on 'em."

Girard mixed himself a second drink. Lyman tapped the bottom of his own glass, long since emptied of the Scotch he'd shared with Casey, on the heel of his hand, but shook his head when Girard offered him the bottle. The two men sat again for several minutes, not speaking.

"My sister's little kid," said bachelor Girard, "would call this Weirdsville. I can't bring myself to think seriously about it."

"That thought has been going through my head too, Paul, but I think I had better proceed on the assumption it might be true."

"Sure." Girard nodded in agreement.

"This could add up to something bad. Something very bad," Lyman said, measuring the words out.

"Yes, it could, boss."

"I'm glad you agree. Then I don't have to spell it out for you."

Lyman walked to the triple window that looked out on the south lawn, swung open the door cut into the right-hand sash, and stepped onto the balcony. The night air felt wonderfully fresh. He stood there looking at the huge obelisk that honored Washington, a good general who'd made a good President too. Out of sight beyond the magnolia tree to his right, he knew, was the memorial to Lincoln, a good President who'd had his troubles—God, hadn't he?—with bad generals. Also out of sight, away up the Mall to the left, was the statue of Grant, that very good general who had made a very bad President. Lyman turned back into the study where Girard waited and went on as if he had not interrupted himself:

"And I think it's just as well, Paul, not to try to spell it out. We might find we were spelling it out all wrong, and that could be very embarrassing."

"Okay," said Girard, "let's play it that way. So what do we do now?"

"If Casey's story means what he thinks it does, we've got only four full days left before Saturday. It's too late to do anything tonight. We've got to start in the morning. Then, if it does check out and we can stop it . . . then what?"

"That's easy," Girard said. "You fire the whole crew and haul 'em into court on a sedition charge."

Lyman shook his head.

"No," he said, "I don't think so. Not in this administration, Paul. Not now and not later either. A trial like that would tear this country apart. Well, think about it. Let's break it up now and I'll see you first thing in the morning."

"Good night, Mr. President," Girard said. "Don't lose your sleep over this thing. There may be some ridiculous explanation that'll give us all a good laugh."

Lyman shrugged. "Maybe. Good night, Paul."

Now the President was alone, except for Trimmer. He tugged at his tie, walked back and forth, then stepped out onto the balcony again. Truman's balcony. Everything in this house was a reminder of the past. One of Jack Kennedy's rocking chairs, its cane seat and wooden back covered with yellow canvas, stood in the corner of this study. The desk, its veneered and inlaid top bulking large on top of delicate tapered legs, had been Monroe's. By the door into the bedroom were two flags, the President's personal standard and the national colors. The latter had stood there unchanged since the day Hawaii was admitted as the fiftieth state in Eisenhower's time.

What a lonely house, Lyman thought. Too big, too empty, no place in it where a man can wall himself off and think his own thoughts undisturbed by the past. What's more, it isn't mine.

From the balcony he could see the intermittent sweep of headlights as motorists curved past the high iron fence at the foot of the White House lawn. As always, they slowed when they came in line with the house, hoping even in the night to catch a glimpse of the inmates.

Fantastic. That was the only word for the colonel's story. Lyman wondered whether the man was sound mentally, despite Girard's assurances. Still, his reactions were normal and average. The way he had been tongue-tied when he came in, the way he had felt about the house, he was just like every other first-time visitor. Maybe a little too much like every other visitor, in fact. Could it possibly be some kind of double play by Scott, to trap him and make him appear a fool before the country, to discredit the treaty? No, that was even more farfetched.

The only prudent course was to check this thing out as quickly and quietly as possible and be done with it. Perhaps, as Girard said, there was some ludicrously simple explanation. Maybe it was a once-in-a-million string of coincidences with no connection whatever. After all, don't they say that if six monkeys hit typewriters long enough, they'd write the Encyclopedia Britannica?

Lyman went back to his armchair and his pipe. It was time to get this thing down to a manageable level. The first thing to do was what Girard said—find out about this ECOMCON business. For that, he'd need someone he could trust. Better start picking the team.

Mentally he began to thumb through his administration, ticking off the men he'd appointed in the sixteen months since his inauguration. Lyman hadn't gone far before he realized what he was doing: he was discarding name after name of men he had picked to do important jobs, but who couldn't be counted on for this one because they weren't tough enough, or trustworthy enough, or close enough to him—or because they might talk about it if it turned out to be a mirage.

Because they might talk. It wasn't that he feared being laughed at. The point was that he wouldn't want even a whisper to get out that he had so much as dreamed it could happen. That would be bad for the country.

And bad for Jordan Lyman too, he thought. Now, isn't *that* a damn-fool way to decide who can be counted on to help preserve the security of the country? Still, face it, Lyman, you're human and that's part of it. All right, then, who won't talk if it turns out to be a phony, but will stay in all the way and do some good if it's not?

He thought at once that both Girard and Ray Clark would

chuckle at his self-analysis and confession. Have to tell them tomorrow. Well, that settled that. There could be no effective defense of his position without Girard and Clark.

Who else? Casey, of course. The colonel might not be the most brilliant officer he'd ever met, but his instincts seemed sound. Let's hope his facts are too. Or hope, dammit, that they aren't. At any rate, Casey was already in this thing up to his eyes.

The Cabinet? Lyman ran swiftly through the list. The Secretary of State would be pedantic, tiresome, and of absolutely no value. The Secretary of Defense talked too much, about everything. Good God, the man was never quiet. Even when he had good ideas, nobody could listen long enough to catch them. Lyman liked Tom Burton, his Secretary of Health, Education and Welfare. In such a power struggle as this one might be, his advice would be good. And he had guts. But the big Negro couldn't slip in and out of the White House without a dozen people noticing it and a hundred questions being asked. His skin makes him risky. Forget it.

Lyman tossed aside one name after another, half wondering whether the process reflected on the men involved or on him for having picked them. He knew he was saving Todd for the last: Christopher Todd, the flinty, cultivated Secretary of the Treasury, the best mind in the government. Furthermore, he had proved he could keep his mouth shut on the President's business. And another big plus—Chris loved a conspiracy. Give him a cloak and he'd invent his own dagger. He also had the Yankee lawyer's ability to spoon through a mass of mush like this and pull out the hard facts. Chris had to be in.

When he ran through the White House staff, beyond Girard, Lyman was surprised how many names fell away like dry leaves in autumn. These were the men who had fought through the campaign with him, had helped set up the administration, but who among them could be relied on in this kind of funny business? Not his press secretary, certainly. Frank Simon skimmed the surface, accurately and swiftly, but this was over his head. He was also too exposed, too much an "outside man." Better for both of us if he doesn't know. Lyman's special counsel? Too legalistic. Law wouldn't help here. His chief lobbyist? Too vain. He'd want to carve out a juicy role for himself.

But there was Art Corwin. The quiet, big-shouldered agent, "Mr. Efficiency" to his men on the White House Secret Service detail, would do anything for the President—for any President. Lyman knew without ever having inquired that Corwin's allegiance was to the Presidency, not to the man who happened to hold it at the moment. What's more, Lyman couldn't move far without Corwin at his side. He had to have him.

Who else, now? The director of the FBI? A powerful man, and thus good to have on your side in a fight. But Lyman hardly knew him; he had spoken to him only three times, always in brisk, formal sessions.

The President took down a copy of the Congressional Directory from a shelf, smiling at the thought that he had to consult a compendium to remember whom he had appointed. He ran through the deputy secretaries and assistant secretaries, the members of commissions, even the courts. The names stared back at him blankly, without sympathy. He really didn't know any of these men that well. For a mission abroad or a legislative opinion, yes. In a fight for the system itself, no.

And so, at last, he came back to six men: himself, Clark, Girard, Casey, Chris Todd, and Art Corwin. And Esther. Good Lord, yes, Esther. He couldn't even make a phone call without her knowing everything. She would be efficient, loyal, cheerful—and she wouldn't be doing it for love of an institution.

At least we're seven to the chiefs' five, Lyman thought. We may lack a few divisions and missiles, but we've got two centuries on our side—and four days. Four days! Casey didn't come here with a dream. He brought an absolute, incredible, fantastic nightmare. It makes no sense at all.

He walked through the door into his bedroom and stood in front of the dresser while he emptied his pants pockets. The whole world to worry about, plus one baffled Marine, plus the chairman of the Joint Chiefs. Oh, quit posing, Lyman, he told himself, and go to sleep.

"Time for bed, Trimmer," he said to the setter. "Out you go." The dog stood patiently by the door until Lyman opened it. Then he trotted across the hall, heading for the stairs and his nightly sleeping spot in the serving pantry just outside the kitchen.

As he buttoned his pajamas, the President watched the lights going on in the parked cars around the Ellipse. Curtain must be down at the National, he thought, noting the little knots of people coming from the direction of the theater into the bright patches under the street lights.

It was the end of the daily cycle for Washington, which goes to bed earlier than any other capital in the world. The night baseball game had ended and the last stragglers scuffed across the outfield grass of the stadium toward the exits. In Arlington Cemetery, the guard changed at the Tomb of the Unknowns, the off-duty squad racking up its gleaming ceremonial rifles before turning in for the night.

At the National Press Club the last strong men threw their cards down on the table, drained their glasses, and headed for home. Among them was Malcolm Waters of the Associated Press, who had allowed himself an evening of poker and Virginia Gentleman because The Man had nothing on his schedule until eleven o'clock tomorrow morning.

On Capitol Hill two tired staff men left the Senate Office Building, commiserating with each other over the piles of pre-recess work that kept them at their desks so late.

In a modest split-level house in Arlington Jiggs Casey rubbed his eyes, turned off the lamp, and laid down a battered copy of the World Almanac. It was the only book he had been able to find in the house that contained the text of the Constitution of the United States.

In the small booths around the White House a new shift of policemen took up the task of guaranteeing that the President would be kept safe—as safe as any human being could be—from harm to his person. They guarded the man. The office he occupied took care of itself. For almost two hundred years it had needed no guard.

Tuesday Morning

Jordan Lyman opened one eye, then shut it again. Rain spattered against the windowpanes in the half-light of early morning. Coming out of his sleep, Lyman listened to the comforting steadiness of the downpour and let the sound take him back to the chill, damp mornings of his Ohio boyhood when he'd stay snuggled in the blankets to await his father's ritual call: "Time to get up, Jordie, the world's waiting for you."

Here in the White House the world was always waiting, but no one dared wake the President without orders—and Lyman had left none for this morning. He stretched and scratched the back of his head. God, what a dismal day. Why hadn't they ever moved the capital to Arizona? Lyman's months as President had confirmed his pet theory about American diplomacy: that it lacked "initiative" primarily because of the Washington climate. The city was always wet, overcast, humidly hot or damply cold. All the bright, cool, cheerful days in a year wouldn't fill one month on the calendar.

He was awake now, but still reluctant to abandon the comfort of his bed. He thought of his daughter Elizabeth in Louisville. I hope the sun is shining on her, poor kid. She's probably in the hospital right now. Well, it will be a good-looking boy, with Liz and her husband as the producers. Boy? Sure, Liz will come through. Better call Doris this morning and see how things are going.

Lyman was swinging himself out of bed, his feet reaching for the floor, when he remembered. That Marine colonel last night and his incredible story. Scott. MacPherson. ECOMCON.

He sat for a few minutes on the edge of the bed, then picked up the phone on the night table.

"Grace," he said to the operator, "good morning. Or it was until I looked out the window. Call Esther at home, will you please, and ask her to come down as soon as she can. Tell her I'll probably still be eating breakfast. Thanks."

Lyman washed, shaved and dressed within fifteen minutes. Leaving his bedroom, he managed a smile for the warrant officer sitting in the hall with his briefcase full of nuclear-war codes. What a way, Lyman thought, to make a President start a rainy day.

He was in the dining room, inwardly fuming again over the grapefruit, when Esther Townsend came in. She was scrubbed and neat, her lipstick very light, the little collar of her blouse tilted upright with starch and the wisp of hair curling over one temple. Why doesn't she get married? thought the President . . . The idea fled before the others crowding in behind it.

"Have some coffee, Esther," he said. "The news is as foul as the weather this morning. Somebody wants my job."

Esther eyed him over her coffee cup as she sat at the corner of the table.

"Now, Governor," she said, using the term she had favored ever since he was attorney general of Ohio and still two years away from the governorship. "Isn't this a little early to be worrying about '76?"

"Somebody wants my job right now, or so I'm informed." Lyman telescoped Casey's story, and his own additions, into about five minutes for her benefit.

"This may be a complete misunderstanding all around,

Esther," he said as he finished the recital, "but we've got to find out fast. For the time being, only five people are going to know about this beyond you and me: Ray Clark, Paul Girard, Colonel Casey, Art Corwin, and Chris Todd. If any one of them calls during the rest of this week, no matter what time of day, I want you to take the message."

"Do you think I'd better sleep here at the House?" she asked. Her tone was neutral, and Lyman had no way of guessing her reaction to the story. Lord, he thought, I wish I knew my own. If the sun was shining now, I'd think the whole thing was cockeyed.

"Yes, I do. I think for the rest of the week you'd better use that cot in the doctor's office. And, Esther, what about the switchboard girls? In a situation like this—I know it's silly—but I'd rather not trust anybody you don't."

"That's easy," Esther said. "Helen Chervasi and I are good friends. I'll get her to set up the two daytime shifts so that calls from any one of those five people will be switched to her. I'll take the overnight shift myself."

"You can't do that, Esther." Lyman was genuinely concerned. "You'd be out on your feet in two days."

She shook her head. "No, I can nap some during the day, and there won't be any calls much after midnight."

"Well, what do you think of it all?" He was curious, for she still had made no comment on this weird new problem of the Lyman administration.

She pointed her index finger at her head in a familiar private signal: Quiet, secretary thinking. They both grinned.

"Actually, Governor, I'm puzzled, just as you are. As a woman, I'd say I'd have to know more about General Scott. I don't have any particular feeling about him, I mean in that kind of thing. If I were you, I'd find out more about his girl friend."

"What girl friend?"

"Oh, haven't you heard *that* old one?" Esther smiled wisely and shook her head as if in pity for the backwardness of the male. "It's been the gossip for a couple of years. The General is supposed to slip up to New York now and then to see a very chi-chi item named Millicent Segnier. She's fashion editor of *Chérie* magazine. They're supposed to have a big thing."

"Well, I'll be damned," Lyman said. "The things a man learns when he lets it drop that somebody is making a pass at his job. That's interesting, dear, but hardly anything to save the Republic with. Look, time's awasting. Get Ray Clark here right away."

The morning papers lay neatly piled on the table behind the desk, still unread, when Clark sailed into Lyman's office.

"What in God's green earth are you gettin' me outa mah bed at this houah fo', Mistuh President?" asked Clark. His face was still wet from the rain. "Ah ain't got me one of them free ten-thousand-dolluh White House funeral wagons to carry me, neither. Ol' Ray gotta drive hisse'f."

Lyman's smile was no more than perfunctory. "Stow the accent this morning, will you, Ray? We've got some fast thinking to do."

He buzzed for Esther and asked her to order a breakfast for Clark.

"Do you know a Marine colonel named Casey, Martin Casey?"

"Sure," Clark said. "If you mean the director of the Joint Staff. He's been before the committee a few times. Did me a favor once, too. The son of a pretty prominent fellow in Atlanta went AWOL from Marine boot camp down at Parris Island. The kid got what was coming to him, but Casey was nice enough to see they kept it out of the papers."

"How do you size him up, Ray?"

"Pretty straight, so far as I know." Clark saw the look on Lyman's face and refined his appraisal. "I'd go a little further. You get a feeling about some people. It's just a hunch, but I'd say Casey was solid. Why? Do you have to trust him on something?"

"We sure as hell do, Ray. Casey came to see me upstairs last night. He thinks he has evidence that there may be a military plot to seize the government on Saturday."

Lyman had expected Clark to explode with a guffaw. Instead, the senator just raised his eyebrows and stared at him.

"You're not surprised? Or do you think I'm a little crazy?" Lyman asked.

"The first, Jordie."

"Why, for God's sake?"

"You tell me the story first. Then I'll tell you why."

This time, as he had with Girard the night before, President Lyman spent almost an hour in the telling, being careful to fit in his own additions, Girard's talk with Bill Fullerton of the Budget Bureau, and even Esther's piece of gossip about Scott. Clark finished his breakfast as Lyman talked.

"Now, my questions," Lyman said as he finished the narrating. "As the ranking member on Armed Services, have *you* ever heard of ECOMCON? And why weren't you surprised?"

"As to the first," Clark said slowly, "I sure haven't. As for the second, I'll tell you why. Goddammit, Mr. President, I've told you at least three times that morale in the services is lousy. They've slipped way behind civilian pay scales, I mean even further than ever before. And the officers—and the regular NCO's and enlisted men too—think your refusal to restore the old fringe benefits is some kind of personal affront on your part."

"Ray, I promised you we'd send up a bill to adjust military pay and benefits, but when I do I want to do it right and give it a real shove. Maybe I have let it slide too long, but the bill's just about ready now." Lyman tugged at his ear. "But you don't really think that the military would try to seize the government just because they're underpaid, do you?"

"No," said Clark. "Of course not. But it's part of the climate. Jordie, this country is in a foul mood. It's not just the treaty, or the missile strikes, or any one thing. It's the awful frustration that just keeps building up and up. They think every new President is going to be the miracle man who'll make the Commies go away. Of course, he never is. But right now it's getting worse. I'll bet I get five hundred letters every time that nut MacPherson goes on the idiot box. And some senators get more."

"But a Pentagon plot?" Lyman's tone was incredulous.

"I'm talking about the climate, Jordie. The move could come from anywhere. I'll bet if that bastard Prentice had a little real guts inside that belly of his he'd be ready to try it too. When you're down to 29 per cent in the polls, they line up to take pot shots at you. Anything can happen."

"You didn't read the Gallup Poll that way yesterday," Lyman said.

"I didn't know General Scott had rented himself a white horse yesterday, either."

"Then you believe it?" Lyman asked.

"I'm like you and Casey. I think we damn well better check it out as fast as we can."

"I knew I could count on you, Ray," Lyman said, his voice showing his relief. "I'm not quite sure where I'd turn if it weren't for you."

Clark stared at Lyman.

"Mr. President, you're the best friend I've got and I'd do almost anything for you," he said, "but if you don't mind my saying so, this might turn out to be something a lot bigger than just helping Jordan Lyman."

Lyman walked around the desk.

"Scratch a true Southerner," he said, "and you find a patriot, despite the Yankees he has to put up with. And now, since we've let our hair down, Ray, I hope you can stay out of trouble for the rest of the week."

Clark's eyes shifted away from the President.

"I don't make promises to other people on that subject. I make 'em to myself."

"Any way you say, Ray," Lyman replied. "But no bottle for the duration. That's an order."

Clark was curt. "I can take care of myself, Mr. President. What do you want me to do next?"

"See if you can't get something out of Scott at the hearing this morning about ECOMCON," Lyman said. "You know, from the side, easy. We can't let him get the least idea that we suspect anything. And be back here at two o'clock sharp. I want a meeting. Come in the east entrance. We'll go up to the solarium. I'm going to talk to Corwin and Chris alone this morning."

Lyman was at the buzzer by the time Clark had shut the door behind him. "Esther, get Art Corwin in here right away. And listen, Esther, tell Paul to go see Fullerton and get a rundown on all the classified military installations in the country. Overseas, too, while he's at it. And tell him to remind Fullerton again not to talk to anybody about last night's call—or today's either. One other thing: I want Chris Todd here at eleven. Okay?"

Arthur M. Corwin, chief of the White House Secret Service detail, came quietly through the door. Corwin seldom smiled, yet no face in the White House seemed so full of good humor. Though his cheeks and mouth remained uncommitted, the little crinkles around his eyes gave him the look of a man who enjoyed everybody and everything about him. After fifteen years as a field agent—dealing primarily with counterfeiters—he had been assigned to the White House under Lyman's predecessor, Edgar Frazier. Lyman had chosen him to head the detail when the job opened up through retirement.

The two men had taken a quick liking to each other on election night, when Corwin showed up at the governor's mansion in Columbus to guard the new President of the United States. Lyman knew without asking that Corwin had never cared for Frazier; his respect for the agent increased when he found that under no circumstances would Corwin reveal this by so much as a single casual word.

Corwin was taller than the President, wide-shouldered and strong, the proud owner of a bristling crew cut. Though his interests were narrow (Lyman was sure his chief bodyguard hadn't read more than half a dozen books since graduating from Holy Cross), he read the newspapers carefully every day, trying to keep one step ahead of his boss in guessing where he might go, whom he might see, and what visitors he might have in.

Now he stood waiting in front of the desk.

"Sit down, Art," Lyman said. "I may be in a jam and I need your help. First, you ought to know that there's another All

Red alert scheduled for Saturday. You weren't to know until the last minute under the security plan."

In his fourth review of Casey's story, Lyman found himself editing it, condensing some points, dwelling at length on others. As the events took sharper focus in his mind, three items—the establishment of ECOMCON, Admiral Barnswell's refusal to join Scott's horse-race pool, and the crumpled note in Hardesty's handwriting—stood out most sharply. Corwin seemed to think so too.

"It's awful hard, Mr. President," he said, "to believe that anybody could fill up a big hunk of desert with men and supplies and buildings and not have word get back to the White House somehow."

"That bothers me, too, Art, most of all," Lyman said. "Of course, Casey is only guessing. He's put two and two together and maybe he's come up with five. But I sat down this morning and tried to list in my own mind all the classified bases we've got, and I couldn't do it. We have so many of them now, and so many levels of classification, that it wouldn't occur to most people to mention a particular one to me unless some decision had to be made about it."

Corwin said nothing. Lyman wondered what this big, quiet man was thinking. Does he share my feeling of outrage at the mere thought that intelligent and capable—and trusted—Americans might be preparing a challenge to the Constitution? Does he feel the same despair and frustration at the idea? Does his loyalty, as a guard, run to the body or to the spirit of what he's protecting?

"What do you think about it, Art?"

"I think I'd better double the detail, with the men I know best," Corwin replied quickly.

"No, no, I don't mean that. What do you think about the whole thing, the idea? Does it make any sense to you?"

Corwin smiled for the first time, and Lyman thought he could read something like affection for him in the agent's face.

"Mr. President," he said, "my predecessor on this job and I get together every once in a while. You'd be surprised how we think of Presidents. As far as we're concerned, in our work, you're all part babe in the woods and part fool.

"Somebody is always trying to knock off the President, in one way or another. We shortstop a hundred letters a year from screwballs who want to cut your throat or poison you or drill you with a rifle."

Lyman smiled ruefully. "And Dr. Gallup must have talked to every one of them last week."

Corwin smiled politely, but was not to be diverted.

"But with all of that, Presidents do the damnedest things. Remember when Truman stuck his head out the window in Blair House, right in the middle of that Puerto Rican thing, to see what all the shooting was about? And Kennedy swimming all by himself fifty yards off his boat in cold water forty feet deep—and him with a bad back? Or Eisenhower playing golf at Burning Tree? Why, the woods are so thick along some of those fairways that a dozen nuts could have a shot out of the trees before the detail could even see them."

Lyman raised a big hand to protest. "But this is different, Art. If it's . . . if it's true, this could be an operation to take over the Presidency, the office itself."

"It's all the same to us, Mr. President," Corwin answered. "We don't trust anybody. Maybe you'll laugh, but I find myself running an eye over some of your top people, even the Cabinet, looking for a bulge under their jackets."

"We're not on the same wave length, Art," Lyman insisted. "There isn't any danger, physical danger, to *me* in this. What this may be is a threat to the office I happen to hold. And, therefore, to the Constitution."

"It comes down to the same thing, sir. If anybody wants to take over the government, they have to get rid of you first somehow, or at least put you away—say in a back room underground at Mount Thunder."

Lyman could see he was wasting time. Corwin refused to follow him into the realm of political philosophy. But did it really matter? Corwin was chained to one task: the protection of the physical person of the President. Well, it might come down to that. And if the thing turned out to be an elaborate tissue of nothing, and Lyman became the laughing-stock of the country, at least Corwin wouldn't join the merriment. Or gossip, either.

"Well, Art. We're all going to meet this afternoon, at two, in the solarium, and I want you there. In the meantime, what would you think about trailing General Scott to see what he's up to?"

Corwin grinned again. "Who says we're not on the same wave length? I was just going to suggest that. And you've got the right man for it. I used to get plenty of practice when I was chasing those funny-money artists."

Esther came in as Corwin was leaving to say that Secretary Todd was waiting, but Lyman asked first for Frank Simon. The thin, wiry young press secretary, looking like a pinched owl behind his horn-rimmed glasses, hurried into the office. He was the best public relations technician in the business, but the mere sight of him always made Lyman feel a little jumpy, as though somebody had just scraped his nerve ends.

"Frank," he said, "I'll have to scrub that eleven o'clock appointment with Donahue of the Fed. There are a lot of loose ends on the implementation of the treaty that some of us have to work out. But don't tell the reporters that. Just say it's been postponed because I'm working on legislative matters. All right?"

Simon twitched his shoulders. "We'll draw some snotty stories if you cancel your only appointment today, after that poll yesterday."

"I can't help that, Frank. If the first stage of this disarmament doesn't come off exactly as we agreed, all of us will be below zero in the next poll."

"All right, Mr. President." Simon's shoulders hunched again. "It's a lot easier to handle these things, though, if you can give me a little advance notice. I don't do my best work in the dark."

If you only knew how dark, Lyman answered silently.

Christopher Todd strode in, carrying his ever-present portfolio. An aura of assurance moved with him: Nothing was ever out of place in Chris Todd's world. At sixty, he had been Wall Street's ranking corporate lawyer when Lyman called him to the Treasury.

A ruddy, leathery tan bespoke his weekends as a yachtsman, formerly on the Sound, now on Chesapeake Bay. He wore a gray suit whose perfect tailoring was as elegantly inconspicuous as its discreet pattern. A darker gray tie was totally plain except for a tiny blue anchor in its center. His black shoes, bench made in England, were impeccably polished but not quite shiny. The gold watch chain across his vest had to be a legacy from his grandfather. The Phi Beta Kappa key which reposed out of sight in a pocket at one end of the chain was his own.

The press sketched Todd as "sharp," "cold," "cultivated," "sardonic." He was all that, and more.

Lyman rose to greet him, then took from a desk drawer the box of fine panatela cigars that he kept there especially for Todd. The President opened his own tobacco pouch and filled his pipe as Todd inspected a cigar, clipped it, and lit it with a kitchen match from a box in his coat pocket. Then Lyman told the story again.

As he recounted it, this time in infinite detail, he could see Todd's eyes brighten. The lawyer sat stiff in his chair, watching Lyman steadily except when he studied the end of his cigar. Lyman knew he was timing the ash. A good cigar, Todd believed (and frequently proclaimed), must go at least fifteen minutes before it needed an ashtray. Lyman finished his recital with a simple question.

"Well, what's the verdict, Chris?"

Todd's gray eyebrows arched upward. Foes of the Secretary found this habit of his particularly annoying, believing it indicated—as it usually did—disdain or reproof. Lyman, however, was merely amused, as he was by many of Todd's calculated traits.

"If I went into court as Scott's counsel against that kind of nonsense," said Todd, "I'd move to quash the indictment and we'd be out of the courthouse in ten minutes."

"I didn't offer it as evidence," Lyman replied gently, "but as a presumption of evidence. You're not the only lawyer in the room, Chris."

Todd's blue eyes snapped. "Mr. President, there are no lawyers in Ohio. Only apprentices in the law. When they become lawyers, they move to New York."

"Or Washington," the President said. He laughed as he relit his cold pipe.

"Let's look at this squarely," Todd began. "You obviously set great store by this ECOMCON business. Nobody has heard of it before. Not you, not Girard, not Fullerton, not this Colonel Casey. Well, then, what makes you think it does in fact exist? We have only the colonel's conjecture. He obviously has no facts."

"And the Hardesty note?" asked Lyman. "That refers to it, and to a Site Y, the designation that Casey's friend uses for his post near El Paso."

"That could easily mean another place. The proliferation of these secret bases has always seemed foolish to me. We confuse ourselves more than we do the Soviets."

"Well, we may have an answer to that this afternoon," Lyman said. "Girard is checking out the location and designation of every classified installation."

"And as for flying troops to big cities in an alert, that seems to me not only logical but prudent." Todd was pressing his case. "Obviously, if the Russians struck, we'd need disciplined troops in the metropolitan areas to keep order and prevent complete breakdown. And, if I may say so, the conversion of a wagering pool on the Preakness into a code for some sinister plot to seize the government seems to me to have no foundation whatsoever. It's sheer guesswork. Everybody knows General Scott loves horse races, and everyone who loves horse races bets on them. Colonel Casey's deductive powers are lurid, to say the least."

Lyman leaned on the desk, supporting his chin in both hands.

"Forget the details for a minute, Chris. What do you think of the over-all probability? Do you think the mood of the country and the climate of military opinion make such an operation, let's say, a possibility?"

"No, I don't." Todd studied the stump of his cigar before dropping it into the big desk ashtray. "But obviously, Mr. President, I realize we must do everything possible to ascertain the facts—and quickly. We'd be guilty of gross negligence if we didn't."

Todd unsnapped his briefcase and took out a long yellow scratch pad. He jotted down a series of numbers with his pen. Opposite the first he wrote: "ECOMCON."

"Let's just run through it all again," he said. "I'll study the list this noon and try to come up with a workable plan of investigation by this afternoon. I must say, though, Mr. President, you don't have many investigators available."

"Try to change places with me in your mind, Chris," Lyman said, "and then run through a list of a thousand friends and associates, and see how many you think you can trust completely. You'll be surprised how few you come up with."

"Especially," said Todd acidly, again arching his gray eyebrows, "if you weed out all those who you think might laugh at you when the monster vanishes out of the bedtime story."

"My, my," said Lyman. "You're not only a good big-city lawyer but a pretty fair country psychologist too."

They enumerated events and circumstances, item by item, until Todd had filled a page and a half with numbered notes.

"A couple of things in here lead me to believe that your Colonel Casey has a vivid imagination," Todd said. "For example, take Fred Prentice's remark about staying 'alert' on Saturday. What earthly excuse is there for linking that to the All Red? 'Alert' is a word that anyone might use."

"I guess you might be right there, Chris. I suppose that once Casey got suspicious every casual remark took on some significance it might not really have. But I think you have to look at it along with everything else."

"Well, I'd better get back to my office," Todd said, sliding the pad back into the case and snapping the catch, "and try to make some sense out of this jumble."

Todd left, carrying his portfolio like a professor on his way to class. Through the door Lyman watched him bowing slightly to Esther as he passed her desk. Then she looked at the President and he beckoned to her.

"Esther," he said, "call Colonel Casey and tell him about the meeting. You don't need to explain. But tell him to use the east entrance again."

Well, Lyman thought, in all of my little band of brothers, only two of us can see the forest for the trees . . . if there is a forest. Only Ray Clark and I can see the big question. There can't be a constitutional struggle unless the atmosphere is right, unless people are really worried deep down in their bellies. Are they? . . . Good old Chris. He's intrigued by the idea of a conspiracy. You can tell it from his eyes, even if he won't admit it. But it's all a matter of evidence, of witnesses, with him. . . . Corwin can't think of anything but the person of the President. Paul sees it as a simple power struggle between Scott and myself. Casey? He's just an officer, doing his duty as he sees it.

They're all on the side of the angels, the President mused, and I couldn't ask for better people. But I can't make them understand *why* it's important. They all think it is, each for his own reasons, but those reasons aren't good enough. I've got to try to make them see it my way, and only Clark sees it that way now . . . but does he? Is he worried about the country? He thinks he is, but I don't know. I don't know if you really can worry about it, no matter who you are and how much you think, unless you sit in this chair here. Alone. Sometimes I think no one except the President ever thinks of the country, all of it. I wonder if anyone else *can*, when you get down to it?

Lyman turned to look out the long windows that stretched from ceiling to floor. The heavy May rain continued to beat down on the hedges, the rose bushes, the rhododendrons, and the big shiny leaves of the magnolia tree. A guard, his head pulled into the turned-up collar of a black rubber raincoat, sloshed along the curving driveway. The President stood watching, smoking, silently cursing the weather—and the myopia of men.

In the pressroom, reporters and photographers were playing wild poker, dealer's choice. Quarters and half dollars clinked noisily on the table. Three telephones were ringing. Milky Waters had his feet on his desk as he talked with Hugh Ulanski of United Press International.

The noncommittal tone Waters used with politicians and other news sources was not in evidence now. As dean of the White House press corps, he spoke with authority among his peers.

"I can't figure the guy," he said. "The day after a national poll comes out showing him up to his ass in unpopularity, he schedules only one appointment—and cancels that one."

"Maybe he's a secret nudist," suggested Ulanski, "and he's contemplating his navel."

"You got the wrong religion for navel watching, son, but the right idea. I like the guy, but if he's a politician I'm a sword swallower."

Simon came into the pressroom. Waters left his feet up but reached for a notebook. The poker game paused expectantly.

"It's nothing much," the press secretary said, fingering his dark-rimmed glasses. "I was asked what 'legislative matters' the President is working on this morning. I haven't got to him yet, but I'll have it for you at the afternoon briefing."

"Frank, you've given me an idea for my overnight." It was Ulanski. "Instead of my day lead, which said the President did nothing, I'll say the President is worn out from doing nothing, and has been ordered to rest tomorrow."

Simon didn't bother to reply. He left. The poker game resumed. The rain continued.

Jiggs Casey's morning in the caverns of the Pentagon was as gloomy as the weather outside. A rising torrent of conflicting conjectures had been flooding his mind from the moment he got out of bed. The ashtray on his desk had doubled its normal accumulation of cigarette stubs, and he had decided that his career as a Marine was finished.

What crazy impulse had sent him to the White House with that nightmare story? How could he have thought of implicating a man of Scott's stature in a plot that had no basis except a frayed string of coincidences? And he had betrayed his own service. Marines don't do that. The feeling of disloyalty to his own kind put Casey in an ugly humor. Every time he tried to think concisely about the episodes that had made such an impression on him yesterday his emotions pulled him back to his own plight. Probably by this time the President had called for his service record and ordered Girard to look for a history of psychiatric trouble. Thank God, at least there's nothing like that in it. Or maybe Lyman had just called General Scott direct and told him the director of the Joint Staff needed a mental examination.

The last possibility was still in Casey's mind when, shortly after ten o'clock, he was summoned to Scott's office. Well, here it comes, he thought as he walked down the hall. Add one Marine to the retired list.

Scott's greeting was friendly as he motioned Casey to a chair. In addition to the usual buoyancy, Casey thought he noted an almost jovial air.

"Jiggs," the General said, "you've been working too hard on the alert. I want you to take the rest of the week off. Why don't you and Marge duck down to White Sulphur and blow yourselves to a good time?"

Casey had expected almost anything but this. He shook his head.

"I couldn't do that, sir," he said. "There are a lot of little details on the All Red, General. I just wouldn't feel right."

Scott waved aside the objection with a sweep of his cigar. "Not a thing to worry about. Murdock can handle anything in that line. You're tired. I can sense it."

"Sir, I want to be up at Mount Thunder with you on Saturday," Casey protested.

"Well, that's all right. You just check back in on the job Saturday morning, then, and pick it up as planned from there. But in the meantime, let's call it a three-day pass."

Casey started to say something, but Scott cut him off.

"Look, Jiggs, I've thought about this. Frankly, word that you're gone will spread around fast. Nobody would think an alert was in the works with the director gone. Consider yourself part of the security cover. And remember, you can't think only about Saturday. I'd rather have you around here in good shape for the next month than have one exercise letter-perfect on Saturday."

Casey tried to keep his voice from faltering. "When do you think I should leave, sir?"

"Right now," boomed Scott. "Walk out and go home. Kiss Marge for me." He walked Casey to the door and squeezed his arm. "See you Saturday, Jiggs. Have fun."

Before his short ride home was half over, Casey had settled on a depressing diagnosis. President Lyman had called Scott, told him of the night visit to the White House, and the two men had agreed that Casey was a good officer who badly needed a rest. Yes, that must be it.

Calm of a kind returned to Casey. He thanked the driver in front of his house and ran for the front door, splashing through the puddles. The empty carport indicated that Marge was out on some kind of errand. That's one break anyway, he thought. It'll give me a little time to figure out a story to tell her.

The telephone was ringing as he opened the door. He answered it while water trickled off his raincoat onto the floor.

"Colonel Casey?"

"This is Colonel Casey." He didn't recognize the caller's voice.

"Colonel, this is Esther Townsend at the White House. Your secretary said you had gone home. You are asked to attend a meeting at two o'clock. Please use the east entrance. The guard will have your name. Take the same elevator you did last night, but go to the third floor. It will be in the solarium, to your left, directly above the study."

"Yes, ma'am. I'll be there."

"Thank you, Colonel. The President said you didn't need to be informed of the subject matter."

Casey removed his raincoat and cap in a daze, ignoring the water that had collected on the floor. He unbuttoned his blouse and loosened his tie, then slumped into a chair in the living room.

He was suddenly relieved. He had been right. It wasn't a bad dream after all. The President must have done some quick checking and decided he was right. That this meant trouble only heightened Casey's excitement.

But why the sudden offer by Scott of a three-day vacation? Offer, hell—he had been ordered to get out of the office. Had the General learned that Casey had driven past his house last night? Maybe a sentry recognized him or wrote down his license number. Or maybe Mutt Henderson had told Broderick of Casey's interest in ECOMCON, and Broderick had tipped off Scott. Had Murdock gotten suspicious? Of what? Casey knew he had given Murdock no cause for alarm. Maybe more coded traffic on the Saturday operation was due to go out and they wanted Casey out of the way so he wouldn't see the dispatches.

In the Armed Services Committee room in the old Senate Office Building, Senator Raymond Clark took his place, just to the right of the chairman's seat at the head of the table. Half a dozen other senators were already in their seats along both sides of the long, baize-covered table.

In the witness chair at the other end, General Scott was waiting to testify. Admiral Lawrence Palmer, the chief of Naval Operations, sat beside him. Behind them, on folding metal chairs, was a row of colonels and commanders, fiddling with the documents in their fat briefcases. Scott whispered with his aide, Colonel Murdock, whose head snipped up and down as he nodded agreement. The left side of Scott's blouse blazed with six rows of battle decorations and service ribbons. He was, as always, totally relaxed and confident in manner.

Clark eyed Scott with fresh interest. There isn't the slightest doubt about it, he thought, that fellow is the most impressive military man this town has seen in twenty years.

Senator Frederick Prentice came in from his private office through a door held open by the committee clerk. The chairman nodded to Scott and Palmer before sitting down in his black-leather chair. He took a deliberate, almost proprietary, look around the room, his glance for a moment putting the other committee members in the same category of personal property as the green-veined marble pillars, the service flags heavy with battle streamers, and the beautifully ornate crystal chandeliers.

Prentice slapped a folder of papers on the table and rapped his gavel once. The clerk hung a sign, "Executive Session," on the outside of the main door, then closed and locked it.

"We are meeting late this morning," Prentice said, "in order to accommodate General Scott. However, we have the consent of the Senate to sit during the session, so we will not have to adjourn at noon. We'll just go ahead until one o'clock, which will give us an hour and a half, if that is satisfactory to the senators."

Prentice looked to his right and left, then tapped the gavel again.

"Very well. General Scott, you may proceed. You had almost finished with your over-all presentation last week, and I would hope there wouldn't be too many interruptions, so that we can get to Admiral Palmer and the Navy. General?"

Scott leaned back in his chair and pressed his fingers down on the edge of the table. His shoulders tightened with the pressure.

He began slowly. "I think we had covered all weapons systems except the ICBM family. Here, as the committee knows, we believe we have more than closed the so-called missile gap of the late fifties and early sixties, and we are now moving rapidly to bring in the Olympus, which should put us well ahead of the Soviet in thrust as well as accuracy.

"Needless to say, the Joint Chiefs view the current missile strikes with the utmost concern, since they involve almost entirely the production lines for Olympus. As you know, the treaty requires us to dismantle only the warheads. The missiles themselves can be built—and should be. They will provide us with some insurance, no matter how fragile, in the very critical months ahead."

Prentice, ignoring his own injunction against interruptions, cut in.

"General," he said, "are you satisfied that other departments of the executive branch are doing all they can to terminate this completely unauthorized stoppage over some petty jurisdictional dispute?"

There was a slight stir among some of the committee Democrats. Scott glanced along the table, and when he replied his words were tactfully restrained.

"I cannot reply directly, Mr. Chairman. I assume that is the case. I know the President called in the head of the AFL-CIO yesterday on the subject. I have not yet been informed of the outcome."

"Don't you think you should be kept up to date," asked Prentice, "considering your responsibilities in this field?"

Scott smiled. "Well, Mr. Chairman, I fully expect to be kept posted, but—"

Senator George Pappas, an Illinois Democrat and a loyal supporter of the Lyman administration, broke in.

"This line of questioning is totally unproductive," he said. "The chairman knows the White House is doing its best in this difficult situation. The senator from Illinois, for one, is confident it will be taken care of. I think we might remember that General Scott isn't supposed to be a labor arbitrator."

"I just want the record clear as to where we stand," Prentice said.

"I think it's already clear where some people stand," snapped Pappas.

Prentice smiled. "Let's move ahead, General, please, now that the distinguished senator from Illinois has cleared the air in his usual fashion."

"Mr. Chairman—" said Pappas angrily, but Prentice snapped the gavel against the table to cut him off.

Scott talked, lucidly and decisively, for a quarter of an hour, ending his discussion of missiles with a summary of the entire defense situation. He wasted no words, yet managed to paint a detailed and vivid picture of the nation's strength.

"Of course," he concluded, "the Joint Chiefs and the ranking field commanders all feel that the next six weeks are critical. Knowing the Soviet record of breaking even the most solemn agreements when it suits their convenience, we intend to maintain our forces on a more or less constant alert until the treaty goes into effect."

Prentice cleared his throat. "Thank you, General. The chairman will confine himself to one question. In connection with your last statement, do you think the United States is in more danger, or less danger, since the ratification of the nuclear disarmament treaty?"

Scott picked up the pencil that lay on the table in front of him and doodled on the memo pad placed there by the committee staff. A good half minute passed before he answered, and when he spoke it was in a measured, almost gentle tone.

"If I might be permitted a personal allusion, Mr. Chairman, this country has been awfully good to me." The committee was intent on Scott's words. "It is probably a cliché to say that I came from humble beginnings, but it is true.

"It never occurred to me, really, until I entered the Military Academy, that I was the beneficiary, along with all citizens, of a really unique system of government.

"I came to the Point in 1934. I think the committee would agree that you could hardly describe that as a year in which our system was operating at its optimum level. But it did not take long for the Academy to make quite clear to me the virtues of our form of government and the differences between the American and other societies.

"Everything that I saw in the war years reinforced my feelings on this subject, as did my contacts with other societies in the Far East and, more recently, the Near East.

"I must say, speaking now on a completely personal basis, and not in my official capacity, that I have been disturbed, over a period of years, at indications that Americans do not always recognize the full dimensions of the threats to them and to this . . . this marvelous system under which we live. I think that an examination of the period of the late thirties, of the late forties, of 1955, of 1959, of early 1961, and of more recent years would indicate at least the shadow of a recurring pattern, a pattern of what might be called 'complacency' or 'wishful thinking.'

"I apologize for this rather indirect answer to your question, Mr. Chairman. But what I would like to say is this, really: I hope we are not now entering another such period. We have, as I said, a system in this country that we all want to protect and preserve. It is my personal feeling that we are approaching a critical period, as critical or more so than any in the past thirty years, because of the fact that the government has decided to attempt a nuclear disarmament treaty.

"The committee is quite familiar with the reasoning of the Joint Chiefs in connection with the treaty. There is no point in my going over that again, except to say that the Chiefs still believe that the treaty is too vague on the question of inspection of new nuclear construction. We still contend, that is, that the Soviet might be able to build ten new Z-4 warheads, for example, at some unknown and undetected location, at the same time that he is disarming ten Z-4's from the stockpile, under inspection, on July 1.

"So I do believe we are entering a period so dangerous that we may face some factors that are totally unexpected. Our system, which has meant so much to me personally and which we all want to see sustained, does contain some features which might make it vulnerable. I am sure that none of us would want to see that system used to bring about the collapse of the very things it has made possible. So, obviously, to the extent that we may encounter new or unexpected problems, to that extent there is increased danger."

Scott stopped speaking and dropped his hands from the edge of the table into his lap.

Senator Raymond Clark squared the papers in front of him. That was quite a testament, General, he thought. I wonder if we've got you figured right?

Prentice made no effort to hide his reactions. He beamed

openly and proudly. "General, I think I speak for the entire committee when I say I regret very much that we have no written record of your magnificent statement. I only wish that all Americans could have heard it. . . . Now, the members of the committee may have some questions. Let's keep them as brief as possible, so we can get on to Admiral Palmer."

He nodded to Clark, the next-ranking Democrat. The Georgian looked at Scott. Well, he thought, it isn't going to sound very good after your lines, but I better go to work.

"General," he began, "I can only echo what the chairman has said about your statement. Now, there is just one point about which I am curious. You may have covered it at a session I missed. What are we doing to safeguard our communications facilities, telephone long lines, television cables, broadcasting facilities, things like that?"

Prentice glanced at Scott in surprise. There was no change in Scott's intent expression.

"Without going into detail, Senator," the General said, "I think I can assure you that adequate provisions have been made. Communications have always been the lifeline of any military establishment, and they are of course far more so today. We fully realize that, and have acted on that realization."

"I'd appreciate it if you could amplify just a bit," Clark suggested.

Scott smiled, almost apologetically. "Senator, this is a quite sensitive subject, and I'm not sure this is the time or place to—"

"The committee simply does not have time." It was Prentice, cutting in. "We can't start into anything of that scope today. We're on the verge of a recess here, Senator Clark, and we must get to Admiral Palmer."

"I notice, Mr. Chairman," said Clark quietly, "that you had time to raise a question about the treaty—for the umpteenth time. I would certainly appreciate it if the committee could indulge me for just a moment."

"Much of the communications field is highly classified,"

Prentice snapped. "The General doesn't have time today to sort out what he can properly tell the committee and what he can't."

"Oh, now, Mr. Chairman." Clark was still slouched in his chair but his voice was cold. "There hasn't been a leak from this committee in my memory. And there is a long record of complete disclosure to it by the defense establishment, going back even as far, if I am correctly informed, as 1945, when details of the Manhattan project were made available several months before the first atomic bomb was used."

Murdock leaned over and whispered to Scott while Clark was talking. The General nodded agreement and gestured to Prentice.

"If I may interject, Mr. Chairman," he said, "the committee knows that we had a practice alert some weeks ago. What it does not know is that it did not come off to our complete satisfaction. We had trouble, in particular, with some of the communications. We are getting the bugs out now, I think, and I'd prefer to wait a few weeks—say, until after the Congressional recess—when we can give the committee a full report that would include any revisions we may decide to make."

Prentice beamed gratefully down at Scott. "Is that a satisfactory solution?" he asked Clark.

"No, it isn't," Clark replied. "I think we are entitled to some information now. Further, I don't want to leave even the slightest impression that the senator from Georgia thinks any member of this committee cannot be trusted with sensitive information."

"There was certainly no such implication intended on my part, Senator," Scott said, "and I would hope there would be no such inference drawn. Frankly, this is an involved subject, on which I think the committee is entitled to a full and detailed review. We just are not equipped to provide that this morning."

Prentice used his gavel. "I can personally assure the distinguished senator," he said, bearing down on the word "distinguished," "that our communications are secure. Now, unless the senator wishes to force a vote of the committee, I think we will proceed. If there are no other questions for General Scott, we will hear Admiral Palmer."

He glanced at the other senators. None of them spoke and Prentice brought the gavel down again. "Without objection. Admiral Palmer."

The Admiral's testimony consumed a half hour. When he finished and the meeting was adjourned, Clark stopped briefly at his own office and then left the building to eat lunch. The rain had slackened to a drizzle, but the overcast still hung oppressively low. From the office building only a faint outline of the Capitol dome, half a block away, could be seen.

General Scott's limousine, its four-star tag on the front bumper, stood at the curb. Scott was holding the door open for someone. Even from behind him Clark recognized the square bulk of Senator Prentice. The two settled on the rear seat and the car pulled away on the wet asphalt.

As it did so, a gray sedan slithered out of a parking place down the block, heading in the same direction. When it passed Clark, he noticed the driver. He had seen him hundreds of times: it was Art Corwin.

So you've put us all to work already, Jordie, thought Clark. Well, you'd better, Yankee boy. There's plenty to find out—and maybe not much time left to find it out in.

Christ, he thought, I need a drink.

Clark hesitated on the sidewalk, made a half-motion to turn back toward his office. Then he jammed his hands in his raincoat pockets and stepped doggedly off the curb toward the restaurant he had decided on earlier. It was only a block away, the food was good—and it was operated by the Methodist Church.

Tuesday Afternoon

Shortly before two o'clock, Esther Townsend brought a brown manila envelope to President Lyman, who was in the upstairs study.

"You didn't ask for this, Governor," she said, "but Art Corwin thought you might want it before the meeting. Don't ask me how he got it."

Lyman cut the envelope open and drew out a thin cardboard folder. The tab on the side, lettered by hand in ink, read: "CASEY, Martin Jerome." It was Colonel Casey's service record; Lyman suddenly realized that though he was commander in chief of the armed forces, he had never before seen an officer's service file. He thumbed through it, retracing Casey's career in the biographical card, proficiency reports, medical examinations, and citations. Quite a substantial officer, he thought. Indeed, quite a brave officer. A sheaf of papers near the end of the file caught his attention and he read them carefully.

Lyman went up to the third floor, crossed the hall, and walked up the little ramp to the solarium. He found Christopher Todd already established in one of the heavy leather chairs. Jordan Lyman didn't use this room often, but he liked it. Added by Harry Truman when the house was rebuilt in 1951, it was all plate glass, steel, and linoleum tile, low-ceilinged and unadorned, completely unlike any other room in the mansion. Eisenhower had used it for bridge games. The Kennedys removed the wicker furniture, added a couple of knee-high sinks in an alcove, and turned it into a playroom for Caroline and John Jr. The Fraziers left it that way for their own grandchildren, but Doris Lyman had redone it as a hideaway for her husband. Lyman retained one memento from Caroline's tenancy—a blue plastic duck which squatted quizzically on the window sill.

The morning rain and noontime drizzle had subsided into a solid mist that beaded the angular, five-panel window and made the room seem almost like the bridge of a ship at sea in a heavy fog.

"This isn't the most cheerful room in the house on a day like this," grumbled Todd. "I feel like a man trying to navigate the Sound in a pea-souper."

"I know what you mean," Lyman said, "but there's no telephone up here and only one door. Maybe no place is secure enough for our kind of business, but I feel better here."

Todd pointed to the little bar in the alcove. A half dozen bottles and an ice bucket stood ready.

"Do you think it's a good idea to tempt Senator Clark that way?" he asked.

"Look, Chris, I know Ray has hit the bottle pretty hard for the last couple of years—since Martha died. But in a pinch he's all right, better than most of us. I happen to know that from Korea."

"In Korea he hadn't met his wife and lost her," Todd argued. "It looks like an engraved invitation to me."

"It's all right," said the President with a note of finality.

Girard, Clark and Corwin turned up, one at a time, in the next few minutes, and Casey stepped through the doorway with military punctuality at just two o'clock. Lyman introduced him to Todd, who had never met him. Casey fidgeted as the Treasury chief appraised him from crew cut to cordovans, much as he might eye the timbers and rigging of a new sloop.

When they were all seated, the President put on his glasses and pulled two pages from the envelope containing Casey's service record.

"This is a report on Colonel Casey's last complete medical examination," he explained. "It was done at Bethesda two years ago, when he was promoted to colonel. I won't read it all, but I think you will be interested in one comment from the psychiatrist who examined him. Quote: 'This officer is normal in all respects. He exhibits no anxieties, has no phobias and is free from even the minor psychiatric disturbances common to a man of his age. Few men examined by this department could be given such a clean bill of mental health.' Unquote."

Lyman, Clark and Corwin grinned at Casey as the Marine reddened slightly.

"Well," Casey said, "I thought I might be going nuts this morning until Miss Townsend called me. It was the longest four hours of my life."

"Be happy to be regarded as totally sane, Colonel," said Todd. "There are few men in this city of whom as much could be said with confidence."

"I took this rather unorthodox step," said Lyman, "because I wanted to settle all doubts at once. Jiggs may be mistaken in his analysis of recent events—that we'll find out—but he's produced it out of a sound mind. Now, I think the best way to proceed is to turn things over to Chris Todd. He's the prosecuting attorney, so to speak, and at least for this afternoon it's his show."

The Cabinet officer pulled black-framed spectacles from his breast pocket and reached into his portfolio for the yellow legal-length scratch pad.

"We all know Colonel Casey's story," Todd began, "but as I understand it, he is not aware of several things President Lyman mentioned to the rest of us."

Speaking to Casey, Todd told of General Rutkowski's call

several months before; of Vice-President Gianelli's revelation that Prentice had suggested he spend the weekend in his ancestral village in Italy; of the FBI file on Harold MacPherson's extremist affiliations, and of Scott's insistence that Lyman fly from Camp David to Mount Thunder for the alert without accompanying newspapermen.

"If you'd known all that, Jiggs, you might have brought the Marines with you last night," quipped Clark.

"The Marines," said Todd coldly, "are reported to be with General Scott this week, Ray, or hadn't you heard?"

Casey looked at Lyman. He was obviously anxious to say something, and the President nodded.

"You don't know it, Mr. Secretary," Casey said, "but General Scott urged me—no, ordered is more like it—to take a three-day leave this morning. I was home before noon."

"Any reason?" asked Todd.

"No, sir, not much. He just said I looked tired and ought to take some time off. Of course, he may have heard something from Murdock or one of the guards at Fort Myer."

"Umm." Todd wrote on his yellow pad, but did not seem overly impressed.

"Is there anything else new bearing on the . . . ah . . . situation?" he asked.

There was an uncomfortable moment of silence. We're a funny crew, Casey thought. Each man here is tied to the President, but not to any of the others. Except me. I don't know any of these men except Paul. I wonder how the President picked this group? Casey was puzzling over the absence of "big" names from Congress and the Cabinet when Clark spoke.

The senator told of questioning Scott on communications, and of Scott's putting him off by explaining that there were changes under way because of failures in the last alert.

"Is that right, Jiggs?" Lyman asked.

"No, sir," said Casey quickly. "That is not true. About the only thing that went *right* with the last All Red was communications. Even the big master cut-in, the one that allows us to take over the networks, worked perfectly, in spite of the fact that it had never been tested before."

"Score another for Gentleman Jim," said Girard. "And I always thought he was a real Boy Scout."

"Well, he gave a wonderful imitation of one this morning," Clark said. "He laid down a personal statement for the committee that was about as fine as I ever heard." He went on to quote the General on the treaty and his fears of Russian duplicity.

"Of course," said Lyman, "that's the real trouble with our conjectures. I mean Scott's character. Even to consider tampering with the Constitution requires a certain kind of personality —overly ambitious and a little bit warped. Scott has always impressed me as just the opposite. I've never doubted his sincerity, nor his feeling for the country either. After all, I appointed him chairman of the Joint Chiefs. How about it, Jiggs?"

"That's why I waited so long yesterday," Casey said hesitantly. "General Scott has never been a conniver. We have them in the service, sir, just like you have them, I guess, in politics. But the General is always straightforward. He always says that he could never have gone so far in any other country."

"As I say," Clark added, "he struck that same note this morning. And I couldn't detect any false overtones either."

"That's what I mean," Casey said. "I guess you all remember that old joke about MacArthur, how he'd turn to his wife when they played the national anthem and say, 'They're playing our song, dear'? Well, I've always kind of thought it *was* Scott's song."

Casey paused a moment, then added: "So his misstatements to me yesterday hit me pretty hard."

"You mean lies, don't you, Colonel?" asked Todd quickly.

"Well, yes, sir."

"I just think we'll make more progress if we're completely frank," Todd said tartly. "It will save time."

They waited for the President to resume his discourse on

Scott, but Lyman, busying himself with the filling and firing of his pipe, said nothing. Todd went back to his check list.

"Anything else new?"

"I followed Scott today," offered Corwin, "as the President directed. When he left the Senate hearing this morning, Senator Prentice got in the car with him. They drove to General Scott's quarters at Fort Myer. A few minutes after they got there, General Hardesty and General Riley drove up, and then General Dieffenbach arrived in an Army car. They were still there when I had to leave. Must be a pretty long lunch."

"Admiral Palmer was not there?" asked Todd.

"Nope. No sign of him."

Todd tapped his pencil on his teeth. His brows gathered in thought. He was clearly enjoying his role as chief diagnostician.

"As you know," he said, "Palmer was not at the chiefs' meeting yesterday. That did not seem particularly significant, but his absence today makes it look more interesting. The only member of the Joint Chiefs not present. Mr. President, I have an idea."

"All right, Chris, shoot."

"Why don't you call Barney Rutkowski? You could remind him of his earlier conversation and find out if anything has developed since that he knows of. Tell him you want him to fly in here and talk to you in confidence. Then, when he gets here, send him over to see Palmer on some pretext and sound him out. It might be very illuminating."

"Do you suppose Barney knows Palmer?" asked Clark.

Casey had an answer. "All the chiefs have visited the Air Defense Command. They go there at least once a year." He chuckled. "So do I. Everybody likes Colorado Springs."

"That's good enough," said Todd. "What do you think, Mr. President?"

Lyman walked to one of the windowpanes and rubbed a finger across it. He didn't improve the visibility; the mist was on the outside.

"I rather like the idea," he said.

"But don't let Rutkowski know what's bothering you," Todd said. "This business, I mean."

Corwin, sitting at the door, snapped his fingers and held up a hand for silence. A moment later there was a knock at the door. The Secret Service man opened it a little—so that others in the room could not be seen from the outside—and then, recognizing Esther Townsend, threw it wide.

The secretary was all smiles.

"Sorry to interrupt, Mr. President," she said, "but you just became a grandfather. A baby girl. Liz is doing fine."

"Oh, my God." Lyman got up quickly. "I completely forgot about that. I meant to call Doris this morning. Gentlemen, excuse me for a minute, will you? I have to call Mrs. Lyman."

"Never mind the cigars," Clark said. "I'll buy for the house —from your stock downstairs."

"While you're down there," said Todd, as if he had not heard Esther, "why not call Rutkowski, Mr. President? Time's running."

The connection to the hospital in Louisville was already open when Lyman reached his bedroom on the floor below. His wife Doris, cheerful as ever, bubbled happily over the wire. Liz was fine, but too groggy to talk to her father. She had waited a few minutes before calling to make sure Liz was all right. The baby was all in one piece, with the right number of everything, and nicely wrinkled. Would it be all right to name it Florence, after Lyman's mother?

"Whatever the kids want," Lyman said happily. "And, honey, kiss Liz for me. And tell Ed he's a great man."

Another button on Lyman's phone winked insistently. He told Doris to hang on and pushed it. It was Frank Simon on the other line.

"Mr. President," said the press secretary, "Esther told me you were calling Louisville. How about letting the photographers come up for a shot of you? We could use it. The boys in the pressroom think you're sick."

"Sure, sure." Lyman was excited. "Bring 'em up, Frank."

The photographers trooped in just as Lyman was telling his wife that much as he wanted her home (and he did) she might as well wait until Monday. Too much doing on the treaty to give him any free time anyway, he said.

"That's an awful serious look for a new grandfather, Mr. President," said Pete Schnure of AP photos. "How about a smile, huh?"

Lyman obliged to the accompaniment of a brief barrage of flashbulbs, but he shook his head when they asked for more. Simon palmed his charges out the door into the oval study. The President wound up his talk with his wife, then made sure they had started down on the elevator before asking Esther to get him General Rutkowski at the Air Defense Command on a normal commercial line. It took several minutes.

"This is Jordan Lyman, Barney. How are you?"

"Fine, Mr. President." The voice was strong and confident.

"Barney, you remember that call you made to me several months ago?"

"Very clearly, sir."

"Has there been anything else said by . . . from the same quarter?"

"No, sir. I indicated at the time I didn't think such a conversation would be proper, and that's the last I heard of it."

"Barney, something quite important may have come up. Could you fly in here tonight?"

"Certainly, sir. I can leave in an hour or two."

"Please keep it in confidence, Barney. Invent some other excuse. I mean I'd rather it wasn't known that you're coming to see me."

"No trouble at all, Mr. President. I always have business in Washington. In fact, I planned to come next week anyway. Shall I call you when I get in?"

"Please. Just ask for Miss Townsend. She'll find me."

Corwin was spluttering with laughter when Lyman returned to the solarium. Casey was wiping his eyes and even Todd wore a smile. Clark had been entertaining.

"And speaking of doctors," he said—Lyman was sure that

Clark had been regaling the company with maternity-ward humor—"reminds me of Ol' Doc, who ran against me in a primary one time. He used to collect his campaign funds on the spot, after he worked the crowds up with a good long speech. He'd stand there, all pink and sweaty with beer and righteousness, and call out the denomination of the bills as they handed 'em to him. 'Ten more for the campaign pot,' like that. Well, one time a fat-cat auto dealer down in south Georgia passed him a fifty-dollar bill. Ol' Doc, he looked at it, and looked at it again, and damn near fainted—and then stuffed it into his pocket and sung out loud and clear, 'Ten more for the campaign pot!' "

They all congratulated Lyman. Clark said it ought to add at least five points to his next poll rating. Girard proposed a toast, nodding toward the portable bar, but the President shook his head. His mind was already back on business.

"Barney's flying in here tonight," he said. "I'll send him over to see Palmer. But, Chris, I want some thought given to the way Barney should be handled. It has to be just right."

Todd nodded and scribbled a note on the top of his pad. Then he ran his pen down his list again.

"The first thing to straighten out," he said, "is this ECOMCON business. Do we have any solid evidence at all that it exists, aside from Colonel Casey's talk with Henderson and the Hardesty note? I gather we don't."

Lyman nodded at Girard. "Paul, give us that list of classified bases you got this morning."

Girard read off a list of seventeen installations. All but five were outside the continental limits. Two of those five, Mount Thunder and a special area at Camp Ritchie in Maryland, were underground retreats for top government officials in case of a nuclear war. The other three were the sites of vaults where nuclear warheads and components were stored. There was no base near El Paso, and none with the ECOMCON designation or a similar mission. Nor was any of the bases, at home or abroad, known to Fullerton by the "Site Y" designation.

"He said the only time that tag was used, so far as he knows, was for Los Alamos where they made the atomic bomb in 1945," Girard said.

"I could not have recited that list from memory," Lyman said, "but I know that each installation on it was specifically authorized by myself or one of my predecessors. Furthermore, on the day after my inauguration I was briefed on each classified base then in existence. I am positive there has never been any discussion of any installation of a secret nature near El Paso."

"That clarifies my point," said Todd. "There appears to be nothing in writing anywhere to indicate that this base does in fact exist. With all due respect to Colonel Casey, perhaps it does not."

"You mean the first order of business is to find out?" asked Lyman.

"Precisely," Todd replied. "But how? Of course, the normal procedure would be for you, Mr. President, to call General Scott and ask him. If he denied it, you would then order him to accompany you on an inspection trip to the El Paso area. If there were no base, you would fire Colonel Casey and apologize to Scott. If there were one, you would disperse the ECOMCON troops and dismiss Scott on a charge of insubordination."

The five men looked at the President. Lyman smiled patiently at Todd.

"Are you seriously suggesting that course of action, Chris?" he asked.

"No," Todd said, "I am merely saying that would be the normal way for a President to act, under normal circumstances."

Girard moved in. "Look, Mr. Secretary. If there turned out to be no base, the story would be plastered all over every paper in the country. The boss would look like a complete fool, and the administration wouldn't be worth the baling wire it would take to hold it together. That's not politics, Mr. Secretary. It's lunacy."

"But of course we assume the base does exist, or we wouldn't be here." Todd's temper was rising.

"Look at the other side, Chris," said Lyman. "Let's say we find the base and I demand Scott's resignation. I suppose his reply would be that I had authorized the base orally. We'd set up a fight in Congress and the newspapers that could literally tear the country in half."

"Christ, yes," added Girard acidly. "The House would vote a bill of impeachment within a week, with the mood the country's in. They'd say the boss was out of his mind. And much as I love him, you put his word against Scott's right now and I wouldn't bet a dime on our man."

"Thanks, Paul," said Lyman. His voice was sarcastic, but his smile was tolerant—and agreeing.

"Wait a minute, all of you," Todd said. "I'm not advocating this. It's just that my instinct always is to sail the shortest course for the harbor in a squall."

"That's why you're the Secretary of the Treasury, by appointment, instead of being a senator or governor by election, Chris." Lyman spoke slowly, in schoolmaster fashion, as men do to friends outside their trade. "We're really at the heart of the matter here, aside from Scott's character itself, and it's a political judgment: Is this thing possible—really? I've spent most of the last twenty-four hours thinking about that."

The President got up from his chair in his gawky way and walked halfway around the room to lean against the center window sill. He crossed his feet as though trying to hide their size and fussed with his pipe for a minute.

"Actually," he said, "Jiggs's visit last night brought into focus a lot of things that have troubled me since I took over this job. I hope you can stand a little philosophy; I think it goes to the guts of this thing.

"Ever since that first atomic explosion at Hiroshima, something has been happening to man's spirit. It's not surprising, really. Up until then a man could have some feeling that even in a terrible war he had some control over his existence.

Not much, maybe, but still some. The bomb finished that. Everybody's first thought was that it would end war. Everybody's second thought was that if it didn't, he was at the mercy of the people who had the bombs. Then came the hydrogen bombs and now these awful neutron weapons.

"Civilization can go with a moan and a whimper overnight. Everybody knows it. But how can an individual feel anything but helpless? He can't grab a rifle and rush out to defend his country. He probably can't even help much by joining the Navy and serving on a missile submarine. He'd know that if he ever got an order to fire, it would mean that his home was probably already a pile of ashes—or would be in fifteen minutes."

The room was still. Todd, sunk in his chair, had let his pad slip to the floor. Corwin sat straight against the door. Casey noiselessly stubbed out a cigarette and clasped his hands behind his thick neck.

"None of that means much to the dictatorships," Lyman went on. "In a monolithic state—and that's what Russia has been for centuries, under czars and commissars both—people never get used to influencing their government, and they don't miss it. But a democracy is different. Each of us has got to feel that we can influence events, no matter how slight the influence. When people start believing they can't they get frustrated, and angry. They feel helpless and they start going to extremes. Look at the history—Joe McCarthy, then the Birch society, now the popularity of this fanatic Mac-Pherson."

Lyman paused and looked at his companions. Todd took the cue.

"Granting all that, Mr. President," he said, "you'll recall that when General Walker—remember, that division commander in Germany—got out of line in 1961, President Kennedy wasted no time relieving him."

"That's exactly my point, Chris, and a good example of it," Lyman said. "Kennedy was quite popular then, and opinion was clearly on his side. But since then this climate

I'm talking about has got steadily worse. People have seriously started looking for a superman. Don't think I couldn't feel that in the campaign. I guess I sounded like one in that acceptance speech, too, thanks to Ray."

Clark chuckled. "We only had eighteen words in that punch line, but I bet we worked on it for two hours."

"Wise men—and I trust that includes everyone here— know there aren't any supermen," Lyman resumed. "The trouble is that democracy works only when a good majority of citizens are willing to give thought and time and effort to their government. The nuclear age, by killing man's faith in his ability to influence what happens, could destroy the United States even if no bombs were ever dropped. That's why I decided I had to bring off that treaty if it was the only thing I ever did."

Lyman shook his head. "I don't know if it's enough, though. Maybe it's coming too late. The climate for democracy in this country is the worst it's ever been. Maybe General Scott thinks he holds salvation in his hands. If he does, he's pitifully mistaken, and I feel sorry for him."

The President sat slouched on the sill of the big window, his wiry hair rumpled and his hands and feet looking ridiculously large and awkward. It occurred to Casey that he looked more like a country poet than a President. The silence lingered until they were all conscious of it. Clark finally broke it with a loud, "A-men, Brother Lyman!"

Lyman chuckled and gestured to Todd.

"That's enough from the revival tent, I guess, even though I really mean it," he said. "Let's get back on the track, Chris."

"Well, I assume that accepting your reasoning leaves only one course open to us," Todd said. "That is to start gathering evidence to see whether there is a . . . an operation, or whether there isn't."

"That'd be my idea," Girard said.

"Then somebody has got to go down to El Paso and see for himself," said Todd, obviously glad to be back on firm factual ground. "We can't phone. We can't ask people. Somebody's got to go."

He looked around the room.

"I'm the one," Clark offered. "I've been around west Texas and New Mexico some with the committee. I don't look like a senator, maybe, but if I get in a jam I can always show my card and claim I'm making an investigation for the committee. It would be natural enough, too, with the recess."

"I guess Ray's right," Lyman said. "But, Ray, I want you back right away. See if you can't get down there tonight or first thing tomorrow, and make it a one-day job. At least be sure you're back here by Thursday night. And keep in touch with Esther."

"Right." Clark stretched, as though his job was already finished. He glanced at the bar.

"You'd better have Henderson's phone number, Senator," Casey said, pulling out his little address book. "And I can brief you on Mutt and his wife after we get through here."

"Okay," said Clark. "And the name's Ray."

"Mr. Secretary," Girard said, "you forgot one thing in your roundup of new stuff since Casey's trip here last night. As I get it, Esther claims Scott has a girl friend in New York. There might be something there."

"You're right," Todd said. "It doesn't bear directly on this thing, but it ought to be investigated right away. Besides, someone has to go to New York to get a better line on Mac-Pherson. If there is a plot, he may be in on it, although I must say that seems unlikely. What possible use could he be to them?"

"That's easy," Girard shot back. "He could be their mouthpiece, the one who tells the country it has a new boss."

"That does not impress me," Todd said, fingering his watch chain. His eyebrows arched in disdain. "I must say all that mumbo-jumbo about some master television switch leaves me unimpressed, too."

Casey, his voice low-keyed but hard, corrected him. "Excuse me, Mr. Secretary, but that happens to be something I know a good deal about. If this is what we think, and they have the use of that master override control, the President could be prevented from speaking to the country for hours —even if he were otherwise free to do so. The way it's set up, you'd never have a chance."

"What's that girl's name again?" asked Corwin.

"Segnier," said Todd, consulting his pad. "S-e-g-n-i-e-r, Millicent Segnier. According to Miss Townsend, she is fashion editor of a magazine called *Chérie*."

"That's right," said Casey. "I met her once."

Todd looked at Casey in surprise. Lyman tapped the Marine's shoulder as he walked behind him to return to his chair.

"Well, well," he said. "I saw nothing in your service jacket to indicate any special proficiency with the ladies, Colonel."

Casey blushed and scratched his head in embarrassment.

"Well, sir," he said, "I know a girl in New York who knows her. Or maybe I ought to say I *knew* a girl in New York who knew her when I knew the girl in New York."

He stopped abruptly, confused by his own words. Clark's booming laugh keynoted a general outburst of mirth at Casey's expense.

"Maybe you'd better start over, Colonel," said Todd.

Now Casey laughed too, but his words came with an effort. "We don't discuss this in the Casey household any more," he said. "But two years ago, before my assignment to the Joint Staff, I ran the Marine security detail for two weeks that time Feemerov came to the UN."

"And?" Todd prompted him.

"And since the New York police were really running the security show, I had quite a bit of free time on my hands. I met a girl who was a television script writer, and . . . well, anyhow, I met Miss Segnier at a party."

"Have you kept in touch with this television female?" Todd asked.

"No, sir." Casey was emphatic, then blushed again as Girard chuckled wickedly. "Well, that is, I haven't seen her, but I know she's still in the TV game up there."

"That seems to solve the problem of who goes to New York," commented Todd.

"Oh, please." Casey recoiled almost visibly at the thought. "Mrs. Casey wouldn't understand a secret mission to New York, not at all. She really wouldn't."

Todd insisted. "You know this woman—the General's woman—and you also know somebody who is in the television business and therefore can easily provide some information on MacPherson. There isn't time to start from scratch on this."

The President intervened, too. "Look, Jiggs, we don't have much choice. Chris has to stay here to co-ordinate things. Obviously I'm a prisoner in this house for more reasons than one. Art's job, and it's one that only he can handle, is to follow Scott. Ray is going to El Paso and I've already picked out a chore for Paul. That leaves you."

"What can I tell Marge, sir?" Casey asked.

"Nothing," said Todd. "But if the domestic pressure gets too strong, perhaps the President could call Mrs. Casey."

"I'd be delighted," said Lyman.

"Lord." Casey was dejected. "If it was any place but New York."

"Don't you wish you'd stayed on Scott's side?" gibed Clark.

"We don't need the name of your friend," Lyman said, "but you'd better leave her phone number with Esther."

Todd returned to his scratch pad and went down his list of items, point by point. Each called for some discussion. Senator Prentice's name, and his connection with the Joint Chiefs, inspired a long inspection of his character. Consensus: While it appeared incredible that Prentice would join a move against a system in which he already held so prominent a place, his campaign contributors included many big defense contractors, he had complete confidence in the military—and he openly doubted the Lyman administration's ability to survive if the

Russians cheated on the nuclear disarmament treaty.

Todd saved the Preakness messages until the last.

"Aside from ECOMCON," he said, "this is the one thing that seems to me the most unlikely. I'm speaking now of Colonel Casey's interpretation of the agreed facts.

"As I see it, these messages can mean three things. First, they may be exactly what they purport to be, a wagering pool. Second, they may be a cover for a proper and prudent military step, to wit, lulling the field commanders before Saturday's alert. Third, the messages may be a coded exchange for a clandestine military operation thus far not revealed to us.

"Let's take the obvious first. Scott is known as a betting man, isn't he?"

"Sure," said Clark. "We joked about it when he came before the committee for confirmation as chairman of the Joint Chiefs last year. Prentice said he guessed it was Scott's only bad habit."

"I've seen his picture in the papers plenty of times, at some track or other," Girard said.

"So it could easily be what the messages say it is," added Todd.

"Wait a minute," Lyman said. "What about his obvious annoyance over Casey's learning of the messages?"

"Well," said Todd, "obviously the government's military radio networks aren't supposed to be used for that kind of thing. So you couldn't blame Scott for wanting to keep it quiet."

"The only thing about that," Casey said, "is that Scott knows I see a lot of his personal traffic, and some of it would cause more rumpus than this if it got around. I remember once he asked the commander of the Army supply depot at Bordeaux to send him a case of claret. He used all-service radio for that, and Code Blue—that's the chairman's personal code. But he never cautioned me about that, or anything else, until yesterday."

"Still," Todd insisted, "there's no hard evidence to prove

these are *not* messages about a horse race. Now, let's examine the second possibility. Is he simply duping his field commanders before an alert?"

Again it was Casey who raised a doubt. "What sticks me there," he said, "is Admiral Wilson. I can't imagine Topping Wilson agreeing to a wager by radio—or any other way. Why, he once banned all gambling on a cruiser division he commanded."

"How do you know that?" asked Todd.

"I had the Marine detachment on the flagship," Casey replied. "But the whole fleet knew about it. Wilson's always been a real sundowner and now that he's CINCPAC, he's even tougher. It doesn't make sense to me that he'd do what he told his entire command not to do."

Todd was obstinate. "Still, you haven't proved anything."

Casey reddened, but not from embarrassment this time. "Look, Mr. Secretary," he began. Lyman cut in fast.

"Calm down, Chris. Jiggs isn't trying to prove anything. By the time we collected enough proof to satisfy a court of law, it might well be too late to stop whatever we proved was going on."

Casey relaxed. Todd grunted unhappily but moved ahead.

"All right, assuming the worst," he said, "and these messages are—"

"Wait a second," Girard interrupted. "Thinking about the alert again made me wonder about something. Mr. President, who decided which people were going to know about the All Red in advance?"

"Why, General Scott did," Lyman said. "That's S.O.P. with us."

Casey spoke up. "You mean, sir, that you didn't ask General Scott to withhold the information from the Secretary of Defense?"

"No, indeed. I didn't think about it at the time, one way or the other."

"That's not the point, Mr. President." Casey was speaking to Lyman, but his words were aimed at Todd. "The General specifically told me, when I asked about it, that you had ordered the Secretary blacked out."

Girard moved his heavy frame uneasily in his chair. "There goes the General again, telling another lie. I'm beginning to feel kind of nervous about our great military leader."

Todd said nothing, but he made another note before going back to his argument.

"Assuming the worst, as I started to say," he said, "and these messages are some kind of private code, when could it have been devised? Has Scott seen these five field commanders recently?"

"The General has toured the overseas bases and commands three times in fifteen months," Casey said.

"Is that customary?" asked Todd.

"No, it's some kind of record. Also, every one of those five officers has been in Washington within the last couple of months."

"They all saw Scott, of course?"

"Yes."

"And all but Wilson," interjected Clark, "appeared before the Armed Services Committee during our general review of the defense situation."

"Still assuming the worst," Todd said, "that brings us down to the Sixth Fleet commander, Admiral Barnswell, the one who replied 'no bet.' Obviously that assumes greater significance if some kind of plot is afoot, which I don't believe, and if the messages are a private code, which I'm not convinced of."

Lyman pushed forward in his chair. "Chris, I've already decided that the only prudent course is to send Paul over to talk to Barnswell. He can go over on the Vice-President's plane tonight without being noticed. I've already talked to Vince about it, and he's glad to do it. I gave him the idea that Paul has a little confidential personal business abroad."

"Good," agreed Todd. "Now, does anyone know anything about Barnswell that would help Paul on this?"

"I've met him," Clark said, "but I really don't know much

about him except that he seems to have a talent for avoiding controversy. He's a mighty bland witness when he testifies."

"That's just it," Casey said. "I thought a lot about that, too, before I called Paul yesterday. You see, Barnswell has quite a reputation around the Pentagon as a, well, a vacillator. He always keeps his nose clean, he never sticks his neck out. He likes to know how the wind's blowing before he commits himself."

"A clean nose and a withdrawn neck in a high wind," commented Todd dryly. "You paint an intriguing portrait, indeed, Colonel."

"I know I don't express it very well, Mr. Secretary." Casey was thoroughly irritated at this crusty old lawyer and his snide cracks. "But, frankly, they say Barnswell's the kind of officer who likes to be with the winner—and usually is."

"My God," Lyman said, "how did a man like that get by the Secretary of the Navy for a key job like the Mediterranean fleet?"

"As a matter of fact, Mr. President," drawled Clark, "how did Secretary Wallstedt get by you?"

His usual joshing tone was missing. It was obvious to the others that some political nerve of the Georgia senator had been touched. Lyman looked embarrassed. There was a hush in the room as the six men looked at each other, all of them realizing in this moment that the Lyman administration could never be quite the same again, no matter what happened or didn't happen on Saturday. From now on there would be those who knew and those who could never know, and the line dividing them would respect neither politics nor position. The thought affected each man in the solarium differently, depending on his degree of intimacy with the President. But whatever that degree, the realization laid a chill upon the room and the darkening mist outside seemed to grow thicker.

Todd busied himself wiping his glasses.

Lyman finally broke the silence. "I think you'd better have a letter from me, Paul, just in case." He went to a little writing desk in the corner and pulled out a sheet of stationery bearing a gold presidential seal on the familiar tan paper that Lyman used for his personal notes. He wrote rapidly:

Dear Admiral Barnswell:
    The bearer, Paul Girard, is my appointments secretary and personal associate. I trust that you will extend him every courtesy of your command and will also answer fully and frankly any questions he may put to you.
    He is acting for me and with my complete trust and support. Your replies will be kept in confidence. Your co-operation will be appreciated.

                    Sincerely,
                    Jordan Lyman

"You'll have to get yourself from Rome to Gibraltar somehow, Paul," said Lyman, handing him the note after sealing it in an envelope.

"And get it in writing, Paul," Todd warned. "You're a gentleman, but your word wouldn't count for much in a court against that of Barnswell or Scott."

The meeting was drawing to a close. Todd looked around the room.

"Everybody plan on being back here by Thursday noon at the latest," he said. "If Casey's right, we'd have only forty-eight hours left after that."

"The code, Chris," Lyman reminded him. The President looked a bit sheepish.

"Oh, yes," Todd said. "If we're up against the real thing, we've got to be careful. I've fixed up a little code for us to use on the phone."

Corwin, still leaning against the door, let his chair down on all four legs with a little thud. "Mr. Secretary, I don't think you need to worry about that. Any time you call into the White House, as long as you know the operator and the person you're talking to—and I gather the President has fixed that up through Miss Townsend—you don't need to worry. These lines are as secure as man could make them."

"Well, what about the phone at the other end?" Todd asked.

"Just stick to public phone booths," Corwin advised. "Nobody could tap that many lines."

"Okay," Lyman said, "I guess it was a little silly. But be careful how you say things, just in case. We'll get the point even if you talk around it some."

"We're all a little old to be playing games," Todd said. "Frankly, I still think the whole thing is absurd, so the quicker we get an explanation the better."

"Ah hope you right, Mistuh Secretary," said Clark, "but ah kin smell a catfish that's been layin' too long in the sun."

As the men filed out, Lyman drew Clark and Girard to one side. He closed the door after Todd, the last of the others to leave.

"Those are three fine men," he said, "but I'm not sure we speak the same language. Especially Chris. Hell, he wants me to climb up in the pulpit and shout 'thief!' and search the whole congregation."

"Let's face it," said Girard. "They aren't politicians."

"That's it, Jordie," Clark said. "Any politician would realize why you can't move in and clobber this thing right away. My God, with our rating today, we'd lose hands down in any showdown with Scott."

"And maybe lose the country with it," mused Lyman. "That's all Feemerov would need for an excuse to junk that treaty—a big brawl in the United States between the military and civilian authorities. I just can't figure Chris. It's funny that he would think we could move openly."

"This one, we play so close to the vest that nobody ever sees the cards," Clark said.

"Exactly," Lyman said. "I made up my mind last night that if there's anything to this, we've got to lick it without the country ever knowing about it. Of course, the only way to do that is to get some evidence that's solid enough to force Scott to resign—on some other pretext."

"Now that Chris is in it," Girard said, "you're going to have to make him see that, boss."

The three sat for another half hour, going over once again the events of Sunday and Monday.

"How about giving him Treatment A?" Girard asked. "That might take care of it, and if the whole thing does turn out to be a phony, we'll still be okay."

"Treatment A?" Lyman was puzzled.

"Oh, hell, you know what I mean, chief." Girard exhibited his wicked grin. "Get him out of town. Send him somewhere —out of the country. Scott can't grab your job if he's five thousand miles away."

Clark chuckled. "It must be something about this house. I remember a fellow who worked here in Kennedy's time—he was a college professor, at that—telling me the best way to liquidate a man was to keep him out of town. Seriously, Jordie, it might be a good idea."

Lyman shook his head. "No, I don't think so. It might work if it were almost any other kind of situation. But you can't just send the chairman of the Joint Chiefs galloping off on some made-up mission. Anyway, I'd just as soon have him right here where Art can keep an eye on him."

It was dark when Clark rose to go. The President shook hands with both men.

"Both of you get back here fast," he said. "I don't want it to be just one politician against nine generals and admirals— or maybe more."

When they had gone, Lyman stood looking out the sweeping window. The mist had begun to break now, leaving a low overcast that reflected the glow of the city's downtown lights.

In the end it's going to be Lyman against Scott, he thought, no matter who else is in it. Somehow he had to get the feel of the man. Sometime, in the not too many hours that were left, he would have to face the General alone.

The President stood in the dark. The old-fashioned globes

on the lights along the back driveway cast little halos in the thinning mist that scudded past them.

They're all good men, Jordie, he thought, but you're on your own in the end. God, what a lonely house. If only Doris were here. It would be nice to have someone to eat dinner with tonight.

Tuesday Night

Art Corwin parked in an apartment driveway across from the main gate of Fort Myer. He picked his spot carefully. The car rested on an incline that sloped down to the highway. A good four feet separated it from the automobile in front, so he could swing clear with one turn of his steering wheel. He was facing an intersection on Route 50, so he could either cut across the divided highway and turn left, toward Washington, or turn right into the outbound lane leading to the Virginia countryside.

The rain had stopped and the mist had lifted, though a low overcast still hid the moon. The wet streets and dripping foliage were dark and soggy, but the weather failed to confine Corwin's spirits. He was alert and cheerful. A beer and a corned-beef-on-rye had tasted just right after the long White House meeting. He had a well-tuned, powerful car that could do better than a hundred miles an hour if necessary. And he was working alone again, back to the feeling of his early days in the Secret Service when the only worry was the next move of some small-time counterfeiter, not the hour-by-hour tension of protecting the President of the United States.

Corwin had driven slowly past Quarters Six, on the hill in-side the old Army post, soon after seven. Both the official limousine of the chairman and Scott's own big Chrysler stood parked in the driveway. Then Corwin chose this spot, across from the Fort Myer entrance, so he could watch all traffic going in and out of the post. He reparked twice to get just the right line of sight on the gate. Now the street light would illuminate the features of anyone who stopped at the guard hut for the routine nighttime check.

This is a strange business, he thought. Whether Scott had designs on the office of the President he didn't know, but it occurred to him that Christopher Todd's doubts were a poor way to begin a defensive operation. Corwin had taught him-self always to assume the worst. Did Scott want the Presi-dency? Well, didn't almost everybody in this town?

He began to estimate how many men he should add to the White House detail later in the week. One thing he would do if he were running this jerry-built show would be to plant a man in the all-service radio room in the Pentagon. It would be tricky, but . . . He wondered if Todd had thought of that. He wondered, in fact, whether Todd's personal reservations about the possibility of a military operation hadn't blinded the Secretary to essential precautions that ought to be taken. Suppose, for instance, Scott moved up the date. What would we do then?

Corwin was deep in the problems of shielding the President when a dark-blue seven-passenger Chrysler slid out of the fort gate into the glare of the street light. The M.P. on duty at the entrance snapped off a salute. At the wheel sat General Scott, apparently in civilian clothes, for he wore no cap. Corwin caught the unmistakable full crop of black hair, sprinkled with white and gray. There was one man beside him—General Billy Riley, the Marine commandant. No other jaw around Washington looked quite like that one.

As the Chrysler wheeled onto Route 50, heading away from Washington, Corwin switched on his parking lights, started his motor and rolled down the hill to the intersection. He let three cars get between him and Scott before he switched on his headlights and pulled out into the traffic. The highway, three lanes wide, rolled out away from the capital. His tires sang on the wet pavement. Corwin liked this. He fixed his eyes on the top of the Chrysler, letting his peripheral vision take care of the normal problems of the evening traffic. He began to hum a song he'd heard at his first Gridiron Club dinner in Washington, a parody to the tune of "Alice Blue Gown":

> . . . I remember the atom blew down
> All the foreign relations in town.

Corwin bore down slightly on the accelerator, as the speed limit increased, to keep his distance behind Scott. With plenty of other cars on the road, it was easy. Where was the General heading?

In the jungle of neon lights and access roads at Seven Corners, Corwin saw Scott bear right onto Route 7, the main road to Leesburg. The two cars moved slowly through Falls Church before the traffic began to thin out and speed up. Corwin dropped farther back. He noted that Scott scrupulously observed the speed limit, holding steady at 55.

As they neared Leesburg, the overcast began to break apart. Corwin caught the outline of a cloud and could pick out one star peeping over its rim. The night began to freshen; he rolled down his window to enjoy the country air. At the fork west of Leesburg, Scott bore right on Route 9, heading toward Charles Town. Now, what gives there, General? wondered Corwin. The night races at Shenandoah Downs?

Tailing became harder work now. There were few cars on the road and Corwin found it difficult to keep more than one automobile between himself and the big Chrysler. With the valleys, hills and turns, he had to stay fairly close. Once or twice he turned out his lights completely, rushed forward at 70, then switched on the headlights again. If Scott was monitoring his rear-view mirror—which he doubted—he would think another car had come onto the road behind him.

They began to climb toward the Blue Ridge, the eastern rim of the Shenandoah Valley. The pursuit became a trial on the roller-coaster dips and twists of the road. Once Corwin turned off onto a gravel road, then made a hurried grinding U-turn to get back onto Route 9. Scott's car was disappearing, its taillights winking as he braked around a curve. Luckily, Corwin was able to get behind a second car that had come along. He looked at his watch: 9:15. The two generals had been on the road for an hour and twenty minutes.

West of Hillsboro, where the road crossed the Blue Ridge before dropping into the valley, the left turn indicator of Scott's car blinked on. Corwin slowed to a crawl. Scott turned left. Corwin followed him onto a black macadam road that ran straight south along the spine of the ridge. He could see Scott's taillights bobbing up and down about half a mile up the road.

So that's it, he thought. Because of his White House job, Corwin knew something about this road that few other Americans did. Virginia 120 appeared to be nothing more than a somewhat better-than-average Blue Ridge byway, but it ran past Mount Thunder, where an underground installation provided one of the several bases from which the President could run the nation in the event of a nuclear attack on Washington. Corwin had come this way at least a dozen times before and knew the road. It was just as well, for some of the rises were so abrupt that it would otherwise be difficult to follow at night. Great trees stood along either side of the paved strip, held back behind the old stone fences.

Once Corwin's headlights picked up two glowing dots beside the road as a rabbit scuttled away to safety behind the rocks.

Assuming that Scott was headed for the Mount Thunder station, a few miles farther on, Corwin turned off his headlights again. God, it's dark, he thought. This is getting a little sticky.

Suddenly he saw Scott's brake lights flash ahead. Corwin stopped. Scott turned sharply and slowly to the left and vanished in the trees. Corwin, using his parking lights, drove on at little more than a walking pace until he reached a point about a hundred yards short of where Scott had turned. He found a wide spot on the shoulder and turned his car completely around, parking on the shoulder with his sedan facing back toward the highway. He tried a start. The ground was too muddy; the wheels spun a bit. He inched the car forward until he found firmer footing in a patch of gravel. Satisfied, he turned off the engine, emptied his right pants pocket of loose change, and put his leather key case, with the ignition key outside, into the empty pocket. You never know, he thought, when you might have to leave in a hurry. He dropped the handful of coins into the glove compartment, pulled out his little flashlight and felt in his coat pocket for notebook and pencil.

Corwin walked along the paved road to the place where Scott had left it. A narrow, unpaved drive cut east, down the side of the ridge, through a thick mixed stand of tulip trees, pine and sumac. On a little marker beside the fence corner Corwin, using his flashlight, could make out the word "Garlock."

More of the same, he thought. This little road must lead down to General Garlock's house.

Brigadier General Matthew H. Garlock was the Mount Thunder station commander. Corwin had met him several times. If there's a conference, he thought, I better get down there.

The gravel road dropped steeply down the slope in a series of turns. Corwin walked along its side on a pad of pine needles, stumbling occasionally on a rock thrown out from the roadbed. He knew the overcast had dispersed overhead, but the woods here were so thick that no light at all penetrated. The heavy moisture from the day's rain and mist clung to trees and ground, wetting his face whenever he brushed a branch but muffling his footsteps. In about a quarter of a mile the road took a final turn and came out into a clearing.

Corwin stopped, caught for a moment by the beauty below him. Set back into the side of the mountain stood a low, rambling log house. Beyond the house the ridge fell away to a far valley. Hundreds of scattered lights shone up through the night haze that drifted across the lowlands. The sky was clear now, the stars crowding one another across the wide arc of the night, brighter by far than they ever seemed in the city. The moon, pale and hesitant, hung in the east like a lantern in a watchtower. That biggest cluster of lights in the valley, Corwin decided, must be Middleburg: the smaller one, to the right, would be Upperville. In the distance, dim in the haze, lay the glow of Warrenton.

Nice duty for General Garlock, he thought, living up here where he can look down on the Virginia horse country.

Corwin inspected the house. To the right, in the kitchen, he could see a woman bending over the sink. The middle of the house, apparently several rooms wide, was dark, but on the left, in a big room with a fireplace, Corwin could see Scott and Riley sitting on a settee, facing him. When Scott flourished a cigar, a third man got out of a chair to light it for him, and Corwin saw that he was Garlock.

The Secret Service agent walked, crouching low, across the lawn, and lowered himself over the edge of a terrace—right into a rosebush. He cursed silently as he sucked the scratches left on the back of his hand by the thorns. Then he circled to his right, in the shadow of the darkened central rooms, tiptoed carefully across the gravel driveway, and took up a position below the lighted windows. He could hear plainly and he knew the three voices, but he was so low that all he could see was the heavy wooden beam in the center of the room's ceiling. He dropped to one knee and used the other to support his notebook. It was awkward to hold both notebook and flashlight in one hand while he took notes with the other, but it seemed the only way. Scott was speaking.

". . . Appreciate your letting us come out at night, General. It's about the only time all week that I'll be free, and I wanted to firm up the details. And after our troubles with the last one, I want to check things myself."

"That's perfectly all right, sir." Garlock was being properly respectful, although he sounded puzzled. "We're open for business twenty-four hours a day up here. Will there be anything special for this alert?"

"Well, the President is coming up to take a look this time," Scott said. "So we decided it might be a good idea to lay on some extra troops."

"Oh." Garlock was surprised. "We've never done that before."

Riley chimed in. "Well, you know, we thought we might put on a little something extra for him. He wasn't very happy about the last All Red."

"And a little extra security, too, with the President here," Scott said. "Accommodations for about two hundred men would do it. You wouldn't have to worry about feeding them. They'll carry full field rations for a couple of days as part of the maneuver. After all, they'll be under full security and won't know where they're headed when they start out."

"Oh, messing the men would be no problem," Garlock said. "We've got plenty of food. But I don't know about the bunks. We're in pretty close quarters down there, General."

"Why can't some of them bivouac aboveground?" asked Riley. "Most of them would be up there anyway, on a perimeter, in case of the real thing."

"Well," said Garlock, "if they're coming in early, I'm afraid it might break security on the alert. A lot of people drive along that ridge road and some of them are service people who keep their eyes open."

"Well, how about lower down on the hill, behind some of those old buildings?" suggested Riley.

"That might do it," Garlock agreed. "By the way, when does the President arrive?"

"About noon Saturday," Scott said. "Of course, the five chiefs will be here by 11:15. If you're worried about any loose ends concerning the President, I can help you wrap them up then. There'll be time."

"The extra security guard is the only problem," said the local commander. "I hadn't realized you planned anything like that. We have almost a hundred men on permanent security detail here, you know."

Corwin thought Garlock sounded a bit miffed, as though the

visiting generals were implying some laxity on his part. Scott apparently had the same reaction.

"Don't take this as any criticism of your command, General," Scott said. "It's just that we've got to learn to move security forces around this country much faster than we have. The last alert showed that clearly."

"If that's what the President wants," said Garlock, "well, of course, I have no objection."

There was silence for a moment and Corwin could imagine Scott's gaze following the smoke from his cigar. When Scott spoke, his voice dropped a tone.

"Actually, this is being done independently of the President," he said. "As you know, he was pretty unhappy with our performance last time, and we want to show him—"

Corwin had stood up to rest his cramped knee and in doing so had brushed against a euonymus bush. A branch, pushed back by his shoulder, was released when he moved again and swung against the side of the house with a wet slap. In the kitchen, a dog growled. The woman said, "Want to go out, Lady?"

Corwin jumped across the gravel driveway and ran up the sloping yard. He threw himself flat on the lawn and squirmed around to peer at the house under a large boxwood which flanked the roses lining the terrace. The kitchen door banged and a shiny black Labrador hustled along the drive to sniff at the shrubbery where Corwin had been.

"Let's go out," said Garlock, opening a door from the room where the three officers had been talking. "We'll have some fun if it's another one of those deer."

Corwin saw him reach up on the mantel for a long flashlight. He crawled across the yard, reaching the edge of the woods just as Garlock, followed by Scott and Riley, came out of the house. Garlock swept the light around in a narrow circle, beginning at the barn and continuing along the terrace where Corwin had been only a moment before. Corwin, now flattening his broad-shouldered frame behind a log, could feel the wet moss soaking his shirt.

The three men walked along the driveway as Garlock probed the yard with his flashlight. The dog sniffed along Corwin's trail up to the terrace, but apparently lost the scent on the flagstones, for he began to run back and forth, barking unhappily.

"A deer's a beautiful sight," Garlock said, "when you catch him in the light. Those eyes look like two hot coals."

He turned back to the house, but Riley took the flashlight from him, and with Scott moved up toward the woods. Garlock stayed near the house, and the dog stayed with him. Riley and Scott were about twenty yards from Corwin when he heard Riley say:

"It might have been an animal, Jim, but I had a funny feeling coming out here tonight."

"I don't think you need to worry," said Scott. "I stood a pretty good watch on that rear-view mirror. I don't think anyone was following us."

Scott and Riley gave up the hunt a few seconds later and rejoined Garlock at the house. They went back to the living room, and the woman in the kitchen called Lady back in. Not until the kitchen door banged shut did Corwin move. When he did, he felt as if he were rolling in an old sleeping bag that had been left out in a downpour. Hardly a patch of clothing was dry. Regaining the gravel road, he broke into a run, and by the time he reached his car he was puffing hard.

My God, he thought, I must be mud and slop all over from shoes to collar. Mr. President, if you think I'm not going to put in for out-of-town per diem for this joyride, plus ten cents a mile for the car, plus a good dry-cleaning bill, you're crazy.

Then Corwin remembered that it would be the Secret Service, not the President, to whom the expense account would have to go. Working for the government, he thought, you can't win.

Corwin drove back about half a mile along the macadam road until he came to a slight bend. He parked a few yards beyond it, calculating that from here he could see Scott's headlights when he came out of Garlock's road. It seemed unlikely that Scott would turn south, for that was the long way around for the return trip to Washington. Garlock might take them that way to Mount Thunder, of course, but Corwin decided that from his position he could go either way without being spotted. He wished he had a cigarette now. He had quit smoking five years ago, but now could recall exactly how good that first big drag on a cigarette used to taste when he came off a long stakeout on some counterfeiting gang.

He didn't have long to wait. Lights swept out from Garlock's road, hesitated, and then came north toward him. He gunned his car over a small hill in the dark. Then he switched his lights on and sped for Route 9, turned toward Washington and drove —too fast—down the winding road which fell off the Blue Ridge. At the bottom, Corwin swung into a dirt road, turned his car around and waited again in the dark. A few minutes later the big Chrysler rolled past, Riley in the front seat with Scott. Corwin picked up the shadow, but much farther back this time.

The ride home seemed to go more quickly. The night was clear now, as the last black cloud moved away to the east. The road had dried and a breeze had come up. The taillights of Scott's car had assumed an identity of their own for Corwin, and he kept his eyes on them.

At the little crossroads in Dranesville, Scott bore off to the left. This will be harder, Corwin thought, he's taking the back road to Chain Bridge. That means he isn't going back to Fort Myer. And he isn't driving Riley home to the Marine Barracks in Southeast Washington, either. He must be heading for some place in Northwest Washington or Maryland.

The road dodged and bent through the trees. Corwin had to stop several times to avoid getting too close to Scott.

Not until the General crossed the Potomac on Chain Bridge did Corwin feel easier. Tailing in city traffic was a cinch; he dropped back four or five cars. Scott drove across to Massachusetts Avenue and turned toward the heart of the city. Corwin followed him through two traffic circles before the chairman turned off into a side street that led to the rear of a huge new apartment building. When Scott drove into the back parking lot, Corwin parked on the street nearby.

He saw Scott and Riley walk past a lighted sign ("The Dobney: Tenant Parking Only") and into the underground garage. From his angle, he could see only their legs and feet as they crossed the room and turned into a side corridor. He waited until they had time to get into an elevator, then followed them. The hallway dead-ended at the freight elevator.

Well now, he thought, that's a strange way for the chairman of the Joint Chiefs to go calling.

Corwin went back to his car, drove into the back lot and parked about a dozen places away from Scott's automobile. On a hunch, he fished into his glove compartment and got out the pocket-sized Congressional Directory he always carried. He looked up Prentice, Frederick, Senator from California. Sure enough. Residence: The Dobney.

A few minutes later a yellow taxicab drove up and parked. Corwin recognized it as belonging to the fleet which had the concession at Dulles International Airport. He also recognized the passenger who got out. He was tall, angular, and walked with a slight forward hunch of his shoulders. He wore a blue lightweight suit with a high sheen—the kind Corwin called an "electric suit."

Well, I've done my homework pretty well, he thought. After his talk with the President that morning, Corwin had done two things before picking up Scott. He had arranged to get Casey's service record, and he had studied the picture of every man mentioned by President Lyman. He hadn't had to hunt for a likeness of the man who had just got out of the cab, because he had obtained a photograph of him at Lyman's request a week ago. He was sure he was right; the man now walking toward the back entrance of the Dobney was the television commentator, Harold MacPherson.

Corwin got out of his car and strolled toward the garage. He saw MacPherson turn left and go down the hallway toward the freight elevator.

It was more than an hour later—almost 1 A.M.—when Scott

and Riley, this time accompanied by MacPherson, reappeared at the garage entrance. The three shook hands and parted, MacPherson going back to the taxi.

Corwin decided to fudge a bit on the President's orders and follow the cab. The quarry was newer—and thus vastly more interesting. Frankly, Corwin thought, I've had about enough of Gentleman Jim for one night.

The new venture, however, proved fruitless. The taxi drove out to Dulles International, as Corwin had suspected it would. He followed MacPherson into the lobby, after brushing the worst of the mud from his shirt and pants, and watched the commentator check in at Eastern Airlines, buy a magazine and stroll down a ramp. Corwin watched him climb onto Flight 348, a night coach to New York.

The Secret Service agent went to a phone booth and called Esther Townsend at the White House. It was 1:55 A.M.

"This is Art," he said. "I've got a report. It's pretty interesting."

"Can it wait until morning?" asked Esther sleepily.

"Early morning, honey," he said, "but awful early."

"How about seven o'clock, upstairs?"

"That's okay. I'll be there."

"I think that's better," Esther explained. "He didn't get to bed until an hour ago and this may be the last night in some time when he'll get a decent rest."

"I'm afraid that goes for all three of us, honey," Corwin said. "I'll be at home."

Flight 348 was lifting off the runway when Corwin drove past the last hanger. God, I'm tired, he thought. And scummy. I smell like a muskrat.

He tramped hard on the accelerator. He began to hum wearily:

> . . . I remember the atom blew down
> All the foreign relations in town.

Wednesday Morning

The night sky began to lighten in the east as Jiggs Casey and Senator Raymond Clark rode through the Virginia countryside. President Lyman's agents were about their business; Casey and Clark were headed for Dulles Airport, which Art Corwin had left only a few hours earlier.

Though they were on their way well before sunrise, they were not the first of the President's little force to start work. About the time Corwin reached home, with the red-clay mud of the Blue Ridge still clinging to his shirt, Paul Girard had flown out over the Atlantic in the after cabin of the big jet transport carrying Vice-President Vincent Gianelli to Rome.

By prearrangement with Casey, Senator Clark was driving his own car to the airport. The two men wanted to be able to talk without worrying about an eavesdropping driver. Clark had beeped gently in front of Casey's Arlington home just after 4 A.M. The colonel, waiting on his front stoop in the dark, climbed into the convertible with the red leather bucket seats and threw his thin dispatch case in the back. He was bound for New York, Clark for El Paso.

"Pretty fancy locomotion, Senator," said Casey.

"Jiggs, if you don't start calling me Ray, I'm going to get Billy Riley to bust you to major."

"Okay, Ray." Casey liked this friendly politician from Georgia. "But it's still a pretty snappy rig."

"Just a widower's consolation, Jiggs. We got to have some fun in life. And what did your wife say about this junket?"

"If you think it's easy to leave home without any explanation, you're crazy," Casey said unhappily. "I couldn't say it was a secret mission because Scott might call. I couldn't say the President sent me. I couldn't say it was duty. Damn it, I couldn't say anything. I just had to stand there and watch those big brown eyes turn green."

"Come off it, Jiggs," Clark said in a mocking tone. "Don't tell me Mrs. Casey has any reason to be suspicious of you."

The merging Virginia suburbs flew past. My God, this guy drives fast, Casey thought. The telephone poles raced by like pickets on a fence.

"Well," said Casey, "she doesn't, no. But if she thought I was going to New York, she would be anyway."

"The gal who works for television?"

"That's right."

"What was that all about, anyway?" asked Clark. "You sounded pretty vague yesterday."

"It was a couple of years ago and it was all over almost before it started." Casey offered nothing more.

"I'm beginning to get a little suspicious myself, Jiggs." Clark's tone was bantering.

"Look," said Casey defensively, "the only reason I know this Segnier dame is because of one weekend in New York two years ago when I was on the UN detail. She's a friend of the girl I met. We . . . well, it was short and it was one of those things. Marge got some word of it somehow and there was hell to pay. And there should have been, I guess. I was a damn fool, but you know how—"

"Yeah, I know," Clark said. "Don't start kicking yourself around all over again."

"It isn't that. It's just that the President is almost forcing me back into something that was dead and buried. I mean, the only way I can find out anything about Scott and Millicent Segnier is through Shoo."

"Shoo?"

"Shoo Holbrook. Eleanor Holbrook. You might as well know. You might have to rescue me up there. She writes scripts for TV shows."

Clark drove a moment in silence.

"Well, take it easy, Jiggs," he said. "A good wife is worth an awful lot."

"I know."

"Worth more than anything," said Clark, suddenly serious, "except a country."

"What do you really think about my story?" Clark was obviously the President's best friend, and Casey was frankly curious about his reaction.

Clark took his eyes off the road and looked at Casey. "I think it's the most harebrained, farfetched yarn I ever heard." He paused. "And I think it's probably true."

"You do?"

"Well, maybe not all the lurid details that your surmises would add up to. That's what we're trying to find out. But the climate's right for something like this, Jiggs, just as the President said yesterday. I've felt it in my stomach for a long time.

"You know, Girard and I stayed behind with the President last night. He needed us. After all, we were the only two politicians in the room besides him. You and Art and Todd are great guys to have in a thing like this, but it takes a professional to kind of weigh what's possible and what isn't."

"What do you think he can do, the President?" Casey asked. "I take it he won't consider a public showdown."

"That's impossible," Clark answered quickly. "Scott would deny it all and his friends would hint that the President had had a mental breakdown—or worse. They might call him insane. He could be impeached, but even if he wasn't, the real power would pass to Scott, and from then on civilian authority wouldn't be worth a nickel."

"So?"

"So the President gets open-and-shut evidence in his hands and then . . ." Clark stopped. Casey looked at him. The Georgian's face had gone hard. ". . . And then he breaks him fast. Forces him to resign. Anything goes at that point."

Casey lit a cigarette. Clark must have been a pretty tough one himself in combat, for all his easy surface manner.

"And what if he can't make the evidence stick?" he asked.

"I've thought some about that," Clark said, "but I don't think the President has. He's too confident that point will never be reached. He's hoping that it's all a dream. One way, of course, would be to fire Scott out of hand without warning, install some guy like Rutkowski as chairman, call off the alert and order Rutkowski to break up ECOMCON—if it's really there."

"You'd have to do that by Friday night," Casey pointed out, "before they start flying troops all over the country."

"I know, I know. But does Jordie . . . does the President know? Jiggs, before we're out of this we may need some professional advice from you. We might reach the point where we'd need to know the exact place to cut the communications and the command chain, so that it belongs to us, not to Scott."

They fell silent. Casey felt small and a bit helpless in the half-light just before sunrise. Six men fumbling with a huge military machine—and no manual to guide them. The great apparatus of the Pentagon stood there, ready to respond automatically to a word from Scott: three million men, guns, ships, planes, missiles. Casey felt as if he'd lost his bearings. Where were the powers of the Presidency, about which he'd heard all his life and for which he himself had jumped on occasion?

"In our system," Clark said, as though reading his thoughts, "a politician without the people isn't much, no matter where he sits."

As they drove into the airport parking lot, Casey copied Mutt Henderson's El Paso phone number out of his address book onto a slip of paper and gave it to Clark.

"Thanks, Jiggs," Clark said, "but I think I better have a look at that base myself. If I don't, we won't be any better off than we are now."

The two men shook hands and parted in the terminal lobby. The sun glowed large and red on the horizon when Casey boarded his shuttle plane to New York. A few minutes later, in the first full daylight, Clark rode the mobile lounge out to the morning jet flight to Dallas and El Paso.

President Lyman's first order of business this morning was an 8:30 call to his wife Doris at their daughter's home in Louisville. Lyman knew that a soft word would keep Doris happy for hours, and he thought wryly that he should be grateful for at least one situation in which a mere expression of approval on his part sufficed to put things right. After chatting with Mrs. Lyman, he called Liz at the hospital, heard her whisper "Grandpa" for the first time and blew her a loud kiss over the phone.

His mood was so cheerful when Secretary Todd telephoned a few minutes later that it earned him a rebuke.

"Good God, Mr. President," Todd said. "The way you sound, Scott must have given up and died."

"No. As a matter of fact, I was just about to call you about that. Can you come over right away?"

By the time Todd arrived from his Treasury office across the street, Lyman had finished two morning papers, informed his protesting press secretary that there would be no formal appointments that day, checked with Esther Townsend to make sure his three emissaries were safely on their way, and finished reading Corwin's notes on his night with Scott.

Todd fingered his watch chain as he read through the Corwin report, handed to him without comment by the President. Lyman removed his glasses, held them lightly in his big hands, and studied them as though inspecting the lenses for flaws.

"I must say that nothing in here tends to undercut Colonel Casey's story," Todd said. "Imagine two grown men sneaking up a freight elevator in the middle of the night to meet with a fringe mental case like MacPherson."

"Incidentally," Lyman said, "we can be pretty sure that it was Prentice's apartment. Esther checked our phone list this morning and Prentice is the only member of Congress of any standing who lives at the Dobney."

"Well, I can understand why Scott would be friendly with Prentice," Todd said. "After all, he's chairman of the Armed Services Committee, even if it was a bit late to call on him. But I can't see him mixing with that MacPherson."

Lyman leaned across his desk. "Look, Chris, if there is something up along the lines Casey suggested, it makes pretty good sense to me. MacPherson has eight or ten million listeners in his audience every night, and they apparently take everything he says as gospel truth. If Scott is planning something, he'll need someone to sell it to the country. And the way MacPherson talks, he'd be willing to do it. What I can't figure out is Prentice's part in this."

Now it was Todd's turn to be slightly patronizing.

"Mr. President, if there's something going on—and I'm still not ready to admit there is—it's quite obvious to me why Senator Prentice might be involved. He has a vested interest in the military not only because of his chairmanship but because of the state he represents. Think of all the defense contracts in California. Almost all our missiles and planes are made there. And it's not just big industry, it's the unions too. You turn on disarmament full steam and there'd be ghost towns all around Los Angeles for a while."

"Prentice is a bigger man than that," Lyman protested. "He throws his weight around, and he fought me on the treaty. But I've always respected him, really."

"I think it could be reflex action, pure and simple. He's no deep thinker. That treaty is a threat to his way of life, that's all." Todd brought the conversation back to specifics. "What about Rutkowski?"

"We talked for about an hour last night," Lyman said. "I found it a little hard to keep my hand hidden. I put it pretty much on the basis of being worried about what the military commanders were doing on the treaty, that kind of thing. Anyhow, Barney agreed to sound out Admiral Palmer this morning."

"Did he—"

The President interrupted. "Yes, there's something else. Barney said he got a call about three weeks ago from Colonel Murdock, asking him to come to Washington for a talk with Scott. Murdock made it plain it wasn't an order, just an invitation to discuss the political situation. Barney told him politics wasn't in his line, but that he'd drop in next time he came here. Murdock got kind of vague then and said 'Yes, do that,' or something like that."

"I don't think Rutkowski should 'drop in' on Scott now," Todd said. "Scott might suspect something."

"I agree," Lyman said. "But I think *I* ought to call Scott right now, and tell him I'm going to skip the alert and go to Maine for the weekend instead."

Todd nodded. "We want to try him out, and that ought to get a reaction. And the sooner the better."

The President buzzed for Esther.

"I have a sneaky job for you, dear," he said. "I want you to get General Scott on the line for me, and then take down the conversation."

Todd stared intently at the President throughout the telephone conversation. Occasionally Lyman nodded at him with a humorless smile. When he hung up, five minutes later, his early-morning buoyancy was gone.

Todd started to ask something, but Lyman cut him off with a wave of his hand and buzzed for Esther. "Come in and read it back to us, Esther."

She came in with her shorthand book, sat down, and read:

THE PRESIDENT: Good morning, General. This is Jordan Lyman.

GENERAL SCOTT: Good morning, Mr. President. I see we're both early birds today.

PRESIDENT: General, to come right to the point, I've been thinking it over and I'm not going to participate in the alert after all. Frankly, I'm tired out. I've decided to go up to my place at Blue Lake and fish for two or three days.

SCOTT: Mr. President, if I may take exception, sir, you really can't do that. You're an integral part of the exercise. Your presence is necessary. In fact, vital.

PRESIDENT: I'm only the last peg on the board, General. You know that. The alert can go through without me.

SCOTT: But you happen to be the Commander in Chief, sir. Certain orders can only be given by you.

PRESIDENT: But those are final orders, and will only be simulated on Saturday anyway.

SCOTT: It's really more than that, Mr. President. Your presence is needed for morale, for the Chiefs and especially for the field commands who'll realize you're watching everything.

PRESIDENT: Don't worry about that. I'll be following things closely at Blue Lake.

SCOTT: If I may say so, sir, I think it would be extremely unwise for you to take a vacation at this stage in our situation with Russia. They won't be very much impressed by an alert which takes place while you go fishing.

PRESIDENT: Suppose you let me be the judge of that, General. I'm afraid my decision is final. I just have to get some time off.

SCOTT: Of course it is up to you, Mr. President, but I must say I can't endorse your decision.

PRESIDENT: Well, I . . .

SCOTT: When do you expect to go to Blue Lake?

PRESIDENT: I'm probably going to fly up Friday afternoon, late.

SCOTT: Well, I envy you. Good luck with the fish.

PRESIDENT: Good-by, General.

SCOTT: Good-by, Mr. President.

Todd waited until the flush of anger faded from Lyman's face. "Not an easy man to cross," Todd remarked. "I'm glad he's on our side and not the Soviets'."

"Our side, Chris?" Lyman said. "Do you still think so?"

"I must admit my doubts are growing," Todd said. "You

certainly drew a reaction from him. Now, what are you going to do about it?"

"I'm going to call Hank up at Blue Lake. If Scott's up to anything, I think he might send someone up there to get a look at it."

It took a minute or two for Esther to get through to Henry Picot, the President's caretaker and fishing guide at his Maine retreat.

"Hank? This is Jordan Lyman. They are, huh? How many? . . . You're a liar, Hank. No, I can't come this weekend, but I want you to make it sound as though I am coming. That's right. Drop the word at the store when you go in to get the mail.

"And listen, I expect a few magazine people might turn up there to look the place over. Maybe in the next day or so. Oh, you know, they always want to get pictures. If you see any strangers around the island, be polite to them, but don't let them on the place. Okay? And, Hank, get a good look at them and give me a call as soon as they leave, will you? . . .

"No, I'm not sure they're coming. It's just a hunch. . . . No, no. You know I don't have any enemies—except you and those fish. Okay. Thanks, Hank."

Todd nodded approvingly at Lyman. "If this thing is as bad as it's beginning to look, your man Picot will have visitors before Friday."

"I think so too."

"Look," Todd said, "I think I ought to go back to the office and work out an alternative plan. Suppose, for example, that we become convinced there's something up, but we can't prove it? In that case, you've got to be ready to act fast."

"I wish you would, Chris," Lyman said. "Frankly, my thinking hasn't gone that far."

When Todd left, Lyman went through Corwin's report again. It read like a two-bit thriller. General Garlock he had met only once, and he couldn't really remember him. Obviously, though, Garlock wasn't in on Scott's plans. Lyman felt strangely upset about General Riley. He remembered an uproarious evening last year when he had given a party for the top Marine commanders, one in a series of military stag dinners he put on. Riley had told story after story of World War II days with earthy, trenchant humor. Few men had made so quick or so favorable an impression on Lyman. Could Riley now really have a hand in challenging the system which had given so much to the country, to the Marines—and to Riley himself?

And how could men of the stature of Scott and Riley bring themselves to sneak into a freight elevator like a couple of burglars for a meeting with such a transparent charlatan as MacPherson? Or had he misjudged MacPherson? Or was Corwin dreaming, too?

Esther's buzzer, announcing General Rutkowski, cut Lyman's thoughts short. He was thankful, for they were beginning to wander and the schedule wouldn't allow much of that.

General Bernard Rutkowski wore his Air Force uniform and command pilot's wings like a man born to them. He was stocky, blond, and just a trifle overweight. A bright, tough Chicago slum kid, he had literally forced his way into West Point, harassing three congressmen until one finally appointed him. He wanted to fly. Now he wanted to command fliers and missiles. He had carefully avoided Pentagon duty over the years; the Air Defense Command was his first completely chairborne assignment and he suffered in it.

Lyman waved at a chair and Rutkowski dropped into it, emphatically. The President offered him a cigar from the box he kept for Todd, and within a few seconds Rutkowski was enveloped in blue smoke.

"That's a good cigar. Well, I had a nice talk with Admiral Palmer," the General said. He blew a hole in his smoke cloud and studied Lyman. "I'm not much good on this espionage stuff, Mr. President, especially when I'm still not quite sure what you wanted me to find out."

Lyman retreated to his veiled language of the night before. I hate doing this to you, Barney, he thought, but that's the way it has to be.

"Really, nothing specific, Barney," he said. "As I told you, I've been a bit worried over the attitude of some of the military commanders since we negotiated the disarmament treaty. I had a feeling there might be some organized resistance from some of your colleagues, and you know that wouldn't be good for the country."

Rutkowski was obviously not satisfied, but he shouldered ahead in his blunt way.

"Anyway," he said, "I told Palmer I had a feeling something was going on here in Washington and as a boy from the sticks I wanted to get the word. I mentioned that call last winter from Daniel at SAC, and then the one a couple of weeks ago from Murdock.

"Palmer fenced awhile, but he isn't much better at it than I am. He likes to get to the point. Finally, he said he felt the same way I did, but he couldn't explain it. He said as far back as last Christmas Scott took him to dinner at the Army-Navy Club one night and talked nothing but politics."

"Did Palmer say what his reaction was?"

"Sure. He's a stand-up guy. He said he didn't like it. He told Scott his job was to run the Navy and help make military strategy in the JCS, and that politics was out of his line."

"Was that the end of it?"

"For about two months. In February Scott had Palmer to dinner over at Quarters Six, with General Riley and General Dieffenbach. This time, Palmer says, all three of them took the same line, very critical of you and your foreign policy."

"Thought I was making a real mess of things?" asked Lyman.

"Well, yes." Rutkowski grinned. "I'm not going to repeat some of the language Palmer used. It got pretty purple."

"Don't bother to spare me," Lyman said, smiling. "That's everyday talk in my business. You should see some of my mail."

"Palmer says he listened but didn't say much, and when the others tried to draw him out, he backed water. That was all for a while, until Palmer denounced the treaty when the Senate

Armed Services Committee questioned him on it. He said
Scott must have heard about his statement through the grapevine, because he called him that night to congratulate him.
That time again Scott wanted to expand into a general political discussion of your administration, but Palmer wouldn't
go for it."

"Is that all?"

"No, it isn't. Palmer says he got a call from Murdock not
too long ago, just about the time I did, inviting him to talk
over the political situation and the 'military responsibility.' Palmer kind of told him off, I gather. He said he'd already said
his piece on the treaty, that it was your show now and that was
that.

"Oh, there was one other thing. Palmer thinks the other
chiefs have had some meetings on this subject that he hasn't
been in on. He figures they're getting ready to back some kind
of citizens' group that will try to get the treaty repealed, or
something. He thinks the chiefs will give it all the covert support they can without having their names appear. He says he
doesn't believe in playing that way."

"What do *you* think of the treaty, Barney?" asked Lyman.

Rutkowski shifted his cigar to the corner of his mouth.
"You want it straight, Mr. President?"

"It wouldn't be much use any other way."

"Okay. I think the Russkis are playing you for a sucker. I
don't think they have any intention of disarming. Oh, they
might dismantle some bombs all right on July 1, but how many
more will they be stockpiling at some new base in Siberia?"

"You don't trust our intelligence?" asked Lyman.

"Not on that one, Mr. President. Russia is too big a country."

"But you wouldn't join some group, say General Scott's if he
has one, to fight the treaty?"

"Nope," Rutkowski said. "You've made the decision. You
asked our advice. We gave it. You didn't take it. All right, now
it's up to you. God bless you, Mr. President, I hope it works.
If it doesn't, we start earning our pay the hard way."

Lyman hoped his smile looked as warm as he felt. "Barney, I wish you'd been in Washington to give me some advice. I like the way you give it. You don't straddle—like some I know."

"If you'll pardon the language, Mr. President," Rutkowski said, "straddling makes my ass tired. So I never got into the habit."

Lyman got up in his angular way and walked around the desk. As they moved toward the door, the President again asked Rutkowski to keep his visit to Palmer and the White House confidential.

"If I need you again in Washington, Barney," Lyman added, "I hope you'll come down and stay awhile."

"As long as the taxpayers let me have that jet," the General replied, "I'm your man in two hours, any time."

When the door closed, Lyman went to the tall window and stood looking out at the rose garden, his hands in his pockets. The sun shone thinly this morning, but even that was a welcome improvement over yesterday's rain. Had there been a similar improvement in his position? Was Palmer right, perhaps, and was Scott merely up to the old military stratagem of quietly sponsoring a civilian organization to say what the generals were not supposed to say for themselves? If that's all it is, Lyman thought, I'll contribute fifty bucks to the pot and lead three cheers for Scott in Garfinckel's window. But what about ECOMCON? Does the chairman need thirty-five hundred trained saboteurs to reinforce public opinion? Is there an ECOMCON, after all? Well, on that one, Ray Clark should know in a few hours.

When Clark stepped out of his plane at El Paso the heat encased his body. It was still early morning in West Texas, but the sun shone with unfamiliar intensity even from its low angle. Clark ran his tongue around the inside of his mouth, grimacing at the taste. He had slept since Dallas, but after boarding the plane in Washington he had drained the half-pint bottle of bourbon in his pocket in a couple of gulps.

His face had the grimy feeling of the overnight traveler and he knew stubble stood out on his cheeks. Clark wasn't sure whether he'd like a drink or breakfast. He decided he'd settle for either.

A lunch counter appeared first. He ordered juice, doughnuts, and coffee and asked the waitress for the name of a good nearby motel.

"Try the Sand 'n' Saddle," she said. "But it's a nice place. Maybe you better shave before you check in, mister."

Clark got the cab driver talking—it wasn't much of a task—on the short ride to the motel.

"Say, I'm looking for an old buddy from down home," Clark said. "You know all the Army bases around here?"

"Ain't many, Mac," the driver replied. "They's just big. You're looking for Fort Bliss, maybe?"

"No, that doesn't sound like it."

"Well, they got White Sands just a little ways up the road in New Mexico. And Holloman airbase, out the same way." The driver studied Clark in the rear-view mirror. "Or Biggs field, here. Any of 'em?"

"Nope," Clark said, "this is a new one. Maybe only a couple months old. Damn, I lost the piece of paper he wrote it down on."

"Well, there's some kinda new base around here somewhere, one they keep pretty quiet. Tell you the truth, Mac, I don't know where it is. We never get no business from it and if Uncle Sam don't want me stickin' my nose in his business, I don't stick it in."

"This buddy," Clark said, "he's in the Signal Corps."

"You got me, pal. I never heard of that neither."

The Sand 'n' Saddle sprawled invitingly in a two-story semi-circle from the office where Clark alighted. Through the open passageways he could see a swimming pool and deck chairs. The air conditioning in the office lowered the temperature to a painless 80 degrees. The senator registered simply as "R. Clark, Macon, Georgia." A Mexican teen-ager with a fixed smile and expressionless eyes took Clark's overnight case and led him to a room on the upper level.

A steady current of cool air poured from the gray machine in the window. Clark stooped over and held his face close to the source, massaging his temples and cheekbones.

"How soon can you get me a little whisky?" he asked the bellboy.

"Sorry, boss, the package store doesn't open until ten," said the youth. "It's far from here, too."

"Come on, son." Clark handed him a $10 bill. "You must have a private stock for your good customers."

The boy disappeared and came back a few minutes later with a pint of blended whisky. Clark winced at the label, but took the bottle without comment. Alone, he wrenched the cap off and took a long drink. He coughed and rubbed his smarting eyes. Then, self-consciously resolute, he walked into the bathroom, put the bottle in the medicine cabinet and banged the little door shut. He returned to the bedroom and picked up the telephone.

"Call me in an hour, please," he told the operator.

He stripped to his shorts, climbed under a sheet and went to sleep almost at once. When the phone rang an hour later he felt better. He shaved, changed into a short-sleeved shirt and lightweight sports jacket, and then sat on the edge of the bed, gazing at the slip of paper Casey had given him. Finally he made up his mind and asked the operator to get him the number. A woman answered.

"Mrs. Henderson?"

"Yes."

"Ma'am, my name is Ray Clark. I'm a friend of Mutt's and Jiggs Casey's. Jiggs gave me your phone number and told me to call when I got to town. I just missed Mutt in Washington."

"Oh, that's too bad," she said. "Mutt got in late Monday, but he had to go right out to the base. I'm afraid he'll be there through the weekend, too."

"Any way I can reach him?"

She laughed. "If you find out, please tell me. I don't even know where it is."

"You mean you've never even seen it?" Clark pumped his voice full of incredulity.

"Well, he did show me the general direction once when we were driving over to White Sands, so at least I know my husband's not in Alaska."

"Service wives have it rough."

"You're not in the service?" Mrs. Henderson's voice became guarded.

"Oh, sure," Clark lied. "That's how I know how it is. Or, rather, my wife does. They keep me traveling all the time on the hardware gadgets."

"Oh." She sounded relieved. "Well, tell me where you're stopping, and if he does get home, I'll have him call you."

"Sorry." He lied again. "I've got to fly to L.A. this afternoon. Just tell him Ray called. And thanks anyway, Mrs. Henderson."

On his way out the door, Clark hesitated, stepped back toward the bathroom, then turned quickly and went out again, banging the door hard. He walked rapidly down to the office, putting a smile back on his face by the time he reached the desk. He handed his room key to the clerk and asked him to arrange a car rental for him.

"Caddy?" asked the clerk. Clark hadn't realized a shave could do that much for a man's appearance.

"No, Chevy or Ford's okay."

While he waited, Clark leaned on the desk and talked with the thin young man who ran the office.

"What road do I take to go to White Sands?" he asked.

"You're on it. Route 54. Take a left out front and then keep straight on out. It's about sixty miles."

"Say, how do I get to that new Army base out that way? I got a friend in the Signal Corps there."

"Search me." The young man shrugged his shoulders. "I heard of some base out that way some place, but from what I hear, it's supposed to be secret."

"What's between here and White Sands?"

The youth grinned quickly. "Desert."

Several miles northeast of El Paso, driving at an unaccustomed 40 miles per hour, Clark had to agree with the description. To his right, the gray-brown land stretched flat to the far horizon, burnished almost white by the unrelenting sun which now rode well up in the sky. Occasional small boulders, clumps of tumbleweed and scattered barrel cactus offered the only relief from the expanse. On Clark's left rose the Franklin Mountains, gray and barren too except for the greasewood clinging to the lower slopes. More than forty million years ago, an ancient agony beneath the earth's surface had thrown up fire and lava to mold a mighty mountain range. Hundreds of centuries of wind and sun had eroded the peaks, inch by inch, until the limestone hills stood like old men, gaunt, withered, timeless.

Despite the heat, the dryness of the air left Clark feeling better than he thought he had a right to feel. He wiped his brow, but found no perspiration on it; evaporation had turned him into a self-cooling machine. Just over the New Mexico state line, he swung into a service station. From the look of the empty road ahead, it would be the last for many miles.

A man, from his stance of casual authority the proprietor, stood in the doorway. He wore a grease-spotted undershirt and his face was seamed and leathery.

"Coke in there?" Clark asked. The man nodded toward a big red box. Clark dropped in his dime and waited for the bottle to thump out of the recesses of the vending machine.

"Have one?"

The man shook his head, but smiled faintly in thanks.

"How far is it to White Sands?" Clark asked.

"About fifty."

"You sure got a hot country here," said Clark, "and I got to make three PX's out that way today."

"Salesman?"

"Yep. Detergents. But this is a new route for me." This evoked no comment. Clark went on: "How many miles to that

Army base, you know, the one they just finished up six, seven weeks ago?"

"Figured you wanted information," said the man in the undershirt, scratching his jaw. "By them tags, you rented the car in El Paso, so you didn't need no gas."

Clark laughed. "Okay, but I did offer to spend another dime. Listen, I'll make a deal with you. I'm breaking in on this territory and I want to sell that new base."

"What kind of deal?"

Clark laid a $20 bill on the glass counter by the cash register. The man made no move to pick it up.

"How do I know you're not some kind of spy?" he asked.

Clark pulled out his wallet again and sorted through his stack of cards, looking for his old Army reserve identification card. He thumbed quickly over several credit cards that listed him as a senator and held out the reserve ID card, with his picture and prints of his right and left index fingers on it.

"Georgia, huh? Whereabouts?"

"Macon, but I'm working out of Dallas now," Clark said. "Listen, all I want is a starter. Tell me where the road to that base turns off and the twenty's yours. And from now on, when I come back, I'll buy my gas here."

The man rang the cash register and carefully placed the twenty under a clamp in the bill compartment.

"Honest, friend," he said, "I don't know much about it. All I know is they built some kinda base over yonder." He pointed vaguely to the northwest. "They got a pretty big airfield there, and lots of buildings, from what I hear, but I ain't never seen nobody from the place. Least, nobody who'd admit it. If I was you, I'd watch my speedometer and when I'd gone about thirty miles, no, make it twenty-seven, twenty-eight, I'd look for a blacktop road off to the left, heading up to a little rise."

"Thanks a lot," said Clark. He drained the last of the soft drink.

"If you get in there to sell any soap, they ought to give you the gold watch, friend," said the station proprietor. "I don't think you will."

As Clark drove off, he watched in the rear-view mirror and saw the man squint at the rear of his car, then wet the stub of a pencil and mark the back of his hand. He's either working for somebody up the line, Clark mused, or he's a very cautious citizen.

Clark pressed the gas pedal down until the car was rolling along at 75 miles an hour. He watched the speedometer; when it showed he had traveled about 25 miles from the gas station, he slowed down. Several cars whizzed by him, the drivers glancing back in irritation. Clark kept his eyes to the left. The mountains reached higher now, though they ran farther from the highway, and the land rolled slightly in the foreground.

He slowed, then stopped. A black asphalt strip, obviously a fairly new road, ran off the highway at a right angle. It was un- marked.

Clark turned left onto it and drove slowly along. The pave- ment was thick. He saw the track of heavy-duty tires printed in faint dust marks on the blacktop. The road ran upward on a gentle grade. The desert stretched away unbroken save for a hill—or rather a domelike swelling of land—several miles off to his right.

Suddenly the road dipped over the rise. About a mile ahead he could see a high wire fence. A wire-mesh gate, closed, blocked the road there and a small hut stood inside. He saw a large sign, but couldn't read it from that distance. He had slowed to less than 20 miles an hour.

"Okay, bud, that's far enough!"

Clark, turning his head toward the source of the shout, saw a soldier coming at him from behind a large rock. He wore khaki shorts and short-sleeved shirt, field shoes and sun helmet, and for an instant Clark recalled the pictures of Montgomery's British desert troops in World War II. But this man carried a modern submachine gun—pointed right at him—and his collar insignia were U.S. government issue.

Clark saw another guard coming from the other side of the road a few yards farther along. He stopped the car.

"Move over, bud." The first soldier opened the door and

shoved Clark to the middle of the seat. He tossed his weapon on the back seat. The other GI squeezed against Clark from the right side and also dropped his weapon in back, but he took a pistol from a holster and held it in his right hand. Both men looked like regulars to Clark. They were about thirty years old, he guessed. Their appearance left nothing to guesswork: they were hard.

The one now behind the wheel gunned the car down the road and pulled up with a screech of brakes in front of the gate. Clark still could see nothing beyond the fence but more desert and tumbleweed. The driver unlocked the gate, went into the little shack, picked up a field telephone, and cranked it. Now Clark could read the sign: "U.S. Government Property. Restricted. Positively No Admittance."

"Gimme the O.D.," said the soldier at the telephone. "Major? This is Corporal Steiner on the gate. We got a snooper here with Texas plates."

Wednesday
Afternoon

The Rock of Gibraltar threw a long shadow on the Mediterranean as the small plane chartered by Paul Girard circled the peninsula to approach the landing strip tucked under the north side of the fortress. It was almost six o'clock, five hours ahead of Washington time, when Girard first sighted the landmark and began to identify the warships of the Sixth Fleet anchored in the Bay of Algeciras. Three carriers lay among the ships dotting the roadstead, but even from the air Girard could pick out the one he wanted—the U.S.S. *Dwight D. Eisenhower,* the 100,000 ton nuclear-powered warship which flew the flag of the Sixth Fleet commander, Vice Admiral Farley C. Barnswell.

The Italian pilot aligned his trim little six-passenger jet with the end of the runway and nosed down. My God, thought Girard, that field looks like a postage stamp in the middle of a bathtub.

Girard had slept soundly crossing the Atlantic with Vice-

163

President Gianelli in the *Buckeye*, which Jordan Lyman had offered for the good-will trip. They had landed at Rome's airport shortly before noon. Gianelli had carefully timed his arrival so that he could drive into town when the streets were crowded with lunch-hour traffic, but a crush of photographers and Italian dignitaries, including the Prime Minister, delayed his departure from the airport almost an hour. Girard, hidden behind a locked door in the private presidential toilet, waited until he could see the last car of Gianelli's motor caravan leave the airfield. An Italian ceremonial platoon, guarding the *Buckeye*, seemed surprised to see one more passenger step off the aircraft an hour after the others, but the captain in command merely smiled and saluted. He made no move to question Girard.

More time was wasted in the red tape over hiring a plane for the run to Gibraltar, although the charter itself presented no problem once Girard displayed a fat roll of United States currency.

There might have been raised eyebrows, however, if the voluble Italian who ran the charter agency had known how Girard acquired the money. Tuesday evening, after leaving the White House, he suddenly realized he would need a sizable amount of cash. He found only $38 in his apartment. He called the President with his "supply and logistics" problem, as he termed it, and Lyman in turn called the president of the Riggs National Bank. The bank official and a teller returned to the financial citadel on Pennsylvania Avenue, drew $2,000 from Lyman's own account, and delivered it by hand to Esther Townsend at the White House. "I not only have to defend the country," Lyman quipped, "but I get stuck with the check too."

In Rome, after Girard hired the plane, another complication arose. The pilot said he wouldn't be able to land at Gibraltar without clearance from British military authorities. Unable to risk using the American Military Air Transport Service office at the field, Girard had to call the British embassy in Rome. A flustered young consular officer drove out to the airport, inspected Girard's White House identity papers and finally made the necessary arrangements after working his way through three echelons of the Royal Air Force. The whole thing took two hours.

Now the charter plane touched down at Gibraltar. Girard stared in disbelief as they rolled past a line of automobiles halted on each side of the landing strip. Apparently there was so little horizontal real estate available that the runway had to be set directly across the main highway.

Girard checked in with the RAF and was courteously remanded to the Royal Navy, which in turn transferred this unexpected caller to the United States Navy. The process consumed another hour, and Girard downed two mugs of milky British tea while he waited.

He bounced into town in a Navy jeep, past the old stone ramparts, soccer field and crowded shops of the lower town. He found that his negotiations had really just begun when he faced the duty officer at the whitewashed building which served as administrative headquarters of the U.S. Naval Facility, Gibraltar. The officer, a spruce young commander, looked through Girard's identification several times.

"This is a bit unusual," the commander said. "We aren't part of Admiral Barnswell's command, you know. We just service him when he's in port."

"Just put me in touch with his flag secretary," said Girard. He had no intention of showing the President's letter until he had to.

The commander surveyed this ungainly man, with his overlarge head and drooping eyelids. Emissaries from Washington didn't just appear unannounced, especially secretaries of the President. Finally, after some hesitation, the officer telephoned the captain in command of the shore base. Good God, thought Girard, by the time they get through, every naval officer from here to Beirut will know I'm around.

The commander listened respectfully on the phone. When he hung up, he summoned a signalman and wrote out a message for him.

"He'll raise the *Eisenhower* by blinker," he explained. "The Admiral's aboard this evening."

Girard stood by the window. The signal station for the fleet was housed in a small tower on the roof of the administration building. In a few minutes, he saw a light on the distant carrier winking toward shore through the deepening twilight. There was a long pause—apparently the sailor upstairs had sent his message and was waiting for an answer. Then the light aboard ship began to blink again. Girard made out a G and an E in the Morse code, but the rest went too fast for him. It had been years since his own two-week cram course in code. The signalman returned to the office and handed a message to the commander.

"The flag secretary wants to know whether this is a request for a personal visit," the officer said, "or official government business?"

Girard decided he'd better not underplay his own status at this stage. The prospect of having to swim a couple of miles out to the carrier did not appeal to him.

"I am representing the President of the United States," he said. "The matter is urgent."

This time only five minutes elapsed in the exchange of messages.

"The Admiral's barge is on the way in for you," the commander said, eying Girard with new respect.

A trim launch with three silver stars on its bow slid quietly into the dock where Girard waited. A boatswain's mate met him at the gangplank and showed him into the handsomely appointed cabin. A mahogany desk stood against one bulkhead; leather swivel chairs, brass-fitted to the deck, were spotted around the compartment. There were even crisp little blue curtains at the portholes. Each metal fitting shone like a jewel.

The Admiral's barge made the run out to the looming bulk of the *Eisenhower* at 15 knots. The huge ship stood out like a mesa in the American Southwest, hardly moving on the gentle bay swells. Behind the ship, Girard could see the glow where the sun was closing fast with the horizon beyond Algeciras. Jet fighters and attack bombers stood in dovetailed rows on the after flight deck. As the barge came into the cool shadow of the *Eisenhower,* Girard heard the heavy murmur that results from the merged small noises of a large warship preparing itself for the night.

A lone civilian aboard a modern man-of-war, with its acres of steel and bristling weapons, is a sorry thing indeed. Girard felt like a castaway space traveler as he climbed the salt-splotched wooden steps of the forward accommodation ladder. The carrier's hull bulked monstrously large now. Below him the Admiral's barge, which had not seemed to him a small boat at all, bobbed like a child's toy in a pond.

At the head of the ladder a tanned young lieutenant, obviously the officer of the deck, cut a prim salute. A commander, apparently the flag secretary, held out his hand.

"Welcome aboard, sir," he said. "I'll take you right up to admiral's country. Just follow me, please."

The knot of sailors who watched Girard cross the flight deck toward the superstructure saw little to impress them. A somewhat ungainly civilian, his suit rumpled, walked with the uncertain gait of a landsman, carrying a small attaché case. Those who hazarded a guess figured him to be some minor civil servant or a technical representative from one of the aircraft or missile contractors. Only the watch on the signal bridge, which had read the messages from shore, eyed him with real interest. They could see Admiral Barnswell, three tiny stars glinting on each point of his starched shirt collar, step from his cabin door and hold out a hand in greeting.

"Nice to see you, sir," they heard him say. "I'm glad we could offer you real Mediterranean weather instead of some of that dirty stuff we get from the Atlantic." The two men stepped into the cabin.

The hours slipped by. With the turn of the tide the carrier heaved gently in a slightly rising swell. Stars, brilliant and sharp, winked on across the sky until they filled the night. The officer of the deck, trying to keep an eye on the Admiral's cabin, knew only that the Old Man had ordered dinner for two sent to his quarters.

More than four hours passed before the watch on the bridge heard the Admiral's door open. Barnswell and the civilian exchanged farewells without banter and their handshake was quick and perfunctory. Neither man smiled.

The officer of the deck noted the grim set to the features of the civilian as he said simply, "Thanks," and lowered himself gingerly down the ladder, descending backward to get a firmer footing. The Admiral's barge purred off to return him to shore.

At the dock Girard turned down the offer of a jeep ride back to the airfield, but asked directions into town. He hurried off, in his long and graceless stride, into the maze of shops and cafés that spread out at the foot of the rock. He looked into several bars before he spotted a public telephone booth in the back of one. He went in, sat down at a table and ordered a sherry from the white-aproned proprietor, then took the little glass into the booth with him.

Making connections with the White House took some time. Girard calculated that it would now be about 7 P.M. there, which meant that most of the switchboard operators would still be on duty. He asked specifically for Helen Chervasi, finally got her and had his collect call approved. She switched him to Esther Townsend without waiting for him to ask.

Esther was cheery and the connection was clear: "And now I suppose you'll be over the border to Spain and the *señoritas.*"

"Why, sure, beautiful," he said, "why do you suppose the boss sent a bachelor over here, anyway?"

"I'll put him on," she said. "He's called down twice about you in the past half hour."

"Paul?" It was Lyman's voice, and Girard could feel the anxiety in it.

"The news is wonderful or awful, boss," said Girard, speaking slowly and clearly. "Depending on how you want to look at it."

"Meaning?"

"Meaning what we suspected is true. All the way. The fellow here is a smooth one. No, make that read slippery. But I got it in writing, signed by both of us and time-dated in his handwriting."

"Oh, God," Lyman said. Girard waited, but he could hear only the heavy breathing of the President.

"Boss?"

"Yes?"

"Don't worry. I hate it too, but we got it all wrapped up. It's locked up tight. I'm on my way home right now."

"How soon can you get here?" Lyman asked.

"I'll get the 11:05 Trans-Ocean out of Madrid right to Dulles. That's 11:05 your time. I'll see you for breakfast, easy."

"No trouble making connections?" The President was still anxious.

"No. The charter's waiting for me. It's a fast little Italian job. I'll have time to kill in Madrid."

"Keep that thing in your pocket." Lyman warned. "Don't trust the briefcase."

"Sure, sure. Remember that cigarette case you gave me for my birthday? Right now we don't store tobacco in it. Paper fits in much better tonight."

"Any chance of your man there talking to our—er—to the other fellow here?"

"Not a snowball's chance in hell, boss. You got to talk to this fellow to know him. Jiggs is right. He goes with the winner. This is the God-damnedest thing you ever read."

"Well, take care, Paul," Lyman said. "We'll call the others in as soon as you and I go over it. And give some thought to just how we do it tomorrow."

"Right. See you at breakfast. Good night, boss."

"Good night, Paul."

When his little twin-jet plane swept off the Gibraltar runway half an hour later, Girard looked back and down at the *Eisenhower*, now a sparkling thicket among the scattered lights of the darkened anchorage. He settled back in his seat, his left hand clutching a silver cigarette case in his coat pocket.

Wednesday Night

Jiggs Casey woke up hot and sticky in his room at the Sherwood Hotel in New York. The light filtering through the window curtains was fading. He looked at his watch. It was 6:30. He'd have to get moving, for he was due at Shoo's apartment at seven.

He had called Eleanor Holbrook at her office as soon as he checked into the hotel. He hadn't heard Shoo's voice in two years, but it was just as he remembered it, the brittle quality of her tone offset by the haphazard pattern of little breathless rushes of speech.

"Hi, Shoo," he said. "You remember a fellow named Casey?"

"Jiggs!"

"What time do you get through work?" he asked.

"Not so fast, Colonel." He heard her quick intake of breath and remembered how she would swallow a cloud of smoke from her cigarette. "I don't make plans for men who vanish from the earth and then come back suddenly, like in a parachute."

"I want to take you to dinner," he said.

"Oh, just like that? And suppose the lady has a date, Colonel, which she happens to have."

"Gee, I wish you'd break it." Casey lowered his voice and promptly felt like a heel for feigning romantic intentions. But he had to see her. There was no place else to begin. "I have to talk to you, Shoo, really."

"Poor little misunderstood married man?" She was sarcastic now.

He could imagine her at her desk, her arms all but bare in a short-sleeved work dress, little golden hairs glinting on her forearm as she tapped ashes from the cigarette held with two fingers in a ridiculous angle. He could see the brown hair fluffed over her forehead; the nose, small and narrow; the full lips that never quite closed over her teeth. She'd be twenty-eight now, this tall, proud girl who hurried so to taste all of life. She was the woman who liked to speak wistfully of a cottage in the country, but who lived in perfect rhythm with the staccato tempo of New York—her world and her hypnosis. In the brief week that Casey had known her, Eleanor Holbrook's lack of affinity for the simple things had irritated and finally (and fortunately) estranged him, but her appetite for the city swept him along. His blood had warmed with the excitement even as he cursed the fascination. She was, indeed, the original Cloud Nine girl.

Now he could feel certain nostalgic tremors and he found it hard to phrase the lighthearted answer that he knew she expected.

"Cat got your tongue, Jiggs?"

When in doubt, charge, he thought. "I'm no traveling salesman, Shoo. I've got two boys at home and a wife I love. What's that got to do with us? I want to see you tonight."

"Where are you?" she asked. He gave her his room number at the Sherwood.

"Wait right there," she said, her words very clipped and businesslike. "I'll call you back. My date tonight was half business anyway. I'll see."

Half business? thought Casey. Mine is *all* business, honey. Or it was when I called you. Damn General Scott for messing up a man's life like this, anyway. What did I ever do to you, General?

Shoo called back promptly. "Come over to my place, sort of sevenish," she said. "We'll have a drink and worry about dinner later."

"What's the address again, Shoo?" It occurred to him that Marge at least would have been pleased that he couldn't remember it.

"Go to hell, Colonel." The voice was brisk, but the little snort was not without affection. "Look it up in the phone book —and I don't mean the yellow pages, big operator!"

He found the number, jotted it down and then went out to saunter along Madison Avenue in the warm May sunshine. Normally the fever of New York repelled him, but today a south wind had blown away the smog and he felt exhilarated. He watched with amusement as sullen, hurried figures pushed past him and the trim legs of the stenographers clip-clipped ever faster along the sidewalks.

He wished he could do something useful before evening, but when he ran through the short list of his friends in New York it added up to nothing. He couldn't approach the military officers he knew, and his few civilian acquaintances worked in fields far distant from Millicent Segnier's magazine *Chérie* or MacPherson's Regal Broadcasting Corporation.

Casey walked on idly, over to Fifth Avenue, up past the Plaza and into the corner of Central Park, then across to Madison again and back to his hotel. He went into the men's bar, now filling with noon-hour trade, and ordered a double martini. The thing to do, he thought, is knock myself out and get a good sleep this afternoon. He was short about ten hours' sleep this week and he realized he couldn't go much longer on reserve energy. Besides, it wouldn't be very smart to get drowsy tonight.

After six hours' sleep, he felt ready for his delicate encounter with Shoo Holbrook. Casey dressed in a dark-blue lightweight suit, the only civilian summer suit he owned, shaved again with the electric razor, and knotted his red-and-black striped tie. He formed the knot carefully; Shoo once complained that the knot in his Marine uniform tie was too big, and it would please her to think he had remembered.

For Christ's sake, he thought, who'd think I'd ever turn into *that* kind of an operator?

He took a cab to her apartment house, in the East Sixties off Park. The doorman, the self-service elevator, the narrow hall with its gray carpeting, even the number 315 on her door, all reminded him again of a weekend he thought he had succeeded in forgetting.

Shoo opened the door and reached for his hand. The brown hair, he noted, still framed her forehead in a soft curve and her nose crinkled prettily in pleasure at seeing him. As usual, she wore little make-up except lipstick. She had on gray toreador pants, quite tight, and a yellow shirt. Her feet were bare inside her sandals.

She stepped back, hands on hips, and surveyed him.

"I never saw you before in civilian clothes," she said. "I like you better in uniform, Jiggs. But you'll do as is. You'll definitely do."

Casey grinned and fingered the knot in his tie. "Small enough, Shoo?"

She stepped quickly to him then, held his face in her hands and kissed him lightly. "That's for remembering," she said.

He lit her cigarette and they sat at opposite ends of the window sofa. The questions came in a rush. What was his job now? What was he doing in New York? Did he still like martinis?

"I do, but I seem to recall that they can be awful dangerous for a married man." His mind jumped back two years to the night when they had started with martinis and had never got around to eating at all. Tonight, he promised himself, is going to be altogether different.

"On the rocks," he said as she went to the kitchen.

"My, you are getting older, Jiggs."

This apartment, he thought, is sure the wrong place for re-
sisting the forcible overthrow of the government—or any
other institution. Shoo's taste in décor was splashy. In a large
semiabstract painting on the wall two bulls, black with green
horns, seemed about to charge each other against background
slashes of crimson and orange. An ivory-colored floor lamp
was topped by four orange shades, each facing in a different
direction. Even the coffee table, a solid chunk of pitted drift-
wood supporting a heavy glass top, ran at weird angles. A
bright orange cloth on the dinette table matched the insides
of the bookcases. Is a person really supposed to live here,
Casey wondered, or just stop by now and then to sin?

The martini pitcher was nicely filled and beaded with con-
densation. Shoo poured his drink over ice, but took her own
with nothing but a tiny olive. They laughed as much as they
talked. Shoo gushed stories of the office politics, sponsor de-
mands, and actor tantrums of what she called "my idiot
trade." They slipped easily into the casual banter of two years
ago.

Finally she fell silent and eyed him for a long moment.

"This atmosphere," she said, "is one of abysmal palship,
Colonel. My little girl's instinct tells me you haven't come
courting at all, Jiggs, you just don't have your radar turned
on tonight. I can see it in that honest face of yours. You want
something else. What is it?"

Casey laughed and winked at her. The evidence was certainly plain before them: she had consumed two drinks while
his glass still stood half full.

"I knew you'd find me out sooner or later, Shoo," he said.
"I'm in New York to find out some things. I thought you might
be willing to help me—in confidence."

"Look, dear," she said, "I don't know a thing about bombs
or the little things that whiz around the world with men in
them. And if you're one of those counterspies, I don't know
a single solitary Russian, thank you."

"This is politics, Shoo." He was going to have to be careful here, but he had rehearsed it. "Washington is a very com-

plicated place, and sometimes a military man does things that have nothing to do with guns or missiles."

"How well I know, sweetheart."

"Anyway, I'm doing a little gumshoe work for some Democrats who are afraid General Scott, my boss, might try to run against President Lyman two years from now."

"Oh, delicious." Shoo curled her feet under her and raised her cigarette like a symphony conductor's baton. "Ask me some questions, quick."

"Will you promise to keep everything we say a secret?"

"Of *course*. I'd love to be an undercover operative in something sordid and political. They call me Little Miss Mum's-the-Word at the office."

Casey fiddled with his drink and loosened his tie. "Well, we hear that General Scott has been having an affair with a good friend of yours, Millicent Segnier. Remember, I met her once?"

"Oh, Milly." Shoo pouted in disappointment. *"That's* no secret. They've had a thing since God knows when. You could announce it in ten-foot lights in Times Square and it wouldn't surprise anybody."

"Maybe not," Casey said, "but I don't think it's ever got into the papers. Anyway, we need to know more about it— from you, if possible."

"Who's 'we'?"

"Let's just say some of the President's friends."

"My, my," she said. "Washington is complicated, isn't it? You work for General Scott by day—and against him by night."

"Well, yes, sort of. How about it?"

"I adore President Lyman," Shoo said, "and I think people are being miserable and unfair to him now when he's trying to get rid of that frightful bomb. I mean it, Jiggs."

Casey took a sip of his drink and said nothing.

"Well, Milly and Jim Scott have had quite a time. At the beginning, Jiggs, it was really torrid. I don't know anything about Mrs. Scott, but the General sure fell hard for Milly. And

she almost loved him. I'm not sure she ever really loved anybody, but she came close with him. She was forever calling
me up and swearing me to secrecy and rattling on about him.
I've been at her place several times when the General was
there. I must admit he's most impressive, even if he's not
my type."

Casey interrupted. "You think Scott ever considered a
divorce?"

"Never," said Shoo flatly. "And Milly didn't want that.
She's *really* a career woman. She's insane about that maga-
zine. She likes the excitement of an affair, but marriage, no."
Shoo peeked at him over the rim of her glass. "I wonder if
I'll get like that, Jiggs?"

"No," he said, imitating the stern father. "We're going to
get you married, young lady. Are Scott and Milly still going
strong?"

"Not really. Oh, he calls up, and he was here a couple of
weeks ago to see her. But it's cooled off some. Milly says he
seems preoccupied about something. The last time, she said,
Scott had his aide, somebody named Murdock, I think, with
him, and they really just used her apartment for some kind of
military business. You know, those things always end, and
knowing Milly, I'm surprised it lasted this long. I think she's
secretly flattered at being the occasional mistress of such an
important military man."

Casey's eyes were on the painting of the two bulls. Why
green horns? he mused. The talk of this romantic liaison had
set his mind wandering and he had to force himself back to
business.

"Is there any evidence of all this?" he asked.

"Evidence? What do you mean?"

"Anything written down on paper or something."

Shoo pulled back her shoulders in feigned distaste. "Now
really, Jiggs, if you're suggesting that I stoop to stealing love
letters for you . . ."

"I don't mean letters," he said, "and I don't want you to
steal anything. But is there an autographed picture, or a gift

that could be traced to General Scott through a bill of sale or anything like that?"

"Oh." Shoo thought a moment. Then she began to giggle. "I don't suppose I ought to tell you this," she said, "but it's so funny. Milly is really a character. She's so feminine and arty and chi-chi, you know, but, God, is she close with a buck! Anyway, she makes gobs of money, and she was crazy to find some new deductions this winter when she made out her tax return. I don't know whether her lawyer advised her on this—I doubt it—but she deducted three thousand dollars for entertaining General Scott last year."

"She did?" Casey was really surprised. "How could she get away with that?"

"Why, military fashions, dear." Shoo threw back her head and hooted. "Isn't that a scream? She decided if she were questioned she'd say she had to entertain General Scott to get the latest word on what the service wives and girls in uniform, the Waves and all, were wearing. I just *loved* her for it. Imagine deducting a love affair. I think it's a howl. *Nobody* but Milly could think it up."

"Did she get away with it, or doesn't she know yet?"

"The story gets even funnier. She filed early, and in March an internal revenue man came around to see her. He wanted her to explain the deduction, and she told him just what I told you. The next thing, she got a note from the tax people saying she couldn't do it and she owed another two thousand or so in taxes.

"Well, Milly got her back up and said nuts, and if the government wanted to sue her, go ahead and sue. I guess the affair was cooling off anyway and Milly was just mad enough to fight. Of course, I knew she didn't have a leg to stand on, but you can't tell Milly a thing where money is concerned."

"So what happened?" Casey tried to make his interest sound casual.

"So they *compromised!*" Shoo broke down in bubbly giggles again. "Isn't that a riot? A little man in the office downtown, all kind of bashful and double-talky, said nobody would want to embarrass General Scott or Miss Segnier, and what would she think if they let her deduct fifteen hundred and pay taxes on the rest? So, she did. She paid about a thousand dollars—she's in one of those dreadful brackets—but everybody's happy. Milly saved a thousand, the government got a thousand, and so far as I know General Scott never heard anything about it. I just love it."

"I thought they had to make those compromises public," Casey said.

"Oh, those are the big ones, where everybody gets lawyers and sits around with portfolios and things," Shoo said. "This was just a little private thing between Milly and the nice little man in the tax office."

Casey let the talk drift back into personal chitchat. Shoo asked about his boys, and whether he was being a good boy himself in Washington. She herself, it seemed, had been on the brink of marriage last year, but discovered just in time that the young man wanted to be "humdrum and dreary and have a lot of babies and live way out in Fairfield County."

She sighed theatrically. "You just can't trust men, not even the best of them. . . . And now, Jiggs, instead of going out and spending a lot of money that Marines don't have, I suggest we be cozy here and let me whip up a nice steak from the freezer."

Casey hesitated. He knew he shouldn't be seen in a New York restaurant if he could help it. On the other hand, the aftermath of a candlelit dinner-for-two here might be more than a man on a mission for his country could handle. He had hoped to compromise on some little cubbyhole restaurant with few patrons.

"Okay," he said. "I'd like that, if you promise you won't do anything elaborate."

"I don't know how to do anything elaborate—in the kitchen." She kissed him on the forehead and went out. He could hear the icebox door open and pans rattling.

"Listen, Shoo," he called. "While you're busy, I'll just run down to the corner and make a call. I have to check in with some people."

"Use my phone in the bedroom, Jiggs," she said. "I promise not to listen, even if it's a call to Mrs. Casey."

"No, this is business, and we're supposed to use public phone booths."

Shoo put her head around the door. "My, my, aren't we being mysterious? I don't think it's very nice, but if that's the way secret agents carry on, go ahead. Back soon?"

"Sure." Casey rebuttoned his shirt collar and fixed his tie. He nodded to the doorman as he left the building and walked toward Lexington Avenue. From a phone booth in a drugstore on the corner he called the White House, asked for Miss Chervasi and was switched to Esther Townsend.

"This is Casey, Miss Townsend."

"Well, everybody's busy. We just had a nice call from Paul, from over the water."

"Did he get it?" asked Casey.

"The Man is feeling much, much better, thanks. And you?"

"Look, Miss Townsend, I'll bring back the details tomorrow. But take him this message: Millicent Segnier deducted quite a bit of dough on her federal tax return for entertaining our friend. It's not quite the kind of evidence we're looking for, but it might be very helpful if we get into a jam. I think the Secretary ought to call for that return. That's M-i-l-l-i—"

"I know how to spell it, Colonel. I'll tell him right away. Anything else?"

"Not yet."

"Well, wipe off the lipstick before you come home. 'Bye, Colonel."

Dinner at Shoo's was predictably intimate. One candle flickered on the table, and after a steak and salad, she brought out a bottle of brandy. They sipped it in the living room, Shoo sitting on the floor with her head against Casey's knee.

"I like this, Jiggs," she said. "I've been here before."

Her low voice and the dim light lulled Casey. He had taken off his coat and now he loosened his tie again. Talk about disarmament treaties, he thought, if I'm not careful I'm going to be disarmed without a treaty. He pulled himself out of the peaceful mood.

"Say," he asked, "did Milly ever say whether Scott knows that TV commentator Harold MacPherson?"

"You bastard," Shoo said quietly. She tilted her head up toward him, rubbing her cheek on his leg. "Even after dinner?"

"I've got to earn my per diem." By the way, he thought, who does pay for this trip? I guess it'll have to be my contribution to the defense of the Constitution. "Come on, Shoo, I thought you loved political intrigue."

"I do," she pouted. "But there's a time and a place for everything, to coin a cliché. Oh, well. Shoot, Mr. District Attorney."

"Well, did she ever say?"

"She didn't have to. MacPherson and his wife were at one of those little dinners-for-eight where I was. I drew the extra man, and was he a drip! But he was better than MacPherson, at that. Those far-out characters give me the creeps. Besides, he's a single-track bore. Against everything from women's suffrage to Congress."

"Did Scott take to him?" Casey asked.

"Oh, he'd met him before. Yes, they were very chummy. When I said earlier I didn't like your Gentleman Jim I think that's what I meant. I don't have much time for anybody who listens to that maniac MacPherson. He's got the country mesmerized, and he's a regular snake-oil salesman."

"You think Scott and MacPherson are pretty thick?"

"I know they are," she said. "That last time he was here a couple of weeks ago, Milly said Scott spent more time with MacPherson than he did with her."

"Look, Shoo, you really could help me. Who can I talk to who knows MacPherson pretty well? You know, maybe somebody around his shop who feels the way you do about him."

"Morton Freeman's your man," she said without hesitation. "He's one of the writers on the show. Morty makes lots of money, but I know he detests MacPherson and is just waiting for a chance to jump to some other show."

"Could you fix me up to see him tomorrow, maybe at lunch?"

"Sure." Shoo got up and took the evening paper from an end table. She fingered several pages, found what she wanted and folded it for Casey.

"Here," she said. "There have been some rumors about a special MacPherson show this weekend. This column seems to have a little more about it."

Shoo left him with the newspaper while she went to telephone. He turned on the floor lamp, managed to get one of the shades twisted his way, and read the television column she had pointed out.

MAC TO BE OWN SPONSOR? . . . Harold MacPherson, video's angry middle-aged man, is browbeating RBC for a solo hour in the 6-to-7 spot this Saturday night. The political gabster, this colyum hears, is so anxious for the time he's willing to foot the bill himself. He won't tell the network biggies what he wants to do, though he sez—despite his already having a five-a-week news show—that he would use the whole hour for commentary. RBC, which gives away that hour for public-service stuff anyhow, is said to be lending a sympathetic ear.

Best Bet: One round, firm and fully packed hour of Mac's antiadministration opinion on Sattidy eve.

Shoo called from the bedroom. "Rockefeller Center at 12:30 okay? By the skating rink?"

"No," Casey said, "the time's all right, but think of someplace a little less public."

When she returned Shoo hopped onto the sofa, her feet tucked under her. "He'll meet you at The Bowl. That's a little hole-in-the-wall on Fifty-fourth, between Madison and Park. 12:30. You'll know him because he wears big, thick glasses and his hair is always tangled. Very, very, serious all the time."

Casey tore the TV column from the paper. "Have you heard anything about this at the office?" he asked.

She snuggled closer to him as she glanced at the story. "I heard some rumor about it last Monday, but that's all. Yesterday there was a one-line squib in the *News*. I guess it must be true. Joe is pretty good on the inside stuff in our business. Oh, that awful MacPherson. If I ran RBC, I'd give him five minutes—to pick up his hat and get out."

Shoo reached across and snapped the lamp off, leaving the candle on the dining table as the only light. They had another brandy. The minutes slipped by into an hour. Shoo nipped playfully at his ear lobe. When he put an arm around her and then withdrew it, she promptly pulled it back.

Shoo ran her fingers through Casey's hair and whispered: "I always did like crew cuts. Remember?"

I'm getting too comfortable, Casey thought, getting to like this too well. He could feel a remembered surge in his pulse and found he could not wish it away. As though to break a spell, he excused himself and went to the bathroom.

It had new wallpaper, printed with little Parisian vignettes: news kiosks, Notre-Dame, bookstalls by the Seine, can-can dancers, sidewalk cafés, and of course the Eiffel Tower. Casey winced at this equation of the natural functions of the lavatory with the gay spirit of Paris.

A little too young and self-consciously naughty, he thought. I graduated from that league two wars ago.

A small sign, handprinted by Shoo and stuck to the cabinet mirror, caught his eye: "Gentlemen do not open strange medicine cabinets."

Yeah, Shoo, you're a very attractive girl and a very compelling one, but you're also still a very young one. I'm forty-four years old and I ought to know better, and if I stay another ten minutes I'll be here all night.

Back in the living room, he straightened his tie and stretched lazily. He wanted to make the exit a graceful one.

"Time for me to get back to the hotel," he said. "We've both got to go to work tomorrow."

"Liar," she said. "You can sleep till noon and you know the mornings never bother me."

Shoo walked over and pressed against him, circling his neck with her arms. "Way back on the closet shelf there's a toothbrush that you've only used a couple of times," she whispered. "I thought you might need it again someday."

He kissed her, hard, and felt the warm suggestion of her thighs. I'm sorry, he thought, awful sorry, Shoo, but it really ended the night it began, and that was two years ago. They stood close together in silence. Then he pulled away.

She stood with legs apart, her head tipped back, smiling at him with a touch of bitterness.

"And so the married man goeth," she said.

"Yeah, I guess he does, Shoo. Thanks for all the—"

"Don't thank me, Jiggs. I'm not going to thank you."

He opened the door tentatively, embarrassed at the way he was going. She stood in the middle of the dark room, silhouetted against the flicker of the guttering candle. Her arms were folded and her face showed no expression at all.

"Good night, Shoo."

"Good-by, Jiggs," she corrected him softly. "You sweet bum."

He hurried down the hall, anxious to be out in the fresh air. He walked the fifteen blocks to the Sherwood, his thoughts cluttered. The night two years ago, deliberately suppressed all evening, now came rushing back to him in infinite detail: the unexpected sudden passion, her hands on him, her gasps of endearment and urging, her complete and utter absorption in the act of love. And the long, gentle hour afterward when they shared a cigarette and were too drained even to speak.

Thank God for that wallpaper, he thought, or I'd have started something that maybe wouldn't have ended this time.

Casey's thoughts were still in the past as he snapped on the light in his hotel room. The sudden brightness brought him back to the present. On the dresser stood the little framed picture of Marge and the boys that he always took with him when he was traveling.

Sitting on the edge of the bed, he picked up the telephone. The operator did not answer immediately.

I might as well call Marge, he thought, just to let her know I'm still alive—and in my own bed, alone.

Then he was suddenly angry. The hell with it, he thought, I've done enough for Marge for one night. More than I wanted to, God knows. Let's be honest about it, Casey. You wanted to stay at Shoo's. You wanted to go to bed with her. And you still wish you had, don't you?

"Your order, please?" It was the operator.

"Never mind," he said, and banged the receiver down. He could still taste Shoo's lipstick. It tasted the same as it had two years ago. He could remember that. He could even remember the brand she used, although he had seen her lipstick only once, one morning when she left it on the washbasin in the apartment: "Raspberry Ice."

Damn, damn, damn.

He was still short on sleep, but he tossed fitfully for most of the night. When he awoke his watch showed it was 7:45 A.M. He washed, shaved, dressed, and went down to the lobby to eat, then decided to call the White House first.

When he got Esther Townsend, she sounded strained and tired.

"I'd better put him on," she said when he identified himself. A moment later a voice said: "Yes?"

"Good morning, sir, this is Colonel Casey," he said. "I'm making good progress. I think I'll have quite a bit to report when I get back this afternoon."

"Do the best you can." Lyman's voice was utterly flat and toneless. "The best you can. Paul Girard is dead."

Thursday Morning

Jordan Lyman put down the telephone. He had hardly heard what Casey said. He stared again at the piece of yellow paper torn from the news ticker in press secretary Frank Simon's office.

UPI-13
    (PLANE)
    MADRID—48 PERSONS, INCLUDING A TOP WHITE HOUSE AIDE, WERE KILLED EARLY TODAY WHEN A TRANS-OCEAN JET AIRLINER CRASHED IN THE RUGGED GUADARRAMA MOUNTAINS NORTHWEST OF MADRID.
    PAUL GIRARD, 45, APPOINTMENTS SECRETARY TO PRESIDENT LYMAN, WAS ONE OF 21 AMERICANS BELIEVED TO HAVE DIED IN THE CRASH. THE PLANE, BOUND FOR NEW YORK, CRASHED AND EXPLODED SHORTLY AFTER ITS PILOT RADIOED THAT HE WAS HAVING "MECHANICAL TROUBLE" AND WAS RETURNING TO MADRID FOR REPAIRS.
    AUTHORITIES SAID THERE WERE NO SURVIVORS. OFFICIALS OF THE AIRLINE, THE NATION'S SECOND LARGEST OVERSEAS AIR CARRIER, COULD OFFER NO IMMEDIATE EXPLANATION FOR THE ACCIDENT.
                5/16—GR712AED

Lyman looked up at Simon, standing in front of his desk. The young man's thin face was drawn tight.

"Jesus, Mr. President, this is awful, isn't it?" Simon said. "I'm so sorry. I didn't even know Paul was out of town until the wires started calling me at four o'clock this morning."

Lyman grasped the arms of his chair and half rose out of it. His voice shook with anger.

"I've just lost my closest friend in this place and you're worrying about what those goddam reporters think of you, Simon. Do you really think that matters to anyone now?"

He sank back again, closed his eyes, and with a visible effort got himself in hand.

"Paul is gone, Frank. That's all that counts."

Simon stood rigid in front of the President's desk, stunned as much by Lyman's interpretation of his remark as by the sudden surge of fury in his voice.

"Please, Mr. President," he said, almost whispering. "Paul was my friend too."

Lyman looked at him, then slowly shook his head as if to clear it. "Of course, Frank. I'm sorry. It's just . . ." He stopped. "Look, we'll have to get out a statement. Would you see if you could draft something for me? You know what I'd want to say."

"About his being away, Mr. President . . ."

"Say he was abroad on vacation, but was returning at my request to handle some details of the missile strike. Don't say much."

No, don't say much, Lyman thought. Don't say that I sent him over there to get killed doing a dirty job for me, trying to save my skin. Don't say he did it just as well as he did everything else for me. Don't say I don't know what I'll do without him. Say he was on vacation.

When Simon returned a few minutes later with the proposed White House statement, he found the President hunched over his desk, chin in his hands, staring at the water color that hung on a side wall. It was a picture of his boyhood home in Norwalk, Ohio. Lyman glanced at the draft.

"It's all right, Frank," he said without looking up at the press secretary.

On the way out of the oval office, Simon stopped at Esther Townsend's desk and motioned over his shoulder with his thumb.

"Gee, Esther, he's really shook up over Paul, isn't he?"

"If you only knew," she said.

"Listen," Simon asked, "is something else the matter? I've had a funny feeling for the last couple of days that things are running downhill around here. No appointments, nothing scheduled."

"He's worrying about the treaty, Frank." She shrugged. "It's a low spot. One of those times."

At his desk, Lyman felt physically faint. He could see Girard's big ugly head before him, could see that half-warm, half-cynical smile, could hear him talking rough common sense on this ghastly business about General Scott. He could hear the voice as it came filtered over the telephone last night. Now Paul was gone and, worse, the evidence gone with him. Pardon me, Paul, wherever you are, Lyman thought, for mentioning the evidence in the same breath. But it *has* made things almost impossible.

He tried to think through the developments since Tuesday. Girard's call last night confirmed the worst. Corwin's report showed that Harold MacPherson was in the middle of whatever Scott was planning. There would be ECOMCON troops, perhaps, at Mount Thunder on Saturday. Casey's story of the income tax return? Mildly interesting, perhaps, but worthless as evidence.

The President felt the breath of panic. He needed hard-rock fact to smash this thing, but where was it? And where was Ray Clark? Not a single word from Ray since he last saw him Tuesday night. Thinking of his predicament—and of Clark—he began to feel the old crawl in his stomach, the same one that had paralyzed him on the line in Korea. Far back in a mist-draped morning, he could see the stubborn set of Clark's jaw and feel the sting as Clark's open hand hit him. His efforts to blank out the scene failed. All at once he realized that his shirt was wet with sweat. Why hadn't Clark called?

Jordan Lyman was calmer, but by no means composed, when Christopher Todd walked into the office half an hour later. Todd's fresh appearance provided some reassurance of reality for Lyman.

They had joked last night, when Lyman called him after Girard's report from Gibraltar. Now, like the President, Todd was somber.

"We're in rough water, Mr. President," he said.

"Terrible," Lyman replied. "Or maybe you still have some doubts left, Chris?"

"Not after Girard's call," said the Secretary. "When a man you trust completely substantiates an allegation, there's not much room left for doubts. The devil of it is we don't know what Barnswell told him."

"No, we don't. I think maybe we better send Corwin over to see him again. Or what about you?"

Todd shook his head. "I've had too much experience with reluctant witnesses, Mr. President. That won't work. Barnswell knows about Girard. If he's as smooth as they say, he'd consider another emissary from you as a sign of panic and slip right back onto Scott's mooring."

The President looked moodily at his Secretary of the Treasury. Todd permitted himself a thin smile.

"But this income tax return of Miss Segnier's is quite interesting, Jordan." Todd leaned forward. "I had the pertinent section read to me a few minutes ago, and it will all be down here this afternoon from the New York office. Really, now—a woman trying to deduct three thousand dollars for entertaining General Scott. You could smash him with that."

Lyman smiled tolerantly at the lawyer as he would at a younger brother. The very effort seemed to lighten his mood a little.

"Chris," he said quietly, "that's blackmail. You don't really think I'd use a thing like that, a man's relations with a woman, to defend my oath of office, do you?"

"By God, Mr. President, if I were sure this was a case of sedition, I'd use anything I could get my hands on."

The light on the President's telephone winked. It was Art Corwin with a report on Scott: The General had just arrived at the Pentagon, but had first gone from Fort Myer to the Dobney, picked up Senator Prentice and driven him to 14th and Constitution before letting him out. Prentice seemed upset, Corwin said, as he stood on the curb trying to flag down a taxi to take him on to Capitol Hill.

Esther Townsend had come in unnoticed. She closed the door behind her as silently as she had opened it.

"Mr. President, excuse me," she said. "I'm holding another call. It's Secretary Burton. He says he must talk to you."

Lyman raised his hands in a signal of protest.

"Esther, I can't talk to Tom right now. Make some excuse for me, will you?"

Todd grunted. "This is hardly the moment to burden your employer with the multifarious problems of health, education and welfare, Miss Townsend."

"Tom doesn't come running down here without a good reason, Chris," Lyman said, "but somebody else will have to handle him today. What's his problem?"

"He says time is running out on those Social Security amendments," Esther said. "You've only got two more days left to decide whether to sign the bill. He says he's got to talk to you about it. He says it's vital."

"Important, yes. Vital, no—not this week. I know how he feels about the bill already, and I'm not going to do anything until I get the report from Budget. He better talk to them."

Esther nodded and started to leave. Then, pausing at the door, she turned back. "Mr. President, Secretary Burton is only one of about two dozen calls I've got stacked up for you. I haven't bothered you with the others."

"I know, Esther, and thank you," Lyman said. "Now, be a good girl and think up something nice to tell Tom."

Todd got to his feet, tugging at his lapels to settle the collar of his jacket properly.

"It's time to hoist the storm warnings, Mr. President," he said. "I'm going back to the office and work out a plan. I've got a feeling you may have to move tonight."

"How?"

"That's what I'm going to figure out."

Lyman glowered at the stack of papers on the right-hand side of his desk—the clerical chores of the Presidency, untouched since Monday. There were commissions and several minor executive orders for his signature, policy papers from State to be read, and several recommendations from the Attorney General for judicial appointments. A pending judgeship in Chicago rested on top of the heap. The Attorney General recommended Benjamin Krakow, a member of the city's leading Democratic law firm. He had backed Lyman before the convention. The Bar Association had him on its list of three men it suggested for the vacancy.

The President wrote "O.K., Jordan Lyman" on the bottom of the sheet and put it over on the left side of his desk. He was reaching for the second paper when Esther came in again.

"It's Saul Lieberman," she said. "He said it's imperative he see you this morning. I didn't encourage him."

Lyman hesitated only a moment. "If Saul says it's imperative, it is. Tell him to come over right away. And, Esther, tell him to come in the front door, and tell Frank Simon to post the appointment in the pressroom. At least they won't think I'm dead."

Saul Lieberman was Director of Central Intelligence. If Lyman had required IQ tests for his appointees, Lieberman would have led the field with twenty points to spare. He had been an enlisted man in the Army Counterintelligence Corps during World War II, then went home to Detroit to found a retail credit agency that spread into half the states and made him rich. Two private missions behind the iron curtain and service on several presidential committees which weighed the shortcomings of the Central Intelligence Agency gained him a small reputation in the elite world of espionage, but Lyman surprised the world at large when he named him to head CIA.

Lieberman was almost aggressively uncouth. He wore his lack of civility as a badge of honor and enjoyed torturing Washington hostesses with the Hamtramck slang of his boyhood. In eighteen months he had become a conversation piece in the capital; never had the Ivy-clad CIA known such a sidewalk product.

"How's the private eye of the cold war?" Lyman asked as Lieberman bustled in ten minutes later.

"Lousy, Mr. President. I was shocked to hear about Paul. Believe me, I wouldn't have bothered you today if this wasn't important."

"That's all right, Saul. I understand."

"After what else I learned this morning," Lieberman said, "I should be spending the day at the health club. Look at this."

He pulled a paper from his coat pocket and slid it across the President's desk. It was a plain outline map of Russia, the kind children use in geography classes for penciling in rivers and cities.

In one area of Siberia someone had marked a cross in red crayon.

"That's Yakutsk," Lieberman said, "and it's bad news. We have it so straight I don't argue with it. Feemerov is starting to assemble the Z-4 at Yakutsk."

Lyman stared at his intelligence chief without expression. The Z-4 was the Russian equivalent of the Olympus, America's neutron-warhead missile. The treaty did not call for scrapping of the missiles themselves, but it did require dismantling of the warheads, with inspection of existing plants to guarantee that no more would be made.

If Feemerov had built a new Z-4 plant in secret, where the treaty inspectors could not see it, the implications were staggering. It meant the Kremlin had decided to cheat on the treaty, taking a calculated risk of being discovered and denounced. It could mean the end of Lyman's meticulous plans and deepest hopes. Indeed—the thought struck him like a blow in the stomach—it might eventually mean the end of civilization.

And more immediately, it meant that General Scott's often-expressed doubts had been proved correct. In the way the mind skitters ahead under tension, playing like summer lightning on infinite possibilities, he could see the headlines:

LYMAN PATSY FOR REDS,
REPUBLICAN CHARGES

And if Scott were correct, what right had he, a President proved gullible, to oppose him now?

Lyman sagged in his swivel chair. His face, to Lieberman, seemed blank and colorless. The intelligence director spoke quickly, as though he were a fresh wind with power to lift a drooping flag.

"We got little bits and pieces of this beginning Monday, Mr. President. But they didn't add up. We knew a special alloy used in the Z-4 was being shipped to Yakutsk. Tuesday, three scientists who are the brains of Z-4 were flown out there from Moscow in a special plane. Then last night the watch officer at the NIC called me. He says, 'Saul, they're building the Z-4 at Yakutsk.'"

The NIC was the intelligence community's National Indications Center in a subbasement of the Pentagon. There specialists from all intelligence services, aided by banks of electronic computers, stood a 24-hour watch on everything that moved in the Communist world. Their mission: to piece together the jigsaw puzzle of Red movements—troops, machines, raw materials, political leaders, scientists, weapons—so as to anticipate any major venture that could threaten the United States.

Lyman said nothing. Lieberman went on with his story.

"I got over there about midnight, real skeptical. In this business I got to be shown. By three this morning I knew the boys were right. They got word on no less than twenty-five or twenty-six items, all exclusive with the Z-4 and all pouring into Yakutsk like rats toward a hanging side of beef."

Lieberman leaned across the desk and began marking the little map. From Moscow he drew a line with his pencil: the three scientists. From Novosibirsk, another line: a new black box for the missile's complex guidance system. From Volgograd, several delicate electronic components made only in one factory there, and used only in the Z-4. The lines multiplied and crisscrossed.

"Has anything like this turned up in China?" asked Lyman.

"Nope," Lieberman said. "Maybe Feemerov's cheating on his Peiping buddies, too."

"If this is true," Lyman said, "the treaty is dead. And maybe the world too."

"It never figured, Mr. President," said Lieberman, "if you'll pardon me for saying it. I mean the Commies never figured to go through with it."

"No, Saul, I guess it never figured." As he said it, Lyman could see the sunrise in Vienna, Feemerov's outstretched hand, the blink of photo flashbulbs. He could feel the dry itch on his skin from lack of sleep. Above all, he could feel again his own relief and elation.

Now he merely sighed.

"I suppose the Joint Chiefs have been notified?" he asked.

"Yes. The NIC duty officer is supposed to be briefing General Scott right now. We knocked off another evaluation conference. It looked too sure to all of us."

Lyman played with the edges of the map as he thought. Lieberman obviously expected action. But there's more than one predicament for the country now, Saul, and which comes first? And where is there help? Girard's advice is gone—forever. Ray Clark is—is where? There's only Chris. No, there's only Jordan Lyman. The President is alone again. Oh, dry up, Jordie. Get back to earth.

Lyman buzzed and Esther came in at once.

"Esther," the President said, "please get word to all members that there will be a special meeting of the National Security Council Tuesday morning. Make it nine o'clock. Say it's important and no deputies should be sent as substitutes."

Esther scribbled swiftly and withdrew.

"Tuesday?" asked Lieberman. "That's five days away, Mr. President."

Lyman nodded. "I want it that way. We've got to be absolutely sure that we're solid on this build-up before we blow the whistle. I can't jeopardize the treaty on flash information, even though you and I believe it. And I want everybody there, including Vince Gianelli, and he won't be back from Italy until then."

Lieberman's mobile features showed his frustration.

"Look, Saul," the President said. "There's more than six weeks to go until July 1. Whatever we do, it's got to be just right."

When the CIA director left, Lyman found himself trying to sweat this new horror down to size. For the first time that day there were no barriers in his mind to inhibit thought. Russian duplicity, at least, was familiar stuff. Unlike the Scott affair, it was not only plausible but could be countered by techniques that were already on the books.

Lyman knew at once that if the CIA evidence held up under further checking, no pale move would suffice. Feemerov's secret audacity demanded a bold public response.

A direct accusation before the United Nations by Lyman? A proposal that Lyman and Feemerov exchange visits to missile-assembly sites, each man to visit a city of his own choosing? Perhaps a televised speech to the world, using the new satellite communications relays, declaring that America had evidence of developments in Yakutsk and demanding that the Kremlin admit the international inspectors at once? Or, bolder yet, why not fly to Moscow and personally challenge Feemerov to accompany him to any United States missile site—stopping first at Yakutsk?

Lyman frothed with ideas. He scribbled notes rapidly on his memo pad. Maybe, he thought, this is actually a blessing. This may be the turning point, after two decades of trying to live with what his national security aides called "the insupportable." Perhaps not even the brutal and opaque Kremlin could withstand the revulsion of world opinion if Feemerov were caught cheating now. Put the facts to him privately, give him a chance to back down and clean out Yakutsk? There were dozens of fruitful alternatives.

But what about Scott? Suppose he seizes on this intelligence and spills it to the country before I can get to him? Suppose we can't stop him before Saturday? How *can* he be stopped?

"Esther," he asked on the intercom, "any word yet from Ray?"

"I'm sorry, Governor. Still not a thing."

Lyman crumpled his notes and Lieberman's little map of Russia, then smoothed them out again and slowly tore them into little pieces. As he dropped the shreds into the waste-basket, a thought struck him. The irony of it forced him to smile.

Do you suppose, he wondered, if General Scott is sitting in this chair next Tuesday, he will wish he had the National Security Council to help him decide what to do about Yakutsk?

Thursday Noon

Jiggs Casey smiled as disarmingly as he knew how while Morton Freeman gulped the last inch of his second gibson and jerked the luncheon menu toward him. The gingham tablecloth wrinkled with the movement and the empty cocktail glass splintered on the floor. The television writer glared at Casey.

"Christ, I can't stand *neutral* people," he complained. "They make me nervous. I said I'd see you as a favor to Shoo, but you sound like a dish of Jell-o."

"I don't want to get into a political discussion, Mr. Freeman. I just want to find out a few things."

Freeman peered through his black-rimmed spectacles and pushed a jumble of hair back off his forehead. He glanced around the crowded restaurant as though seeking allies. Casey felt vaguely like a foreigner, as if he should have shown his passport to the headwaiter.

"I can't figure you, Casey," Freeman said. "You say you want the lowdown on MacPherson so Washington can cut off his water, but you won't commit yourself on anything. Don't you ever stick that big fat neck of yours out?"

It had started peacefully enough. Casey recognized Morty Freeman at once from Shoo's description. When they were settled in a back booth at The Bowl, he stated his business simply, if untruthfully. He said he was a Democrat, in a modest federal job, one of many friends of President Lyman who were concerned about the increasing virulence of Harold MacPherson's attacks on the administration and the nuclear disarmament treaty.

Freeman promptly plunged into a passionate denunciation of nuclear weapons and previous United States policies, praising Lyman for "having the courage" to understand that "the Communists want to live too." When he went on to declare that Eisenhower-Kennedy distrust of the Russians had set civilization back two decades, Casey offered a mild dissent. Freeman rushed on anyway. He blasted military officers as "latter-day Francos," damned the Republican party, the Chamber of Commerce, and the American Medical Association, and called Lyman "the only world statesman since Nehru."

When Casey suggested that the two men represented completely different philosophies, Freeman stopped talking and looked at his luncheon companion as if he had just noticed him for the first time. "Say," he said, "just where *do* you stand?"

Casey tried to backpedal into a compromise, but Freeman blocked his retreat. Casey decided he had better concentrate on simply holding onto his temper long enough to get out of this place with some information. Freeman continued to demand that he take the stand and testify.

"Look," Casey finally said, "I've stuck my neck out once or twice, but that isn't my job right now. I'm trying to get some facts that will put MacPherson where he belongs, and what I believe about birth control or aid to Yugoslavia hasn't a thing to do with that. Are you going to help me or not?"

Freeman squeezed into the corner of the booth. "How do I know you're not some frigging FBI agent and this isn't some trick to blacklist me?"

Good God, Casey thought, they complain about Scott having right-wing oddballs on his side. Well, it looks like

Lyman has managed to collect at least one lulu from deep left field. He covered the thought with a smile.

"You don't, unless you think Shoo, who happens to be an old friend of mine, would deliberately trap you. Come on, let's talk sense."

"Piss on you," said Freeman, but his belligerence began to fade. "Let's order, since you're buying, and then you ask your questions—and maybe I'll answer them."

Casey revised his plan of attack while the writer buried his head behind the menu card. They both ordered lunch, but Freeman decided he needed a third gibson first.

"Actually," Casey said, "I only want a couple of things, in confidence. The main thing we need is some idea of the relationship between MacPherson and General Scott, the chairman of the Joint Chiefs."

"They're thick as thieving bastards," said Freeman bitterly. "Scott's been up to Mac's place in Connecticut two or three times. Mac has had some of those private 'briefings' for conservatives only. You know, the General tells 'em that Social Security is original sin and that we're all going Communist tomorrow. They love it, and they all line up to back him for President."

"Are you serious about Scott running for President?"

"You kidding? Of course he is. And MacPherson wants to be the big kingmaker."

"When did these sessions take place?" Casey asked.

Freeman clutched his drink as though it was about to run away. "He had one last winter sometime, then one in April. I remember the last time because Mac had me come up there to work out some changes in a show, to get in something Scott said. The usual craperoo."

"What about this Saturday night? We hear he's cooking up something special."

"You got me there. He won't tell me a goddam thing about this super one-hour special of his. Which is something for him, because he pays me seven hundred a week as a writer just so he can pump me dry. Claims he's gonna write this one himself." Freeman grimaced. "I advise you to buy earplugs, Casey. Mac can ooze like ointment, but he can't write his own name."

"Then the gossip columns are right? I mean, he has asked for time from the network?"

"Oh, sure. He did that last week, and he got it, too. He told me this morning that RBC has agreed. He'll get the whole hour, six to seven, no sponsor. He's putting out sixty-five grand of his own for the time."

"Does he have to submit his script?" Casey asked.

"No, he doesn't. Technically he's supposed to, but they've got an unwritten understanding on that. He's never libeled anybody. He just calls anybody he doesn't like an ignoramus, which is supposed to be fair political comment."

Freeman rattled on about MacPherson, delving with practiced relish into his personality as though he were a psychiatrist analyzing the devil. Casey's attention waned. Freeman had run out of facts, and his opinions were hardly worth the price of the lunch, which, when the check arrived, turned out to be $12.75.

"Only one thing puzzles me," Casey said as he paid the bill. "If you hate MacPherson so much, why do you work for him?"

Freeman flashed his first real grin. "He bugs me so bad I spend everything I make trying to forget my work. Any decent liberal commentator who offers me a job can have me at bargain-basement rates—down to six ninety-five a week."

Casey followed Freeman out, turning his head slightly away from the diners packed into the little restaurant. His New York mission was ending and he felt he had failed. He had been able to do little more than confirm what they already knew or suspected, and he surmised that Millicent Segnier's tax return wouldn't count for much in this kind of struggle. He thought of Girard. What a lousy thing to happen to a swell guy. And what a spot it puts the President in. Still, Miss Townsend said Girard had telephoned good news. Was anything pinned down? He wondered how soon he could get a plane out of LaGuardia.

On the sidewalk under the canopy, Freeman squinted in the sunlight. He jabbed a finger at Casey's chest.

"You don't look like the man for it, but for the sake of sanity, I hope your bunch can dump MacPherson and Scott both."

Casey held out his hand. "Well, thanks, Mr. Freeman. I'll keep anything you've told me under my hat."

Freeman ignored the offered handshake and his voice bristled with parting sarcasm. "Try taking sides sometime, Casey. It'll do you good to bloody your nose for something you believe in. So long, pal."

Casey watched him walk off along the street. Sonny, he thought, if I didn't have to get back to Washington, I'd bloody someone's nose for something I believe in—right now.

At the White House, Jordan Lyman chewed absently on a sandwich while he read the sheets of news copy brought him by Frank Simon. There were three adds to the first story he'd seen that morning, each supplying a few more details, and then a new night lead, apparently written by a correspondent who had reached the crash scene:

UPI-104

(CRASH)

LA GRANJA, SPAIN—SMASHED AND CHARRED WRECKAGE STREWN OVER A BARREN CASTILIAN HILLSIDE WAS ALL THAT REMAINED OF THE GIANT TRANS-OCEAN JETLINER WHICH CRASHED HERE EARLY THURSDAY.

POLICE AND RESCUE WORKERS WERE STILL COMBING THE SCATTERED FRAGMENTS OF THE PLANE FOR THE BODIES OF PASSENGERS, WHO INCLUDED PAUL GIRARD, 45, APPOINTMENTS SECRETARY TO PRESIDENT LYMAN.

WING AND ENGINE DEBRIS WAS FOUND SOME DISTANCE FROM THE MAIN WRECKAGE, INDICATING A TERRIFIC IMPACT. CAUSE OF THE CRASH WAS UNDETERMINED, ALTHOUGH THE PILOT HAD RADIOED THE MADRID CONTROL TOWER SHORTLY AFTER HIS TAKE-OFF FOR NEW YORK THAT HE HAD "MECHANICAL TROUBLE" AND WAS RETURNING TO THE SPANISH CAPITAL FOR REPAIRS.

AIRLINE OFFICIALS SAID THEY HOPED TO BE ABLE TO FIND OUT WHAT HAD GONE WRONG. THOUGH MOST OF THE AIRCRAFT BURNED, OFFICIALS HOPED TO SALVAGE COCKPIT INSTRUMENTS

AND RECORDING DEVICES THAT MIGHT GIVE THEM A CLUE TO THE ACCIDENT, WORST TRANS-OCEAN CRASH IN FIVE YEARS.

5/16—WO232PED

Well, thought Lyman, that ends the chance of finding a small piece of paper that might force Scott to resign. About the only remaining hope of any substantial evidence would be a report by Clark—good God, why doesn't Ray call?—from El Paso. But Lyman realized with a sinking sensation that even proof of a secret base, not authorized by the President, would be a flimsy basis for firing the chairman of the Joint Chiefs of Staff and his fellow four-star generals. The nation simply would not understand why a popular officer should be dismissed for taking measures, even in secret, to safeguard communications facilities.

Perhaps Chris is right, he thought, and we'll have to move openly.

Almost as bad was Saul Lieberman's report. Lyman felt like a preacher whose congregation suddenly deserts him on the morning of the ground-breaking ceremony for a new church. But at least this one, he thought grimly, I can cope with. In fact, a plan was already beginning to shape up in his mind. It was bold and risky, but it just might work.

Esther opened the door just enough to put her head into the office. "Dr. Kramer reminds that you're due in his office for your physical in five minutes," she said.

Lyman stepped through the French doors onto the veranda that led around the rose garden and across from the west wing to the mansion, where his doctor had a ground-floor office.

At least the weather had improved. The early-afternoon sun shone through a thin drifting cloud, and there was the pleasant smell of the grass, newly mown that morning. Lyman heard a blue jay, creaking like a garden gate, and saw the bird fuming at a sparrow in the big magnolia tree. He nodded to a Secret Service agent standing unobtrusively against the wall.

Dr. Horace Kramer, Lyman's long-time personal physician who had left his practice in Columbus to attend the President, chatted about the break in the weather as he busied himself with the weekly checkup: stethoscope, the inflated band on the arm for blood pressure, a lighted magnifier probing eyes, ears, nose and throat. When Kramer had finished he sat on a stool and swung his stethoscope idly, looking at his patient.

"How long has it been since you had a vacation?" he asked.

Kramer was a swarthy man, with deep-set eyes that dwelled diagnostically on his patients.

"I've been up to Blue Lake two weekends this spring," Lyman said defensively.

"I said a vacation, Mr. President." Kramer's voice was patient but firm.

"Well, let's see," said Lyman. "There was that week at the lake last summer."

Kramer shook his head, his eyes never leaving Lyman's. "That just won't do either, Mr. President. You had two conferences a day that week, and by my count you went fishing only three times."

Lyman said nothing. His thoughts were far from the clinic, on a hillside in Spain, on a handsome general in the Pentagon, on a desert waste in the Southwest.

"I'm going to be blunt, Jordan," Kramer said. "Your blood pressure is up again, and I don't like it one little bit. From now on you're going to obey orders. You go away and stay away at least two weeks. You can have one conference each week and damned few phone calls."

Lyman shook his head and smiled wanly at the physician. "I can't, Horace. We'll just have to wait until July—until after the treaty goes into effect."

Kramer tried a new tack. "If you don't care whether you ruin yourself, think of *my* reputation. How can I make any money back in Columbus if you die on me?"

Lyman grinned. "That's easy. You'd just announce that you were pleased to bury your biggest mistake."

Kramer shrugged his shoulders as Lyman took his coat from the hanger and put it on. He walked back toward his office, unaware that his doctor stood in the clinic doorway watching him go. The physician dropped his stethoscope on his desk and turned to his nurse, who had re-entered the office after Lyman left.

"It doesn't make any sense," Kramer said to her. "We elect a man President and then try to see how fast we can kill him. I sometimes think it's a perpetual race to see which breaks first —the President or the country."

Jordan Lyman paused to look at the magnolia tree again. The birds had left and the only sound penetrating his consciousness was the distant drone of an airplane. It reminded him of Paul Girard and of an institution that seemed suddenly to be crumbling about him. This time he walked unseeing past the Secret Service man.

Thursday
Afternoon

The thing about the diplomatic service, Henry Whitney thought as he drove out of Madrid, is the strange mixture of good and bad in the jobs they give you.

Here he was on an errand that could only be described as grisly, and it was costing him his first quiet evening at home in three weeks. All because the ambassador thought the situation called for rank, to flatter the White House, even though the most junior officer in Whitney's section could have—and should have—handled it. Politics, that's all it was.

So he ought to be sore about it. But this assignment would take him across some of the country he loved best in all the world, and that thought cheered him as he drove the Mercedes up the main highway leading northwest toward the mountains. He had discovered them when he was a brand-new foreign service officer in his first overseas post, and he still loved them. He would cut off Route VI at Villalba, on the near side of the pass, and climb over to La Granja on the back road. It wasn't the shortest route across the Sierra de Guadarrama, but it was the one he liked, and he hadn't driven it in a long time. He would reach the scene with plenty of daylight left. He could look at the wreckage, do what had to be done with the police, and still have time for a decent dinner and a good sleep. There wasn't any need for him to get back until tomorrow.

Whitney slowed down for Torrelodones and devoted his full attention to threading his way through the customary tangle of burros, casual pedestrians, and gracefully ineffective traffic cops in the center of town. As he speeded up on the other side, he fell to musing again.

What ever possessed old Archie to work up such a flap over this plane crash, anyway? No one else in the embassy had been particularly excited just because the name of a White House aide turned up on the passenger list. Few, indeed, had ever heard of Paul Girard. The first secretary finally caught the name, remembering him as appointments secretary to the President. No one had known he was even in the country. He couldn't have been in Spain long, because Whitney's consular boys had strict, if entirely informal, orders to let him know whenever a White House or Congressional passport turned up at their entry points.

But as soon as Ambassador Archibald Lytle heard about it, just before noon, he got Whitney on the intercom, and half an hour later the consul general had his orders: go up there yourself and see if there's anything left that we should take care of. Whitney asked if there had been orders from Washington. The ambassador said, a little brusquely, no—but it never hurt to let the department, to say nothing of the White House, know that the mission cared about the important *little* things too. Besides, Whitney should be prepared to cable details on the state of Girard's remains and stand by for instructions from Washington. That, at least, made some sense to Whitney, although it certainly was a job for one of his subordinates.

Well, he thought, that's how Father Archibald got where he is today, and you have to expect him to keep it up, even if it doesn't make sense to think that President Lyman will care much of a damn now about the rank of the consular officer who goes up to collect the remains of his late assistant.

Whitney dropped this line of thought as "counterproductive," to use the department's cherished phrase, wiping it away as he had long ago learned to erase worries that merely wasted his time. There were too many men in the service who had been bleeding incessantly for years over damn-fool little things that would take more time to correct than they were worth.

Instead he concentrated on his driving and on the scenery. He had a wonderful little car—one of the fringe benefits you never told visiting senators about was the low price of good cars here—and it made the twisting mountain road seem like a boulevard. Moreover, Whitney knew no more fetching twenty kilometers in the world than this stretch up to the Navacerrada Pass, down through the woods on the north side and then into La Granja, where the handsome summer palace of the Hapsburgs stood amid its lovely gardens and fountains.

Coming up the road to the pass, the country rose bare and gaunt almost to the top. Just below the divide stood a cluster of ski resorts, shuttered and locked for the summer, their terraces overlooking the wide, flat valleys below. The beauty of the Puerto de Navacerrada was in the contrast between this and the other side. At the very top the mountains seemed to drop away in a great tilted bowl, and instead of the rocks and brush of the southern slopes a deep pine forest covered everything.

Whitney passed the marker at the crest, and now he was into the pines and starting down through the patched light and shadow of the woods where the road turned and turned again, dropping away. This was big woods, the trees well spaced, the ground all pine needles except in the little grassy clearings.

He had hiked here twenty years ago. He drove on down, around the curves and across the white cement bridge that was supposed to be the one the guerrillas blew up in Hemingway's novel about the civil war. Whitney remembered it because he had tucked the book into his rucksack that spring. He had walked through the whole story, full of romance and nostalgia, lacking only a girl to come to his sleeping bag at night.

An hour later Henry Whitney was all business as he climbed a little knoll above La Granja with Juan Ortega, the officer of the local *Guardia Civil* detachment. They came over the rise to the wreck. In a fat, ugly scar along the ridge, burned and twisted metal still smoked in little piles. A much larger heap marked what must have been the fuselage. Two hundred yards farther along lay the only recognizable piece, the crumpled remains of the cockpit and nose section. He must have gone in with his nose up, Whitney thought, and that piece was thrown out beyond the fire.

"If it would not be a great imposition," Whitney said in Spanish as they picked their way through the mess, "could you perhaps keep a few of your men here until the investigators from the airline arrive? In these matters there is much that trained eyes can see to help discover why it happened, and it is better if nothing is disturbed."

"Certainly," Ortega replied. "As you can see, I have men here now, to prevent the curious from interfering." Three men in the gray-green uniform of the *Guardia* stood together off to one side, weapons slung over their shoulders. "There will be no meddling. Nothing has been moved, except for a few little things that were scattered about. They are safe in my office, and I will give them to you."

Whitney's stomach turned at the sight of several charred fragments of bodies, and he looked away. He asked if any attempt at identification had been made. Ortega shrugged and said it was impossible, except for the recognizable bodies of three crew members found in the cockpit wreckage.

They walked together down the slope again, climbed into Whitney's car and drove into town. In his office Ortega ordered one of his men to bring sherry, then hauled an old wooden ammunition box out of a corner and set it on the desk.

"This is all, *señor*," he said. "As you saw, there was a great fire."

It wasn't much. Whitney picked gingerly at two scorched books, a single earring, a ripped flight bag reeking of brandy from the broken little souvenir bottle of Fundador inside, a man's hat, a woman's torn purse, half of a flight steward's cap, and a crumpled cigarette case, its silver cover jammed shut.

Whitney, reluctantly looking at all that remained of forty-eight human beings, felt hot and sickened in the musty office. Dammit, I'm too old for this kind of thing, he thought, that's what the young guys are for. But he sipped the sherry, forcing himself to appear unhurried and unruffled.

"Many thanks," he said when both glasses were empty. "Now I must go. With your permission, I will take the box with me."

"Of course," the officer replied. He rose with his visitor. "I hope I may have the good fortune to meet you again, *señor,* on a more pleasant occasion."

Whitney walked out of the building. The fresh evening air tasted good. He opened the trunk of the Mercedes, lifted the box in, slammed the lid and locked it. What I need is a slug of good whisky and a quiet meal, he thought. I can go over that stuff later. What I really ought to do is dump it on Archie's desk just as it is.

Thursday Evening

Hank Picot first heard the outboard motor coming around the island while he was cleaning a mess of fish down on the big flat rock just beyond the dock. Although the motor was running so slowly that the noise was muffled, he recognized it by its deep-throated tone as one of those big rental rigs from Edwards' place over at the landing.

Goddam, he thought, here it is only the middle of May and already the sports are beginning to show up. Pretty soon a man won't have this place to himself even in the winter, and it'll be all fished out too.

He watched the boat out of the corner of his eye as it slid around into view. In the fading daylight, he could see that it was one of Edwards' boats, all right, bigger than it needed to be and pushed by a 40-horse motor that was a lot more than enough for this little lake. The three men in the boat were not fishing at all, but were studying the island as they chugged along.

Then he remembered Jordan Lyman's call. Oh, those magazine people. Always wanting more pictures. You'd think they would have got enough last summer to last all the magazines in the country for a lifetime.

Picot had just finished gutting the last fish when the man in the bow of the boat pointed to him and spoke to the others. The man in the stern, who was running the engine, swung the boat toward the dock.

Picot stood up as they cut the motor and eased alongside the dock. They don't look like city fellows, he thought, at least not like any I've ever seen around Blue Lake before. Those three live outdoors somewhere, from their looks, and they're in good shape. Sure look like they can take care of themselves.

And only one small camera. Funny-looking crew for photographers. Picot swished his knife in the lake, dried it on his pants and slipped it back in its belt sheath. Then he washed his hands in the cold water. He said nothing.

"You take care of this place?" The speaker was the one in the bow, a black-haired man with heavy eyebrows and a scar along his jaw.

"That's about it," said Picot. "Something I can do for you?"

"Secret Service," said the black-haired one. "Just checking things out for the President's next trip, just checking things out."

Oh, is that so? thought Picot. Never seen them before, and when it's Secret Service it's always the same bunch. Besides, Lyman's already been here twice this year, and he didn't say anything on the phone about another check. Maybe they don't figure a Canuck fishing guide knows the difference.

The man who had spoken to him ran the bow line through one of the rings on the dock, and started to step out.

"Just a minute there," Picot said, moving from the flat rock onto the dock himself. "This here's private property."

The big man heaved himself onto the dock anyway and stood facing Picot. "Take it easy, friend, take it easy. We're just the advance men from Washington. We want to check out the island and run over the communications, the radio and stuff. They come through the winter all right?"

Picot took time to pull a cigarette from the pack in his shirt pocket, light it, and rebutton the pocket. This fellow, he thought, is as ugly as a porcupine—and not a whole lot smarter. If he really was Secret Service he'd know all that from two weeks ago, and the Signal Corps men okayed the generators and transmitters a month before that.

"You got some kind of identification?" he asked.

The black-haired man stared at him. The one sitting in the middle of the boat tugged at his companion's trouser leg to get his attention, then clenched his fist in an unspoken question. The black-haired one, obviously in charge, shrugged but shook his head. He untied the line from the dock and got back into the boat.

"Well, I guess we don't need to go over everything," he said, "if you say it's all in good shape."

I didn't say no such a damn thing, Picot thought, but he said nothing.

The black-haired man signaled his assistant in the stern. He started the motor and the boat swung away from the dock and headed slowly toward the far end of the island.

Picot collected his fish and walked up to the house along the pine-needle path from the dock. He threw the fish in the refrigerator and then went out onto the porch. Although the house stood at the highest point on the small island, the trees around it hid much of the shoreline from view. But he could follow the boat's course by the sound of the outboard as it slowly went around. Once it stopped briefly at the far end, where the radio mast was set up and the telephone cable came out of the water, but it started up again in a minute and finally droned off at full throttle in the direction of the landing.

Well, Lyman had it figured right about visitors, thought Picot, but they didn't look like they worked for any magazine. They were up to something else, and whatever it was it wasn't good. Fact is, they looked more like they might have been figuring to steal something.

A loon broke the stillness with its rattling call. Picot shivered as he looked out across the lake, dead calm now in the final windless moments of twilight. Damn, he thought, it still gets cold at night. He turned and went inside the house to call Jordan Lyman.

When the phone rang in President Lyman's second-floor study, four men were sitting amid the litter of dinner dishes. Lyman, Christopher Todd, Art Corwin and Jiggs Casey had eaten at the long coffee table. The President's food was almost untouched; he had drunk two cups of coffee and tried vainly to keep his pipe lighted while the others ate.

Lyman had the instrument off the cradle almost before the first ring ended.

"Maybe it's Ray," he said, as if apologizing for his haste.

His face slackened in disappointment when he heard the voice at the other end, but he listened intently. After he hung up, he relayed Picot's account and his description of the three men in the boat.

"That's Broderick," Casey said. "That description couldn't fit one other guy in a million."

"He's a long way from home," said Corwin. "It's a couple of thousand miles from El Paso to Maine, isn't it?"

Todd tugged at the bottom of his vest like a lawyer who has just demolished a witness on cross-examination. He smiled confidently at Lyman, who was still frowning at the phone.

"Mr. President," he said crisply, "you're in luck."

"Luck?" asked Lyman. "Is that what you call it when the bottom drops out of everything?"

"Look," said Todd. He drew a silver-cased pencil out of an upper vest pocket and tapped it on the large yellow pad that now seemed as permanent a part of his attire as his watch chain or cuff links. "Ever since I became convinced of the existence of this operation—"

The President interrupted. "Which was all of twelve hours ago, Chris, as I recall it."

Except for a twinge of a smile, the lawyer ignored the remark.

"Ever since I became convinced of it," he said, "I've been

wondering about one very important element, namely: how many allies does Scott have? If he has a great many, and this thing involves a lot of military units, large and small, we're in shoal waters. But if it comprises only a few men, even though they are the top commanders, the odds are all on our side."

"So?" Lyman was puzzled.

"So if General Scott has to dispatch Colonel Broderick all the way from El Paso, where he holds a command vital to this operation, up to Maine to do a job that any ordinary investigator could do, it means that Scott's trying to sail with a jury rig."

Lyman failed to brighten. He had been nervous and ill at ease ever since the little group had gathered an hour before. Corwin, who watched for such signs as part of his trade, was worried. Jittery Presidents meant more care and more work for him. Lyman stood up and paced the room, hands jammed in his pants pockets.

"I don't see how that helps much, Chris," he said.

"It helps if you decide to smash this thing out of hand," Todd replied, "and the time for that decision is getting mighty close."

Lyman's thoughts were elsewhere. "We've got to find out about Ray. My God, a United States senator can't just vanish." He looked at his wrist watch. "It's been more than thirty-six hours since Jiggs left him at the airport. I just don't understand it."

Todd was tempted to point to the bottles on the tray set against the wall of the study, but thought better of it. There was no use in flaying the President's temper any further. But what else could it be? They had called Clark's office. No one there knew his whereabouts. They had called his home repeatedly. No answer. They had tried the hotel in Macon where he stayed on his visits to Georgia, but that was a forlorn gesture. He must be somewhere around El Paso. Lyman had even suggested calling all the hotels and motels in the El Paso area, but Todd convinced him it would be dangerous.

"Jiggs," the President said now, "I think you better call Colonel Henderson's house in El Paso."

"I'm not so sure, Mr. President," Casey said, "that we ought to . . ."

"I think you'd better try," said Lyman.

Casey knew an order when he heard one. He fished the Henderson number from his pocket and placed the call through Esther. Mrs. Henderson answered. Mutt was at the base and had said he probably would be there through the weekend. Yes, a Mr. Clark had called yesterday, but he said he was flying on to Los Angeles. No, nothing more from Mr. Clark. Why, was anything the matter?

The three others received Casey's account of his phone conversation in silence. Lyman poured himself another cup of coffee. That's three, thought Corwin, he's really getting the jitters.

Todd's face was wrinkled in thought. He rapped his yellow pad with a knuckle.

"I'd like to ask a blunt question," he said. "Is there anyone here who thinks that a military coup is *not* afoot?"

Corwin and Casey sat mute. Lyman said, "I wish there weren't. I think there is."

"So do I," said Todd. "Everything Casey and Corwin have found out indicates it. Girard's call told us so flatly. I think even General Rutkowski suspects more than just some covered-up propaganda effort by the chiefs opposing the treaty. And I think Admiral Palmer does too."

Todd paused, then bit out his next words like a prosecutor explaining a case to his staff. "But we have no evidence that a jury would believe, to say nothing of a public that's already in love with General Scott. Furthermore, I don't think we're going to get any—unless Senator Clark comes through soon."

"I'm counting on Ray," said Lyman stubbornly.

"That's a hope, not a fact, Mr. President," Todd said. "Getting any evidence that would force Scott to resign seems a remote possibility to me, at best. I suggest that now is the time to come to grips with this thing."

"What do you mean?"

"I mean we have to decide right now—tonight—how you can break Scott and preserve your authority."

"What do you suggest, Chris?" Lyman's voice lacked interest, like that of a man resigned to hearing a sales talk when he is in no mood to buy.

"I've got a few ideas," said Todd. "We ought to thrash out every angle of this thoroughly, but if it were up to me, I'd do these things tonight:

"First, I'd get General Garlock down here and order him to put a reinforced, twenty-four-hour guard on that switch that controls the television and radio networks.

"And I'd order him to lock the gates at Mount Thunder and let no one—military or civilian—inside until I told him to, on pain of court-martial.

"Second, I'd call Scott over here and fire him—"

Lyman interrupted. "And what's the excuse?"

"Unauthorized establishment of ECOMCON."

"He wouldn't swallow that, Chris, and you know it," Lyman said.

"If he balked at that, I'd threaten him with the Segnier tax return, and if that didn't do it, I'd fire him anyway and lock him in a room in this house under guard by Art's people.

"Third, I'd dismiss Hardesty, Dieffenbach and Riley as members of the Joint Chiefs and heads of their services, for conspiring to nullify a treaty executed by the President and ratified by the Senate."

Todd was barking out plans like a top sergeant. No one moved to interrupt him and he plunged on.

"Fourth, I'd install somebody I trusted, maybe Admiral Palmer, as chairman of the Joint Chiefs and order him to dissolve ECOMCON at once. I'd recall General Rutkowski, commission him as head of the Air Force, and tell him to make sure that any orders for flying troop carriers to that base near El Paso are canceled at once. If some planes had already gone out, I'd tell him to get them back.

"Finally, I'd get a company from the Third Infantry and station them here, around the White House grounds, for a couple of days."

Casey was surprised that the Secretary even knew of the existence of the ceremonial regiment at Fort Myer, much less its proper designation. He had obviously done his homework.

Lyman had slipped down in his armchair, his thumbs hooked under his chin and his fingers pressing against his nose. He smiled wanly when Todd stopped.

"Well, Chris," he said, "that's quite a package. Are you sure you didn't forget anything?"

"Oh, yes." Todd seemed to be ticking off points like an accountant checking a balance sheet. "I'd call up the head of that network and ask him, as a personal favor, to keep that lunatic MacPherson from getting any time on the air Saturday."

Lyman said nothing to Todd, but turned instead to Casey. "What do you think of it all, Jiggs?"

"You mean, should you do it?" Casey hadn't expected to be asked for advice.

"No, I mean do you think it's feasible, as a military man?"

"I think it might work, sir, but only if you got a new chairman in immediately. And you'd be better off if you backed him up with a new chief in each service, so there'd be no confusion about the chain of command. I think I'd have the new chairman send out an all-service message, canceling all plans for an alert Saturday. That might surprise the people who didn't know there was one scheduled, but for anybody like General Seager at Vandenberg or Admiral Wilson at Pearl, it would mean the thing had collapsed."

"All points noted and accepted," Todd said. "Anything else?"

"Well, about confining General Scott here, sir," Casey said. "I'm not so sure about that. It's a cinch he couldn't run a revolution cooped up in a bedroom. But . . ."

Lyman smiled. "But you think it might be rather poor public relations for our side."

"Well, yes, sir. There would be some repercussions, certainly among military people."

"Art?" Lyman had turned to his Secret Service man.

Corwin shrugged his heavy shoulders. "Don't ask me about heading off any political plots, Mr. President. But, strictly from a legal standpoint, I'd rather have you use soldiers, if you can, to guard General Scott. Our only excuse to do that would be to claim he had threatened your life. Still, in a way I suppose he has. Well, we'd do whatever you wanted."

Lyman walked over to the tray of liquor and looked at the others inquiringly. Casey and Corwin shook their heads. "Scotch and soda, please," said Todd.

The President mixed a drink and handed it to Todd, then made one for himself. He remained apart from the others a moment, squinting reflectively at the bubbles rising in his glass. Without turning, he began to talk.

"Chris, the only thing wrong with that is the same thing that was wrong with it Tuesday when somebody brought it up. The newspapers would go wild, yelling for my scalp. Congress would come back in a rage, ten bills of impeachment would be introduced the first day, and there'd be investigations till hell wouldn't have 'em. The country would demand a court-martial of Scott to 'get the facts.' "

He swung around to face the Treasury Secretary.

"My God, man, before it was over, they'd have me in St. Elizabeth's with half the head shrinkers in the country certifying I was suffering from delusions of persecution."

Todd leveled a finger at Lyman. "Granting all that, Mr. President—which I don't, by the way—isn't it true that it would leave Gianelli as president and the Constitution still operating?"

"For how long, Chris?" Lyman waved his glass as if to sweep away the other man's argument. "Scott would own this country, lock, stock and barrel. It would be a military dictatorship and Vince would be nothing but a figurehead."

"But Scott would be out," protested Todd, his voice rising again.

"Not for more than a week, if that long," countered Lyman. "There'd be so much pressure that Vince would have to fire Palmer, or whoever it was, and give the job back to Scott. From then on he could run the country."

"Confound it, Mr. President, you're conjuring up all kinds of fantastic visions," Todd snapped. "The fact is that you took an oath to defend the Constitution of the United States against all enemies, and unless you act fast you'll be violating that oath."

Todd had risen to his feet in the heat of his exposition. He and the President stood, no more than two feet apart, in the center of the room. Each held his drink as though brandishing a weapon. Both men were flushed now.

"Don't tell me about my oath," barked Lyman. "You may be a great lawyer, but how I do my job is my business."

"This happens to be my country as well as yours, Jordan," rasped Todd, "and I don't intend to stand by while it slips away because you can't face reality."

They had forgotten all about the Marine and the Secret Service agent as they stood arguing. Todd blazed and bit, aroused almost to fury. Lyman was on the defensive, his anger that of a sad and tired man who snarls when cornered.

"Chris, you just couldn't possibly understand it." The President's voice was infinitely weary. "No man who hasn't gone to the voters can."

"I've never noticed that the mere process of running for office conferred wisdom on a man."

"Chris, you couldn't be elected dog catcher." There was no trace of humor left in Lyman's tone.

"Well, at least now we know where we stand . . . Mr. President." Todd bit off the title as though Lyman were unworthy of it.

Lyman glared at the lawyer, and for a moment Casey actually feared the two men might come to blows. Then Todd picked up his briefcase, pulled out Millicent Segnier's tax return, and flourished it in front of Lyman's face.

"Why don't you use this?" Todd's voice had risen sharply.

"No."

"You haven't got the guts."

"I do not participate in blackmail," said Lyman, "and I'm surprised that it seems to be accepted as a matter of course on Wall Street."

Todd waved the paper. "For God's sake, Mr. President,

we're facing the destruction of the greatest system of government on earth and you insist on acting like some Victorian prude."

"Oh, Christ, quit waving that thing, Chris," Lyman complained. "You remind me of Joe McCarthy."

Todd crammed the tax return back into his brief case and threw the portfolio into a chair.

"And furthermore," Lyman added, "your idea of surrounding this house with troops is just plain childish. I'd be the laughingstock of the Western world."

"You seem to be more concerned with your image than with your country," said Todd frigidly.

"Throwing troops around the White House would be the act of a coward." Lyman said it stubbornly.

"Well, confound it, then *you* suggest something—anything. I'm sick of talk. It's time to act. You're behaving like an ostrich."

Todd and Lyman were oblivious of the other men in the room. Corwin and Casey, for their part, were too embarrassed to look at each other. Corwin had seen emotion among high officials before, but never anything like this. Casey simply wanted to get out of the room; he felt like a neighbor who had blundered into a domestic squabble. He felt he had no right to look at the President. A feeling of great pity for this troubled man came over him, and he silently pleaded with Todd to stop.

But it was Lyman who subsided first.

"We'd just be cutting our own throats, Chris," he said. "It just can't be done your way." His voice trailed off. "I wish Ray was here."

"My God, Mr. President," Todd exploded, "can't you make up your mind without the senator from Georgia holding your hand?"

"At least I can count on him for some realistic advice," Lyman shot back. Then, shaking his head as if to clear it, he smiled wearily and put his big hand on Todd's shoulder.

"I'm afraid the General has succeeded in dividing the

allies," he said. "Chris, it isn't that I'm afraid to act. I just don't know how yet. We're still dealing with a bowl of mush and we really don't know any more than we did two days ago."

Lyman turned to the other two men as if he had just noticed for the first time that they were in the room. His eyes silently beseeched them for advice. But neither Corwin nor Casey had anything to offer.

"Let's sleep on it," Lyman said finally, his eyes on the floor. "Something may turn up in the morning. If not, well, we'll see."

Todd led Casey and Corwin toward the door. With his hand on the knob he turned and spoke in a voice that was almost forcibly restrained.

"Let's just make sure we act before it's too late," he said. "It takes only one administration to throw the country away."

Lyman was standing by the tall window, swinging his glasses by an earpiece and looking out toward the lonely, dim figure of Jefferson in his rotunda down by the Tidal Basin. His shoulders seemed to droop with fatigue.

"That's right, Chris," he said softly. "You just reminded me of something. Good night, gentlemen."

My God, thought Casey as he left the room, he isn't even talking sense any more. He felt sudden exhaustion in his own neck and shoulders. If Lyman feels the way I do, he thought, he's done for.

But Jordan Lyman, though physically exhausted, was not done for, nor was he done with that day's work. As the door closed behind his three guests, he picked up the phone.

"Esther? Please get me the Secretary of State."

The Secretary was on the line in less than a minute. Apparently Esther had reached him at his home.

"George? This is the President. I'm sorry to bother you, but this ought to be taken care of tonight, I think. I want to meet with Feemerov no later than the end of next week. That's right. Well, I don't care where—maybe Vienna again—but I want him there. Can you get a cable off to Moscow and have the ambassador go to the Foreign Ministry first thing tomorrow? No, he can't tell him why, but you know. Our friend from Detroit talked to you today, didn't he? I've got an idea that I think might do it. I'll go wherever Feemerov suggests, but tell them to put it to him hard. All right. Thanks very much, George. I'll explain it all to you as soon as I can."

Lyman hung up. It's got to work, he thought, because Chris is right: it takes only one administration to throw the country away. And it isn't going to be Jordan Lyman's administration if I can help it.

His eye fell on the liquor bottles on the tray by the wall. Where, he thought, where *is* Ray Clark?

Thursday Night

Senator Raymond Clark sat in a sparsely furnished, air-conditioned Quonset hut on the New Mexico desert, almost in the foothills of the barren San Andres Mountains. When he peeked through the lowered Venetian blinds, as he did at regular intervals, he could see a sentry standing in front of the hut. Like all the other soldiers Clark had seen in the past two days on this post, the guard was no boy, but a man with the patiently relaxed carriage of a toughened combat veteran.

Beyond the sentry Clark could see—in the bright light of the rising moon—a few other Quonsets, a half-dozen radio antenna towers scattered over several square miles, a number of windowless concrete-block buildings, and what appeared to be an endless stretch of desert. The last time he had looked out the window, before dark, Clark had seen a convoy of trucks, led by a jeep, rumble past on a gravel road that seemed to go nowhere. He had counted the vehicles and added a few marks to the notes he was compiling on the back of an envelope.

Now, sitting in a folding canvas armchair, Clark reviewed what he had listed:

—Airstrip. Fighters. F-112?
          2—Twinjet transports
—Towers. Microwave relay?
—Towers, radio transmitter
—Mobile radio trucks. H̶H̶1̶ 11
—Jeeps, command cars. Many
—Armored Personnel Carriers. H̶H̶1̶ H̶H̶1̶ H̶H̶1̶ 1
—Infantry approx 1 Bn
—Hvy cargo planes. Troop carrier? landed Wed Nite
—Trucks, 6x6. H̶H̶1̶ H̶H̶1̶ H̶H̶1̶ H̶H̶1̶ 111

Clark put the envelope back in his pocket and lapsed into another review of the events that had put him in this place. Maybe, he thought, I can stretch this playback out until I fall asleep again.

He had been held in the stuffy little shack at the gate Wednesday morning for almost an hour. The corporal—the one who had identified himself as Steiner on the telephone—picked his teeth and looked at Clark sourly. Both he and his companion ignored all Clark's attempts at conversation.

Then a colonel, black-browed and with a scarred cheek, raced up to the shack in a jeep that trailed a rising funnel of dust behind it. Clark could see a look of startled half-recognition on the officer's face as he entered the shelter. Suspecting he had been identified, Clark decided it would be foolish to try to play a role. Instead, he held out his hand.

"I'm Senator Raymond Clark of Georgia," he said. "I suppose you must be Colonel Broderick."

Now Broderick was really surprised, hearing himself identified, but he returned the handshake. "Nice to meet you, Senator," he said. "Nice to meet you. I've heard a great deal about you."

"Your people are a little gung-ho, Colonel."

"Yeah. Let's get out of the sun. I'll take you up to the guest hut, Senator, it's air conditioned and we can talk there. We don't have many visitors."

The road ran straight west over the flat, parched land. Clark, shading his eyes against the glare, could see nothing for miles except the bulk of mountains against the horizon. They drove for perhaps twenty minutes. Then the road dropped down a slope and Clark saw a whole military community spread out ahead: buildings, smaller huts, towers and a wide, single concrete runway which he guessed was at least two miles long. A few jet fighters and transports stood beside the strip.

Clark's inquiries during the drive got little response from Broderick. The colonel's eyes were hidden by his sunglasses and he wore a fixed, somewhat forced smile. He evaded direct answers. The whole base was highly classified, he said. Some of Clark's questions were answered with no more than a grunt.

Broderick stopped in front of a lone Quonset, separated from the nearest building by over a hundred yards. Carrying Clark's jacket for him, he fumbled with a ring of keys, found the right one and unlocked the door. The window air conditioner whirred at full speed and Clark stood by it thankfully as he surveyed the room. There was little to see. Tan bedspreads covered two narrow cots. An unpainted wooden desk and small chair were in one corner. The other corner was occupied by a floor lamp and a folding canvas camp chair. The small bathroom at the rear was barely big enough to hold a shower stall. The rounded ceiling came down to shoulder height on each side of the room.

Broderick stepped to the front window and lowered the blind, then sat down on a bed and gestured to Clark to take the armchair.

"Now, Senator," he said, "what's this all about?"

"Nothing mysterious," Clark said brightly. "I'm just moseying around on a little inspection trip of my own during the Senate recess, so I stopped by."

"It's somewhat irregular, Senator, somewhat irregular." Broderick scratched the back of one of his hairy hands. "I'm sure you know the top-secret classification of this base. Your committee chairman assured us there would be no visits here. We don't want to tip off the location."

"Well, now, that *is* mysterious, even if I'm not," Clark said. "Colonel, I never heard of this base before in my life."

Broderick looked at him from under his black eyebrows. It was not a friendly look. "Then how did you know where it was?"

"Heard about it in El Paso," said Clark, trying a bland smile. "I was on my way up to Holloman Air Force Base and White Sands."

"Who told you?"

"Now, Colonel, I'm the visiting senator. I think I'm supposed to ask the questions."

"Frankly, I don't believe you. Nobody in El Paso knows about this base."

"I don't intend to argue about it, Colonel." Clark stood up. "Now, if you don't mind, I'd like to call my office and let them know my whereabouts. After that, you can show me around the base and then I'll be on my way."

"I'm afraid that won't be possible, Senator," Broderick said. "No calls are permitted that would reveal the location of the base. There's only one line out of here, and that's in my office for my use."

Clark pointed to a telephone on the writing table. "What's that?"

"That's connected to the same line, but its use is restricted to me. No one but the commanding officer calls out of here."

"Say now, cousin," said Clark, putting on his Georgia drawl, "y'all ain't so hospitable to strangers out west heah. Now, down home we'd break out the catfish and hushpuppies and treat a feller like he was kinfolk."

"You're wasting your time," Broderick said brusquely, "and mine too. Your committee knows all it needs to about this base already."

"I wouldn't want to call you a liar, Broderick," said Clark, "but nobody on Armed Services ever heard of this base."

"Well, Senator, why don't we just call Senator Prentice in Washington and ask him?"

Clark tried to hide his surprise. "That would be just fine,

Colonel. It'll be a distinct pleasure to talk to someone in the outside world."

Broderick picked up the phone. "Sergeant," he said, "get me Senator Prentice in Washington. Try his office first, then his home." Broderick wore the abused expression of a floor-walker trying to handle an unreasonable customer.

Apparently talking to Prentice is a routine thing around here, Clark thought. I wonder how the sergeant makes connections? Maybe that phone line runs to a switchboard terminal in Washington.

"Senator? Hello," said Broderick into the phone. "This is Colonel Broderick. I have a friend of yours here, Senator Raymond Clark. Yes, that's right, Senator Clark of Georgia. He thinks there's something irregular about our base. Yes, sir, I will."

Broderick handed the phone to Clark with an I-told-you-so smile.

"Ray?" It was Prentice's heavy voice. "What are you doing in that hothouse, son?"

"Fred," said Clark, "what the hell's going on? Broderick insists the committee knows all about this place. I never heard of it before."

Prentice chuckled. "I warned you that you'd miss some important meetings if you went back to Georgia so often this spring. The committee had a long briefing on Site Y when you were away."

"It's damn strange nobody ever mentioned it to me," said Clark. "Especially you, Fred. And General Scott didn't say anything about it yesterday. It seems to me if the committee knew all about it he might at least have referred to it when I asked him about communications."

There was a pause at the other end. Oh-oh, Clark thought, I'm not supposed to know this has anything to do with communications. He forced himself not to look at Broderick.

"Now, simmer down, Ray," said Prentice soothingly. "Nothing to get all worked up about. You let Broderick show you all over the place and then you can give the committee a personal report after the recess. Say, put Broderick back on a minute."

The colonel took the phone and listened. "Yes, sir. Of course." He listened some more, nodding. "Yes, Senator. I understand perfectly. Right. Good-by, sir."

"Well, I hope that satisfied you, Senator," he said to Clark. "You just make yourself at home. I've got a few things to attend to, and I'll be back in an hour or so to show you our base. We're mighty proud of it."

"We'll take that tour right now if you don't mind," said Clark.

"That won't be possible, Senator, that won't be possible. I'll see you later. We'll look around when it's cooler, and then we can have dinner."

Broderick unplugged the phone from the wall and tucked it under his arm.

"What the hell gives here?" Clark spluttered.

Broderick merely winked, stepped out and slammed the door. Clark tried to open it. It was locked. When he lifted the Venetian blind a few minutes later, there was a sentry walking back and forth. Well, for Christ's sweet sake, he thought, they've locked me up.

A half hour later there was a rap on the door and a corporal let himself into the room with a key. He set a brown paper sack on the floor.

"Compliments of the colonel, sir," the corporal said. "He says to make yourself at home. We'll bring dinner over at 1745."

"Look, son," Clark said, "I don't intend to stay cooped up in this room. I'll walk back with you."

"Sorry, sir." The door had shut again, and the corporal was outside.

Clark lifted the two bottles from the paper bag. One was soda water. The other was Old Benjamin, his favorite brand of bourbon. He set the quart of soda and the fifth of whisky on the writing table, then went over to the bed and sat down. He stared at the bottles for perhaps ten minutes. Then he went to the table, drew the cork from the whisky and sniffed it. Old Benjamin, all right.

Clark walked slowly to the bathroom with the bottle. He upended it over the toilet bowl and watched the liquor splash into the water. When the pouring ceased, he shook the bottle. Several last drops ran out. He flushed the toilet. Then, finally, he ran a finger around the inside of the bottle neck and licked the finger.

"Bastards!" he growled. He slammed the bottle to the floor, but it failed to break. He picked it up and started to throw it again, but stopped himself and set it in the corner of the shower stall.

I don't know about Scott, Clark thought, but I'm going to get even with Prentice and Broderick if I never do anything else.

The minutes dragged by interminably. There was no book, no magazine, nothing to read in the room. He found a pamphlet in his coat pocket, a what-to-do-in-El Paso folder that he must have picked up at the motel, and read its sixteen small pages so many times he could almost recite them. He sat in the armchair. He lay on the bed. He tried the floor. He lifted the blind and banged on the window. That merely drew a rebuke from the sentry.

After several hours he began making notes on the back of an envelope. He raised one corner of a slat in the blind and tried to fix each object he could see in his memory. There wasn't much in his line of vision, although he could see the end of the runway and a wind sock far to his right.

At 5:45, as promised, the corporal brought dinner on a tray. A folded newspaper lay alongside the food. Clark again started to argue about leaving, but this time the soldier refused to talk at all. He also kept himself between Clark and the door, watching the senator as he set the tray on the table and backed out. The lock clicked behind him.

The food, at least, was good. After steak, peas, a baked potato, two rolls, peach pie, and coffee—he realized he had eaten nothing since breakfast—Clark felt reasonably at ease for the moment. He stretched out on the bed to read the paper. It turned out to be a day old, however, and except for local items he could find nothing that he hadn't known when he left Washington. Gianelli would depart for Italy. Labor refused to heed the President's plea to end the missile strikes. The West Virginia Rhododendron Queen had been unable to see Lyman, but had been kissed by the Secretary of the Interior instead. A wirephoto of the President talking on the phone in his bedroom, a wide smile on his face, was printed over a bulletin telling of the birth of his first grandchild in Kentucky.

The night seemed almost as long to Clark as those on the line in Korea. Every half hour, he lifted a slat to peek out at the silent base. Once he tried to knock a hole in the tiny frosted window in the bathroom, but it was too thick. He thumped on the walls from floor to ceiling and finally decided that without a sledge hammer or a crowbar there was no way to get out of the hut.

Just as he finally stripped to his shorts to try to get some sleep, he heard the growing roar of an approaching airplane. Through the blind, he watched a big jet, apparently a transport or cargo plane, drop onto the runway and flash out of sight. Other planes of the same type landed at intervals of three minutes; he counted a full dozen. By his watch he noted that the last one touched down at 2:26 A.M. When the whine of taxiing jets died away, he lay down and at last dropped off to sleep.

In the morning Clark had to reach under the cot for the paper to remind himself what day it was. It seemed as though he had been in this room for a month, but this must be Thursday. Yes. This was a Tuesday evening paper. He had arrived in El Paso Wednesday morning, and only one night had passed.

Then he saw it.

On the floor, by the door, was another bottle of Old Benjamin. Without hesitation, he carried it to the toilet and emptied it. This time he didn't bother to save a taste with his finger, but merely set the empty bottle beside the other one. Well, Broderick, he thought, we're getting a nice little row of dead soldiers.

Breakfast came at 7:30. Again the orderly hastily slipped it onto the table, retrieved the tray from the night before, and left. Clark didn't try to talk to him.

The morning, it seemed, would never go by. The air conditioner droned on without pause. Another sentry paced out front. Clark watched the tiny lines of light that came through the blind inch their way across the floor as the sun moved higher in the sky.

A new man brought the soup, sandwich and milk that made up lunch. He wouldn't talk either.

The first faint hint of panic settled down on Clark. He had never known fear and could never recall a time when his nerves had failed him. But now a gnawing frustration made it increasingly hard to concentrate. What should he do if he ever got out of this room? Where was his car? How would he get off the base? He found it difficult to pursue a line of thought through to its finish. Instead, his mind jumped from subject to subject. Girard should be back by now. Would he have something in writing? Let's hope so, for God's sake. What did Lyman think had happened to his old buddy Ray? Was that skeptic Todd still in doubt about Scott's venture? If he was, Clark wished he could change places with him. Could the others block this crazy operation without him?

He paced the room, counting his steps. He did deep knee bends and push-ups. He counted the rivets in the metal arch of the hut. He thought of his wife and how he had missed her since her death three years ago. He wondered what Scott would do with Congress if he succeeded on Saturday. Or with Russia, for that matter. He washed out his undershirt in the bathroom, hung it up to dry in front of the air conditioner, then took a shower himself. He was sweaty—and he needed something to do.

Propped on the bed once more, he vowed to read through the newspaper, but it slipped from his hands as he dozed off.

When he woke he knew it was evening, for the little bars of light had marched to the edge of the floor and partway up the wall, and they weren't nearly so bright as before. Once more he lifted a slat. The only thing that had changed was the shadow from the mountains, now reaching out across the desert. Dinner arrived, and Clark forced himself to eat it. Later, in the twilight, a line of trucks appeared, in convoy, with a jeep in front. He counted them and made a few more marks on the envelope.

Clark's rambling review of his troubles was interrupted by a knock on the door.

"Senator Clark?"

Clark didn't recognize the voice. Since the newcomer was making no effort to enter, as had his other visitors, he said, "Come in."

An officer wearing the eagles of a full colonel on his open-necked shirt stepped into the room. He had a round, red face, curly black hair and jug-handle ears.

Clark's heart beat heavily. This must be Jiggs's friend Henderson, he thought. At least he fits the description.

"I'm Colonel Henderson, sir," said the officer, putting out his hand and smiling a bit sheepishly, "acting C.O. in Colonel Broderick's absence."

Absence, thought Clark. Ray ol' boy, this is your chance to prove you could have been the best salesman in the whole state of Georgia if you had wanted to.

"Glad to know you," the senator said. "What's the matter with Colonel Broderick?"

"Orders, sir," said Henderson. "He's been called away for a day or so. I'm awfully sorry about having to ask you to stay in this hut, Senator. Frankly, I can't understand it, but the orders are specific."

"Aw, it's not your fault, Colonel." Clark decided to play this one slow and easy. "Just some misunderstanding, probably. We can win wars, but we can't get rid of the peacetime snafu."

Henderson grinned. "That's about it, Senator, but I *am* sorry I can't do anything about it."

"Forget it and sit down a minute," said Clark. "Say, your pal Casey is a good friend of mine. Thinks a lot of you . . . Mutt, isn't it?"

"Yes, sir. How do you know Jiggs?"

"Call me Ray, Mutt," Clark said, as cheerfully and confidently as a man who had recently sweat his undershirt into a stinking mess could say it. "Oh, Casey has been up before our committee a lot. Matter of fact, he did a helluva favor once for a friend of mine in Atlanta. I guess we're kind of whittled off the same broom handle—you know, we may not be brilliant, but we mean well."

Henderson relaxed a little. He had no idea why this senator was locked up, but he seemed like a nice guy anyway, and there weren't many of them at Site Y.

"Anything I can get for you, Senator?" he asked. "How about a drink?"

Clark eyed Henderson sharply, but could see only innocent hospitality in his face. Well, he thought, we might as well start right now.

"That's one goddam thing I don't need," he said. "Come here."

Clark led Henderson into the bathroom and showed him the two empty bottles.

"Your commanding officer was kind enough—or rather bastard enough—to provide me with those. I poured it down the can."

Henderson was puzzled. "I don't follow you, Senator. Why two bottles? And why did you throw it all away?"

"I got a little drinking problem, Mutt," Clark said, "and your boss knows it. Or at least he knew it after he talked to Senator Prentice."

"Prentice?"

"Yeah, Prentice. *My* chairman." Clark's voice was sarcastic. "Broderick called him from this room. After they finished talking, he took the phone away, and I got the whisky —and a prison number too, I guess."

It was plain from Henderson's look that he was now suspicious as well as confused. He edged toward the door of the hut and muttered something about pressing duties. But Clark held his elbow.

"Look, Colonel, don't go. My mind's sound, in spite of the fact that I've been cooped up in this place for two days. How about having the mess send over some coffee? There's an awful lot I want to tell you, and you've got to hear it."

Henderson, somewhat reluctantly, agreed. He opened the door and spoke to the sentry, then came back and sat down again. This time, however, he chose the chair nearest the door.

"Mutt," Clark asked, "how much do you trust Jiggs Casey?"

"You name it and he can have it," Henderson said. "Why?"

"If Jiggs told you something in complete seriousness, would you believe him?"

"Sure."

"All right. Do you know," said Clark slowly, "that when you told Casey about ECOMCON on Sunday he had never heard of it before?"

Henderson was startled, and could not hide it.

"How do you know about my seeing Jiggs on Sunday?"

"He told me," Clark snapped, "and he told some other people, too. He never heard of it."

"Really?" Henderson was frowning and his round face was troubled. "But he sounded like he knew all about it."

"He was faking," Clark said. "When he got back to his office after having lunch with you, he went through all the JCS orders for a year back. He couldn't find a thing about ECOMCON or anything like it. What's more, President Lyman had never heard of this base. Neither had I."

"I can't believe that, sir," said Henderson. "Colonel Broderick goes to Washington all the time to brief brass."

"Some of the brass, maybe, but not the Commander in Chief. Mutt, you listen to me now. I'm going to tell you the

God-damnedest story you ever heard in your life."

Clark began by recounting everything that Casey had encountered on Sunday and Monday. A sergeant knocked at the door, entered and put a tray with two mugs of coffee on the little table. As the two men sipped, Clark described Casey's first visit to the White House in minute detail, trying to impress Henderson. Then he sketched the meeting in the solarium on Tuesday, told of Girard and Casey's missions, and explained how he had made his own way from El Paso International Airport to the gates of Site Y.

Henderson was not convinced.

"That's pretty hard to believe, Senator, all of it. Why, General Scott has flown in here several times in the last few weeks with other members of the Joint Chiefs, and there was never the slightest hint that this was anything . . . anything it shouldn't be."

"Was Admiral Palmer ever here?" asked Clark quickly.

"No, but—"

"And my being locked up? And two bottles of my favorite bourbon to get me drunk? Do you people usually put a fifth of whisky inside the guest hut before breakfast?"

"No, sir, I admit it's awful strange, the whole thing, the way you put it together."

"That's the only way it fits together, Colonel. And it's worse than strange." Clark was deliberately harsh. "It's a planned, premeditated attempt to overthrow the government of the United States, in violation of the Constitution. And that, my friend, is sedition, and it's mutiny, and anybody who does it or helps someone do it can get twenty years in the penitentiary."

Henderson looked lost and irresolute, not at all the hearty officer of an hour before. "What do you expect me to do about it, Senator?"

"When will Broderick be back?"

"Sometime tomorrow, he said."

"Then you've got to get me off this base tonight. And I want you to fly back to Washington with me."

Henderson shook his head. "Senator, you know I can't do that. I'm an Army officer under orders. I've never disobeyed or ignored an order."

"Never, Mutt?"

"Never."

"Well, I'm ordering you now, by direction of the Commander in Chief, to get me out of here and to come to Washington with me."

"But—"

"And if you're worried about it," Clark went on, "you don't need to be. Look, if Casey and the President and I are wrong, and there's nothing to this, I'll guarantee that you'll get a letter for your C.O., or for your file, or for whatever you want, from the President of the United States. And if we're right, you won't need any excuses—if you get me out of here. Now how about it?"

"That's not what I mean," said Henderson, plainly disturbed and even angry at being caught between two fires. "I got an order from my commanding officer not to let you out of this hut. I guess the President could countermand that, but you can't, Senator."

"Colonel, if you persist in that argument, you can throw your country right down the drain all by yourself."

Henderson merely shook his head again. Clark tried a new tack, arguing that Casey had already done far more than he was asking Henderson to do. Casey had gone to the President on his own, risking a long and proud career in the Marines. He had gone—Clark spoke as persuasively as he knew how—because he knew in his heart it was right.

"Yeah," said Henderson. "But maybe Jiggs is all wrong, even if you're quoting him right."

Clark kept on, for he thought he detected signs that Henderson was weakening. He felt sorry for the officer, knowing the conflict that must be churning inside him, but he could not let up. He argued his side of the issue with a determination he wished he could bring to Senate debate.

"Why all these bully-boy troops?" he demanded, his voice

filling the room. "You know you've got the hardest bunch in the Army here. Why has it been kept a secret from the President? Why would Scott give command of it to a man who is openly contemptuous of civilian authority? Just what the hell do you think is going on here, Mutt, if it isn't an attempt to overthrow the government?"

Henderson sat studying his hands, clasped on his knees. His round face, usually cheerful, wrinkled in thought and his big ears heightened his forlorn appearance. When he spoke, there was a dogged quality to his voice.

"Gee, Senator, for antisabotage work, you want 'em tough."

"Antisabotage? Mutt, wasn't it you who told Jiggs you thought it was strange that you spent more time training to seize things than to protect them, or something like that?"

"Yes, but—"

"And why a man who says right out that he favors a dictatorship as the commanding officer?"

"Colonel Broderick's pretty conservative, I guess you'd say, but—"

Clark flashed in again. "Conservative, hell, Mutt. He's an out-and-out Fascist and you know it."

Henderson brought his eyes up to meet Clark's.

"Look, I'll level with you, Senator," he said. "I admit I've had some doubts about this outfit, and Broderick, but your story is pretty far out. How do I know you're not up to something?"

"You mean, off my rocker?"

"No, sir, not that, but maybe some kind of trick. You know, maybe General Scott sent you here to test our security."

"Even if that were true, which it isn't, what would you lose by leaving with me?"

"I'd just be a deserter, that's all." Henderson's tone was moody. "In wartime they can shoot you for that. In peacetime—in this outfit—it would be good for maybe twenty years in jail."

"Leaving with a United States senator?"

"You're just a civilian. It all boils down to that. I can't take orders from you."

Clark tried to ignore the flutter of anxiety in his stomach. "If we could get Casey on the phone, would you listen to him?"

"Sure. Well, at least I think I would."

Clark knew at once he had made a mistake. It would be folly to try to put a call through to Casey. What was the switchboard setup in Washington? Probably every call had to be reported to Scott or Murdock. He improvised hastily.

"All right," he said. "Obviously we can't use the base line, so let's just go off the post long enough to find a coin booth and call Casey. You have my word I'll come back with you if you're not satisfied."

Henderson shook his head. "You still don't understand, Senator. My orders are to keep you here."

"And you still don't understand, either. I have a verbal directive from the Commander in Chief to order you."

Henderson shook his head doggedly. Clark tried again.

"Look, Mutt, how about this? We go off this base and drive toward El Paso until we hit the first phone booth. Then you drop in the dime and ask the operator to give you the White House collect. When they answer, I'll go on the line and get you the President. You explain the situation to him and ask for instructions. Christ, man, that ought to satisfy anybody in uniform. I don't care what his rank is."

Clark pulled out his wallet and handed Henderson a dozen identification cards: credit, reserve Army officer, honorary Georgia Highway Patrol officer, driver's license. Six or seven identified him as a United States senator. Henderson studied one intently. Embossed in gold, it was titled "For Lyman Before Chicago Club" and listed Lyman as president, Clark as vice-president, and half a dozen prominent Democrats as incorporators. The card was signed with Lyman's unmistakable flourish and carried on its back a handwritten inscription: "For Ray, the man who made it possible, Jordie."

Henderson toyed with the card, inspecting both sides. As he did so, Clark returned to his philosophical gambit. He spoke eloquently of the American system, of Lyman's high esteem for the military, of values handed down untarnished from generation to generation. He was trying to repeat, word for word, Lyman's moving dissertation in the White House solarium on Tuesday afternoon. He talked for almost fifteen minutes without interruption from Henderson. When he finished, there was silence.

Henderson, who had stood up and walked around the room as Clark lectured him, stopped pacing and stared at the senator for a minute. Then, finally, he stepped to the door.

"I'll go over to my quarters and get a few things and give a few orders," he said, almost in a whisper. "Don't worry, I'll be back."

Clark threw himself down on the bed, emotionally exhausted. God, I'm used up, he thought. Henderson's admonition not to worry didn't help. Clark began to wonder whether he'd ever see him again—or whether Henderson would come back with a doctor and a strait jacket.

The next sound he heard, almost an hour later, was that of a car pulling up outside. "That'll be all for tonight, sergeant." It was Henderson's voice. "You're relieved. I'm taking the civilian in my custody. You can go on back to barracks."

Henderson put his head in the door. "Get your coat and let's go."

Clark's rented Ford was outside. Henderson motioned the senator behind the wheel and gave directions as they drove off. The night was cool, almost cold, now that the sun had been down for five hours. Clark's wrist watch, still on Washington time, showed 2:30. That makes it 11:30 here, he thought.

Henderson said nothing, merely pointing out a turn whenever one was required. They soon reached the flat, straight road that cut across the desert to the chain-link fence. The air felt wonderful; Clark realized that two days of air conditioning was about all that a man could take at one stretch. The land rolled out flat and bare except for the tiny shadows of the tumbleweed under the moonlight.

"You won't have to call the President for me," Henderson said abruptly.

"I'm a man of my word, Mutt," Clark replied.

"No," said Henderson, "once I'm off this base, I've had it if you're not telling the truth. Even the President couldn't help much."

Clark peered at him in the dark, realizing almost for the first time the true breadth of the gulf between a politician and a military man. For Clark, an order was merely a statement of opinion, something to be analyzed and questioned, contested at the most, compromised at the least. For Henderson, it was something absolute, rocklike, immutable. Clark sighed.

"I've got to call him anyway," he said, "if we have time. We may be pushed to get a plane out of here."

At the gate a sergeant came out of the hut, saluted Henderson, and peered across him at Clark.

"I'm sorry, Colonel," the soldier said to Henderson, "but I have orders that the civilian is not to leave the base, sir."

"That's all right, sergeant," Henderson answered. "I'm acting C.O. now, and I'm escorting him into town."

"Colonel Broderick said 'no,' sir." The sergeant was emphatic. "He stopped here when he left this afternoon and said that under no circumstances was the civilian, or anyone else, to leave the base." The guard stood beside the car, his rifle held in front of him, his face impassive.

Without warning Henderson reached through the window, grabbed the stock of the rifle and slammed the barrel against the soldier's cheekbone. Almost in the same movement, he opened the car door and jumped out as the soldier reeled backward. He wrenched the rifle out of his hands, ejected the clip and threw the weapon as far as he could.

Then keeping the dazed guard covered with his own .45—Clark wondered where Mutt had been carrying *that*—Henderson unlatched the wire gate and pushed it open. My God, thought Clark, once this guy makes up his mind he means business.

Clark drove through the gate, then halted for Henderson. The colonel still kept his pistol pointed at the sentry. "Step on it, Senator," he said. "There won't be any more like him now. We pull them all inside the fence at night."

Clark gunned the Ford down the macadam road. He drove as fast as he could all the way to the main highway, then turned right and sped through the moonlight toward El Paso.

Friday Morning

Clark and Henderson drove sleepily into Washington from Dulles Airport. As they crossed Key Bridge, the clock on the dashboard of the senator's convertible showed one minute past eight o'clock. Clark, fighting exhaustion, had kicked off his right shoe in hopes that the engine vibration transmitted through the accelerator pedal would help keep him awake. Henderson, mouth open, slumped in his seat. He had fallen asleep almost the minute Clark unlocked the door of the car at the airport parking lot.

As he fought the morning rush-hour traffic streaming over the bridge toward the Pentagon and other federal agencies in Virginia, Clark felt as if some personal antagonist had pumped grit under his eyelids. It had been a long night. Racing to El Paso airport in the rented sedan, they had decided not to risk interception by showing themselves in the commercial terminal. Henderson pointed out that although Site Y might be nonexistent on paper, any officer from the base could order M.P.'s to arrest him and detain Clark. So they bypassed the terminal and drove to a far hangar where, after a jittery half hour, Clark was able to charter a small plane. He telephoned ahead to Dallas for seats on a commercial flight to Washington, and the charter pilot got them into Dallas with minutes to spare.

Even Clark's "sunshine bit," as President Lyman termed his talent for turning on the full warmth of his Georgia charm, failed to relax his companion's nerves on the flight to Washington. Mutt Henderson was a soldier undone. He was assailed by second thoughts. Long periods of moody silence were punctuated by feverish questions directed at Clark. The senator tried jokes, but Henderson sometimes failed to manage even a routine smile. At last it became obvious to Clark that only the voice or face of Jiggs Casey could restore Henderson to normal. He was a man who had made his decision—and rued it. The nearer the plane came to Washington the nearer drew the inevitable court-martial—or so Clark surmised that Henderson was thinking. He was almost thankful that Henderson had finally fallen asleep in the car.

Clark pulled up in front of a white-painted brick house in Georgetown that was only a foot or two wider than the little car was long. Henderson followed him groggily across the sidewalk and waited while Clark fumbled with the doorkey.

"Well, here we are," said the senator. Books, old newspapers and magazines littered the couch and floor of the small living room. A sweater hung from a corner of the mantel and gray rings marked tables where too many highball glasses had been left overnight too often.

"The maid comes once a week," Clark said, by way of apology. "Sit down and I'll see if I can get Jiggs on the phone."

He found Casey's home number in the book and dialed it while both men remained standing. Henderson's normally ruddy complexion was dulled by fatigue and tension.

"Jiggs?" said the senator. "This is Ray Clark. Yeah, you're telling me. I'm lucky I'm not still stuck in the middle of the desert. Listen, I've got a pal of yours with me. He looks awful. Either he just swallowed a green watermelon or he thinks he picked the wrong side. Give him the word, will you? His name is Mutt Henderson."

Henderson's face slowly relaxed as he listened on the phone. He grinned weakly. Finally he laughed and hung up.

"Jiggs says to take off my girdle and have a good cry," Henderson said happily. "He can't say much because Marge is there, but he says he'll see us soon. I'm supposed to do whatever you tell me."

"Right now you're going to bed," Clark said. He pushed Henderson up the stairs ahead of him and showed him into a back bedroom.

"Now it's your turn to be under house arrest," Clark said, "except we don't have armed guards around the place. We get along without strong-arm men in Washington. But no phone calls, and don't leave the house until I come to fetch you. If you're hungry when you wake up, you can find something to eat in the kitchen. The coffee is in the cupboard over the stove."

Henderson was already untying his shoelaces when Clark closed the bedroom door. The senator went down the stairs, taking them two at a time, and called Esther Townsend at the White House.

"Senator!" He had seldom heard a woman's voice so relieved. "Where are you?"

"At home, honey, where all good boys should be at breakfast time."

"Can you get here right away?" she asked, her tone quickly serious. "He's in trouble and he needs you."

"On the way," he said.

Clark drove into the back driveway at the White House and parked by the big magnolia tree at the entrance to the ground-floor reception room. Guards and White House police nodded to him. The Georgia senator needed no identification; his face was his passport here. He strode into the mansion and took the little walnut-paneled elevator to the second floor.

Lyman was hunched over a breakfast tray in his study, but he rose quickly as Clark knocked and entered. The President came across the room in three big steps to meet him. Trimmer, his tail wagging happily, sniffed at Clark's trouser cuffs.

"God, I'm glad to see you, Ray. I thought you'd fallen off the planet somewhere." He gripped Clark's hand and squeezed his arm, as if to assure himself that this was flesh and blood and not an apparition.

Lyman's appearance stunned Clark. His face was colorless and an unnatural puffiness hung about his eyes. There seemed to be more gray in his hair, and it took Clark a moment to realize that it was merely a matter of Lyman's having missed his regular weekly trim. The middle-aged man of fifty-two whom Clark had seen Tuesday night now seemed almost old. It was obvious to the Georgian that his friend had slept but little.

"Ah'm back from the desert," Clark said, "an' this ol' boy has had mo' adventures than Ali Baba an' his fo'ty thieves. Ah got mo' tall tales than Lyndon Johnson's camel driver."

Clark stood casually with one hand on the high white marble mantel. Lyman sat down in his easy chair and leaned forward, forearms on his knees. He seemed spent and spiritless.

"Ray," he said quietly. "I guess you haven't heard. Paul Girard is dead. His plane crashed on the way home."

Clark stared at the President.

"I'm sorry, Jordie," he said quietly. "I hadn't heard."

He sat down on the sofa opposite Lyman's chair. The President pulled off his glasses and held them in front of him, eying them as if looking for some tiny scratch on the lenses.

"He got a signed statement from Barnswell. He called me up before he started back and he said that much. And also that Casey had guessed right. Then he went up to Madrid and got onto a Trans-Ocean jet and it flew into a mountain."

Clark could think of nothing to say. Lyman went on, almost as if his friend were not there, to recount the events of Wednesday and Thursday, including Saul Lieberman's shattering news of Russia's apparent intention to assemble new nuclear warheads in violation of the treaty. Much of the time his eyes wandered over the pattern of the rug at his feet. His hands hung limp, the wrists sticking out of his shirt cuffs, the eyeglasses dangling and twitching. The hunch of his shoulders bore the imprint of resignation, almost defeat, as he told of his argument with Todd the night before in front of Casey and Corwin.

"Feemerov I can handle, but on this other thing I can't see my way out, Ray," he concluded.

Clark's mind ran back to that morning in Korea. He could feel the sting on his palms as he slapped the face of a much younger Jordan Lyman. He put into his voice a heartiness he did not feel.

"Aw, come on, Jordie," he said, "there's always a way out. But there isn't much time left. Listen to this."

Clark told of his experiences in detail. As he talked, the anger mounted in him. "Bastards, *double* bastards," he said as he described the two bottles of bourbon pressed on him.

Lyman's got to get mad, too, he thought, as he told of Henderson's quick knockout of the guard at the Site Y gate the night before.

"Broderick is probably back at the base now," he said, "and you can bet that Scott and Prentice and those other sons of bitches are either in a huddle or will be soon. Now they know that we know, and that's not good, Jordie. What worries me is whether they can move up the time."

"Did any more of those transports come in last night?"

That's it, Yankee boy, thought Clark. You got to start thinking fast to stop this. We need a little fight spirit right now.

"No," he said, "except for those twelve big jets that came in Wednesday night, there weren't any landings. But if they bring 'em in today they might be able to move things up a few hours."

A knock on the door brought a "Come in" from Lyman. Christopher Todd, dressed, as always, as though on his way to a directors' meeting, entered with briefcase in hand. He smiled briefly at Lyman and nodded somewhat noncommittally at Clark.

"Ah, the prodigal son returns," he said. Though the morning sunlight filtering through the mesh curtains promised another warm spring day, Todd's manner was frosty.

Clark quickly retold his story while the President poured himself a cup of hot coffee and sipped at it.

"Well, Mr. President," Todd said when Clark finished, "there's one thing to be done at once."

"What's that, Chris?"

"Call Prentice. Let's find out what he has to say about putting a colleague under arrest."

"Won't that tip our hand?"

"They already know we're onto it. It's time to start finding out what they're planning today. A call from you just might upset Prentice enough so you could get some information from him."

When Lyman got Prentice on the phone, the other two men listened. The President began in a firm, almost harsh voice.

"Good morning, Fred, this is the President. I want to hear your version of that telephone conversation you had with Senator Clark out in New Mexico Wednesday."

Clark and Todd could hear the deep, cadenced voice of Frederick Prentice booming through the instrument. Lyman's face set in weary, rigid lines.

He's tired, tired, tired, thought Clark—but who isn't? He poured himself a cup of coffee to help fight off torpor.

"Frankly, I don't believe you, Fred," Lyman said. "Will you please tell me the present whereabouts of Colonel Broderick? He seems to be quite a tourist."

The President shook his head and bit his lower lip as he listened again. "You've been as helpful as ever, Senator," he said, and brought the phone down heavily in its cradle.

"He says he never talked to Ray Wednesday, or since, in New Mexico or anywhere else. He says he's heard of a Colonel Broderick, he thinks, but he can't recall ever talking to him, and says he hasn't the vaguest idea of where he might be."

"Liar." Clark bit off the word angrily.

"He says you must have been . . . dreaming, Ray."

"I know what he said. If I was dreaming I've got a real live colonel out at my place who shared the nightmare."

"I think we ought to have Colonel Henderson here with us for the rest of the day," Todd said. "He ought to be able to tell us how that infernal place works."

Lyman agreed. "Yes, I think you better go get him, Ray. We'll get Casey and Corwin in too while you're gone."

Clark drove the twenty blocks to his Georgetown house at a fast clip, running two red lights on the way. He pulled into the alley and squeezed the car against the high brick wall of his garden. At the back door he was surprised to find a pane of glass broken. It was the one just above the lock. Clark let himself in and ran up the narrow flight of stairs.

The guestroom at the rear of the house was empty. Rumpled sheets lay in a heap on the bed where he had left Henderson. A blanket trailed off on the floor. Clark looked into the closet. The hangers were bare; Henderson's clothes were nowhere to be seen.

"Mutt?" Clark shouted from the head of the stairs. No answer.

He hurried through the front bedroom and the rooms downstairs, but found nothing. At the back door he noted that the slivers of glass from the broken pane lay scattered on the kitchen floor. The window had been smashed from the outside.

He drove back to the White House as fast as he could. Corwin and Casey were there to hear his bad news. Both swore softly as Clark explained.

"And I told Henderson we don't use thugs in Washington," he concluded ruefully. "A lot I know."

Lyman said nothing. Todd was the first to speak.

"Either Senator Clark is completely out of his mind, which seems unlikely, or you'd better start moving right now, Mr. President."

"The first thing is to get Henderson back," Clark said, trying to lend momentum to Todd's urgings. "He didn't just walk out. The way the window was broken tells us that. Somebody shanghaied him. They're starting to play rough."

"What do you think, Jiggs?" asked Lyman.

"I think Mutt and the senator were followed from the airport," Casey said. "My guess is they'd put Mutt in a military guardhouse somewhere. They could charge him with going AWOL, or with assaulting an enlisted man, or both."

Corwin looked at the President. Lyman nodded. "You better get on it right away, Art," he said. "We've got to find him."

"It's just as I said last night," Todd began after the Secret Service agent had left the room. "We don't have one scrap of evidence that could be used in court, but every one of us knows that a big operation is under way. We don't know its exact purpose, but it has to be smashed today, and the sooner the better."

Todd fixed his eyes on the President as though to stare him into action. Lyman looked at Clark.

"I think Chris is right," Clark said. "You got to move."

"How?"

"Call Scott over here and fire him," Clark replied quickly. Then, obviously thinking as he spoke, he went on more slowly: "Then put out a message to all commands that an alert, scheduled for Saturday, has been canceled. And forbid any major troop movements without express permission from you. Then get Barney Rutkowski to fly down to Site Y and bust the place up."

"What's our excuse with Scott—and with the country?"

"Why, establishment of this goddam ECOMCON thing without authority, and airlifting troops all over hellandgone in secret," Clark said. "And don't forget that tax return. You can wave that under his nose."

Lyman twirled a pipe on the coffee table and watched as the stem swung in an arc around the bowl. He knocked the pipe out in the ashtray. Todd started to speak, but the President held up his hand.

"No," he said slowly, "not yet. There's got to be a better way. Anything sudden like that, and General Scott would own the country by Monday morning. People just wouldn't understand it—or stand for it."

"Maybe so," argued Clark, "but you've got to run that risk now. This thing has gone far enough."

Lyman walked to the tall windows and looked down across the big lawn toward the fountain, glistening in the morning sun. Two gardeners were working in the flower bed that surrounded the pool. After a moment the President turned and faced the group.

"No, not yet," he said again. "My hand would be immeasurably strengthened if we could get Henderson back here. He's really our only impartial witness, you know."

"You're gambling with the whole country," Todd said roughly. "Suppose Scott moves up the deadline and doesn't wait until tomorrow?"

Lyman passed up the opportunity to start another debate with Todd. Instead, he looked to Casey.

"Is that feasible, Jiggs? Could an operation like this, with that airlift, be speeded up?"

"I doubt it, Mr. President. It's taken weeks of preparation as is. It's possible, I suppose, but hardly probable." He grinned. "Anyway, if I were running it, I don't think I could move it up."

"I'll accept that military judgment," said Lyman. "We'll sit tight a few more hours before we decide and hope we get Henderson back in the meantime."

"I think that decision, or lack of it, is insane, Mr. President," said Todd.

"We had a full exploration of your views last night, Chris," Lyman said, "and you are clearly on record. I think we can dispense with any further summations to the jury, thank you."

Lyman walked Todd and Casey to the door. "Stay by the phone," he said. "I may need you both back here at any moment. I'm afraid it's going to be a long day."

As the Marine and the lawyer crossed the great hallway to the elevator, Todd eyed an Army warrant officer who sat woodenly in a chair, a small briefcase clasped between his knees.

"Say, Colonel," asked Todd when they were inside the elevator, "who are those people? One of them is always sitting just outside the President's door, wherever he is."

"I don't know. It's some kind of classified deal, I think, Mr. Secretary," said Casey vaguely. What a complicated thing this government is, he thought. There sits the man with the code that could launch a nuclear war, and the Secretary of tĺ Treasury doesn't even know it.

"Well, I just hope he isn't on Scott's list," Todd said.

Casey said: "Yeah, me too." Casey thought: But even the Commander in Chief couldn't order him away. And maybe— just maybe—this whole thing is so intricate, and has so many little compartments like that one, that even General Scott can't break through it. Let's hope so.

Casey's thoughts turned to personal matters as he drove home. He still had explained nothing about his trip to New York, or his absence again last night, to Marge. The time was coming, if he knew her, when she would demand some an-swers.

He was right. Instead of her usual morning work costume, she had on a green print dress and her high heels. That meant either a luncheon date or talk-talk with him. Casey guessed from her set smile that it was the latter.

"You look pretty classy for so early in the morning, honey," he said.

Casey followed her into the living room. She sat down on a leather hassock and tucked one nylon-clad leg under her.

"Colonel Casey," she said, "I think it's time you started trusting your service wife."

"Meaning?"

"Meaning where were you Wednesday night and what are all these comings and goings about?"

"Marge, I'm sorry, but I went out of town on a confidential assignment."

"I know that, dear. Very confidential." Marge smiled. He could see the little space between her teeth, but it definitely did not make her look innocent at this moment. "But you're on leave, remember? So let's not pretend it was business, shall we?"

Casey tried to look hurt and misunderstood. It required very little effort. He felt both.

"It *was* business, Marge. Official, government business."

"And did that business require you to contact a tall bitch named Eleanor Holbrook in New York, maybe?"

"Aw, cut it out, Marge," he said. "We went all through that a long time ago and I'm not going to go through it again."

"You were in New York." It was an accusation, not a question.

"No, I wasn't," he lied. Could some friend of Marge's have seen him at the Sherwood? Or at that restaurant? Or—God forbid—at Shoo's apartment house?

"You're too honest, Jiggs. You never have learned to lie well."

He bristled. "Marge, now, dammit, lay off. I'm not going to discuss any of this. Maybe I can tell you something about it Sunday. Maybe I can't. It's just going to have to be that way."

Her nose crinkled—but not with affection. This was the Angry Crinkle. Jiggs saw it only rarely, but it always meant trouble.

"I may just go off on a little confidential 'assignment' of my own this weekend," she said, "so I may not be available to have the pleasure of listening to your story—if you can make one up by then."

"Oh, for Christ's sake, Marge!" he exploded. But Mrs. Casey, in her best dramatic manner, rose from the hassock and clicked down the hall to the little room where she kept her sewing machine, her golf clubs, her writing desk, and her extension telephone. The door slammed behind her.

Casey kicked the hassock as hard as he could, and succeeded only in hurting his toes. Thank God, he thought, a fellow doesn't have to help save his country more than once in a lifetime.

Friday Noon

Art Corwin, swinging down from one doorstep and heading to the next, decided that if this week had accomplished nothing else, it had provided him with a thorough refresher course in the techniques of his business. *Not that I really needed it,* he thought. *I may have spent a couple of years on my can in the west wing, but I haven't forgotten everything.*

By the time he had rung three more Georgetown doorbells, he had it spelled out to his satisfaction. Two maids and one very attractive young wife, the last in tight black stretch pants and a scarlet house jacket, remembered seeing an Army sedan parked on the street about 8:30 that morning. All three women agreed there were two soldiers in it. It had been parked some forty feet from Senator Clark's door. One of the maids said she had seen the senator drive away shortly before nine, and noticed that the two uniformed men went up to the house right afterwards and tried the door. She was about to step out and tell them that there was nobody home when the two—one apparently an officer, because he had "shiny things on his shoulders"—went back to their car and drove off.

An elderly woman on the next street, whose rear garden faced Clark's across the alley, said she saw two Army men come out of the senator's back door a little after nine.

"They had another one with them, and they seemed to be *supporting* him. I must say I was a little surprised. I've heard that some people who come out of that house have to be held up by their friends, but I'd never seen it myself. And at nine o'clock in the morning!"

She sniffed. "You sometimes wonder how this government manages to do anything, with that kind of people in it."

Corwin climbed back into his car, thought a minute, and then on a hunch drove to the Dobney. He obtained Senator Prentice's apartment number from the clerk in the ornate marble lobby, then spent fifteen minutes prowling the halls on Prentice's floor. Learning nothing, he descended on the freight elevator and quizzed several maintenance men in the garage—without results. He walked through the parking lot, looking for an Army sedan. Then he drove slowly around the block, but saw no government vehicle.

Corwin drove down Massachusetts Avenue and cut right at Sheridan Circle into Rock Creek Park. He followed the parkway to the Constitution Avenue bridge, where he crossed into Virginia. At Fort Myer he parked just inside the gate and walked back to the sentry house. He showed his Secret Service credentials to the guard on duty and asked to speak to the man who had been on the gate about nine o'clock or shortly thereafter.

"That was me," said the guard, a young M.P.

"Maybe you can help me, then," Corwin said. He lowered his voice. "I'm working with CIC on a security case."

"Sure."

"Did an Army sedan come in here a little after nine with three men, a couple of officers and an enlisted man?"

"Yeah, I think so," said the M.P., obviously intrigued to be involved in a security case. "Sure. There was this colonel, and a major, and a sergeant. I remember because I thought it was kind of funny. The major was driving and the sergeant was riding in back with the colonel. The colonel had a mouse under his eye, like he might have been slugged or something."

"Were any of them post personnel, so far as you knew?"

"No, sir, I don't think so. Least I never saw them before."

"You know where they went?" asked Corwin.

"No, but I can guess. They asked directions to the stockade, so I told 'em and they went in."

"Thanks, soldier," said Corwin. "Please keep this to yourself. This case is pretty highly classified."

"Yes, sir."

Ten minutes later Corwin was in the White House, reporting to the President in his west wing office.

"I didn't want to take a chance on nosing around the post stockade, Mr. President," he explained. "My mug is pretty well known around town, and I've worked a lot with the officers of those ceremonial troops over at Myer."

"I've got an idea," Lyman said. He picked up the phone and asked Esther to get him Casey's home.

"Hello," he said. "You must be Mrs. Casey. This is Jordan Lyman. Could I speak to Jiggs, please?"

Lyman covered the mouthpiece and grinned at Corwin. "We may be in a jam, Art, but I think we just got Colonel Casey out of one. She almost bit the phone off when she answered, but when I said who I was she just gulped and said 'yes, sir'—*very* faintly."

Corwin chuckled. "I had a cop's hunch that he didn't tell us quite everything about that New York trip." He fell silent as Lyman began speaking again.

"Jiggs? Art thinks he's traced your friend to the Fort Myer guardhouse. He thinks a major and a sergeant took him there. Have you got a friend you can call over there? . . . Well, that would do it, I guess. Yes, please. And call me right back, will you?"

Casey was back on the phone in a few minutes. Lyman said, "Wait a minute, Jiggs, I want Art in on this too," and waved Corwin to an extension.

"That was good deduction," Casey said. "I called the duty sergeant at the Myer stockade and asked him if they were 'still holding' a Colonel William Henderson. He said yes. So I said I'd been appointed as his defense counsel and asked what the booking charge was. The duty sergeant said he didn't know yet, that the major who brought him in just said he struck an enlisted man and went AWOL from his post. He's being held on verbal orders from his commanding officer—whose name turns out to be Broderick."

"Thanks, Jiggs," Lyman said. "I'm afraid we're back where we started, almost, but at least we know where he is. There wouldn't be any way of getting him out without kicking up a big rumpus, would there?"

"I'm afraid not, sir," Casey said. "But I think he'll be all right there for a while."

"You better come back over here, Jiggs. We're going to have to do something pretty quickly, I'm afraid."

Lyman turned back to Corwin as he hung up.

"Art, you better go back to the Pentagon and pick up Scott," he said. "I want to know everywhere he goes this afternoon, if you can possibly manage it. And call Esther every half hour or so anyway. We may need you in a hurry."

"Right, sir."

When Corwin had left, Lyman walked back from his office to the mansion and took the little elevator up to the third floor. Clark was asleep in one of the guest rooms tucked under the roof. The President knocked gently on the door.

"Ray," he said, putting his head just inside the door, "come on down, will you? We're coming up against the gun on this thing. I'll be in the study."

When Clark came down he was still red-eyed and yawning, but a borrowed shirt—the tiny initials J.L. were embroidered in blue on the pocket—gave him some appearance of freshness.

Lyman, Todd and Casey were eating ham sandwiches and milk. The President looked cheerless, but at least, Clark thought, he was eating again. Trimmer lay curled contentedly on his rug.

"No, thanks, not yet," Clark said when Lyman offered him a plate of sandwiches. "Just a little coffee."

When the others had finished eating, Lyman pushed back his plate.

"Ray, we found Colonel Henderson," the President said. "He's in the stockade over at Fort Myer. He was kidnapped out of your house about nine o'clock and locked up on orders from Broderick. Jiggs thinks he'll be all right there, and there isn't much we can do about it right now anyway."

Clark put down his coffee cup. "You know," he said, "I think the other fellows are getting a little panicky. That's not very smooth, grabbing him like that. To say nothing of sticking him in the first place you'd think of looking for him."

"A typical example of the military mind at work, Senator." Todd was as biting as usual, and Casey stirred in his chair. The Cabinet member bowed slightly toward him. "Present company excepted, of course."

Lyman picked up a pipe and tamped it full of tobacco before he spoke again.

"Well, after all, Scott's people aren't trained spies, even if they are in a conspiracy. They're amateurs." He struck a match and lit his pipe. "Thank God for small favors. And this must have caught them by surprise. They had to improvise."

"And so do we." It was Todd again. "Right now, Mr. President."

"Yes, I guess we do," Lyman said reluctantly. "We can't put things off much longer."

"Good," said Todd. Casey thought the Secretary spoke with just a bit too much relish.

"I am now willing to consider a plan of action that can be put into effect tonight. But I want every step thought out with extreme care, and we must consider every possible result of any move we make. I am convinced that one false step will ruin everything. In fact, I have grave doubts that we can succeed, no matter what we do."

"Dammit, Mr. President, that's no way to—" began Todd. The ringing of the phone interrupted him. Lyman answered, listened a moment and said, "Yes, put him on."

The President turned to the others.

"It's Barney Rutkowski from Colorado Springs," he said. "He's calling on the command line."

Friday, 1:30 P.M

General Bernard Rutkowski, his cap set at a slightly rakish angle, strode along the tunnel. His short, plump body rolled as he walked, and his chubby cheeks glowed with the exertion. His well-polished buttons and the silver decorations on his cap visor gleamed under the bright overhead lights.

It was 1:30 in Washington, and thus 10:30 in the morning in Colorado. But here, half a mile inside Cheyenne Mountain, it might as well have been midnight. General Rutkowski was making his daily visit to the Combat Operations Center of the North American Air Defense Command. As boss of NORAD, Rutkowski never let a day get by without inspecting the center—the focal point of the nation's air defense—but he tried to stagger the pattern and the hours to keep the staff alert.

Today he had ridden from the outside portal along the curving half mile of main tunnel, wide as a highway, that led to the primary lateral. Then he jumped out of his jeep and walked the rest of the way into the self-contained three-story steel blockhouse that cradled the operations center.

He entered the center as an air police sentry at the door

cut away a salute so smart that it almost whistled. There were more guards and more salutes inside as Rutkowski hurried to the long, theaterlike room where some forty people, working in two tiers, kept track of every missile, satellite and aircraft aloft over North America.

The General climbed to a balcony and took up a position behind a desk console rimmed with dials, telephones, switches and buttons. The duty controller, Colonel Francis O'Malley, popped up from his chair and stood at attention beside it.

"At ease, Frank," said Rutkowski. "Any problems today?"

O'Malley turned over his duty seat to an assistant and sank into a chair beside the General. In front of them was a huge screen—some public-relations man had christened it "Iconorama"—which showed everything moving in the air over the continent. An electronic computer, fed by wire, telephone and teleprinter from hundreds of airports and military bases, changed the symbols on the screen every few seconds.

"No problems, sir," said O'Malley. "We had a flap a while ago, when they shot a couple of big ones out of Vandenberg without bothering to cut us in on the countdown. The damn things were off the pads before we knew about them."

"That's inexcusable. Did you chew somebody out over there?"

O'Malley grinned in the half-light of the theaterlike room.

"Don't worry, sir. I did. That controller at Vandenberg must have thought he was back at the Springs as a Doolie again."

Rutkowski liked this trim young officer. The earliest graduates of the Air Force Academy were beginning to come into responsible positions now, and Rutkowski rated them, on the average, as far superior to his own age group which had schooled at West Point and then transferred to aircraft. These youngsters, he thought, were all Air Force. They had it drilled into them as shaven-headed "Doolies," or first-year men, at the Academy, where no effort was spared to weed out those who might later decide to give up a military career. They were run, shouted at, and worked until instant obedience was instinctive and the hunger for responsibility, for a chance to prove themselves, was ravenous. They were bright and smart and they loved the service. Rutkowski could ask no more of an Air Force man.

The major who had substituted for O'Malley at the controller's post turned around and beckoned with his head. The colonel excused himself and stepped down to the desk. The major handed him a piece of paper and he brought it back to the General.

"We're getting a little static this week, sir," he said. "I thought I could get it cleared up before this, but the thing is getting to be a headache."

Rutkowski took the slip from O'Malley. It was a dispatch on yellow paper, torn from a teleprinter:

O'MALLEY
COC
NORAD
TRANSPORTS LEAVE OUR FREQUENCY FIVE ZERO MILES OUT. DESTINATION CLASSIFIED.

> THOMAS
> OPERATIONS
> BIGGS FIELD

"What's this all about, Frank?" asked Rutkowski.

"That's what I'd decided to ask you this afternoon, sir," the colonel said. "Wednesday night we were notified of clearance for twelve troop carriers, out of Pope Air Base at Fort Bragg. They were cleared for Biggs Field at El Paso. But they didn't go there. Instead, they went somewhere north and landed. We had them on the radar maybe ten minutes after they should have landed at Biggs. They dropped off the screens out in the New Mexico desert somewhere."

"What were they?"

"By the size and speed of the blips, the controllers figured they were K-212's," O'Malley said. "And that's what they turned out to be."

"Airborne maneuvers?"

"I suppose so, but dammit, General, we can't have planes wandering around our screens and landing God knows where."

"This ever happen before, Frank?"

"Well, yes, sir. It turns out it has, although I never knew about it until Wednesday night. Single planes have landed and taken off from some place between Biggs and Holloman Air Base. Nobody paid much attention until we got this flight of twelve."

"Did you check it out anywhere?"

"Yes, sir," said the colonel. "At Pope and Biggs both. I got Pope operations on the phone. They said they filed a flight plan and clearance for twelve K-212's to Biggs Field. They thought that's where they went. Otherwise they didn't know anything about the flight. Then the officer at Biggs operations told me they switched off his frequency some miles out and he didn't know where they went."

"What about this message?" asked Rutkowski, tapping the yellow sheet in his hand.

"This morning, Biggs notified us that thirty more K-212's would be coming in there at 0700 tomorrow. So I asked Thomas at Biggs operations where the planes would be landing. That's his answer."

Rutkowski studied the slip for a moment, then handed it back to the controller. "Probably something ordered out of Washington, Frank. I'll check it and let you know. But you're sure right—we can't have planes disappearing into the desert. Not if we're supposed to be running an airtight defense. I'm glad you hollered about it."

The General resumed his walk around the big room. He stopped for a moment to say hello to the Canadian officer who shared the control desk with O'Malley, then descended to the floor level, made the rounds there and left the center.

Half an hour later he was back in his "topside" office— seven miles from the main tunnel portal, back in Colorado Springs. Barney Rutkowski lit a cigar and ran his eyes across the great colored map of the continent which covered the end wall of his office.

He was annoyed. His professional competence was involved in this thing. According to the book, his command was supposed to be informed—well in advance—of every friendly airplane, missile, balloon or miscellaneous object that might make the airspace over the United States its habitat for any period, however brief. Sure, the regulations had been violated now and then. Little private planes were always hopping from one cow-pasture airfield to another without filing flight plans. But twelve big jets—Air Force jets!

And a secret destination. That *really* irritated him. Two years ago he had gone to the mat with General Hardesty, the Air Force Chief of Staff. It made absolutely no sense, Rutkowski argued, to classify a base so highly that NORAD wasn't aware of its existence. How could his command police the skies if planes were flipping across the continent to some secret base, such as that place in northern Alberta where they were doing some kind of satellite research? Hardesty agreed with him, fought the case through the Joint Chiefs, and won. In early January of the previous year a JCS directive specifically stipulated that any installation, whatever its classification, had to be registered with the commanding general of NORAD if it expected to receive or discharge "flying objects" of any kind. Someone was ignoring—or disobeying—that directive now.

The more Rutkowski thought about this New Mexico business the angrier he became. He had a low boiling point, and his instinct was to pick up the command phone and ask Hardesty in Washington just what the hell was going on. But his years in service had taught him that, angry or not, you do better to stay in channels. The thing to do, he decided, was to call Tommy Hastings at Fort Bragg. Strictly speaking, those troop carriers belonged to the Tactical Air Force, and he ought to call them; but he knew Tommy, and liked him, and might learn more from him. He asked his secretary to place the call: "Lieutenant General Thomas R. Hastings, Commander First Airborne Corps, U.S. Army, Fort Bragg, Fayetteville, North Carolina."

Rutkowski stared at the wall map as he waited. When his phone rang, he shifted his cold cigar to the corner of his mouth.

"Tommy? This is Barney Rutkowski. Say, young feller, where the hell are those K-212's out of your place headed for? I'm supposed to keep everything on my board, but those troop carriers of yours are giving my people fits. They all drop out of sight somewhere north of El Paso."

The voice of Lieutenant General Hastings was calm and unruffled. "You got me, Barney. Those babies don't belong to me. They're all Air Force—all yours. All I do is feed and bed down the pilots."

"Oh, I know, Tommy," Rutkowski said. "Don't give me that jurisdictional crap. You sound like a labor leader. You must know what it's all about. After all, they come out of your shop."

"Look, Barney, don't press me on that one, pal. This is a classified maneuver. You've got to go higher up than me for your answers."

"Thanks, buddy," said Rutkowski testily. "Any time I can do you a favor in return, just whistle."

"Barney!" Hastings' tone was wounded.

"Any time, Tommy," said Rutkowski as he hung up.

The NORAD commander stared unhappily at his phone for a moment and then called his C.O.C controller on the direct line.

"Frank," he asked, "did you say those planes were due at that piss-ant base tonight or tomorrow?"

"Originally they had an ETA of 0700 Saturday, sir," said O'Malley, "but we just got a second message from Biggs pushing it up to 2300 tonight."

"Where do you figure the goddam landing strip is, anyhow?"

"It has to be pretty close to El Paso, sir. The planes leave the Biggs frequency about fifty miles east and turn northwest. They keep coming on that heading for a few more minutes before we lose them."

"Thanks, Frank," Rutkowski growled. He was thoroughly

mad now. It galled him to think that a man could wear four stars, hold complete responsibility for the air defense of his country—and still have vital information denied him. The fact that the man was Barney Rutkowski was doubly infuriating.

He didn't bother his secretary for the next call. He got Parker Hardesty himself on the direct Air Force Washington line.

"This is Rutkowski, General," he said. "I got troubles. Some bureaucrat down there figures I can't be trusted with the nation's business."

"Easy, Barney."

Rutkowski could see Hardesty's smooth, unlined face and wavy brown hair. The voice, as always, was serene.

"I mean it," Rutkowski protested. "Some son-of-a-bitch thinks I can run an Air Defense Command without knowing what's in the air."

"How about explaining, Barney?"

"Look, there are about thirty troop carriers coming into some secret base near El Paso tonight, out of Pope Field at Fort Bragg, and we don't get a damn flight plan. What's more, they're blacked out for the last hundred miles."

"Well, now, you don't think they're bandits, do you?"

"Oh, hell, General, that's not the point," said Rutkowski wearily. "Either we run this show by the book or we don't."

Hardesty sought to soothe.

"Of course we go by the book, Barney, but I wouldn't worry about this operation. You know they're friendlies. You know they come from Fort Bragg. If I were you, I'd just swallow those last few miles and forget it."

"Do you know what the hell this desert base is all about?"

Hardesty was silent for a moment. Then he answered in even, careful words.

"I think we'd better just cut it off there, Barney. We all know there are certain levels of classification. We don't like them, perhaps, but we learn to live with them."

"You mean I'm not supposed to know?"

"I didn't say that."

"Well, you meant it, General. If that's the policy, it stinks. I can't do a job for you in the dark."

"I'm sorry, Barney." Hardesty was closing the conversation.

"Okay," Rutkowski said. "Good-by."

By now he was seething, and he squashed his cigar butt in the ashtray with an angry stab. He felt hot, although the thermometer outside his window showed only 67 degrees; he jerked off his jacket and loosened his collar. Hardesty, who got his fourth star only a couple of months ahead of him, was treating him like some kid reserve officer. Here he sat with the third most important command in the Air Force, and Washington was short-circuiting him. He wondered if Ted Daniel, the SAC commander over at Omaha, knew about this base or those flights. He thought of calling Daniel, but decided against it a second later. If Daniel knew, that would only make it harder to take.

God damn. Some of those guys around General Scott spent too much time worrying about politics and international affairs and not enough time running the military services. Rutkowski lit another cigar and leaned back in his swivel chair. That was a funny business, Lyman calling him in for those talks Tuesday night and Wednesday morning. And they were funny talks. Why had the President hauled him to Washington instead of just calling him on the phone? And when he got there, Lyman seemed to be talking all around the subject—whatever it was —instead of leveling with him. That wasn't like him.

But anyway he did the President the favor he had asked for and sounded out Admiral Palmer. And now, for Christ's sake, the President had authorized some kind of secret operation— with his NORAD commander deliberately cut off the need-to-know list. That's a hell of a way to treat a guy, especially when it's something essential to his job. That's the thing, he repeated to himself, it's essential to the job.

Well, if the President could call *him* in confidence, why couldn't he call the President? Rutkowski disliked end runs and despised officers who didn't have the guts to speak up to their superiors. But this was different. Lyman had obviously set up some kind of secret exercise and had decided himself who needed to know about it. The President was a civilian, and probably just didn't realize what a mess NORAD would be in if it couldn't keep tabs on traffic. It was dangerous as hell. Dangerous? It might be suicidal.

His mind made up, Rutkowski lifted the receiver of the white phone which connected directly to the White House switchboard. In his two years at NORAD he had never used it. The only times it had rung were on equipment tests. Now the answer was instantaneous.

"White House."

"The President, please," Rutkowski said. That took the heat off. If he had used the code word it would have meant a war emergency. Plain language merely meant "urgent." Even so, it took only a few seconds to get the President on the line.

"What's up, Barney?"

"This is a personal complaint, Mr. President, but I think it's important or I wouldn't bother you. I gathered from what you said the other day you want me to talk frankly."

"I wouldn't want it any other way."

"Okay, Mr. President. Well, here it is: I think you've made a serious military error in setting up this troop carrier exercise without cutting my command in on the security arrangements. And I think you made another one when you put a base with an airstrip out in the desert without letting me know."

There was a pause.

"Could you amplify that a bit, Barney?"

"Yes, sir. In order for NORAD to work, it has to know about every single friendly aircraft or missile or anything else over this continent. You blank us out on just one operation and the whole system is compromised."

"Barney, without taking issue with you on that point, would you mind telling me how you learned about this?"

"Sure. We try to drill it into every duty officer here that he's got to question everything he sees. One of my controllers was watching the first flight Wednesday night. The planes were headed for El Paso, then turned northwest and dropped off our radar screens. He tried to find out about it through channels, and when he couldn't, he took it up with me this noon."

"First flight?" the President said. "Is there another one, you think?"

"Yes, sir, as you probably know. Thirty of the transports were due at this damn classified place at 0700—7 A.M.—tomorrow. Then I learned that it's been moved up to 2300 tonight."

"Eleven o'clock tonight?"

"Yes, sir."

"Hold on a minute, Barney, will you?" The phone seemed to go dead, and Rutkowski guessed the President had placed his hand over the mouthpiece. Perhaps General Scott or some other officer had been conferring with Lyman on the subject when he called. Rutkowski fiddled with his dead cigar in the ashtray and waited. Several minutes went by. Then the President came back on.

"Barney, something very serious has come up. It has critical military aspects and I need your advice. Could you come down here again—right away?"

"Well, yes, I suppose so. Couldn't be handled on the phone, sir?"

"No. I'd have to have you here in person."

"Of course, Mr. President. But what about these troop carriers?"

"Barney, that's part of my problem. When could you come?"

"Mr. President, with driving time to and from the airports, I could be there in three hours. Is that all right?"

"Fine, fine. No, wait a second." Once more the President went off the line, but this time he was back quickly.

"Barney, the speed is less important than the security. Could you fly yourself down? I mean solo?"

"Sure." He chuckled. "I need the flying time anyhow. I can take one of the fighters, but I'll have to refuel once. Give me four hours."

"That's plenty of time. Now, Barney, I want this really private. Don't tell anyone where you're going, please. And when you land at Andrews, make up some personal excuse. You know, say you're going to see a sick sister or somebody somewhere in Maryland. Anywhere but here. Then take a cab and come to the east entrance of the White House. The guard will be expecting you. Can you wear civilian clothes?"

"Yes, sir." Rutkowski was baffled, but the President offered no further explanation.

"Okay, Barney. See you this evening, then."

"Right, Mr. President."

General Rutkowski took his jacket off the back of the chair and absently slid one arm into a sleeve. "Well, I'll be Goddamned," he said, half aloud. He straightened his tie and hurried out the door, whistling tunelessly through his teeth.

Jordan Lyman turned away from the phone and looked toward the three men sitting in his study. He said nothing for a moment. His eyes seemed to be focused on something far beyond them. Ray Clark had never seen his old friend looking so tired, so sad, so remote. Christopher Todd, a tight smile on his face and his eyes triumphant, watched the President closely. Casey, on the other hand, looked away from Lyman's face and concentrated on the bright shaft of the Washington Monument in the sunlight.

A plane droned over the city. A mockingbird flew into the top of the big magnolia tree. Its song, pouring into the room through the open windows, accented the silence inside.

Lyman jammed his hands into his coat pockets and bit his lip. When he spoke, his voice had the weariness of old age.

"I've got to act tonight," he said. "There aren't many hours left."

"We're right with you, Mr. President," said Clark.

"I wish prayer came easily to me," Lyman said. He seemed not to have heard Clark at all. Todd raised his voice as if to break his mood.

"You'll win, Mr. President. You'll come out on top—if we

act with precision and speed."

Lyman's smile was one of tolerance and sympathy. He scuffed the rug gently.

"There won't be any winner tonight, Chris. Let's just hope the country stays calm."

The President shook his head, like a man waking from a deep sleep, and lowered himself into his big chair.

"All right," he said, "let's get down to business."

"As I see it," said Todd briskly, "three steps are called for at the start. First, you call Scott over here and fire him. Second, you send a message to all commands over your signature, announcing the resignation and ordering that no troop movements be made in the next forty-eight hours without your express authority. Third, you send General Rutkowski to that base with orders to close it down immediately."

"Jiggs?" The President looked at Casey.

"I'm worried about that override switch, Mr. President, the one that cuts into the TV network programs," said Casey. "I think someone should carry a letter up to Mount Thunder, from you to General Garlock, stating that no interference with commercial programs is to be permitted until further notice from you."

Lyman thought a moment. "I don't think we need to send Barney back to New Mexico," he said to Todd. "I'd rather have him right here. There are a hundred and one details of command communications procedure he could handle for us. I'm not even sure what they all are."

"That's right," Clark said. "And I'd have Rutkowski order those troop carrier planes to stay on the ground at Fort Bragg —under penalty of court-martial, if he thinks he has to go that far."

"Of course," said the President, "we've got to tell Barney everything. The way he sounded on the phone, I don't think he'll need much persuasion. The facts are too glaring to be ignored by anyone now."

Casey ran a hand over his close-cropped hair. "Mr. President," he said, "I don't like to say anything against a general officer, but you'd be in a lot firmer position if you dismissed General Hardesty too and turned his command over to General Rutkowski. Then he could issue orders with authority."

"I've already decided to do that, Jiggs," Lyman said. "And of course I'll have to announce everything to the country."

"But not tonight, Jordan," cut in Clark. "Save that for tomorrow. Besides, Frank Simon will probably faint dead away when you tell him you've fired Scott."

"Poor Frank," said the President. "I haven't been very good to him this week, have I?"

Casey was still concerned. "Mr. President, if I may say so, I think you'd do better to call General Hastings yourself, down at Fort Bragg, and tell him none of those planes are to leave the ground. I'm not sure he would obey General Rutkowski."

"I thought instant obedience was the lifeblood of the military," said Todd, his voice edged with sarcasm.

Casey flushed. "It is, sir. But the response to command gets kind of shaky when there's a big upheaval at the top all of a sudden. You've got to give each officer a little while to adjust to the change. Otherwise he's not sure who does have the authority. Besides, Hastings is Army and Rutkowski is Air Force. But if it's the President, there's no doubt about it."

"I don't see why we have to worry about that goddam ECOMCON bunch tonight," said Clark. "If Broderick doesn't have any planes, he can't get his people out of there."

"But he does have twelve planes already," Todd pointed out. "You saw them land."

"I think we can take Barney's advice on that one when he gets here," Lyman said. "Obviously, nothing is scheduled out of there until midnight at the earliest."

"If I could suggest one more thing, Mr. President," Casey said.

"Please."

"I think it would be wise if you called each one of the field commanders listed in General Scott's 'Preakness' message. Just tell them that the alert has been canceled and that they are to stand by until further notice."

"That'll jar 'em." Clark said with a grin. "The Commander in Chief canceling an alert that they don't know he knows about and that they aren't supposed to know has even been scheduled."

"I think Casey's right again," Lyman said. "Chris, are you making notes on all this?"

The answer was obvious. Todd, his face wreathed in busy satisfaction, was scribbling on his big yellow pad.

"Well," Lyman said, "we finally come up to what I hoped would never be. I must say I have absolutely no faith that we can succeed. I'm afraid the country may be on the verge of rebellion by Monday. Can you imagine Scott on television?"

"That reminds me," Clark said. "One more thing for your list, Chris. The President has got to call up the head of RBC and get him, as a personal favor, to cancel out MacPherson's time tomorrow."

"That's right," said Lyman. He stood up again and walked over to the windows. Once more he seemed to drop a curtain between himself and the others in the room.

Why, he thought, did this have to happen to me? Even Lincoln had an easier decision—the other side fired first. This thing looks so simple to the others, but it just won't work. Scott will tell the country that the Russians are building a stack of new warheads, and he'll say I failed to protect the country. What's my answer? If I get into a shouting match with him, we might wind up in a war with Russia. If I don't answer him, the House will pass a bill of impeachment. There isn't a man on the Hill who could stop it. And who's the winner then, Mr. Todd?

Lyman's eye ranged across the Ellipse and over the Tidal Basin to Jefferson's columned portico, and he thought: Wasn't it Jefferson who said, "I tremble for my country"? Well, now I know what he was talking about. If we'd got the evidence of this plot in writing, I could have pulled it off, forced Scott out quietly, used the treaty fight as an excuse, and the country would never have known. But this way? This way we have one chance in a thousand of succeeding. Todd and Casey, even

Ray, don't understand that. But they can't. Only the President can, and you're it, Lyman, and there isn't any choice now.

Oh, quit playing wise old man, Jordie, and get on with the job.

He was still standing by the window when a loud rap on the door startled them all. Esther Townsend came in.

"Excuse me, Mr. President," she said, "but there's a man downstairs who insists he has to see you right away. His name is Henry Whitney." The secretary's voice trembled. "He's our consul general in Spain."

Friday, 4 P.M.

Henry Whitney had spent twenty years schooling himself not to show uneasiness or emotion no matter what kind of company he might find himself in. But here he was in the private quarters of the President of the United States, unbidden, uninvited, and out of channels. That was the most unsettling part of it: out of channels. He followed Miss Townsend across the vaulted hall.

"The President is waiting in the Monroe Room," she said, and steered him through a doorway without bothering to knock. "Mr. President, this is Mr. Henry Whitney."

Jordan Lyman came quickly forward, hand outstretched. "Nice to see you, Mr. Whitney."

"How do you do, sir," the consul general replied. He stood awkwardly, conscious of his soiled shirt, his rumpled suit and scuffed shoes. There had been no time to clean up. After a wild drive from La Granja to the Madrid airport, he had flown to New York, hurried across Long Island in a taxi and caught another plane to Washington. There had been just barely time to wash his face and run an electric shaver over it at Dulles Airport.

274

"Is it about Paul—about Girard?" asked Lyman. His voice was eager.

"Yes, sir. It is about Mr. Girard. I'm not sure how to begin, sir. I guess I better just give it to you."

Whitney put his thin attaché case on a chair, snapped the catches open, and took out a bent silver cigarette case.

"Look inside, Mr. President."

Lyman almost snatched the case out of Whitney's hand. He struggled with it and tore a thumbnail trying to open it.

"Here, sir." Whitney produced a little penknife and pried open the catch.

Lyman took out two sheets of folded paper, scorched brown at the edges and along the folds, but otherwise undamaged. He glanced quickly at the first few sentences, then turned to the second page and looked at the bottom.

"Sit down, sit down," he said to Whitney. "I'm awfully sorry. Just let me read this."

Lyman took the papers over to a window, adjusted his glasses and began reading. When he finished he went back over it to reread several passages.

"Have you read this?" he asked Whitney suddenly.

"Yes, sir." Whitney was sitting uncomfortably in a curved-back armchair across the room.

Lyman looked at the foreign service officer with the pleased curiosity of a man studying a stranger who has just done him an unexpected favor. He saw a slightly built man with red hair and thin features. Large blue eyes gave him an air of innocence that seemed incongruous in the light of his presence in the White House at this moment.

"Understand it?" asked Lyman.

"Not altogether, sir. I could only add two and two. But I thought it would be . . . important for you to have it. So I brought it."

"Did you discuss it with anyone?" asked Lyman. "Or show it to anyone? How about the ambassador?"

"No, sir, perhaps I should have, but I did not. No one has seen it except you and me. It seemed to be an eyes-only kind of paper. I'm quite sure the Spanish police at La Granja never thought to look inside. The ambassador doesn't know I've come. I suppose I may have been missed by now."

"Ambassador Lytle knows nothing about this?"

"No, sir," Whitney said. "You see, Mr. President, the police chief at La Granja—that's where the plane crashed—gave me a box of things found in the wreckage. There was precious little, but what there was he turned over to me. I put the box in my car and had dinner. Then, before I went back to the scene to meet the investigators, I decided to see if any of the belongings could be identified as to owner. The cigarette case had no markings on the outside, and when I opened it, I . . . well, I read it, and I thought you ought to have it right away."

Lyman folded the papers, put them carefully back in the silver case and slipped it into his pocket. He pulled a chair up close to Whitney and sat down.

"Mr. Whitney, I have other questions," he said. "But first, about Paul. Was he . . . was there . . . ?"

"No, Mr. President. Very few bodies were even whole, except those in the cockpit. The others were all burned." Then, seeing the look on Lyman's face, he added: "I'm quite sure that it all happened very quickly, sir. On impact."

Lyman looked away toward the window. Strangely, what he saw was Girard on Inauguration Day, his big head looking ridiculous under his rented silk top hat. They had joked about that; Paul had compared himself to the cartoonists' standard personification of prohibition and blue laws. Now he was gone, and Lyman knew how old men feel when they pick up the newspaper in the morning and see their lives flaking away each time they turn to the obituary page.

"He must have had that case in his hand when the plane crashed," Whitney said.

"Yes, he would have been trying to save it," Lyman said, almost to himself. Then, to Whitney: "We were very close, Mr. Whitney."

"I'm sorry, Mr. President."

Lyman forced himself back to questioning.

"So you didn't inform Ambassador Lytle?"

"No, sir." Whitney's blue eyes held Lyman's without blinking and there was no apology in his voice. "After reading the paper, I gave the box with the other stuff to a Trans-Ocean man, and then just drove to Madrid and got on the first plane to the States. I . . . well, I don't even have a clean shirt with me."

Lyman waved away the sartorial reference. "I don't need to tell you that this is the most important paper handed to me by any State Department officer this year. You did the right thing. I don't suppose I need to tell you, either, that you must never mention what you read to anybody."

"I realize that, sir."

"And that you are never to disclose, or even hint at, its existence."

"No, sir."

"I emphasize the word 'never.' "

"Yes, sir."

"I have your word on that, Mr. Whitney?"

"Absolutely, sir."

Lyman spoke slowly. "Nothing like this"—he tapped his pocket—"has ever happened in this country. Needless to say, I don't want it to happen, but just as important, I don't want anyone ever to think that it might have happened. Thanks to you, I can now hope to deal with this privately."

"I understand, sir."

"Good." Lyman smiled. "Mr. Whitney, I think you have something of a future in your profession."

"Thank you, Mr. President. I hope so."

Whitney stood up, sensing that the President had neared the end of his questions. Lyman searched the diplomat's thin features for a clue to his reactions to this strange conversation, but found none. He merely stood politely, awaiting the President's next move.

"Now, you go clear yourself with the department. Make up

any story you want to, and if they give you any trouble, just call Miss Townsend. She's a wonder at helping people. By the way, how did you get to her?"

"Well, to be honest, sir, the only names I knew in the White House—besides yours, of course—were Frank Simon and Esther Townsend. Under the circumstances, I thought I ought to talk to Miss Townsend. It took quite a while to get through to her."

"Good man. You go get some sleep now and forget all about it."

"Yes, sir. Is that all, sir?"

"That's all, yes. Except, again, thank you."

Lyman escorted Whitney to the elevator, waited until he started down, then walked swiftly back to the study. He threw open the door.

"Break out the Scotch!" His voice was suddenly triumphant. "Drinks are on the house!"

Todd stared at him, for once stripped of his poise. "My God! Did he bring it?"

Lyman pulled the case from his pocket and held it up.

"All there," he said. A real smile, the first in four days, spread across his face. "I think we're out of the woods, thanks to Brother Whitney"—he looked at the case again, then added gently—"and Paul."

"Mr. President," said Clark, shaking his head, "you're nothing but a goddam luckpot."

"Does it say everything you need?" asked Casey anxiously. "The paper, I mean?"

"This is the damnedest thing I ever read," Lyman said. "Let's just say it's enough to get a resignation from Scott."

Lyman wanted to take Ray Clark next door into the Monroe Room and go over the memorandum, sentence by sentence. But protocol—and Todd's presence—said the Secretary of the Treasury had to see it first.

"Chris, read through it," the President said. "Then I want the others to take a good look at it too."

The silver case opened more easily this time. The President

extracted the papers and handed them to Todd. As the Secretary read, Lyman gestured to the others, offering drinks. Clark shook his head. Todd, deep in the memo, picked up his glass without looking at it. The President touched his own glass to Casey's and smiled at the Marine.

Todd read it through twice, slowly.

"I agree, Mr. President," he said. "This is indeed the Goddamnedest thing I ever read. It tells quite a lot about Barnswell, too. He's slippery, all right. I'm glad we didn't call him."

Clark also read the papers while the others remained silent. But when it was Casey's turn, he shook his head.

"Sir, if you don't mind, I'd just as soon not. I take it there's enough there to meet your needs, and I don't think I need to see it all. In case anybody ever asks me, I'd rather say I haven't any idea."

Lyman grinned. "Jiggs, as that script writer said to you in New York the other day, you're kind of neutral."

"Sir, I'm still a Marine. And if any guy sticks his neck out farther than I already have, he'll be a giraffe."

For a few minutes the atmosphere of the room, which had been leaden for so long, lightened as the four men relaxed. Clark offered another Georgia political story. Lyman recalled the time, during his campaign for governor of Ohio, when he received a call from one of his opponent's advisers by mistake and poured forth counsel which thoroughly confused the opposition. Even Todd let down and told how his sloop once lost the Bermuda race because some pranksters bribed a Newport lady of easy virtue to stow away.

But Todd also brought the group back to reality with a law-school definition of "enthusiast": "One who believes without proof—and whose proof nobody will believe."

"The question is," he said, "what do we enthusiasts do now?"

"I've decided that, Chris," said Lyman without hesitation. "I'm going to call Scott tonight and tell him I've decided to go to Mount Thunder after all. I'll get him over here to give me a briefing. Then we'll have a little talk and I'll get his resignation."

"Sounds too easy," Todd said doubtfully. "How are you going to do it?"

"I intend to confront him with ECOMCON, with holding Ray a prisoner, with kidnaping Henderson, with sending out a fake message that actually was a code for a military take-over—the whole ball of wax."

Todd and Clark objected simultaneously.

"How about the tax return?" asked Todd.

"You mean you aren't going to use the Girard paper?" said Clark.

"Miss Segnier's tax return is out," Lyman answered. "I said that before, and I meant it. That's Scott's private business."

He tapped his glass on the arm of his chair and spoke almost as though to himself. "As for that memorandum, the less said about it the better. If I use Paul's report, Scott will know we have it, and it would be that much harder to keep it secret over the long run.

"We've still got a long way to go on the treaty, one hell of a long way, and I don't want to muddy it up with this. There are enough problems already without tossing in a military coup too. And even if there weren't, I can't afford to let that kind of poison get around."

The president paused and stared at Clark before continuing.

"Look, I hope the people of this country feel the way I do— that what is outlined in that paper is unthinkable here. Ray, you know how I feel about politicians who don't tell the truth. But I promise you right now that I'll lie about this one without the slightest hesitation if I have to. I think it's that important that the public never even suspects this kind of thing was attempted."

"Then why, for God's sake, all this fuss about getting the memorandum?" Clark asked. "If you aren't going to use it, why are we all as happy as goats in a junk yard?"

Lyman smiled. "Because it's insurance, Ray. Because I'm going to feel a whole lot better with it in my pocket."

"Suppose he denies everything?" asked Todd. "Or claims he had nothing to do with it?"

"I'll face that when I get to it," said Lyman stubbornly.

"If you can pull it off your way, you're a miracle man," Clark said dubiously. "Frankly, I think we ought to have something a little stronger in reserve."

"We will," Lyman said. "For one thing, Barney Rutkowski is going to keep those troop-carrier planes on the ground at Fort Bragg. And I'm going to put out that all-service message canceling a scheduled alert."

The phone rang. Lyman answered.

"Okay, Art," he said after listening a moment. "Come on in." To the others, he explained:

"Corwin says Prentice, Riley and Hardesty just left Quarters Six. They've been with Scott all afternoon."

Todd banged a fist into the open palm of his other hand. "I wish we had it on tape. They know that we know now. I wonder what I'd do in Scott's position?"

Casey frowned professionally for a moment. "That's not so hard," he said. "As long as he's got control of the all-service radio and the override switch for the TV networks, he can afford to wait. He thinks his troops are going to move tonight, and he probably figures he has the President blocked."

"Say, cousin," drawled Clark, "next time I decide to take over this house, I want you on my team."

"Any time, Senator." Casey was beginning to feel a bit lightheaded. Lyman's new confidence was contagious.

"Unless I overestimate the man," Todd said, "he has studied President Lyman's character and has decided the President will not oppose him with an open move—and he thinks he's got it fixed so we can't move otherwise."

"I'll buy that if you include the damn Gallup Poll," offered Clark. "I think he might figure that anybody with only 29 per cent of the country back of him isn't a helluva lot of opposition."

"Go right ahead, gentlemen," Lyman said cheerfully. "Just pretend I'm not in the room."

Todd turned to him, his face serious. "Are you still going to tell Rutkowski what's up?"

"I think I'll have to," Lyman said. "I think he's already figured most of it out."

The President picked up his phone.

"Esther," he said, "please get me General Scott. I believe he's at his quarters. Fort Myer." He put his hand over the mouthpiece. "Ray, get on that other extension. I want you to listen."

The call was put through in less than a minute.

"General, this is the President." Lyman began briskly. "I've changed my mind again. I've decided to stick around tomorrow and do my duty instead of going fishing."

"Fine, fine, Mr. President," said Scott. "I'm glad you decided that."

"I thought you would be," said Lyman, measuring his words. "I thought it would make things smoother all around. And I decided I'd better keep in close touch right at this particular time."

"Yes, sir."

"Now, so I'll know enough to make it useful, I think I ought to have a rundown of the current force dispositions both here and overseas before we go up to the mountain."

"That's a good idea, sir. I'll have one of the Joint Staff officers from the war room over there at your convenience in the morning."

"If you don't mind, General, I'd rather have you take me through it yourself."

"Well, sir, I had planned to go up a little early tomorrow, you know, just to get on the ground . . ."

"No, no," Lyman said. "I mean tonight."

"Oh. Tonight. I see."

"Yes, tonight. If you don't mind, I'd like you to come here, General. Would, say, eight o'clock suit you?"

"Well . . . yes, sir. That would be fine."

"Good," said Lyman. "Then I'll expect you at eight. In the upstairs study. Just have your man park in the back driveway and come on up."

"All right, Mr. President. I'll be there."

Lyman hung up. Clark, dropping his phone in its cradle, shook his head.

"What do you think, Ray?" Lyman asked.

"How the hell could you tell from that voice?" said Clark. "That fellow doesn't scare easy, that's for sure."

Lyman looked at his wrist watch, then at Todd and Casey.

"It's five-fifteen now," he said. "I'd like you both back here at seven-thirty. Ray and I'll stay here and meet Barney when he arrives."

The President saw the two men out at the study door, then sank into the big yellow-covered armchair, undid his shoelaces and kicked the shoes off.

Clark looked at Lyman's unshod feet and shook his head dolefully. "Thank God, no photographer got a shot of those during the campaign, or the gag men would have been asking whether you expected to fill Ed Frazier's shoes—or surround them."

Lyman grinned, but then spoke seriously. "Ray, I'm proud of you out there in New Mexico, pouring two fifths down the drain."

Clark grunted. "Close call, Jordie. I killed half a pint on the flight out to El Paso. Oh, well. If I was a saint I wouldn't be mixed up in anything as crummy as this."

Lyman leaned forward and put his elbows on his knees. Twirling his glasses in one hand, he began ruminating out loud about the reported Russian duplicity in opening a new Z-4 assembly plant at Yakutsk.

"You know, it isn't just that it lessens the chances of peace," he said. "It's that Feemerov can't imagine how much it lessens them. Look what it does for Scott and his case. General Scott, the American military idol—and the man who said all along he would never have agreed to any kind of disarmament treaty."

"Feemerov's word is worth about as much as Khrushchev's was," said Clark in disgust. "To think that I toasted the bastard in his own vodka in Vienna. The guy must be nuts."

"No, I don't think so," Lyman said. "I wouldn't have signed

anything with him if I thought that. It's just that treachery has been a way of life in Russian politics for five hundred years, and they can't break the habit in foreign relations."

"Any word from Moscow yet?"

"No, but I'm not worried about it. At least not the first part. I'm pretty sure he'll agree to a meeting. The visit to Yakutsk is another matter."

"You think your plan will work?"

"I don't know, Ray. Who can tell? All I can do is try," Lyman said. "But, God, this will be dynamite in Scott's hands, whether or not he resigns. I just can't let him tell the country about it."

They talked at length about the confrontation with Scott. Clark funneled suggestions to Lyman and the President's mind sorted, filed or discarded them. They were still deep in analysis of Scott's probable reactions when Esther called to say that General Rutkowski had arrived.

"Send him up," Lyman said, reaching for his shoes.

In civilian clothes Rutkowski looked more like an off-duty bartender than a four-star general. He wore a sports shirt buttoned at the collar and a suit jacket, but no tie. His heavy-jowled face, blond hair and pudgy body made him seem no match for the trim, handsome Scott. But his first words dispelled any illusions of flabbiness: he spoke with the authority of the command post.

"Mr. President, I should get portal-to-portal pay. I made it in three hours and seventeen minutes."

Lyman put out his hand. "Barney, you know Senator Raymond Clark of Georgia, don't you?"

"Sure," said Rutkowski. "I spend too much of my life either before his committee or somebody else's."

"Look, Barney, I know you like straight talk," Lyman said. "The senator was held prisoner for about thirty-six hours at that classified base you were worrying about in New Mexico."

"What?" Rutkowski was incredulous. His match went out

on the way to the tip of his cigar, and he had to strike another one.

"Also," Lyman added, "that base was started months ago—but I never knew it until Monday night."

The President went on to sketch the whole affair, skipping some details but leaving in everything the NORAD commander would need to make his own judgment. When Lyman finished, Rutkowski was folded in a haze of cigar smoke. He said nothing.

"If I nominated you for chief of staff of the Air Force tonight, assuming I get Hardesty's resignation, what could you do to stop this thing?" Lyman asked.

"Well, one thing I sure could do, Mr. President, is stop those planes from leaving Pope." Rutkowski looked at his watch. "If they've got an ETA in New Mexico at 2300 mountain time, that means they'll be leaving Pope about the same time by Eastern Daylight."

"You mean eleven our time?" Lyman asked.

"Yes, sir." Rutkowski grinned. "That's slicing the salami pretty thin for you, I know. But don't worry. It'll take them another hour to load in New Mexico, at least, even if they get in there."

"Would you take the job?" Lyman asked.

Rutkowski smiled again. "I take any orders the Commander in Chief gives me. It's strictly no sweat, Mr. President. If you have to fire Scott and Hardesty, and you make me chief of staff, we'll shut things down tight in half an hour."

"But apparently there's only one telephone line out of Site Y, connecting with some private switchboard in Scott's office —or somewhere else around the Pentagon."

"You leave all that to me," Rutkowski said. "Just give me a couple of guys with good legs to run errands around midnight."

Clark looked at the General with a puzzled air.

"You don't seem surprised, General," he said. "Aren't you a little thrown by this thing?"

"I did a lot of putting two and two together on the way

over here, Senator. People always say it can't happen here, and I'm one of those people. But all of a sudden I figured out I was wrong. Given the right circumstances, it can happen anywhere. And don't quote me in the Senate, but the military has been riding awful high-wide-and-handsome in this country ever since World War II." He showed his teeth once more in his confident grin. "I ought to know, too. I've been doing some of the riding. But that's thirty years—and that's a long time."

Lyman pulled off his glasses again and chewed an earpiece. "You know, although I never thought about it from that angle, it's true. We never had so much military for so long before. But the idea still staggers me, Barney."

Rutkowski lifted his hands as if to say that he had no further answer. "Maybe my—pardon the expression—my boss, General Scott, will explain it all tonight."

"I wish he could," said Lyman unhappily. "I wish he could."

The President asked Clark to wait, then took Rutkowski to the third floor and showed him to a guest suite. He called the kitchen, ordered dinner for the General, and told him to relax until 7:30.

When he returned to the study, Esther Townsend was standing in the fading light with Clark.

"Mr. President, there's one thing you have to do right now," she said, holding out some papers. "Tonight's the deadline for you to act on that Social Security bill."

Lyman took the documents and riffled absently through them, trying to force himself back to routine.

"I never did talk to Tom Burton, did I?" he mused. Then, more crisply, he asked Esther, "What about the Budget Bureau?"

"Their report's in there, Mr. President. They raise some questions about interpretation and administration of the new sections, but they recommend approval."

"All right," Lyman said, sitting down and spreading the papers out. "They can work that out with Tom and his people." He scribbled his name on the bill. Esther scooped up the papers and disappeared.

"Ray, it's going to be a long evening," Lyman said. "Let's get a quick swim in before we eat."

"You're on, Jordie."

A few minutes later, the two old friends were cavorting in the basement pool that Franklin Roosevelt had installed to exercise his crippled legs. Clark spouted like a whale, swam underwater and demonstrated what he called "the Lyman crawl"—a mere flutter of the hands on the surface, but a powerful kick underwater. The President, sticking to a more sedate breast stroke, swam methodically up and down. They wound up, breathing hard, hanging on the drain trough at the shallow end of the little pool.

"Listen, Ray, I want you next door in the Monroe Room when I talk to Scott. I may need some help."

"Jordie," said Clark, "you know I'm always right next door."

Friday, 8 P.M.

The President reviewed the arrangements again. On the coffee table, behind the cigar box and out of sight from the chair in which General Scott would sit, was a slip of paper with twenty numbered items written on it in Chris Todd's small, precise hand. In Lyman's coat pocket was the silver cigarette case. Inside it were the two sheets of paper. In a drawer of the writing desk, over against the wall, lay the Segnier tax return. Todd had insisted on leaving it there despite the President's continued refusal even to consider using it.

Lyman stood at the window and waited. The evening was serene, the fountain playing steadily on the south lawn, the traffic thinned out and leisurely. The city's downtown streets were quiet in the twilight pause between day and night. The Irish setter Trimmer, exiled for this evening from the study, loped across the lawn.

But try as he would Jordan Lyman found it impossible to relax. His shoulders and neck felt tight, and he found it easier to stand than to sit. Although he had eaten some of his dinner and had swallowed two glasses of milk, there was a knot in his stomach. As he looked out across the White House grounds, he saw a black limousine pull up at the southwest entrance, pause while the guard opened the gates, and roll on up the drive. Lyman stepped quickly from the window, picked up a book from the end table and settled himself into his arm-chair. He would at least appear at ease when his visitor arrived, even though he was alone, as he had to be, always and finally, for the showdown.

Lyman's allies had scattered after supper. General Rutkowski and Colonel Casey left in a White House car equipped with a radio-telephone. They were to wait in the Pentagon parking lot until Esther Townsend informed them that General Scott had arrived in the mansion. Then they would go to the Joint Chiefs' war room.

Todd was downstairs in the Cabinet room near a telephone. Without telling the President or the others, he had assembled agents of the Narcotics Bureau and the Alcohol Tax Unit—both under the jurisdiction of the Secretary of the Treasury—in his office across the street from the White House. More than thirty agents, hurriedly called in by their supervisors at Todd's order, milled around the Secretary's reception room, drinking coffee, playing cards, and trying to figure out what was up.

Ray Clark sat in the Monroe Room, separated from the President by only a wall. His feet were propped up on a sofa. He was reading, carefully, an annotated copy of the Constitution of the United States—something he had not done since law school.

Art Corwin had twenty-four Secret Service agents scattered through the White House and around the grounds. He had told them only that the President might decide to leave that night for either Blue Lake or Camp David, and he wanted to be prepared for a quick move in any direction. Corwin himself stood outside the oval study in the second-floor hall. Across from him sat the omnipresent warrant officer, his slim portfolio gripped between his knees. At the west end of the great vaulted hall, where chairs and sofas were grouped to make a family sitting room, sat two senior members of Corwin's White House detail.

General James Mattoon Scott stepped off the elevator at 7:59 P.M. His tan Air Force uniform, four silver stars glinting on each shoulder, clung to his big frame without a wrinkle. Six rows of decorations blazed from his chest. His hair, the gray sprinkling the black like the first snowflakes on a plowed field, was neatly combed. A pleasant smile softened the rugged jaw as he nodded to Corwin and the warrant officer.

"Good evening, gentlemen," he said. Corwin responded politely and opened the study door for the General.

Scott strode purposefully into the room. His smile flashed confidence as he watched Lyman put down his book, stand up and come toward him.

He intends to dominate it from the start, Lyman thought. You've got to be good for this, Jordie. This is the big one.

Lyman gestured toward the couch, then seated himself again in the armchair. They were alone now, under the prim portrait of Euphemia Van Rensselaer. One window was open to the warm May air; through it came the occasional distant sound of passing traffic.

Scott had a map folder with him. He laid it on the coffee table and started to undo the strap holding the covers with their TOP SECRET stamps.

"Don't bother about that, General," said Lyman. "We don't need it tonight. We aren't going to have an alert tomorrow."

Scott straightened and stared at Lyman. His face was without expression. Lyman saw no surprise, no anger, not even curiosity. Scott's eyes held his and the President knew at once that this would be a long, difficult night.

"I beg your pardon, Mr. President," Scott said. "You wish the alert canceled?"

"I do. I intend to cancel it."

"May I ask why?"

"Certain facts have come to my attention in the past few days, General," said Lyman. His eyes were locked with

Scott's. He forced himself to keep them that way. "I will not waste time by detailing them all now. I will simply say that I want your resignation tonight, and those of Generals Hardesty, Riley and Dieffenbach as well."

The little wrinkles around Scott's eyes tightened. He continued to stare at the President until the silence became a physical fact in the room.

"Either you are joking or you have taken leave of your senses, Mr. President," Scott said in a low voice. "I know of no reason why I should remove my name from the active list voluntarily. Certainly not without a full explanation for such a—shall we say unusual?—request."

Lyman dropped his eyes to the little sheet of notebook paper on his side of the cigar box. "I had hoped we could avoid this, General. It seems redundant to tell you what you already know."

"I think that remark is extremely odd, to say the least."

Lyman sighed.

"It has come to my attention, General," he said, "that you have, without my authority, used substantial sums from the Joint Chiefs' contingency fund to establish a base and to train a special unit of troops whose purpose and even whose existence has been kept secret from me—and from responsible officials of the Bureau of the Budget and members of Congress. This is in clear violation of the statutes."

"Just what unit are you referring to, Mr. President?"

"I believe its designation is ECOMCON. I take it that stands for Emergency Communications Control."

Scott smiled easily and settled back on the couch. He spoke almost soothingly, as he might to a frightened child.

"I'm afraid your memory fails you, Mr. President. You gave me verbal authorization for both the base and the unit. As I recall it, there were a number of items that we covered that day, and perhaps you didn't pay too much attention to this. I guess I just assumed that you would inform the Director of the Budget."

"What was the date of that meeting, General?" Lyman had

to struggle to hide his anger, but he kept his voice as even as Scott's.

"I can't recall exactly, but it was in your office downstairs, some time last fall. Late November, I believe."

"You have a record of the date and subject?"

"Oh, certainly. In my office. If you care to make a point of it, I can drive over to the Pentagon right now and get it."

"That will not be necessary, General."

"Well," said Scott casually, "it's really not important anyway. My aide, Colonel Murdock, sat in on the meeting and can substantiate my memorandum of the date and discussion."

Oh, so that's how it is, thought Lyman. There's a witness to corroborate your statements. He wondered if anything he said tonight would catch Scott by surprise.

"As for not informing Congress," Scott continued, "this matter of protecting communications from Soviet sabotage seemed to us so sensitive that we thought it wiser not to discuss it with the committees."

"But you did discuss it with Senator Prentice, General," Lyman shot back. "In fact, you seem to have discussed quite a number of things with him this week, in quite a few places."

The statement had small effect on Scott. He merely hunched himself a bit closer to the table and put his hands on it. Lyman watched his fingers on the edge of the table, the tips going white with the pressure, as though Scott were trying to lock the tabletop with his hands.

"Senator Prentice knows nothing about ECOMCON," the General said.

"When Senator Raymond Clark was at the base Wednesday," Lyman said, "he talked with Prentice on the telephone. He reports that Prentice told him the Armed Services Committee knew all about it."

Scott shrugged. "I didn't know Senator Clark had visited the base. As for differences between members of Congress, I must say I learned long ago not to get involved in that kind of thing."

Lyman would not drop the subject. "Perhaps you can explain why you selected a commanding officer for that unit who is openly contemptuous of civilian authority and who has made statements which come close to violation of the sedition laws?"

"I never in my life discussed an officer's political views with him." Scott's voice had an indignant ring. "The officer in question has an excellent combat record and is one of the most competent officers in the Signal Corps."

Lyman persisted. "He also has an interesting travel record. What was Colonel Broderick doing last night in an outboard motorboat, cruising around my island at Blue Lake, Maine?"

"That's fantastic, Mr. President." Scott looked at Lyman with an odd expression, as though doubting his own ears—or the President's sanity. "Colonel Broderick left Site Y yesterday to come to Washington to confer with me."

"The description given by my caretaker fits Colonel Broderick quite closely. Black brows, swarthy complexion, tough face and all."

"Thousands of men could be mistaken for Broderick."

"And the scar on his right cheek?" asked Lyman.

"Didn't you say this was at night, Mr. President? I'd say your man can't see very well in the dark."

"It was not yet dark, General," said Lyman flatly.

"Mistaken identity, obviously," said Scott. He offered nothing more.

"Well, General, perhaps you also have an explanation for the detention at Site Y of Senator Clark?"

"I would say such a charge is somewhat reckless, Mr. President. As I understand it, the senator from Georgia has some . . . ah . . . personal problems and might be inclined to imagine things under certain circumstances."

Lyman flared. "I think you'd better withdraw that statement, General. Ray had nothing to drink at your base—no thanks to Broderick, who put two bottles of whisky in his room."

Scott's voice was emotionless but hard. "I think that if Senator Clark told you any such story, the fantasy of it is plain on its face. I can't imagine any court in the land accepting that kind of testimony."

"Are you implying that there is going to be some kind of trial?"

"Of course not, Mr. President." There was a patronizing overtone in Scott's voice. "I just think that here again we have Clark's word against Colonel Broderick's, and, frankly, we have no evidence that Clark was ever on the base."

"You deny that Senator Clark was there?"

"I don't deny it or affirm it. I don't know one way or the other. I do know that Broderick didn't mention it to me last night."

Lyman glanced at his list again.

"Now, General, there is the matter of the arrest and present detention in the Fort Myer stockade of Colonel William Henderson," the President said.

"You mean the deputy commander at Site Y?"

"You know very well whom I mean, General."

"This case I do happen to be familiar with," Scott said. "Colonel Broderick informed me this noon that Colonel Henderson was apprehended for deserting his post of duty and for striking an enlisted man with the barrel of the man's rifle."

"And did Broderick tell you where Henderson was picked up?"

"The military police picked him up on a downtown street here in Washington, as I understand it."

Lyman shook his head in impatience. "General, Colonel Henderson was kidnaped. He was taken forcibly from Senator Clark's home in Georgetown."

Scott threw back his head and laughed.

"Mr. President, let's get back to earth. I don't know who's providing your information, but he has a vivid imagination."

"We will go to another subject," said Lyman coldly.

"Before we do, Mr. President, would you mind if I had one of those excellent cigars from your box?"

Lyman had no intention of letting the General relax in a cloud of easy cigar smoke.

"I'm sorry," he lied, "but Esther must have forgotten to fill it today. I looked just before you came in."

"Well, then." Scott unbuttoned his jacket and reached into a shirt pocket. "I trust you don't mind if I have one of my own."

"Not at all." Lyman felt that he had been outmaneuvered.

Scott lit the cigar and watched reflectively as the first few puffs of smoke rose toward the ceiling. He settled back on the couch and smiled.

"There was something else, Mr. President?"

Boy, this is a tough customer, Lyman thought. The muscles between his shoulder blades hurt, and he could feel the strain in his face. He hoped he looked half as confident to Scott as the General did to him.

"Indeed there is," Lyman said. "I would like an explanation of your wagering activities, in particular your betting pool on the Preakness."

"Oh, come now, Mr. President. Certainly you do not intend to try to pillory me for making a bet?"

"I would like an explanation, General."

"There's really nothing to explain," Scott replied. "Oh, I know all-service radio isn't supposed to be used for personal traffic of that kind. But the chairman traditionally has been granted small courtesies."

"I understand you transferred a young naval officer who talked about the betting messages."

"Cryptographic officers are not supposed to talk about any messages," Scott snapped. "And I see that Colonel Casey has been talking about my personal affairs as well. Frankly, Mr. President, I am surprised and disappointed."

"How do you know I've been talking to Colonel Casey?" Lyman's voice was sharp.

"I didn't say you had. I merely said Colonel Casey had talked to someone. He came to you, then?"

"If you don't mind, General," Lyman said, "I'll ask the questions. Why did you excuse Casey from his work for four days this week?"

"He was tired."

"And why did Admiral Barnswell refuse to join the wagering pool?"

"I really have no idea, Mr. President," said Scott. "I guess some men just don't like to gamble. I love it." He was expansive. "It's one of my many failings."

Lyman eyed Scott closely. There was no indication that he knew of Girard's trip or that he had talked to Barnswell. The President waited a moment, hoping the General would say something more that might offer a clue on the point, but when Scott spoke after several contemplative puffs on his cigar his voice was even and natural.

"If I might ask just one question, Mr. President, what is the purpose of these inquiries about my little Preakness pool? Surely you're not indicating that I am being asked to resign because I sent a personal message?"

"Of course not, General," Lyman said. "Now, on another point. Will you please explain why you and the Joint Chiefs scheduled the alert for a day when Congress will be in recess and its members scattered all over the country?"

"No better way to throw the field commanders off guard," Scott said quickly. "If you recall, you yourself said as much when you approved the date."

"Was Admiral Palmer present at the meeting when the time was fixed?"

"No-o." For the first time, Scott seemed just a trifle taken aback. "No, he wasn't."

"His deputy?"

"No, as I recall," said Scott slowly, "the Navy was absent that day."

"And there have been several other recent meetings when neither Admiral Palmer nor his deputy was present?"

"Well, yes. Now that you mention it, there have been."

"Isn't that highly unusual?"

"Unusual, perhaps, but not highly. The Navy just couldn't make it the last few times. Admiral Palmer, as I understand it, has been preoccupied with some special problems in his missile cruisers lately."

"That's not what Admiral Palmer says, General. He was not notified of certain meetings of the Joint Chiefs. That is certainly highly unusual."

"I gather that Admiral Palmer, as well as Colonel Casey, has been voicing complaints. The Navy and Marines seem to be doing some talking out of channels—from lieutenants junior grade clear up to flag rank."

Lyman offered no response to this, but went to the next point on his list. Scott waited tranquilly.

"You and General Riley made a visit to General Garlock's home Tuesday night," Lyman said.

"Yes, we did. We wanted to make sure everything was in shape at Mount Thunder for the alert."

"And to make arrangements for bivouacking some special troops there Saturday?"

"I take it I have been followed all week." Scott ignored Lyman's question.

"I'd like an answer, General."

"First I'd like to know why the President of the United States feels it necessary to follow the chairman of the Joint Chiefs of Staff like a common criminal," Scott said.

"You will answer my question, General."

"Not until you answer mine, Mr. President."

Scott stood up, towering above the seated President. He held his cigar between thumb and forefinger and pointed it accusingly at Lyman.

"I don't propose to stay in this room and be questioned any further." Command authority rang out like a chisel on granite. "I will not resign and I will answer no more questions. But I intend to say a few things, Mr. President."

Lyman felt inadequate and puny sitting under this tall, imposing officer who held a cigar pointed at him like a weapon. The President stood up and took a step forward, putting the two men on more equal physical terms as they stood facing each other, no more than two feet apart. Scott kept on talking.

"The information put together yesterday morning by the National Indications Center, and reported to both of us by Mr. Lieberman, substantiates all the misgivings of the Joint Chiefs," he said. "We told you time and time again that the Russians would never adhere to the spirit of the treaty. And we emphasized until we were blue in the face that it was folly to sign a document which left a clear loophole—namely, that one country or the other could assemble warheads in one place as fast as it took them apart in another under the eyes of the neutral inspectors. The United States, of course, would never do that. But the Russians would—and they are doing precisely that."

"I know all that as well as you do, General." Lyman began to feel old and tired again, as weary as he had been all week until Henry Whitney's sudden appearance that afternoon.

"I must say further, Mr. President, that it borders on criminal negligence not to take some immediate action. If you persist in that path, I shall have no recourse as a patriotic American but to go to the country with the facts."

"You refuse to resign, but you would do something that would assure your removal," Lyman commented. Scott said nothing.

"Well," the President went on defiantly, "I have moved. But something just as important to this country—perhaps more important—has to be settled first."

"Meaning what?"

"I think you know, General."

"I have no more idea of what you mean by that than I have concerning a dozen other things you have said tonight."

Lyman stared quizzically at Scott. "General," he asked, "what would you have done with Saul Lieberman's information if you had been President yesterday?"

"I said I would answer no more questions."

"This has nothing to do with what we were talking about before," Lyman said. "Frankly, I'm curious. A President needs all the help he can get, and you're a resourceful thinker, General—to put it mildly."

"I would never have signed that treaty."

"I know that. But suppose you became President after one was signed and ratified. How would you have responded yesterday?"

Scott had turned as if to go to the door, but now he paused and looked at the President, apparently searching Lyman's face for a clue to his sincerity. The General gripped his right fist with the palm and fingers of his left hand. Obviously intrigued with the problem, he frowned in concentration.

"Are you serious, Mr. President?"

"I have never been more serious, General."

"Well, then." Scott's grip on his fist tightened. Clearly all the other arguments of the evening were erased from his mind for the moment. He stood in silence.

"First," he said slowly, "I would have contacted the Russians and demanded an immediate meeting with Feemerov."

Lyman smiled for the first time in half an hour. When he had conceived the idea of a confrontation with the Soviet Premier, the thought had taken almost precisely the same number of seconds to form in his mind.

"It may surprise you, General," he said, "but I've already done that. The Secretary of State, at my request, has ordered our embassy in Moscow to set up a session with Feemerov. I propose to meet him at the earliest opportunity next week."

Scott's face showed genuine surprise, but he shook his head.

"I'm not sure I can believe that, Mr. President," he said.

"There's the phone," said Lyman, pointing to it. "You are welcome to call the Secretary and check it with him if you like."

Scott shrugged off the suggestion in the manner of one gentleman willing to take the word of another. "And what do you plan to do when you meet him?" he asked.

"No, General," Lyman said, "I'm the one who needs the advice, remember? What would *you* do at such a meeting?"

It was apparent that, however distasteful Scott found the

line of inquiry into which Lyman was pushing him, his mind was eager to cope with the problem. The little net of wrinkles around his eyes pulled together.

"My course," he said, "would be simple and direct. I would demand to visit Yakutsk. If the Communist refused, I would go before the United Nations and denounce him as a fraud and a cheat. Then I would start assembling more warheads for the Olympus."

Lyman burst into laughter, surprising himself almost as much as Scott.

"You regard that line of action as funny?" asked Scott.

"Not at all, not at all." Lyman tapered off into chuckles and shook his head. "It's just the irony of the situation, General."

Scott bristled. "I fail to see the humor in it."

"Sit down, General." Lyman, with his awkward gesture, indicated the couch. "I want to tell you something about the office which you apparently intended to seize tomorrow."

"That's a lie."

"Sit down."

Scott hesitated a moment, then seated himself. Curiosity, thought Lyman, is a wonderful thing. The President sat down again in his armchair.

"What struck me as funny," he said, "was that you proposed almost the same steps that I've contemplated myself—at least up to a point. I intend to try to use this Yakutsk business as the lever to force Feemerov to accept a foolproof inspection system—for assembly plants as well as the dismantling sites. Now that we've caught him in the act, we can make him choose between being exposed as a traitor to civilization or letting the inspectors go anywhere in Russia. At any rate, I'm going to try it before I go to the UN or start assembling more Olympus warheads."

Scott said nothing, though his face reflected disbelief.

"So," continued Lyman, "if you were charged with directing the foreign policy of this country you would start out on this thing about the way I'm starting. And I'm sure that if you had my responsibilities you'd make that last try to get really thorough inspection controls, too. So you'd act pretty much as I am going to. And yet you want to dislodge this administration. Doesn't that strike you as—well—somewhat odd, General?"

"I deny the allegation," Scott said angrily. "And I must say most of this conversation seems odd to me."

Lyman crossed his legs in an effort at relaxation and the big feet stuck out like misplaced logs in a woodpile. He felt tense and tired, but he struggled to make himself understood.

"It's really too bad, General. We could have worked so well as a team, with each of us exercising his proper and traditional responsibility. Your answers to my questions show how much alike we think. Actually, you know, there isn't really much that a man with average intelligence can overlook in this job. And there isn't much that another man could do differently—no matter what the cut of his clothes."

"Is that intended as some kind of slur on my uniform?"

"Oh, good God, no," Lyman said. "No, I'm just trying to say that the great problems of this office, so many of them really insoluble, are not susceptible to superior handling by —let's say—the military rather than the civilian. The problems, General, remain the same."

"Some men act. Others talk," Scott snapped.

Lyman shook his head sadly. "General, you have a real blind spot. Can't you see how close together we are on this thing? Can't you now, really?"

"Frankly, Mr. President, I think you've lost touch with reality. And I think this kind of rambling self-analysis proves it."

Scott's words came out harshly. Fatigue again engulfed Lyman. I can't get through to this man, he thought, I just can't get through. He felt a sudden knot in his stomach, and he could see a mist drifting—years ago—across a Korean ridge.

"Listen, Mr. President." Scott spoke softly, but his voice seemed to hammer at Lyman. "You have lost the respect of the country. Your policies have brought us to the edge of disaster. Business does not trust you. Labor flaunts its disdain for you with those missile strikes. Military morale has sunk to the lowest point in thirty years, thanks to your stubborn refusal to provide even decent minimum compensation for service to the nation. Your treaty was the act of a naïve boy."

"That's ugly talk, General." Lyman's voice seemed weak by contrast.

"Those are facts," said Scott. "The public has no faith in you. The Gallup Poll may not be exactly accurate, but it's pretty close. Unless the country is rallied by a voice of authority and discipline, it can be lost in a month."

"And that voice is yours, General?" The way Lyman said it, the question was almost a statement of fact.

"I didn't say that," Scott replied. "But certainly you cannot expect me to pretend that I would act as you would, and so assume at least partial responsibility for the bankruptcy of the Lyman administration."

This man is immovable, thought Lyman. I simply cannot make him understand. Has my administration failed in the same way to explain itself to the country? Is that the meaning of what he's saying? Is he right in saying the time for talk is past? Doesn't anyone understand what's at stake here?

He felt faint, and the mist rose again in the mind's eye, drifting across the rugged, treeless ridges.

I've got to talk to Ray, he thought. Yes, Ray. Where is he? I've got to see him. Why, he's right next door, in the Monroe Room. I can just walk in there and talk to him. He'll know what to do.

Lyman sat still, staring at Scott, but his mind swung erratically. He ought to get into the Monroe Room, get to Ray, get his help, get the strength he could always draw from his friend. Hadn't Ray saved his life—and his pride, his courage, his self-respect—on the ridge in Korea? Couldn't he do it once more, just once more, to help him get over this ridge too? He felt, and wanted to feel again, Clark's open hand across his face, driving strength back into him.

But that was twenty years ago, Jordie, and you weren't the

President of the United States then. It isn't going to do any good to get slapped now. You may lose this without someone else's help, but you can only win it that way too. You've got all you need if you know how to use it.

As if to reassure himself, Lyman rubbed his hand across the front of his suit coat. He felt the hardness of the object in the pocket inside, and confidence began to flow back into him like a turning tide, floating his spirit. It had come at last to the memorandum. He had been blissfully optimistic to think that he could avoid using it. Chris and Ray had been right.

He had been staring at Scott as he thought it out. The General was sitting as still as he, and his face had not moved as he waited. Now Lyman searched that face again, with his mind as well as his eyes focused on it.

And, finally, he saw something in the face. The complex of tiny wrinkles around the eyes had shifted into a different pattern. No other muscles in the face had moved, but there was a change, a new attitude. What was it? Was it wariness? Concern? Uncertainty?

Uncertainty. Yes. Lyman's mind shouted the word at him. Uncertainty. Why, this man was unsure of himself. He had seemed so sure all evening, but he was not sure now. Maybe that look had been there all along, if only Lyman had had eyes to see it.

The President sat back, almost relaxed now. You know, he thought, this fellow can be taken. He really doesn't have things going for him at all. Lyman let his eyes fall away from Scott. He didn't have to duel him that way. He looked around the room: there were Eisenhower's flags, Kennedy's chair, Monroe's ornate desk. Reminders of the Presidency, of the strength of the office he now held.

He bent himself to business, and the effort lent him added strength.

"General," he said evenly, "I want to read you something." He drew the cigarette case from his pocket.

"I intend to leave right now," Scott said quickly.

"No," the President said. Oh, I saw something, all right, he thought. "No, you sit right there and listen. I'll tell you when you may leave."

Scott watched as Lyman pried open the case and took out the two sheets of scorched paper. He placed them on the table, smoothed them carefully and hitched his glasses closer to his eyes.

"This was saved from the wreckage of the plane in which Paul Girard was killed," he said. "He was on his way home from Gibraltar."

Now Scott could not have gone if Lyman had ordered him out. Curiosity pinned him to the couch. Lyman began to read:

MEMORANDUM FOR THE PRESIDENT

Gibraltar, May 15

The undersigned, who have also initialed each page, agree that this is the substance of a conversation had in Admiral Barnswell's cabin aboard the U.S.S. Eisenhower on this date.

Lyman looked at Scott. The General's face remained impassive, but his eyelids had come down over his eyes.

Late in December, Adm. Barnswell, while on an official trip to Washington, met with General Scott, Chairman, JCS, in his quarters at Fort Myer. Also present were Gen. Riley, Commandant, U.S.M.C., and Gen. Dieffenbach, Chief of Staff, U.S. Army.

There was considerable discussion of the state of the nation, and general agreement that the Lyman administration was losing public confidence and that there was general public dissatisfaction. It was also agreed that the proposed nuclear disarmament treaty would expose the nation to surprise attack. These matters, added to the dangerous loss of morale in the armed forces because of administration refusal to support needed benefits, led all present to the conclusion that the nation faced its most critical time in history.

Gen. Scott said that under such circumstances military commanders should make themselves available, under their oaths to uphold the Constitution, to take whatever steps seemed necessary. It was agreed that if some action should be required, commanders who felt as those present did could be alerted by orders from Gen. Scott.

On 26 February, during an inspection trip to the Mediterranean, Gen. Scott visited Adm. Barnswell aboard this ship. During an extended private talk, Scott said the conditions outlined at the December meeting had further deteriorated. Barnswell agreed that military commanders had a duty to the nation, but asked what Scott proposed to do. Scott said they must act "to uphold the authority of the nation." Barnswell asked if this meant upholding constituted authority, such as the President. Scott said of course, unless such authority had been so undermined or weakened by outside events as to be meaningless. Barnswell told Scott that he was ready as always to do his duty.

On 23-24 April, Adm. Barnswell was again in Washington, and had another talk with Scott. Scott said at this time that should action become necessary Barnswell and others would be informed by a code message in the form of a pool wager on a horse race, the message to include the time for taking necessary action. Agreement to enter the pool in return message would be sufficient acknowledgment.

Adm. Barnswell at this time again sought assurance that such action would not conflict in any way with constituted civilian authority. Scott gave this assurance "subject to conditions existing at the time." Adm. Barnswell then asked what Scott meant by "conditions existing at the time." Scott replied that by this he meant that recent developments indicated that the President might not be fulfilling his responsibility for the national security, and that if this were in fact proven to be the case, it might be necessary for the good of the country to supersede him.

Adm. Barnswell on May 12 received a message from Gen. Scott inviting participation in a pool wager on the Preakness, Saturday, May 18, and advising of a "post time" for the race. After consideration Adm. Barnswell replied "No Bet." By this Adm. Barnswell meant to indicate that he desired more details and assurance that any plans had the approval of the President.

At the time of this conversation, Adm. Barnswell has received no further word from Gen. Scott. Adm. Barnswell is surprised and dismayed to learn, according to the report of Mr. Girard, that no information of the pending action had been transmitted to the

President, and that he therefore had not approved it. Under these circumstances, Adm. Barnswell could not obey any orders that might be forthcoming without the express direction of the President.

> Farley C. Barnswell, Vice Admiral, USN
> 2200Z 15 May
> Paul Girard

"Do you wish to comment?" Lyman asked Scott.

"That thing is a fake."

"A *fake?*" Lyman was incredulous.

"That is what I said, Mr. President."

A flush rose on Lyman's face and he folded his long arms across his chest. "Are you accusing me of forging a document, General?"

"I accuse nobody. I merely say that the events set out on those scraps of paper never occurred. I had no such conversations with Admiral Barnswell. It's a pity Mr. Girard isn't here to tell us the circumstances under which that was written."

Lyman flared. "It's a pity Paul lost his life trying to save his country."

"If that is intended as a reflection on my patriotism, I'll ignore it."

Lyman waved the papers. "Do you deny that this is Admiral Barnswell's signature?"

Scott shrugged. "How would I know? If it's my word against Barnswell's, I have no doubt of the outcome."

"Once again you seem to be hinting at some kind of hearing, General."

"If it should ever come to that, the American people will never believe this story you've cooked up."

"I'll take my chances on that," said Lyman, "even without going into a number of other questions." He pulled the little slip of paper from under the cigar box and read from it.

"There is your statement to the Senate Armed Services Committee that communications did not work properly in the last alert, when in fact they were almost the only thing that did function properly. There is your extended and intimate acquaintance with Harold MacPherson, a figure whose associations are extremely questionable. There is your action in attempting to hide by taking a freight elevator at midnight to visit Senator Prentice at his apartment. There are others, a good many more. But I don't think we need to belabor this. I want your resignation and those of the other three generals on the JCS within the hour."

The uncertainty Lyman had noticed earlier seemed to take hold of Scott more strongly now. His eyes sought out the scorched papers and the list in Lyman's hand, then searched the President's face.

"Perhaps fake was too strong a word," he conceded. "But there is no proof of the authenticity of those papers."

"No, General, I'm afraid that won't wash," Lyman said. "This has been signed by two men, one of whom is still alive. Girard called me to say he had obtained a written statement and was placing it in his cigarette case for safekeeping. A Spanish police officer found the case and turned it over to an American foreign service officer. That officer is in Washington now. He gave it to me this afternoon."

"His name?"

"I am not going to tell you," Lyman said. "But you may be assured that he has read the contents and would so testify. The Spanish police officer could, of course, identify the cigarette case. As for the document itself, there are handwriting experts."

Scott smiled wanly. "Is this at the trial you accuse me of inviting, Mr. President?"

Lyman said nothing. Scott sat motionless. There was no change in his bearing, but his eyes gave him away before he spoke.

"If I submit my resignation, will you destroy that paper?"

Scott was bargaining now. Lyman, who hadn't considered the possibility, thought for several minutes. The only sounds in the room were the breathing of the two men and the intermittent hum of traffic through the open window.

"Yes, I will, General," Lyman said. "Not for the reason you have in mind, but I will. In fact, I think that's the only thing to do with it. I will burn it, in that fireplace, with you watching if you wish, as soon as I have those four resignations in my hands."

Scott stood up. He stared down at the President, and Lyman for a moment had not the least idea whether the General was about to surrender—or stalk from the room. The two men eyed each other. Then Scott spoke quietly.

"May I use your writing desk?"

"Certainly."

Scott straightened his shoulders and stepped briskly to the little walnut desk against the wall. Lyman, holding his knee against the lower drawer to make sure it remained shut, pulled open the top drawer for Scott. The General took out a single sheet of stationery, and under the gold presidential crest he wrote:

17 May

I hereby tender my resignation as Chairman of the Joint Chiefs of Staff of the United States, effective immediately upon its acceptance.

James M. Scott, General USAF

Lyman took the sheet, blew on it to dry the ink, leaned over the desk and scribbled across the bottom:

Above resignation accepted, May 17, 9:39 P.M.
Jordan Lyman

The President picked up the sheet of paper and went to the telephone.

"Esther," he said, "General Scott will be using this phone for a few minutes to call several of his colleagues. Please put through any call he wishes. But first, please connect me with General Rutkowski at the Joint War Room."

Scott, standing in the middle of the study, could not hide his surprise when he heard Rutkowski's name.

"Barney," Lyman said, "this is Jordan Lyman. General

Scott has just tendered his resignation and I have accepted it. Please send out an urgent message to all commands, signed by me as commander in chief, stating that an alert scheduled for tomorrow afternoon has been canceled. And, Barney, order those K-212's to remain at Fort Bragg. If they've left already, get them diverted or turned back in flight. If you have to, put my name on that too."

Lyman hung up and turned to Scott. The General wore a bleak smile. You can't be sure, Lyman thought, but I believe there's actually some reluctant admiration there.

"General, I don't propose that the country ever know the real reason for your resignation," he said. "I don't know whether you appreciate that or not, but that's the way it's going to be."

"You're assigning a reason, then?"

"Yes. Our differences over the treaty. God knows they are real enough. I will make a speech to the country tomorrow, saying that I asked for your resignation and the other three because you insisted on opposing settled national policy on a vital matter after the decision was made final."

"Suppose I say otherwise?"

"You may, of course, say whatever you please. The Constitution remains in force, and so do its guarantees of free speech." Lyman smiled. "But if you mention the real reason, I'll deny it from every soapbox I can climb up on."

Scott drew himself up in front of the President.

"Mr. President, there is no 'real reason,' as you call it. I have done absolutely nothing wrong, or illegal, or seditious, as you have implied. My resignation was forced by a man who has lost his . . . bearings."

"Have it any way you want, General," Lyman replied, "but I must have your word that you will say nothing until I have announced this. Otherwise, I shall be required to keep you in this house through tomorrow."

"You have my word on that," said Scott. "When I speak out, if I do, it will not be until the public is thoroughly familiar with the facts in this matter."

Lyman moved toward the door.

"I'll leave you alone for a while, General. Please tell Riley, Hardesty and Dieffenbach to come to this room at once. They can come in by the back gate as you did. When any one of them is here, call Miss Townsend on the phone. She'll get me."

Lyman stepped out into the hall, closed the door behind him, and gave Corwin an all's-well signal with circled thumb and forefinger. Then he stepped to the door of the Monroe Room. He threw it open and was about to call "Ray!" when he saw that the room was empty.

The President beckoned to Corwin.

"Art, where's Ray? He was supposed to be standing by in here."

"Oh, he hasn't been there in over an hour," said Corwin. "He's down in the Cabinet room with Secretary Todd."

As he rode down in the little elevator, Lyman thought: Ray wasn't there at all in the clutch. What if I had needed him? But I didn't need him. Maybe he knew I wouldn't . . . Lyman felt like whistling as he hurried along the covered passageway past the rose garden to the west wing.

The President stepped into the Cabinet room as his two associates came forward anxiously. Lyman stood there smiling, awkward and angular as always, but obviously in command. He pulled the sheet of stationery from his pocket.

"General Scott has resigned," he said.

Todd's gray eyebrows arched upward, but his look was anything but disapproving. He grasped the President's hand.

"You weathered the point, Mr. President," he said. "The rest is smooth sailing."

Clark feinted a punch off Lyman's jaw and grinned at his old friend. His eyes were serious—and admiring.

"You did it, Jordie," he said. "Nice going, Yankee boy!"

Friday, 11 P.M.

Cleaning up the "sad debris of surrender," as Todd called it, took time. Corwin, Todd, Casey and Rutkowski—the last two hastily recalled from the Pentagon—milled around restlessly in the Monroe Room as President Lyman officiated alone at the stiff and painful business in the oval study.

Hardesty of the Air Force, smooth, outwardly untroubled, came first. Only a single, self-conscious sweep of a hand through his wavy brown hair indicated his concern.

As soon as Hardesty left, Lyman slipped back next door and appointed General Bernard Rutkowski as the new Air Force Chief of Staff. The one-time Polish slum kid from Chicago stood with one hand on the President's boyhood Bible while Secretary Todd swore him in.

Then Rutkowski promptly phoned NORAD headquarters in Colorado, got Colonel O'Malley on the wire, and ordered him to report immediately if the radar screen showed any planes taking off from the secret base in New Mexico.

General Dieffenbach of the Army wrote out his resignation without exchanging a single word with the President. He

311

merely bowed slightly as he left and readjusted the black patch over his bad eye.

When Dieffenbach's signature was on paper, Rutkowski phoned the Army vice chief of staff and requested, in the name of the President, the release of a prisoner named Colonel William Henderson from the Fort Myer stockade. Casey left, with a note from Lyman, to pick up his friend.

Last came General Billy Riley, his jaw as pugnacious as ever and his eyes dark with anger, and then suddenly it was all over. At the door of the Monroe Room, Corwin signaled to the others.

"General Scott is on his way out," he said.

Clark and Todd hurried out of the room together. They caught Scott by the elevator.

"Could I have a word with you, General?" asked Clark.

As he spoke, and Lyman looked on from where he stood in the hall, Todd stepped into the study and went to the little writing desk. He drew a manila envelope from the lower drawer, stuffed it in an inside coat pocket and quickly rejoined Clark and Scott at the elevator. The three rode down together in silence.

Outside the White House, the night was warm. Although clouds hid the moon, a pale diffused light gave form to trees and shrubs. The three men stood under the canopy leading from the ground-floor diplomatic reception room to the curved south driveway.

"General," said Todd, "the President is a statesman and a gentleman."

"The first had escaped my notice," said Scott curtly.

Todd ignored the remark. "But he is, above all, a gentleman. I'm not. I'm a crusty, mean trial lawyer. Senator Clark is a politician. Neither of us cares much for unnecessary amenities."

"I've had enough roundabout conversation for one night, thanks," said Scott. "If you don't mind, I'll just get in my car and leave."

Todd, half a head shorter than Scott, skipped around him to block the sidewalk.

"I don't think you will, General," he said, "until we're finished."

He pulled the manila envelope from his pocket.

"This is this year's federal income tax return," he said, "filed by Miss Millicent Segnier of New York City."

Scott stood still. In the dark under the canopy, they could not read his face. He said only "Yes?"

"I'm not sure whether you're aware of it," Todd said, "but Miss Segnier deducted three thousand and seventy-nine dollars for entertaining the chairman of the Joint Chiefs of Staff last year. When the Internal Revenue Service questioned it, she said she had to entertain you in connection with the apparel and fashions of female military personnel."

"That's interesting—but hardly enlightening," Scott said coldly.

"We have other evidence, a great deal of evidence," said Todd, "indicating conclusively a long and somewhat cordial relationship between yourself and Miss Segnier. The President was too much of a gentleman to mention it tonight."

"Well, now that you've exacted your own extra pound of flesh," the General said, "I think I'll say good night."

Clark interposed himself. "Y'know, Ah don't think you git the point, really Ah don't, Gin'rul. If you step one teeny-weeny little step out of line, the Secretary an' me are gonna jam this goddam tax return right down your throat."

"What does that mean?" Scott almost shouted. "Nobody says what he means around this place."

Clark spoke again, careful and precise this time. "I mean I'm a politician and a member of the President's party, and if you make any anti-administration speeches, or let anybody make a martyr out of you, I'm going to spread your little romance over every front page in this country."

"I'm sure Mrs. Scott would love you for that," the General said bitterly.

"Evoking the tears of wives, widows or even orphans won't help you a bit, General," said Todd. "Upstairs, President Lyman was working only for his country. The senator and I are working at politics."

Clark jabbed a finger at Scott's tunic.

"Specifically, General," he said, "you are not going to run for President against Jordan Lyman two years from now, treaty or no treaty, polls or no polls. You aren't even going to think about it. If you do, the Secretary and I will hang Miss Millicent Segnier right around your neck. Now you tell that to the kingmakers when they come calling on you."

Scott grunted. "I have just met two plain, ordinary bastards."

Clark's laugh was almost a whoop. "Hell, General, you've met worse than that. Roll both of us down the hill in a barrel and there'll always be a son-of-a-bitch on top."

Scott pushed his way past the two men and walked to his car. His big frame was erect, his shoulders squared, his stride emphatic. At the door of the limousine he turned.

"You may both pride yourselves on the cheapest, filthiest little trick of the year," he said.

"At least we didn't need thirty-five hundred hired thugs and a twenty-million-dollar base in the desert to back us up," Clark shot back.

Scott slammed the door without answering and the big car slid away. Todd and Clark watched its taillights until they disappeared beyond the southwest gate, then turned and went back inside the house. As they opened the door to enter, Trimmer—as if sensing that he would now be welcome again in his master's study—galloped up and shoved past them.

The dog ran to the big stairway and rushed upstairs while Todd and Clark waited for the elevator. Todd pulled out a long cigar, rolled it between his thumb and forefinger, and put it into his mouth.

In the elevator Clark shook his head. "I shouldn't have made that last crack. He made me lose my temper."

Todd extracted one of his big wooden kitchen matches from a vest pocket and lit it with a snap of the thumbnail. He got the cigar going before he answered.

"Forget it," he advised. "But you've got to admire the way he went down. You'd almost have thought he was standing on the bridge with the water up to his waist, listening to the band play 'Nearer My God to Thee.' "

"Yeah. Too bad he wasn't on the right side."

They found Lyman standing beside the marble fireplace, staring at a puff of ash no bigger than a fist that smoked on the grate. The President looked at his friends. His eyes glistened and he shook his head.

"It's such a pity," he whispered. "Paul will never know that he saved his country after all."

Clark stared at the grate. Then, not able to look at Lyman, he said:

"He helped, Jordie. He surely did. But he couldn't do it, any more than the rest of us could. Only you could—and you did."

Saturday, 1 P.M.

A mass of newspapermen, so tightly packed that some men had to take notes against the backs of others, pushed and heaved in Frank Simon's west wing press office like a great school of mackerel rushing inshore to feed. The room, heated by two hundred bodies and a sudden early blast of Washington summer weather, was as sticky as a steam bath. Shouted questions spurted from the over-all uproar. Nobody could hear anything.

Simon climbed on his swivel chair and waved his hands to abate the din. He finally managed to cut the noise by perhaps half. Now the shouted questions came through.

"When do we get text?"

"Is Lyman quitting?"

"Did he get all the networks?"

"What the hell is it all about?"

Simon, his thin face twitching, beads of sweat standing on his forehead, continued to flail the air with his hands. At last the room subsided into something approaching order.

"If you'll be quiet for one minute," he yelled, his voice

hoarse, "I'll try to tell you what I know. First, the President requested fifteen minutes of time on all networks for a speech of major national importance. He got it, and he goes on the air at one o'clock, Eastern Daylight. He will speak from the Cabinet room. There's space for three poolers. Second, there will be no advance text, but . . ."

Groans and curses crackled in the crowd and ran like a lighted fuse out of the room into the overflow filling the corridor and part of the lobby.

"Okay, okay," shouted Simon. "Could we have some quiet, for God's sake? Stan, get down from there or somebody's going to get hurt."

A photographer had boosted himself on top of a filing cabinet to get a picture of the crowd. He stood precariously on one leg. He paid no attention to Simon's order.

"Whose idea was this no text?" It was the booming voice of Hal Brennan of the *New York Times,* a hulking extrovert who regarded his trade as a primeval struggle between reporter and news source.

"Nobody's," snapped Simon. "It just isn't written yet. Now listen, dammit! We're putting a relay of stenotypists by a TV set, and you'll have transcript, in takes, starting right after the President begins speaking. We'll set up a distribution table in the lobby. You'll have the whole thing by one-thirty."

"Frank," asked a voice from somewhere in the rear, "there's a report General Dieffenbach has quit as Army chief of staff. How about it?"

"I'm sorry," Simon answered, "I don't know a thing. There are a lot of rumors. We'll just have to wait until one o'clock."

"Who's writing the speech?"

"The President. And I honestly don't have the least idea of what he's going to talk about."

A derisive laugh sputtered through the crowd, but the throng began to break up. Within a few minutes, by chattering threes and fours, it had been transplanted to the lobby to wait in customary bedlam.

Malcolm Waters lingered by Simon's desk. The press secretary nervously lit a cigarette and leaned confidentially toward the AP correspondent.

"So help me Hannah, Milky," he said, "I don't know any more about this than you do. Probably less."

Waters dropped his voice. "Something funny's going on. They had about thirty Treasury agents in the Secretary's office across the street last night until almost midnight. None of them knew why they'd been called in. And I heard Art Corwin had his whole detail on duty last night."

"I know, I know," Simon said bleakly. "Milky, he won't tell me a thing. Whatever it is, he cut me out completely."

Several reporters had lingered inside Simon's doorway. Waters put his face close to the press secretary's ear. "Was General Scott over here last night?"

Simon looked startled. "Scott? You got me, Milky. For all he's told me, he could have had Alexander the Great in here last night."

Sixty feet away President Lyman sat at his office desk in shirt sleeves. A half dozen sheets of paper, covered with scribbling, were strewn around the desktop. Christopher Todd, immaculate as usual in gray suit and figured tie, sat across from the President, writing on a large yellow lined pad. Ray Clark, his collar undone and tie drooping, sat at the corner of the desk. He tapped his teeth with a pencil as he stared at a page of notes. Outside, the noon heat of the first real summer day shimmered on the rosebushes and the shiny magnolia leaves, but the air conditioning kept the President's office comfortable.

"I didn't feel easy about all those troops at Site Y," Lyman said, "but Barney says they can't go anywhere without planes. He thought it would be better not to spring that on the Army vice chief until after the speech."

"He's right." Todd nodded. "That gang has to be broken up with the utmost care or we could have some ugly stories on our hands."

"I don't see why we can't keep the base," said Clark, "for the same type of training, and just bring in some new officers, maybe make Henderson the C.O., and weed out the bad apples in the noncoms. It's a pity to break up an outfit with that much morale."

"Maybe that's not such a bad idea, Ray," said Lyman. "I'll talk to Barney about it."

"Does Admiral Palmer know about his future yet?" asked Todd.

"No." Lyman grinned. "If he listens this afternoon, he'll get a surprise. I'd like to see his face. Well, come on. I like the beginning, but the end's still pretty weak."

The three men worked on, largely in silence. Occasionally Todd or Clark, reviewing a page, would offer a phrase. If the President nodded, it would go in. A Filipino messboy brought in three sandwiches, milk and coffee. Soon crumbs and coffee stains marred the scattered papers.

At 12:30 Esther Townsend opened the door.

"The girls will have to have that in five minutes," she said, "if you want a clean copy to read."

Lyman handed her a sheaf of papers. Whole lines were crossed out. Smudges mingled with inked insertions.

"You read it to the girls," he said. "That's everything but the last two or three minutes."

She was back again at 12:45. "You'll have to give me the rest now, or we can't make it."

Lyman handed her two more pages. "That's enough," he said. "I'll go with this for the last page or so. It isn't all legible, but I know what I want to say now anyway."

A few minutes before one o'clock, the three men walked into the Cabinet room. Lyman held ten sheets of clean manuscript, typed in large print on the special speech typewriter for easy reading. On the bottom were two handwritten pages, messy with last-minute corrections.

At the door of the Cabinet room Lyman paused in front of Esther.

"How do I look?" he asked. "Doris and Liz will be watching in Louisville, and I don't want the family to be ashamed of the old man."

Esther grinned at him and pointed her forefinger at her temple in their private code: Quiet, secretary thinking. Then she checked his appearance, straightened his tie, and flicked a crumb off his shirt.

"Okay, Governor, you'll do," she said. "Of course, those bags under your eyes are big enough to frighten a redcap, but they make you look more like a statesman."

Clark whispered to his friend, "Be good."

The room was in hushed turmoil. Five television cameras, one for each major network, were aimed at the center of the long Cabinet table. A half-dozen sound engineers, wearing earphones, tried to avoid tripping over the tangle of wires and cables as they checked their control boxes and connections. Still and newsreel photographers squeezed in on both sides of the big TV cameras.

Lyman took his place behind a small portable podium, adorned with the presidential seal, which rested on the table. On each side of him stood a flag standard, one bearing the national colors, the other his own flag. Esther, Todd, Clark and Art Corwin stood against the side wall behind the three "pool" newspapermen who would report personal touches and color for the rest of the press contingent, now crowded around four television sets in the pressroom, lobby and Simon's office.

As the door closed, Lyman caught a glimpse of an Army warrant officer, his face blank, sitting in the outer hall, a black briefcase lying in his lap.

One of the men wearing earphones held up his index finger to the President: one minute to go. He bent his finger: 30 seconds. The murmuring in the room quieted. The director closed his fist as five television newsmen said, each into his own microphone, "Ladies and gentlemen, the President of the United States."

The fist came up again, the index finger shot imperiously at Lyman, and the President was on the air.

My fellow citizens:
I am sorry to interrupt you in the middle of a pleasant day when you are relaxing after a busy week of work. It is beautiful here in Washington today, and I understand it is pretty

*much the same all across the country—really the first day of
summer for all of us. So I am grateful to you for taking a few
minutes to listen to me.*

In front of the TV set in Frank Simon's office, Hugh Ulanski
of the UPI snorted. "What the hell is this, anyway—a new
weather forecast program?" The crowd of reporters snickered.
Simon growled, "Shut up, Hugh."

*I would not take your time today for anything less than a
question of grave concern to every American. For some of us
in the White House, this has been a week of heavy trial, and
in some respects of heartbreak and deep disappointment.
There are three matters on which I felt it was my duty to report to you without delay.*

In an Italian mountain village, Vice-President Vincent Gianelli sat at an ancient wooden table in a café. Gianelli
cocked his head in puzzlement as he listened to the President
on his little portable radio. What was this all about? That
Gallup Poll must've shaken Jordan Lyman up more than he
realized.

*First, I must announce with regret that I have today asked
the Attorney General to prepare to go into court on Monday
morning to seek an injunction to end the missile strikes. I
realize that responsible segments of organized labor—and
that includes, of course, the vast majority of working men and
women, as well as their union leaders—are as distressed about
these work stoppages as I am. I appreciate the efforts of President Lindsay of the AFL-CIO and his colleagues. But the
strike still continues, and it is my responsibility to protect the
national interest. In this critical time there can be no gambling
with the safety of the United States.*

In his new, rambling home in suburban Maryland Cliff Lindsay rose from his chair in a flush of anger. "Double-cross," he
muttered to himself. "He gave me until Monday and now he's
beat me out of forty-eight hours." Lindsay stamped to the
telephone to call the head of the Teamsters on the West Coast.

In his bombproof underground office at Vandenberg Missile base, General George Seager, overseer of the nation's intercontinental missiles, nodded his head grudgingly. Cancellation of the alert had come last night, and this morning a rumor came through the Air Force grapevine that Jim Scott had been fired. But, thank God, the President was showing some steel at last on these strikes. It was about time. Seager moved his chair closer to the TV set. What about Operation Preakness?

Second, my fellow Americans, I must inform you that a most critical problem has arisen with regard to the nuclear disarmament treaty recently ratified by the Senate. It is so serious as to raise doubts whether the implementation of the treaty can begin, as scheduled, on July first.

Senator Frederick Prentice of California listened to his car radio as he drove his Thunderbird convertible along Route 9 toward the Blue Ridge—and Mount Thunder. He had spent the night at his hilltop cabin north of Leesburg, a retreat without a telephone where he went to relax. Now, by prearrangement with General Scott, he was on his way to Mount Thunder to help give the nation the firm leadership it deserved. It will not serve you now, Jordan Lyman, to have second thoughts about that treaty. The fat's in the fire, and you're too late.

Security prohibits me from discussing the exact nature of this problem. All I can say now is that I hope to resolve it. We must resolve it, and do so quickly, if we are to be able to see this treaty, for which we all have such great hopes, go into effect. Therefore, two days ago I asked our ambassador in Moscow to request Chairman Feemerov to meet me at once. He has agreed, and I plan to meet him Wednesday in Vienna.

At the office of United Press International a few blocks from the White House a news editor swung away from his TV set and shouted to a teletype operator waiting a few feet away: "Bulletin. President will meet Feemerov in Vienna Wednesday." In the Associated Press office on Connecticut Avenue two precious seconds were saved, for the bureau chief himself sat at the "A" wire teletype. When he heard Lyman's announcement, his fingers hurried over the keyboard:

FLASH
LYMAN MEETS FEEMEROV IN VIENNA WEDNESDAY.

The bureau chief turned back to his TV set—but stayed by the teletype.

I shall be accompanied by the Secretary of State and others of my associates. We go with concern, of course, but I say to you—and to others who may hear me—that we go without fear. I have every hope that the meeting will resolve the problems that have arisen, and that the treaty will go into effect at Los Alamos and Semipalatinsk as planned on July 1. I regret that I can say no more on this matter at the present time.

In his office at the Central Intelligence Agency, across the Potomac River in Virginia, Saul Lieberman nodded his head approvingly. Just right. The odds are ten to one against success, but we can try. Lyman was good on this one. He's a real clutch hitter, all right.

In a Louisville hospital room Doris Lyman reached over to the bed and took her daughter's hand. "Oh, Liz. I should have gone home yesterday." Elizabeth replied quietly: "You go this afternoon, Mom. I'm all right now."

In a long, high-ceilinged room in the Kremlin, thin shadows stretched in the fading Moscow twilight. Premier Feemerov cocked his bushy head to listen to the translation. The satellite relay system was working perfectly today, and he could study the American President's features on the television screen as the interpreter spoke rapidly. Does Lyman know of Yakutsk? No, that's impossible. He must have some trick of his own up his sleeve.

And now I turn to the third subject which I must discuss with you today. I do so with a heavy heart, for an event has occurred which has disturbed me more than any other since I took up the duties of this office.

It is no secret to any of you that the ratification of the nuclear disarmament treaty inspired a national debate even more vigorous than the one over the original signing of that instrument.

Stewart Dillard, sitting on the porch of his fashionable Chevy Chase home, turned to his wife and chuckled: "It sure wasn't any secret around this house. Lyman should have heard the ruckus Fred Prentice kicked up on the lawn Sunday night." Francine Dillard pouted. "Well, I got nothing but compliments on the party next day, Stew."

Morton Freeman sat in his New York apartment and glowered at a TV set. Wait'll Lyman hears doll-baby MacPherson tonight, he thought, and he'll think the last couple of months have been a finger-painting duel in a nursery. Why wouldn't that Fascist bastard let me have a look at his script for tonight? Somebody ought to castrate him.

It was not the argument that you carried on in your homes and offices, nor the public debate that took place in the Senate, that disturbed me. That is the way this country decides, and we pray that it may ever be so. But hidden from public view, there developed also a bitter opposition to the treaty among some of our highest military leaders.

"Here it comes," Milky Waters whispered to the reporter sitting next to him in Simon's office. "Ten will get you twenty General Scott gets the ax." His colleague looked at Waters in bewilderment. "Scott?"

In the Cabinet room, Clark watched Lyman and thought: Don't rush this now, Jordie, or you'll panic them. Take it slow and easy.

I should take a moment here to explain my own concept of the civilian-military relationship under our system of government. I deeply believe, as I know the overwhelming majority of Americans do, that our military leaders—tempered by battle, matured by countless command decisions, dedicating their entire lives to the service of the nation—should always be afforded every opportunity to speak their views. In the case of the treaty, they were of course given that opportunity.

Admiral Lawrence Palmer, seated at his desk in the Pentagon suite of the chief of Naval Operations, nodded to the aide who sat beside him. "He's right about that," he said. "I testified against it at least five times." The aide protested: "But, sir, they were all executive sessions." Palmer agreed: "Sure. But I got listened to where it counted."

General Parker Hardesty, at home with his wife, exploded. "That's a barefaced lie," he said. "I tried to slip just one paragraph in my Chicago speech and the Secretary's goddam censors killed it."

But once the President and the Senate, as the responsible authorities, make a decision, then, my fellow citizens, debate and opposition among the military must come to an end. That is the way in war: the commander solicits every possible view from his staff, but once he decides on his plan of battle, there can be no disputing it. Any other way would mean confusion, chaos and certain defeat. And so it also must be in the councils of government here in Washington.

In Quarters Six at Fort Myer, General Scott lounged in sports clothes in front of a portable TV set in his second-floor study. Generals Riley and Dieffenbach flanked him.

"You've got to hand it to him," Scott said. "For a man who's dead wrong, he's putting on the best possible face. If only he was that way where it counted."

Riley shrugged. "I'm not impressed, Jim," he said. "The country's had it. He'll blow everything at Vienna."

Dieffenbach pulled out his wallet. "Not that anybody cares much," he said, "but I've got ten bucks that says Barney Rutkowski is the next chairman."

Scott smiled. "You're playing to my weakness, Ed. You're on. I think it'll be Palmer."

Early this week it came to my attention that the chairman of the Joint Chiefs of Staff, General Scott, and three other members of the Joint Chiefs were not only still opposing the treaty, despite its ratification, but were in fact organizing a formal group in an effort to prevent its implementation on the first of July.

Millicent Segnier and Eleanor Holbrook sipped highballs as they watched together in New York. "Ye gods," Milly cried, "don't tell me he's going to fire Jim?" Shoo recalled a Marine's arms around her neck, and thought: Jiggs must have done his job well. Maybe they'll make him a general or something. Aloud, she said: "Who cares, Milly? Love that Lyman."

I have the highest regard for General Scott. He possesses one of the finest minds in the government. His advice, over the months, has been of great value, often indispensable, on a hundred and one problems facing me and other civilian authorities. I know he ranks high in the esteem of his countrymen. So he does in mine too. When reports of his participation in an organized plan of opposition to the treaty reached me, I did not credit them. But General Scott, honest and forthright as he is, conceded frankly to me that such was the case.

In a Navy code room at Pearl Harbor, Hawaii, Lieutenant (jg) Dorsey Hough had a radio turned on full blast so he could hear it over the chatter of typewriters as sailors with headsets kept the message traffic of the Pacific Fleet flowing to Okinawa, San Francisco, Midway Island, and the ships at sea. Hough's feet were propped on a desk and a magazine lay open in his lap. "That's awful damn fancy language to use to fire a guy just because he bets on the horses," he muttered, half to himself. "That Lyman must be death on gambling."

In a Quonset hut on the New Mexico desert, Colonel John Broderick kicked angrily at the leg of the tripod holding his TV set. The machine crashed to the floor. "I've heard enough of that frigging lecture," he snarled to the major at his side. "If you ask me, we've got a Commie right in the White House, right in the White House!"

Furthermore, and I grant him the courage of his convictions, the General declined to abandon his plans for opposing the treaty further. That being the case, I had no choice but to ask for General Scott's resignation. He tendered it to me last night. Despite my great regret that the nation will be deprived of the talents of this able officer, I accepted his resignation.

Bells rang on teleprinters in newspaper offices across the country:

BULLETIN
    GENERAL SCOTT FIRED

Admiral Farley Barnswell, in his cabin aboard the U.S.S. *Eisenhower* at Gibraltar, tugged at his ear and considered his own position. With Girard dead, did the President have any way of knowing about that memorandum he had signed? No, of course not. Could Girard have telephoned the President between the time he went ashore and the time his plane took off from Madrid? Maybe, but he doubted it. Girard had made no call from the Navy's shore facility at Gibraltar, and he wouldn't have had much time anywhere else. Barnswell rubbed his palms together nervously. Nothing to do now but wait this one out.

I also asked for and received, at the same time, promptly and with every courtesy and consideration, the resignations of three other fine officers: General Hardesty and General Dieffenbach, the Chiefs of Staff of the Air Force and Army, and General Riley, the Commandant of the Marine Corps. Since all these men followed their convictions with honor and courage, I shall request of the Congress that no attempt be made to deprive any of these officers of the full retirement benefits due them. These are small compensation for a lifetime of service to the country. In passing, I might say that I shall present to the Congress, soon after it reconvenes, proposed

*legislation to liberalize not only such benefits but also the basic
pay scales of the armed forces.*

Admiral Topping Wilson, commander of the Pacific Fleet,
sat in his hilltop house in Honolulu, listening to the President's
voice but looking across his porch to Diamond Head and the
blue-green Pacific beyond. That message twelve hours ago
from the President, canceling the Saturday alert, indicated that
Operation Preakness had collapsed. Now his reactions were
numbed. Whatever possessed him to join Jim Scott in such a
wild venture? He was glad it was over. Honestly, what could
Scott have done that Lyman wasn't doing already? Wilson
fingered the silver stars on his collar and thought of the days
when he stood on the bridge of a cruiser, leading his division
into Pearl past the headland over there. He could feel salt spray
on his cheeks, and he felt infinitely old.

In the den of a handsomely restored house in the Connecticut countryside, Harold MacPherson slumped in a chair in
front of his typewriter. He had pulled out the last sheet just before the President went on the air. Now he slowly tore the
whole sheaf of typescript in half, then into quarters, and finally
into eighths. He walked to a wicker wastebasket and dropped
the pieces in, letting the last shreds flutter off his fingertips. The
country is dead, he thought. Dead. Ready to be buried. The
Communists have gotten to Jordan Lyman and everything
we've worked for so long is finished. He poured two fingers of
whisky into a glass and downed it at a gulp. He stared moodily
at the initials cut into the glass, turning the tumbler in his two
hands, and then hurled it across the room to shatter in the old
stone fireplace.

*I am taking immediate action, of course, to fill the vacan-
cies created by these resignations, so that there need be no concern about the security of the United States. I am appointing
Admiral Lawrence Palmer, now chief of Naval Operations, as
the new chairman of the Joint Chiefs of Staff. The Chief
Justice of the United States has kindly consented to administer*

*the oath of office to Admiral Palmer in my office this after-
noon.*

*It will doubtless be suggested that Admiral Palmer was no
less opposed to the treaty than his former colleagues on the
Joint Chiefs. That is true. However, once the decision was
made by the President and approved by the Senate, he stilled
his voice and joined the many other military leaders who
closed ranks behind their commander in chief. He acted in the
tradition of the Constitution and of the military academies,
which have given this country a career officer corps that is not
only professionally skilled but is also a bulwark of our liberties. Admiral Palmer is an officer of unexcelled ability, foresight and military knowledge, and I am sure he will discharge
his new responsibilities well.*

In Quarters Six, Dieffenbach silently pulled a $10 bill from his
wallet and handed it to Scott. The former chairman squinted
and looked out the window toward the Mall and the Capitol,
bright in the midday sun. "I could never budge Palmer," he
mused.

At Mount Thunder, General Garlock stared at his TV set.
The whole thing baffled him. That visit to his home by Gentleman Jim Scott and Billy Riley Tuesday night had been bothering him for four days. Did the President really know something
more than he was saying? Should he ask for an appointment
at the White House and tell him about the visit? What was his
duty? He leaned forward to hear the rest of Lyman's speech.

*A new chief of staff for the Air Force has already been ap-
pointed. He is General Bernard Rutkowski, until now the
commander of our North American Air Defense Command.
His life and career exemplify the promise of America; his fine
combat record and unique abilities as military tactician and
strategist speak for themselves. He was sworn into office last
night in this house. I am confident he will serve with distinc-
tion alongside Admiral Palmer.*

The Army and Marines, and the Navy, have fully qualified

deputy commanders who have assumed, for the time being, the command of their services.

Jiggs Casey sat in his living room in Arlington, between his wife and his old friend Mutt Henderson. Marge put her mouth to Casey's ear and whispered, "I'm sorry I made such a fuss about New York, honey. I had no idea that something important really *was* going on." Casey merely grinned down at her.

Henderson got up from the sofa, absently exploring the purple lump under his left eye with his fingertips. "Jeez, this is an awful lot for a simple country boy to take in one week. How about a guy mixing himself a drink?"

Casey said, "Sure. And fix one for Marge and me too."

When Henderson had gone into the kitchen, Marge asked, "Jiggs, was there some kind of plot, or something, going on this week?" Casey looked at her in surprise.

"I don't know, Marge, I really don't," he said. "I have no certain knowledge—and I have no doubts."

In another suburban subdivision, across the river in Bethesda, Bill Fullerton stood in the shade of the big beech tree behind his home as he listened to the radio resting on the cook-out table. Just what the devil was the connection between this and that call from Paul Girard Monday night? And that list of classified bases President Lyman wanted Tuesday morning? After thirty years of sitting in the Budget Bureau and dealing with the Pentagon, he thought, I can smell fish when they're hidden somewhere around, and this thing sure smells fishy. Do you suppose some kind of military operation was involved? And what about Site Y—just where the hell is the place, anyway?

There may be some who believe that these changes in our military high command will weaken the nation in a critical time. To them I say with complete confidence: Put aside your fears. Admiral Palmer, General Rutkowski and the other officers now in charge of our defenses have served in high councils for many years and they are fully prepared and able to assume their new responsibilities.

As I set out for Vienna next week I shall need your support and your prayers, but I shall go in confidence, with the assurance that all is well at home and that the nation, having made its decisions in our traditional way, remains devoted to the basic principles handed to us by the founding fathers.

Henry Whitney listened in rapt attention to the President's voice. He was in the home of a fellow foreign service officer in Georgetown. When he had checked in with the Spanish desk at the department that morning, they read him an angry cable from Father Archibald at the embassy in Madrid. Whitney hadn't figured out how to handle that one yet, but now he was thinking of other things. Yes, he thought, I'll pray for you, Mr. President, wherever you go and whatever you do. Then he thought of Jordan Lyman's parting pledge to him. Maybe Miss Townsend could arrange something to cool Ambassador Lytle's anger. Better call right after the broadcast is over.

And now, if I may, let me make a few general observations. No matter what convictions and deeply felt motives moved General Scott and his colleagues to act as they did, I had no choice, as President and commander in chief of the armed forces, but to act as I did. To have done otherwise would have been to betray the great trust handed down to us across two centuries by the men who wrote the Constitution.

This is a republic, managed by a President freely elected by all the people. Sometimes the President has been a military man. Sometimes he has been a civilian. It matters not from what profession he may come; once he is elected, he must assume full responsibility, under the Constitution, for the foreign relations and the defense of the United States. He may make mistakes; his decisions may be popular or unpopular; but so long as he remains in office, he may not avoid the responsibility for decision. And it must follow that once he has made a decision—whether for better or for worse—members of the government which he directs must give his policies full support.

It was not the opposition of General Scott and his col-

leagues which required their resignations. It was the timing of that opposition. Until the Senate ratified the treaty, they had every right—indeed a duty—to speak their views frankly and fully. But once the Senate voted, making the treaty an established national policy of the United States, they were then duty-bound to render it every support within their power as long as they remained on active duty. That they refused to do; and that refusal no President could countenance.

Somewhere, this afternoon, there are listening men who will one day occupy this office. I would betray my obligation to them and to their generation of Americans, as well as my duty to the past and to all of you today, if I failed to act as I have.

I would close with one final observation. There has been abroad in this land, in recent months, a whisper that we have somehow lost our greatness; that we do not have the strength to win—without war—the struggle for liberty throughout the world; that we do not have the fortitude to face, without either surrender or blind violence, the present challenge of men who would use tools as old as tyranny itself to make the future theirs.

I say to you today that this whisper is a vile slander—a slander on America, on its people, on the institutions which we hold dear and which in turn sustain us. Our country is strong—strong enough to be a peacemaker. It is proud— proud enough to be patient. We love our good life—love it enough to die for it if need be, or to forgo some of its benefits to help others less fortunate come closer to achieving it.

So, my fellow citizens, go back to this lovely day in May. Do not weep for your country. Do not listen to the whispers, for they are wrong. We remain strong and proud, peaceful and patient, ready to sacrifice, always willing to help others who seek their way out of the long tunnels of tyranny into the bright sunshine of liberty. Good-by, and God bless you all.

President Lyman's closing sentence crackled incongruously from the radio in the smashed automobile as a Virginia highway patrolman swung his squad car off Route 120. The trooper hurried across the road to the car, which lay on its side against a stone wall. The dust and smoke of violent collision still drifted upward from the wreck.

An Army bus was stopped on the road, and a dozen or so soldiers stood in a little circle around a body lying on the gravel shoulder. A sergeant stepped forward as the patrolman approached.

"We tried first aid, officer," he said, "but he was gone. Died on impact, I guess."

"How'd it happen?"

"We couldn't see too well. One of the boys had a portable radio and we were mostly in the back of the bus listening to the President. The driver says that all of a sudden this car came around the bend right in front of us, going real fast, and swerved off and piled into the wall. Maybe he wasn't paying attention and got scared when he saw us."

The highway patrolman walked over to the battered car, reached inside and switched off the radio. Then he noticed the license tags of the car and swore under his breath. Damn, he thought, I'll be tied up on this one all week.

The rear license plate of the Thunderbird convertible was bent, but easily legible. It was a California plate: USS 1.

Epilogue

Monday, May 20, 10:30 A.M.

(In attendance: 483)

THE PRESIDENT: Good morning. I have several announce-
ments.

First, the arrangements for the trip to Vienna are now complete, and Mr. Simon will have detailed information on that for
you by noon today.

Second, I have one diplomatic appointment. When the
Senate reconvenes I will send up a nomination for ambassador
to Chile, to fill the vacancy which has existed in that post for
the past several weeks. I am appointing Mr. Henry Whitney, a
career foreign service officer who has demonstrated unusual
initiative and skill. He is currently serving as consul general in
Spain.

Third, I have accepted a number of resignations in the
armed services. The officers are General George Seager and
General Theodore F. Daniel of the Air Force. There will be a
list available after the press conference, by the way. General

334

Seager is commander of Vandenberg missile base, and General Daniel is commander of the Strategic Air Command. Also Admiral Topping Wilson, commander of the Pacific Fleet, and Admiral Farley C. Barnswell, commander of the Sixth Fleet in the Mediterranean, and Lieutenant General Thomas R. Hastings, commander of the First Airborne Corps of the Army at Fort Bragg.

MALCOLM WATERS, Associated Press: Mr. President?

THE PRESIDENT: Excuse me, Mr. Waters, I have one further announcement. As you all know, the President has traditionally had three military aides—one each from the Army, Navy and Air Force. I thought it was about time a Marine was added, and I am appointing Colonel Casey as my Marine aide. He will be promoted to brigadier general. That's all I have.

HUGH ULANSKI, United Press International: Could we have the full name of that Colonel Casey, sir?

THE PRESIDENT: I'm sorry. That is Colonel Martin J. Casey. He is currently serving as director of the Joint Staff. I think some of you may know him.

MERRILL STANLEY, NBC: Mr. President, are we to understand that these five resignations you just gave us are in the same category as the Joint Chiefs, that is, because they opposed the treaty?

THE PRESIDENT: Now, let's get one thing cleared up. It wasn't opposition to the treaty that brought on these resignations, but opposition of a formal and persistent nature after the policy of the government had been firmly settled. With that proviso, the answer to your question is yes. The five field commanders proposed to ally themselves with General Scott in formal defiance of government policy. That could not be tolerated.

MERRILL STANLEY, NBC: Mr. President, our switchboard has been swamped with calls on this Joint Chiefs thing.

THE PRESIDENT: So has mine. (Laughter)

MERRILL STANLEY, NBC: Yes, sir. And most of them are to the effect that the public doesn't understand why so many had to be fired.

THE PRESIDENT: Well, they weren't fired. They resigned. It is true, of course, that I requested the resignations, but the officers in question could have refused to submit them and could have carried the matter further. They preferred not to do that, and I think they were wise. Now, why so many? The resignations involved only those military officers who proposed to defy established national policy after it had been settled. As I said Saturday, we could not operate in that situation. No military leader has been disturbed because he expressed opposition to the treaty before it was ratified. In fact, Admiral Palmer has been advanced to a more responsible assignment, as has General Rutkowski. General Rutkowski argued very strongly against the treaty last year.

JAMES COMPTON, Knight Newspapers: Sir, you didn't make it clear in your speech Saturday to what extent you encouraged them to resign.

THE PRESIDENT: Jim, I'll assume that's a question even though I couldn't hear a question mark on it. Let's just say I advised them to resign and they accepted my advice. (Laughter)

HAL BRENNAN, *New York Times:* Mr. President, we have an authoritative report that some intelligence information, involving Russia's intentions to abide by the treaty, accounts for your trip to Vienna to see Mr. Feemerov. Is that correct, sir?

THE PRESIDENT: I'm sorry, but I will have nothing more to say on the Vienna conference until it is over.

HAL BRENNAN, *New York Times:* Then we may assume the report is correct?

THE PRESIDENT: Now, Mr. Brennan, I am neither confirming nor denying anything. I am simply not discussing the subject. I'd like to be helpful, but I think it would not be useful for me to discuss it just now. You'll all be informed in good time.

RUTH EVERSON, New Orleans *Times-Picayune:* Mr. President, people in Louisiana are very worried about our country's safety with all these top officers being fired. Have you thought about that?

THE PRESIDENT: I thought I made it clear on Saturday that I myself have no qualms. Every branch of the military establishment has many fine, experienced and devoted officers ready to assume command responsibilities. I think that is one of the great successes of our service academy system, and of course we have many fine officers from the ranks and from the civilian colleges.

THOMAS HODGES, *Minneapolis Star and Tribune:* Mr. President, did you consult with the National Security Council or the Cabinet or other advisers on this?

THE PRESIDENT: Not the NSC or the Cabinet as such, but I did consult most earnestly, and at some length, with certain of my advisers.

THOMAS HODGES, Minneapolis *Star and Tribune:* I wonder if you could give us their names, please, sir?

THE PRESIDENT: In this particular case, I don't believe it would be useful.

ROGER SWENSSON, Chicago *Tribune:* Mr. President, many people find it hard to believe that the treaty alone was the cause of this mass exodus. Was anything else involved?

THE PRESIDENT: The treaty stirred very deep feelings in this country. Men in high positions are not immune to deep feelings.

ROGER SWENSSON, Chicago *Tribune:* Are you saying, sir, that this was also partly a matter of personalities?

THE PRESIDENT: No, I am not. I am saying that the chiefs and I differed one hundred and eighty degrees on a matter vital to the security and future of this country and of the whole world. These differences were not susceptible of resolution.

GRANT CHURCH, Washington *Star:* Mr. President, you said Saturday that you would go into court today on the missile strikes. Is that still your intention?

THE PRESIDENT: Well, on that I have asked the Attorney General to wait until this afternoon. I understand that there now seems an excellent prospect that the problem may be solved by then without our seeking an injunction, so I have asked him to wait, and keep in touch with the Secretary of Labor, who has been working over the weekend on the matter. But if there is no progress this morning, yes, we will go into court this afternoon as I indicated.

EDGAR ST. JOHN, Washington *Post:* Mr. President, there's

been quite a lot of speculation over the weekend about the political implications of these resignations, since General Scott has been highly favored by many Republicans and even some Democrats. Do you foresee him as a possible Republican nominee against you next time?

THE PRESIDENT: Eddie, you are not going to get me to announce for re-election. (Laughter) At least not today. (Laughter) It's possible that General Scott might be interested. Of course, I don't think he could win if I did run again, despite my, well, somewhat modest standing in a certain recent poll. (Laughter) Seriously, things do change quickly in politics, but I would be very much surprised, on the basis of certain information given me over the weekend, if General Scott decided to seek elective office. But let me say right here that I have the highest regard for his intelligence, character and dedication. I just happen to believe that he is misguided on some things.

A. H. COOLEDGE, King Features: Mr. President, you said "some things." What are the others, please, sir?

THE PRESIDENT: I meant that I believe him to be wrong on the central issue in this whole matter. By "some things" I meant the auxiliary questions that stem from the central issue.

ERNEST DUBOIS, Los Angeles *Times:* Mr. President, have you had a chance to talk yet with the governor of California about the appointment of a successor to Senator Prentice?

THE PRESIDENT: I think it would be in poor taste for me to do anything like that now, and it would be improper, and unnecessary, in any event. I am sure the governor will discharge his responsibility, at the proper time, without any help from me. I do want to say that it was most untimely, Senator Prentice's death, and his loss will be felt keenly in the Senate. It is no secret that we differed on some matters, but that did not diminish his stature, and I might say his influence, in my eyes.

HELEN UPDYKE, CBS: Mr. President, on those field commanders you listed at the beginning, who is replacing them?

THE PRESIDENT: In each case the deputy commander or chief of staff is taking over, for the time being.

KYLE MORRISON, Baltimore *Sun:* Mr. President, no doubt you have heard that, in addition to the treaty, many military men felt that you have been remiss in not moving to restore some of the fringe benefits which have been eroded away from the services, and, according to some critics, have hurt morale. Would you have any comment on that, sir?

THE PRESIDENT: Well, yes, Mr. Morrison. I spoke briefly of that on Saturday, as you know. I think their feeling has considerable justification. Morale in the services, or in some branches of them, could be improved, and I think this is one factor. We hope to send a bill to the Hill within two weeks. It will be sound financially, but it will be generous. I think we can work out the details quite quickly. I may have been a little slow on this, but only because there was so much else that had to come first, as I saw it.

JOHN HUTCHINSON, Chicago *Sun-Times:* Mr. President, on a different subject, have you made a decision yet on that vacancy on the district court in Illinois?

THE PRESIDENT: Yes, I have, but I'm afraid that, with everything else that's happened in the past few days, I've forgotten. Just a minute.

(The President conferred with Mr. Simon.)

THE PRESIDENT: Oh, yes. Frank reminds me. It is . . . I intend to nominate Benjamin Krakow of Chicago. Mr. Simon says he was endorsed by the *Sun-Times* (Laughter) as well as by the bar association.

ALAN ANGELL, Newark *Star-Ledger:* Mr. President, how did you learn that the officers you named today were still opposing the treaty? I mean the field commanders.

THE PRESIDENT: Well, a president does have his sources of information. It so happens that the five whose resignations I announced today were all allied with General Scott in support of his planned course of action.

OSCAR LEWIS, Des Moines *Register:* Mr. President, are you indicating there was some sort of military cabal, or something, on this thing?

THE PRESIDENT: No, I'm just stating the facts. All the men

who resigned knew each other well, and they exchanged their views rather openly, and they did not keep their attitude a secret. They were just pulling the wrong way on a matter of established national policy, and you can't have that.

MARVIN O'ROURKE, Gannett Newspapers: Mr. President, there's been quite a mystery about a force of Treasury agents called into their offices Friday night. Could you help us on that, sir?

THE PRESIDENT: No, I really can't. My understanding is that Secretary Todd had information of some kind of criminal operation afoot in the metropolitan area, but that it never really materialized. I will inquire into it, though, and see that Mr. Simon has information for you later.

WILLIAM SEATON, RBC: Mr. President, it was before my time, but I think that when President Truman fired General MacArthur in 1951 he did not object when MacArthur addressed Congress. How would you feel about that now as far as General Scott is concerned?

THE PRESIDENT: I really don't think you can make a comparison of the two situations. President Truman took the action he did—I think you will find this to be the case, if you look at the record—primarily as a disciplinary matter. General Scott and I differed over something that went far beyond that, to the question of our national survival and our world leadership, our existence as a nation for many . . . for many years of what I hope will be peace. I think your question is one of those "iffy" ones, really. I don't think Congressional leaders have it in mind, and I would rather doubt that General Scott would be receptive.

PETER BENJAMIN, United Features: Mr. President, this is a delicate question, and I'll try to phrase it rather precisely. There have been many rumors around here in the past few days that far more than the treaty was involved and that perhaps there was some idea, some indication, of . . . well, of upsetting the government. Do you have any knowledge of anything in the military, the military forces, that would have been intended to alter or upset any of our present setup?

THE PRESIDENT: I'm sure you would not want to be suggesting, Mr. Benjamin, even by a question, that General Scott sought to usurp any powers of the civilian authorities. That of course would be beyond understanding. I am aware, though, of these rumors, and I'd like to try to answer you as exactly as I can. I think then I won't have anything more to say today.

Now, this country has been in existence almost two hundred years, and our roots as a republic go back much farther than that. We were given the finest Constitution ever written by men. You know, it is unique. There is no political document like it in history, because it was written all at once, from scratch, but it still has lasted and it has been adaptable to changes the founding fathers could not have dreamed of.

That Constitution and the whole governmental structure that flows from it are taught as basic subjects, bread-and-butter, at the service academies, even more than at our other colleges and schools. The cadets and midshipmen there absorb it. And throughout their careers they live with it much more than do most civilians. They read it on their commissions, and it is part of their oath of office. They fight for it, of course, as junior officers, and as senior officers they never question its arrangements for ultimate civilian authority, no matter how much they may differ with the elected officials on some particular issue.

So, when you think about it, this is perhaps the finest tradition of our military services, and it is certainly one of the most important now, because with missiles and satellites and nuclear weapons, military commanders could take control of any nation by just pushing some buttons.

I am sure the American people do not believe that any such thought ever entered the mind of any general officer in our services since the day the country began. Let us pray that it never will.

MALCOLM WATERS, Associated Press: Thank you, Mr. President.

ABOUT THE AUTHORS

Fletcher Knebel and Charles W. Bailey II are both with the Washington Bureau of Cowles Publications.

Mr. Knebel graduated from Miami University, Oxford, Ohio, and worked as a reporter in Pennsylvania, Ohio and Tennessee before going to Washington. His daily political column, *Potomac Fever,* appears in eighty major newspapers.

Mr. Bailey went to work as a reporter for the *Minneapolis Star and Tribune* after attending Phillips Exeter Academy and Harvard University, and came to the Cowles Washington Bureau in 1954.

Knebel and Bailey have collaborated on a previous book, *No High Ground,* the story of the Hiroshima bomb, published by Harper & Brothers in 1960. They were both contributors to *Candidates: 1960,* edited by Eric Sevareid.